FRANCIS

THE Poet's War

A NOVEL

Published by
Gustav Press
Salzburg, Austria

ISBN: 978-3-9519796-0-1

eISBN: 978-3-9519796-1-8

Cover Illustration: Mark Leithauser

GIUSEPPE UNGARETTI. Giuseppe Ungaretti, who was born in Alexandria in 1888 and died in Milan in 1970, fought in WWI and received the Neustadt International Prize for Literature in the year of his death. His war poetry brought the starkness of his style into dramatic effect. He was one of the leading avant-garde poets between the wars. An English version of his selected poems, translated by Allen Mandelbaum, was published in 1975.

W. H. AUDEN. W. H. Auden's *Goethe's Italian Journey* is outside the poetic production he is better known for. How his translation differs from Alistair and Ottavia's is noted in the book and need not be laid out here. A few lines of Goethe's geological notes here use Auden's translation.

WILLIAM BUTLER YEATS. William Butler Yeats (1865–1939) was, as much as any one influence, the lodestone of Alistair Stears' poetic vision and of much of his personal philosophy. Literate readers can follow much of this *passim* throughout the book, though underground and rarely quoted.

The Gods did this, and spun the destruction of people,
For the sake of the singing of men hereafter.

—DEMODOCUS

The bard of the Phaecians, singing to the weeping Odysseus
and the Phaecian lords of the horrors of the sack of Troy

PART I

1

In November of 1915, the youth who became the soldier and American poet Alistair Stears took his horses by wartime train from Rome to Venice. He had just lost his first mistress, while his mother, the sculptor Anna Stears, had found the love of her life. Maggiore—for he was, in fact, an Italian major— had been posted to northeastern Italy, the Austrian front, and Anna's palazzo in Rome was already in the contortions of being closed. She was moving the household to Venice to be closer to him; the three of them—Anna, Maggiore, and Alistair—felt themselves a family, since love and trust had made them one. Alistair's horses, who shared him just now with no serious female unless poetry counts as one, were chief among his present cares.

On one of their last nights in the palazzo, where so much had happened—for Alistair and his mother, so much in the four swift years since Boston—Alistair honored his mother with an appearance at dinner. The dining room ceiling showed, as far as anyone could work it out, Ceres on her annual return to Olympus from Hades. She looked down this evening at Maggiore and Anna and Alistair in evening dress, many candles, Capo di Monte plates—the palazzo's very best—and excellent Champagne.

Alistair said, "I was going to send Filippo with them, the head groom. He's a good man. The *barone* was pretty decent about it."

Anna said, "Considering that I have been paying that man's wages for a year, the barone's decency was within bounds."

"True. And thank you, Mamma. But it doesn't matter, because Filippo's gone. He got conscripted."

Maggiore nodded. "Not a surprise," he said.

"Bernardo knows the work, and he's good when he's sober," Alistair said. "But he won't stay sober between here and Venice, so I can't use him. That leaves Roberto. He's good with the horses, and he's strong as an ox. But he's also dumb as an ox, and he can't read, obviously. Which means I have to go too."

"That is not very suitable, Alistair," said Anna. "Three days in a horse car."

"That is not very optional, Mamma. I can't give them a map and tell them to walk. And Vipero won't like to be handled by people he doesn't know."

"Three days will be damn lucky in a war," said Maggiore. "Do you know anything about how to do this, Alistair?" With Maggiore, they spoke Italian.

"I am hoping very much that you will tell me, Maggiore."

"Oh dear," said Maggiore. "You would do much better talking to a corporal. I will tell you what I know. Bran. Plenty of bran. Soft hay, no alfalfa. No oats except by hand, for treats. Start cutting them now. Two sets of blankets. Secure a third stall for yourselves and supplies . . ."

Alistair took notes on a small pad. Anna, who had spent an Irish childhood breathing horses and dreaming fox hunts, listened closely. A platter of cheeses was brought and dealt with. Maggiore finished as a crème caramel in a little cup with Capo di Monte sheep and shepherds on the bowl and clouds with skylarks on the lid was placed before each: "You'll be a very tired, dirty, and sore young man."

Alistair looked up at the ceiling. "I'm going to miss her," he said. "She always looks so happy getting home."

He meant Ceres.

"I expect she has friends there," said Maggiore.

He meant Olympus.

"We should all miss her," said Anna. "As we should and shall miss much of Rome. And she is not bad. Look at how her sheaf of wheat balances her skirt, the diagonal line, and how it passes from the gold of the wheat and sun to the darker woods and fields below. Not great, but not bad. To me."

She meant to herself as an artist, which she was.

IN WHAT SHE HAD happily taken to calling "our bedroom," Anna said, "Can he really do this, Gianfranco?" Her dress was easier to drop than his stiff shirt and studs, and she was in bed first. Warm October was over. November was chilly even in Rome. The fireplaces had not been lit.

"He's about to find out, Anna. It's better that he knows what he can do and what he can't. I can't see anything terrible happening. If I did, I'd ask you to put a stop to it. You'd better have a bath, a meal, and a bed ready in Venice."

"Could you send a soldier with him? A reliable one?"

"Not in wartime, Anna. Some officers might. I can't."

She got up on an elbow. "If I come back to this world after I die, Gianfranco, I am going to spend my life with men with no sense of honor. It's going to be so relaxing."

The head of her bed was in the shape of a scallop shell, and her auburn hair coursed on the snowy cover. He declared a truce with the shirt stud, walked over, and kissed her.

"But I'm very glad to have you, Gianfranco, even as you are. And soon we'll be almost together again. I'm glad you were here in Rome at the end."

In the night, she woke. She always woke now with sorrow at leaving Rome, where her childhood had grown into a happy youth, whose master sculptors informed her own slight art. When she thought of her son and his horses alone on those miles and miles of track, it all seemed terribly rocky and steep. Her authority was ebbing, but she could still put her foot down. He was only seventeen. She thought a long while, then put her head on Maggiore's shoulder and felt herself sigh. Her loyalty to him went beyond a wife's because she was not a wife and only love held them, and loyalty was anyway her best thing and she would go with him to Venice and far beyond. To be posted was not a soldier's fault. He was there. Her head was on his shoulder. She went back to sleep.

ALISTAIR MET HIS BEST friend, Manfredi, and Helene, Manfredi's new fiancée, for a farewell luncheon at the Hassler. Since Helene was an innocent young girl in love, this was like sitting next to a peach blossom, in November. The peach blossom wore a loose blue dress, which somehow absorbed the coral from the Hassler's walls as ripples. He realized with surprise that it must be the same stuff that Miss Schrauler, his very new friend in Venice, liked. *Fortunatus,* was it? *Fortuny?* The Hassler was a drain on the young men's pockets, but Helene's parents preferred places for their daughter where they knew the headwaiter.

Alistair asked carefully of Helene, *"Vos freres?"* (Your brothers?)

"Ils sont bien. Tous les deux. Toujours. Merci, Alistair." (Well. Still. Both. Thank you.) "But Lucien gets out of St. Cyr next week, so then he's in the war. Pharamond's regiment's in the rear for a little while."

Alistair nodded. "I'm glad they're well." Which was what you could say.

He told Manfredi what he was planning to do with the horses. His friend looked serious and said, "You've bitten off quite a lot, Alistair." He added, "Maybe I should come too. Won't be quite as much fun as Capri."

Vivid in all their minds was a recent sail with fresh wind and sparkling spray in Manfredi's family yacht, from Posilillipo to Capri, and a night in the villa there.

Helene looked appalled.

Alistair said, "Don't be an idiot, Manfredi. You're leaving soon too. You've got lots to do. I can easily manage."

He was rewarded with a blast of violet eyes. *"Manfredi vous aime tellement, Alistair."*

"How's little Ottavia?" said Alistair.

"Hasn't turned into a gargoyle yet," said Manfredi. "She'll manage." Ottavia was Manfredi's little sister, eight, there at the villa with her nanny, found making faces to herself among the rocks.

"My best to her," said Alistair.

"She rather took to you," said Manfredi. "Bad luck."

Manfredi ordered turbot for them after the fettucine. He ordered Champagne. "You must watch out for the remount squads," he said to Alistair. "They're hungry for horses."

Italy, a country plowed by oxen, had always been short of horses, even of mules. The Italian army now needed more than three hundred thousand. In the mountains, they were getting through them at a great rate.

"I have an American passport," said Alistair and almost blushed. "It might help." Indeed, he did have one. He had formerly traveled on his mother's but now had his own. It had been brought over by the kind consul general when he came by for tea several months before and had since been stuffed in the back of an underwear drawer, like a ticket of leave from a leper colony. When he had opened it the night before, he saw that the consul general had put in a handwritten list of the consuls in Italy and their addresses, which was nice of him.

"It probably might," said Manfredi. "Actually, they don't have a right to requisition horses yet. Doesn't mean they don't act as though they have. We had to ship some mules to the place in Umbria and it was an issue." Then he had a thought. "Why don't you ask Simon if he'd go with you?" Simon Cartwright, who fenced with them at the Palazzo Colonna, was the son of the American first secretary and sailed his family's Alden on the Chesapeake.

"Not a horseman. Sails and sabres for our Simon. No saddles. No go," said Alistair.

"I think I'm glad you're going," said Manfredi. "You'd be apt just to mope here. I'm terribly sorry about Serafina and all. I liked her, you know."

Helene now imitated herself looking out of a window, the casement closed. She was in favor of love, that enchanting new invention. She was really fond of Alistair, knew that a girl he thought he loved was gone, and would have liked to show sympathy. Since the girl was only a model he slept with who'd posed for his mother's pieces, even the stark naked ones, that was quite different, and she could not. She looked out of her window, serious but encouraging.

Late that afternoon, Alistair was given a package, long and slender, brought by hand. There was a letter wrapped around it. It was in Manfredi's writing, with ramrod verticals and almost womanly loops.

"I should come with you," it read, "but I'm facing a mutiny by every female on the planet. First Helene, then my mother. Ottavia not heard from yet. She'll be next. Probably her nanny. Here's this. My father doesn't exactly know I've borrowed it, so I need it back. Maybe it could come in handy. If they get stones in their hooves. M."

It was a sabre. The light cavalry kind, not the dragoons' scythe, so somewhat like a fencing sabre. Alistair tried the balance. It was quite a good sword. It was extremely sharp. For neither one of them was it a toy. They fenced twice a week under an excellent maître d'armes, training that had reached a new intensity with Manfredi's imminent cadetship. They had even attempted a mounted duel, until their horses turned it into a fiasco such that they could only sit down on hay and laugh. He smiled at it, though it was lethal, mainly with affection. For one who was also thinking to be a pilot, Manfredi was cavalry to his toes.

xxx

It was the kind of operation that shows its hand by starting at a hellish hour, before dawn. In the outer circle of an arc lamp's light, on a siding hard to find even with a drawing, he saw his railroad wagon. It was alone. It seemed thoughtful in the night.

"That's it," Alistair said.

"Looking just like home," said Manfredi, whose help at this phase Alistair couldn't have turned down even had he wanted to. Manfredi eased the car toward it. He had learned to change gear, just recently.

It did look rather smug. So that shunting crews might see that there were creatures in it, not pig iron, there was a hay bale tied to each corner of the roof. Under the light, this was festive. It had been well disinfected and smelled of pine.

Manfredi sniffed. "You've got that right," he said.

The loading gate was down. They went on board. Manfredi scuffed his heel on the ramp and nodded. "Not too slippery, and it's got slats. I've been reading the army manuals."

Alistair had engaged the whole car, on Maggiore's later advice. Four of the eight stalls were set up: mattresses for Roberto and himself in one, deep straw, stuffed sacks for buffers and rings, polished, for the horses, stocks of hay and bran, blankets and wraps, and bright new canvas buckets in the last. Manfredi pointed at the buckets.

"Good thinkin', Lincoln," he said suddenly, in English.

"Come?" said Alistair, in Italian.

Manfredi laughed. "I heard a man in Baltimore say that. I've been waiting for a chance." He said, "This looks good, Alistair. I'd have you as my sergeant any day. God, I should be going with you."

"Every time you say that," said Alistair, "I think you're sending me to my death while you go and have another drink. So shut up, would you?"

"OK," said Manfredi. They walked back down the ramp. It was cold, not bitter. Manfredi said, "Will your horses mind the disinfectant?"

"They're used to it."

"I think I see lights," said Manfredi.

The rail yard looked like a spider's web, some strands of it burning under the arc lights, others like ice on a window. A few locomotives crept about it, with stomachs of fire, but far off at the edge of the dark there were lights with the wavering, moth-like quality of a motor.

"I hope they loaded them right," said Manfredi. "We don't want two maniacs."

"Probably did," said Alistair.

They watched the lights, like weak eyes, move about uncertainly, never far from the regions where the iron maze ended at darkness. Manfredi got into the Alfa-Romeo, turned it to face the lights, and began to flash its headlamps. The weak eyes stopped, were crushed by a passing freight, and then were seen to pick their way toward them. Yes, it was a flatbed truck with two stalls jury-rigged out of wood and a big board for unloading carried on top. Much suaver versions would soon be called "horse boxes."

It could have been worse. Vipero felt he should have been consulted and made trouble, but that was mainly out of form for him. They got him up the ramp, Bernardo at his head, Alistair and Manfredi behind him on either side with a rope against his arse. Manfredi said to him cheerfully, "You're off to Venice, old boy. Pretty girls and tiramisu." Vipero indicated that he was a gelding, thank you very much, didn't waste his time with the one and didn't know much about the other.

Manfredi put his hand on Alistair's shoulder. "Pretty girls goes for you, too, old boy. Find one there."

"I have, rather," said Alistair. Just for an instant, lovely Miss Schrauler, beautiful silks and golden hair, the most joyful accident of his and his mother's reconnaissance in Venice, flickered on the platform and was gone.

"That was fast work," said Manfredi.

"No work. Only the canvas. Blank."

The smell of horse now overlying oil and grease made them all feel warmer. Manfredi produced a thermos of coffee and grappa and handed it first to the older groom.

"Grazie, Marchese," said Bernardo. He looked spry, sober, and entertained to be doing a new thing. He raised his cup to both of them. *"Signori!"* Alistair realized

at that moment that he should have taken him and not the boy. Roberto's face was heavy and sad, an Italian peasant's asked to do what he didn't understand. "Cheer up," said Alistair. "Just do what I say."

"Sisignore," said Roberto. He mumbled it. Well, he knew the work and could lug things.

There was suddenly nothing to do. Alistair and Manfredi pretended to check around. Manfredi's sword had been stuck up to its hilt in a lower bale of hay. "Don't forget that," said Manfredi. From down the track, a locomotive began to back down on them. They could hear the slow gasps of its steam and once the scrape of shoveled coal.

"This could be it," said Alistair to Manfredi.

Manfredi nodded. "When you buy me lunch up north, it's truffles."

Men dropped off the locomotive. They were sooty as they passed in front of the firebox flames.

The coupling was done with exemplary manners, thought Alistair. He heard just the snort of one of the horses. He motioned Roberto into the car, shook Manfredi's hand, shook Bernardo's and put something in it, and followed Roberto. The men from the locomotive came to the loading ramp and showed him the inside bolts to be shut. They raised the ramp, grunting. Manfredi's salute was swallowed up by a narrowing arc. He shot the bolts. He could smell coal over all else. He heard two motors start. He heard steam fill the pistons. They moved out of the arc lamp, and it was dark.

The dark suited him. He could see the outline of the stalls. He could hear the horses standing easy. In the dark his lost, his only, Serafina, came back to him, as she usually did. His memory stroked her light, warm shoulder. He held her still, hushed her mouth, and contemplated her. From time to time a bright light whipped through the hatches across the car. He saw that he should check that they could be shut in serious cold. They could be. Serafina had left. They were not covering ground. The train went forward and back. There were jolts, not so slight as the first but none really to unsettle, as cars were added, seemingly further and further away. He breathed deep, trying to hold the shape of the next four days within him, so he could carry it to its end. He acknowledged one mistake, his choice of servant, but he did not think it a grave one.

They ran a little further. Then stopped. There was solid light outside. To his surprise, the personnel door, though not the ramp, was opened. He went to it and saw they were at a platform, well lit, where trucks with boxes of small items—canned food, boots, and the like—were set around. There was the freight agent he had dealt with two days before, still with the same pencil, the same fardel of rumpled papers, the same bristles on his jowl, and the same smell, as though he dressed in stale sausage. There was a man with a horse. The agent took a step toward Alistair and half bowed.

"*Signore.* Signor Stears," said the agent.

Alistair looked at the man with the horse. He was a solid man, poorly built for shuffling, and said simply, *"Bon di."* And a moment later, "Signore." "Bon di" for *"buon giorno"* was the far north.

The agent was saying, "A very great favor, signore. Half your car is empty." He poured more butter on. "*Commendatore,* the horse who needs a place is a nobleman's. Cars are so short in this war. The army. I know this groom. If the *commendatore* could offer space to Bologna, then he can find a final train there. He is a serious man. No gypsy." And carries money, obviously.

The horse was properly blanketed, was a gelding, his legs bandaged rightly for travel, was a good horse, had a clean, bright eye, stood calm.

Alistair said to the groom, "You are from the north."

"Bergamo." He did not say "signore."

"You know this work?"

"It is what I do."

"You have supplies for the time?"

The man pointed to a neat pile of bales and such like. "Yes," he said.

Alistair said, "You may come. A good horse should not spend his life on platforms."

The man slightly smiled. "Grazie, signore. I am grateful." He touched the horse's neck. "We are."

The agent bowed again. They dropped the ramp. Alistair watched the man load. He rejected Roberto's help, which was offered poorly. It was properly done. Alistair felt the shape of the coming days rest calm inside his chest.

This time when they were off, they were off. The sun was rising now, and the winter morning light was sweet. They ran on the track, Rome to Florence, that he would come to know in every weather of his life. Through the hatch he watched the noble roofs of Rome that Serafina had leaned across him to see. They rotated this time as on a failing turntable. The Via Flaminia where, once riding, he had seen the column of guns and the pennants, and the men and the sabres came by as well. There was not much to do right now. He remembered himself lounging on a sun-warmed step asking heaven how to bring his column into a verse and knew that now he would be at his desk looking down a pen as down a lancet. Vipero was playing with his tether ring like a solemn child. Pompey, the grey, looked bemused. He went quietly into each stall and ran a hand down each. He wondered whether Pompey could remember the Via Flaminia and their great jump.

They picked up speed somewhat. He was dozing, having slept little the night before. Serafina slept beside him, dark and sweet. Of a sudden she rose up, high and black, face averted, surging away from him. He reached for her hand, but there was suddenly a blow of pressure on his ear, a sucking away of the light, and a rage of sound. Vipero screamed. Both horses plunged. They were in a tunnel. He jumped to his feet. He saw Roberto in Vipero's stall. He went into Pompey's, held his head as best he could, tried to soothe him, thought the horse's head hit the ceiling as he tried to rear. They came out of the tunnel. Roberto had Vipero under good control, but both horses were panting and deeply insulted. He knew that he was panting, too, but they were undamaged, out of trouble. Then there was another tunnel, somewhat longer.

After that one, as he wiped his face, the groom he had allowed onboard spoke for the first time since Rome.

"It gets better. They learn it doesn't hurt them. This one's done it before. Doesn't bother him a bit."

Alistair said, "It's the first time I have done this. As I suppose you know."

The groom said, "There is always a first time. I respect you for doing it at all. Very few gentlemen do."

"They conscripted my best groom," said Alistair.

The groom smiled, or showed his teeth. "That is quite funny," he said, "for the same has just happened to my master. They say my papers are waiting at home. This is my last run. But I doubt my master will be doing as you are doing. Still, of course, you are quite young. Are these horses yours or your father's?"

"Mine," said Alistair.

"They look useful, at least."

"They are," said Alistair. "This one is the better of the two but a little difficult."

"That is often the case," said the groom. "As with women."

Alistair went over to the other end of the car and offered his hand. "My name is Alistair Stears," he said.

The smooth hand was taken into the rough. "And mine is Daniele. Signore, I believe you are not Italian."

"Irlandese," said Alistair, inaccurately. He had recently decided that he believed his mother's Catholic Irish a great deal more distinguished than all of his father's Yankees.

The tunnels got better.

He stayed awake. It was safer so. Rome passed behind him. Its painted ceilings, ten thousand like that of Ceres and her friends, moved safely inside their walls. One could have been of him waking with his mother's model, with drapings as Baroque as you please. Let us have a frieze around it, line drawings, Rococo now, of the two of them united even more than in flesh, in marvelously ingenious games not to be caught. Now a panel, night, a great ship sinking, fire showing bodies on the waves. And to balance it, something like an expulsion from Eden, but also at night, and rocky. And there you had it. His mother, suddenly affrighted by her passion for Maggiore, guilty though it was still unconsummated, had been on the very brink of return to Boston, husband, virtue, discontent. Serafina, seeing herself left behind, had vanished. Two days later, the *Lusitania* was horribly torpedoed, horribly sunk. His mother gave virtue and discontent a cooler look. Maggiore, whom Alistair already loved, entered their lives.

Leave to the light, which gives to paint all its grace, that Serafina, slight and unschooled, had given a stilted New England boy Italy and joy and, though she had none of her own, had unlocked the poetry inside him.

Leave completely out of the composition his promise to her three nights before the end, that her firstborn would be his heir. You cannot make a promise to the empty night. And Roman ceilings have no place for the Brothers Grimm.

He slept. They stopped. It seemed deliberate and luxurious, as though the train had put down a basket. When there was a voice outside, Daniele the groom opened the door and called a question. He looked back in. "Long stop," he said. "Maybe an hour. Maybe more." He went to his stall, picked up the water bucket, emptied what was left over the rails, and climbed down.

Alistair said to Roberto, "Follow him." Roberto made for the door. "With the buckets. One bucket. Two. Follow him to the water. Fill the buckets. One. Two. Bring them back. All right?"

"Sisignore," said Roberto, got the buckets, climbed down, followed Daniele at a run.

Alistair mucked out the stalls, quickly, with economy of straw. He gave each of his horses a handful of sweet feed and a muzzle rub and so calmed his own irritation. He pitched the bucketful a little down the track then, braced with both arms, leaned all the way out of the door into a part of Italy he had always loved—loved the low hills with the ridges sharp in the clear light, loved the poplars and the chestnuts, loved the vines and villages with their roofs as uneven as a small boy's steps, and, God almighty, they had a band to greet him.

They were in a village with a town just up the track, which had to be Orvieto. The train went the full length of a side of the village and could have served it as a wall. The band was in the center, of course, in the square outside the church, where the police station was, and an inn, a nice broad tree, and a fountain now covered with dead leaves. The band was dressed in military uniforms of a time long gone, and its members had no doubt worn them new. There was a dais on which roosted black suits tending to the stout, a priest in his soutane, and, to give the composition life, an officer, with sword and braid, to sparkle in the sun. The band picked up a patriotic tune one had begun to hear everywhere of late, though clearly not in this village. Alistair wondered what in the world it was all about. There were lots of flags. He got down from the car.

And Carabinieri, whose black hats, if one was a little above them, did look a little bit like flies, especially when the Carabinieri, perhaps at the sun's rising heat, began to dart about. For the sun was also drawing into the square, first by ones and twos and then as of a vapor much the same color as the stones, young workmen and peasants, whose clothes seemed straight from field or forge, and upon these the Carabinieri darted, taking papers, asking questions, pointing where to go. Where to go was a table, and more Carabinieri, opposite the shade tree, between the church and the inn, at the head of a street in which—his eyes were working now—there was line of army-grey FIAT trucks. The band gave up the new hit as a bad job, took a deep breath, and happily went off with that fine old chestnut, "Mia Savoia." The officer leaned forward, becoming a blaze of sparks, and folded his hands over his sword's hilt. Now behind the men, being barked into rough ranks lined up between the table and the trucks, came a second presence out of the narrow streets—young women, most carrying one child and followed by a brood. They moved more slowly than the men but much more steadily, and the Caribinieri ignored them, so that before long they were mixed with the men, two liquids of different colors, the girls much brighter. An onlooker might expect a rousing chorus, a quartet or so to wrap up the action, a country dance (a hornpipe for the Carabinieri), and a general bow.

The country dance was impeded by the girls losing their partners, as the men were pulled from them into the trucks. There was a good deal of boo-hooing, which the band had to work up a sweat to drown. When the square was all women, and some crones and old men, the officer rose, coruscated, and said the village, it was called something like Domatumno, had done its duty. The mayor rose and said it was glad it had. The priest was happy to report God's sentiments, which were the same. The band played the national anthem, causing all on the dais to rise, the better afterward to follow the mayor, the officer, and the priest toward the inn. An old woman in black screamed at the lot of them, *"Bastardi neri!"* and was ignored. A sergeant barked, corporals yelped, and the lines of men slouched toward the trucks. Alistair, looking at females as usual, found his eye fixed on one, her neck with the milky innocence of a young girl's, only one baby and that at her breast, her face beyond tears and in a set, hard, dry despair forty years older than herself. She looked toward the trucks, but he did not think she saw. She neither moved nor saw him. He could not turn his gaze and was looking at her still when Daniele and Roberto came back, the latter breathing hard and with wet pants but buckets mostly full.

Alistair said quietly, "It is not very nice to take men from their women. I had not thought of that, in war."

Daniele lifted up his bucket and set it precisely on the edge of the door then turned around and followed Alistair's eye. "She may be thinking of how empty her bed will be this winter. I do not know her and I cannot say. She is certainly wondering what she is going to find to eat."

When the girl moved, she did not look up, never saw him, and Alistair was thankful, though did not know why. He saw her much longer than that. Hers is the earliest face that exists in the surviving works, though in them she is transposed in time and place to the last days of the war. She is the ghost of the "Tagliamento" poems of 1918. Throughout them she is half-seen through the smoke of burning Fruili—waif, witch, and fury.

They plodded through Orvieto and did not yet close the door. Alistair stood in it. The locomotive's thoughtful breathing, well down the track, was easy to hear. Just outside the passenger station, they passed a troop train, packed and still. Carabinieri guarded it, standing back so that one covered three doors. So their car drifted very close to them, the sweat stains under their arms, skin of hands a little white where they held the carbines, sweat on necks in the sun. One turned around as the wheels clumped over a point, and Alistair looked into the mild brown peasant eyes; an order would fall into them as easily as a coin into a collection plate, fall softly, and stay.

Daniele the groom said, "Would you like to extend your life a little?"

Alistair said, "Well, yes."

"Do not stand in that door. If the train stopped suddenly, and it rolled, it would crush you."

So, after that, Alistair stood to the side of it, with an arm braced.

THEY REACHED THE YARDS outside Florence in the night and stood becalmed on another steel maze prowled by creeping dragons. Their own train, though stopped, had become a living creature, making sleepy sounds. He knew there were other cars of horses, maybe of mules. Pompey and Vipero knew it, too, and listened to faint whinnies without comment. For himself, he felt tired, alone, would have loved a friend. They barely moved but crept up to a platform of unplaned wood then nestled there. The platform carried sound. Far up the train, Alistair began to hear footfalls of groups of men, with purpose, then, very faintly, voices. He heard all this through a light mist of half sleep until another noise, horses' hooves, cleared his brow, and a group of mules was lead past by Carabinieri. Daniele the groom was motionless, had withdrawn into himself. Alistair looked up the platform. Most of the horse cars had their loading ramps down. Very slowly, he bent down, pulled Manfredi's sabre from the hay bale, put it behind him, and stood straight. Roberto saw him, which he had not wished, and his eyes went wide. Three horses were led past. They were mainly just horses but serviceable. The footsteps and voices now were closer. More horses.

So the Carabinieri came in. They were good, he admitted, at seeming intrusive and at filling, just two of them, sergeant and private, the whole car. The private shot the bolts of the ramp and lowered it to the second private outside. Then there were three. By luck, they started on Daniele. Alistair stood at ease in front of the latch of Vipero's stall and motioned Roberto to do the same with Pompey. But Roberto sidled out of the car and down the ramp and into the shadows. A horse could not have rolled his eyes better. Alistair swallowed a bolt of fury, and, even more at ease, moved the point of the sabre to the bottom of Pompey's door, so it just showed from behind his leg.

The first private, not the sergeant, looked at Daniele's horse. He looked appreciative. He was perhaps the horseman of the three. He nodded to the sergeant. Who said, "We are requisitioning this horse in the name of the king." The soldier went into the stall.

Daniele said, "You cannot requisition, and I am not authorized to sell."

The sergeant looked at him, in the face but without interest. "Why are you not in the army? Your papers, please."

Daniele gave him papers, said, "I am not in the army because my conscription papers are dated next week, not this. They came in my absence. They are in Bergamo."

The private had his hand on the horse's tether rope. The sergeant said, "If you have received your papers, you are under orders and you will turn over this horse. It is perfectly regular." He gave back the groom's papers, politely enough, and pulled one of his own out of a pouch by his side. Daniele started to speak. The sergeant said, "Don't be a fool. I have put this horse down as 'Officer's Charger.' Your master can take this paper and get quite a lot of money. And you have obviously not stolen the horse. Two copies. I sign one. You the other. Make your mark if you can't write."

The groom said, "My master does not authorize . . ."

The sergeant sighed, to be heard. He put his hand into his pocket and took out some small bills. Alistair thought it was about two weeks' wages.

"I suppose you know your orders," said the groom. He signed the paper.

The sergeant gave him the bills. The sergeant gave him the other copy. The horse was led away. The sergeant turned to Alistair. "Don't get ideas," he said.

Alistair's idea was that he had seen yet one more ignobility, and that the car, after Roberto, was turning greasy with it.

Alistair did not move, and said to the men, "My situation is special. It will require an officer."

The first private looked at the horses. His enthusiasm returned, refreshed. The sergeant said, patiently and almost pleasantly, "Your master will understand perfectly well. Don't get in trouble, young fellow."

Alistair said, "I am that master, and I do not understand." The private made to open Pompey's stall. Alistair raised the sabre point two inches. The private stopped. Alistair looked the sergeant in the face and said, *"Transmetti ad onorevole il tuo ufficiere I mei complimenti eggregi e lo prega che Egli mi faccia il piacere dal suo coloquio."* He said it pleasantly. It meant, in all its shades of grammar, "You, fellow, convey to your distinguished officer my highest compliments and request his honor, fellow, to afford me the pleasure of his interview." It mixed as much offense and grace possible in one sentence in the time and his Italian allowed, and he was proud of it. It made the air fit to breathe. The sergeant took a moment to digest it. Then he turned darker and stepped forward.

"You'll get your officer, you little prick," he said.

So Alistair relaxed.

Actually, he got two. A *tenente* of Carabinieri, voice and skin from Naples south, smooth muscled and with the kind of military collar that pushes the chin toward the ears and turns an intelligent young Italian into a throttled pig. The other tenente, he was delighted to see, was cavalry, had the thoughtful presence of a crane, more thoughtful yet with a bad limp; he was evidently senior to the first in the sense that a man is senior to his mastiff, and, like a man with a mastiff, walked behind.

"Thank you, tenente. I am glad of your presence." He spoke to the crane.

Of course, he kept his horses. It was easy. He did not need the officers.

An authority, tenente, to requisition, that does not exist. Am I not right?

An authority that a sergeant, confronted by the passport of a major power, would never have used. Not as Alistair presented it, only now, handing it past the first officer, roast beef past a mastiff's nose, to the second, who, cranes having spectacles at will, read it at leisure.

And, apart from that, tenente, the question of nationality. These horses are American.

No. The sergeant would have looked cloudy, then foggy, then muttered something, then turned away. So why all this?

Because with the bullying, with the bribes, with the girl left bereft, Roberto skulking, his beloved Italy was turning gangrenous. Only by confronting it fair and square could he try to counter the disease. Corruption of form is dissolution, and that is death.

"The consulate here is on the Lungarno. I can be there at nine. The consul general in Rome is my family's friend. But my own friends are fighting with you. One day my government will wake up. Then I will be with you. Stealing my horses is a bad way to begin."

"Stealing's a bit hard. We do pay. Are they yours?"

"Of course."

"Where are you going? Why are you doing this?"

"My mother is moving from Rome to Venice. You conscripted my groom. I have to get them there."

Through an Italy to which I have given my heart's fealty, and please, please do not give me cause to look away.

"I doubt that anybody closer than Rome has any idea whether we have authority over you or not. I think we are wishing you a pleasant trip. Though maybe we should conscript your horses with your groom and get you out of this car. Actually I will do better." He took a paper from a dispatch case, signed, and gave it to Alistair with the passport. "If people like us bother you again, this may help. Or it might not. There are troubles further north. Keep your eyes open. Where in God's name did you get that? The sabre?"

"A friend at Pinerolo." Manfredi's school.

"Dear God. Don't wave it around. That really might be trouble. The last time I used one, an Austrian gave me this." He touched his thigh. "We use carbines now. Like these gentlemen. The Carabinieri."

"Thank you, tenente. I hope your leg heals. Maybe we will meet again."

"Thank you. I, too, would rather ride than walk."

"Pretty damn good," said Daniele, the groom. The loading ramp had been shut.

Alistair looked bleakly at him. He said nothing.

The man looked him back. He said, "The war changes everything. I do not belong to me. Conscription changes everything. The horse did not belong to me. My master is not my master. I have some money in my pocket. I did not steal the horse. Our conditions are different, signore."

Alistair nodded, not to agree.

The man said, "I would like to stay on as far as Bologna, still. I can at least show your boy where to find water."

"You may as well," said Alistair.

WHEN THEY WERE WELL clear of Florence, he lay down. They went slowly through the mountains, and the swaying of the car was not much. He on the whole resisted sleep but was aware of rising through its surface in the first light through the hatch. He thought vaguely of the very pleasant Miss Schrauler he would certainly see again in Venice and her beautiful silks. *The liquefaction of her clothes.* He drove himself to his feet, went to the door, and slipped it open a little way. They were crawling through the Apennine valleys—there were sheep in the fields and the skeletons of beans—not very far from Sabbioni, almost through the hills and putting on speed. The air was chill but not bitter. He splashed some water from a bucket on his face and let the cold peel through a tiredness he did not admit, but he was already dull. He got the horses' morning hay, arranging it befittingly, for it was inconceivable to him that the most beautiful beings in the world (if you thought about it, they had it all over even girls) could lack a sense of the comely. They had been far too long in their stalls already. He ran his arms firmly down each neck, under their blankets, and along their bellies. Vipero found his belt and tugged at it, causing Alistair to reprove him, chastising his muzzle with a finger. They were warm. Their blankets were dry. They were in a cocoon of bran and hay and humans they knew. They were fine. Roberto slept, snoring just over the noise of the train. Alistair looked at him with disgust and would let him sleep until there was something to pick up.

They crept into Bologna, the first of the cities of the north. There were recruits here too. Very far from the dove-grey university, down a long stark warehouse avenue they were being marched by military police. There was no band here, no gold and blue officer, no priest. There were women, girls to ancient, a ragged pack of shawls and dirty aprons, shrieking and throwing what came handy, from cabbage stalks to bricks, at the police. Pretty often, the recruits got hit as well. The women pressed against the walls along the street and rushed out sometimes, and sometimes the police rushed out, found a woman to club, and then jumped back again. Up the avenue, a squad of mounted police was getting ready join in. Though structures sometimes swam into the way, the train was about fifty yards from this. The women's voices had less of battle than despair. It was a picture that smelled of ashes and stale soup. Alistair stood in the door and watched. His heart covered its face.

They were still in Bologna at night. The train was broken up and reformed, Milan, Turin, and France, or Venice and the war. Things were not well here. After dark found them in a string of cars and no locomotive far out on the web of track. There was not much around. Daniele had left, at a place that did not look promising to Alistair. He walked off down the track, carrying two blankets and so like a peddler. Should I send the boy for water? Alistair had said. Not here. Wait until they are making up the train. Then it will be close. There were no farewells.

He heard voices in the dark, a group, men's, closer and farther, moving about. Eventually they appeared, in and out of the patches of light around the cars. They were about a dozen men, just short of ragged, a pack not quite formed. He stood in the door, nothing coy about the sabre now. They tried the doors of cars, broke into one, broke things up in it, and some came out carrying boots. They were not quiet. He had no idea what they were, nor even how unusual. Deserters, he guessed. He considered closing the door, disliked the thought of listening to them try it, and stood in it instead. They came to the track below him. They were older than he, all of military age, so deserters might be right. They were less vicious than they might have liked, but tough they were.

One said, "There's horses in there."

Another said, "Give us the horses, boy, and we'll leave you alone."

He looked back. He was not in much trouble. There was only one way into the car. He was vastly more dangerous than they knew. They could not expect to walk out of a railroad yard with two horses. And, though this would be too late to help, if they somehow untied Vipero and put a hand on him, their troubles, whatever they might be now, would just have begun.

He heard, "No use in fucking horses."

A rangy man, something black, oil, smeared on his brow, said, "He'll have money, that one." He shoved others aside and pushed to the car. One sleeve was ragged, and the shoulder, strong. He said, straight to Alistair, "Give us the money and you and your horsies can go." His face was at the level of Alistair's shin. His eyes were not calculating, but they were off their balance.

Alistair looked down at his throat and drew a line in his eye between just below the Adam's apple and the sabre point. He did not move the point but knew that if the man grabbed or tried to rise up, he would hurt him badly enough to shock them all.

"No," he said. For a moment the man's shoulders flexed, and for a moment Alistair's hand tightened on the hilt. But the wild eyes did not resolve. The group did not tighten but wavered.

Then they heard something they did not like. They broke apart. They drifted from the car. Alistair, too, heard distant hoof falls of ridden horses. They ran, boots bouncing in their hands. He did not move. The man at the car, his enemy, stayed, as though tied to him. His eyes now flicked from side to side, washed in need and panic.

Alistair raised the sabre now. "Go," he said.

The man went. Ran fast enough to join his friends.

Alistair looked out at the blighted wilderness he had come to, where people would hurt him if they could and a sword stopped them, and dissolution felt cold on his brow. When they were at a distant platform and the train was making up, he pointed to the buckets and said to Roberto, "Ask where the water is and fill them."

Roberto backed away. "The soldiers might take me," he said.

"They may," said Alistair. "But if you do not take the buckets, you will not stay in this car, and if you come back with them empty, you are not getting back on." He touched the sabre's hilt. "Then you will have to beg your way to Rome, the police will pick you up, and the army will quite certainly take you. Do you doubt me?"

Roberto flinched.

"So take them."

Roberto did. And came back.

This trip was fairly simple, thought Alistair. Stand in the door and scare Roberto worse than the army. He was just so tired.

THEY AMBLED INTO MESTRE in the late afternoon of the fourth day. They were by no means done. Out on another wilderness of track, the train was broken up again: Treviso, Belluna, Udine, Monfalcone, the Serenissima. He had not slept properly for four days, his clothes were a disease, he had not eaten for a day and was too tired to want to. But the shape of the venture nestled inside him as soft as a girl after love. A tank engine turned up, collared the few cars for Mestre, mostly machines for Miss

Schrauler's father's excavation, and brought them to a platform siding. There was a motor box there, rather senior to the barone's, two men from the stable Pietro had found, his mother, and his tutor, Mr. Featherstonhaugh. The cars drifted in slowly enough that, when they stopped, all were by the door. He got out, and his mother, long light grey dress and ghost of a scent of freesia, put her hands on his shoulders and considered him.

She said, "Dear God, Alistair, you look awful. Are you all right, child?"

"I'm OK, Mamma. It was a bit long."

He gently disengaged her hands and turned to the two men from the stables. They looked competent, as Pietro the Venetian, though he was no horseman, had assured him that they would be. One had taken Vipero, who did not protest. Both horses had to think about getting down the ramp. Alistair said to him, "I think they're fine. Walk them, please. Forty minutes gently, that would be good. Hay tonight then start the hard feed in the morning. Just two kilos to start with. You can turn them out together in the morning; they're pretty good friends. The one you've got is a little tricky, but he's not nasty. Take this," he pointed to Roberto, "and give it a bed. I'll decide what to do with him tomorrow. Understood, or do you want me to come?"

"Capisco, signore. Il signore deve allentarsi." Understood. Relax.

"Wasn't easy to find you. Where or when. We've been here hours," said Mr. Featherstonhaugh.

"Sorry," he said.

"For God's sake, Alistair," said his mother. "You're here, child."

So, to his surprise, was Miss Schrauler's father's speedboat.

His mother said, "She twigged where we were coming and insisted we take it. She said you liked it. Actually, she made her father's people find out where you'd turn up. She seems a nicer young woman than one might have thought, whatever her father may be." When Mr. Featherstonhaugh was out of hearing, she said, "Alistair, are you involved with her? She seemed quite concerned."

He said, "Of course not." He was shocked. "She's not even Italian," he added, and, though he always liked his mother's laugh, was too tired to figure out the joke.

In the boat, she said, "It's back to the Gritti, I'm afraid. The palazzo has no plumbing. Two days, they say. At least the Gritti has baths. Which you do badly need, my dear."

On the Gritti's wide stairs, they met the Schrauler family coming down, two stumps with the fair tree, Victoria, behind. Victoria at once detached herself and came swiftly over.

She looked at him, without disguise. "Mr. Stears," she said. "What have they done to you?"

"A rather long trip, Miss Schrauler, " he said. "But the company was good, and your boat was even better."

She looked him up and down, more closely, and then almost angry, "Why did you do this? Somebody could have brought them. Somebody."

He was annoyed at her annoyance. He said, "I am their master. Who else do they have?" And, hearing how pompous that was, smiled at her and said, "It was a lark, Miss Schrauler. Just a lark."

This time she looked him in the face and said quietly, "No it was not, Mr. Stears. It wasn't a lark at all." She smelled of lilac. He did not.

2

When Alistair woke the next morning he knew that the train had stopped again, then that this was not a bed you got in a horse car, then that he was damnably hungry, and finally that when he drew the curtains, there would be the Grand Canal. He dressed, went down, and ordered the kind of breakfast he had not thought of since Maine mornings in another life, where there was no prosciutto. He found himself looking vaguely around for Miss Schrauler and annoyed himself.

He went straight out after breakfast. From the dining room, he had seen bright white wavelets winking on the Grand Canal. He started up a narrow *calle*, built indeed for slinking cats, but where the eye could rise up to Santa Maria dei Gigli at the end, turned and was soon in the Campo San Stefano, already his favorite, airy and quiet. Breezy this morning, he pulled his jacket around him. He went up onto the Academia Bridge. There were gondolas out on the canal. Their sterns were blown a little askew by the wind as they rounded the bend to the Rialto. They were scattered petals, one could say, he would have said, but now see the gondoliers: the oar feathered through the water looks light, it's true, a darting fish, but then the heavy punch from the spine, the wince of hip, the thighs inclining forward, the weight driven into the counterstroke, like pushing logs. In this light and air, very unlike their leaden arrival the first day, the *palazzi* of the canal were at their foamiest, the roof over San Stefano's brick barn sides was ready to shake its white turrets and fly away. He saw it all from the bottom, heavy on its pilings, pressed into mud, built stone by stone, hungry for labor, ladders of workmen carrying up, clambering down. A country bought and rebought at great price, the final account never paid. In this clear air, the line of the Dolomites cut the horizon again, the breeze prevailing over guns, though it came from their kingdom. There went the troop trains, the horses led past him on the platform in the night, the Umbrian girl's young husband, the current payment, many more to come.

It was cold up here for his clothes. He went down, back through the *campo* and the calle to where the Gritti's late geraniums shivered in their boxes and dropped real petals into the canal. The lobby's warmth made him shiver the first instant, and there was Miss Schrauler at the concierge's desk. In blue-grey this morning, pale art nouveau lilies growing up toward her bust, somewhat like last time, but now on top a dragon, made of its own pale smoke, its talons skimming her breasts, one guessed, its body as a halter, its neck and twisting tail descending her shoulders. She saw him and turned. *Ambush?* he thought and didn't care. She did improve the view. He had thought of her since last night on the stairs.

"Could you endure company, Mr. Stears?"

Actually, yes, he easily could.

"Could you stand to watch me eat breakfast?"

"I'll take you to a local place," he said. "It's more fun." He had seen one such in the Campo S. Maurizio, just short of San Stefano. "But you need to put more on. It's chilly. Unless your dragon keeps you warm."

She laughed. "What fun!" she said. "I'll be just a minute."

When she came down, he said, "I looked for you at my own breakfast."

"Did you?" she said and smiled.

The place he had seen was down a couple of steps. Inside, it was smoky enough that the exciting photographs of the collapse of the great campanile of St. Mark's into a heap of brick had turned historical, although the event was recent and the rebuilt tower still garishly new. The tables were tin, the menu in chalk on the wall, and they did not often get the likes of Miss Schrauler. But she sat with an interested, pleased look that he liked, so apparently did the waiting girl, and they were pleasantly served in the soft shoo-shoo Venetian he was trying to get a handle on. He pointed to the third thing on the menu.

"That's what you should have," he said.

"OK," she said.

He spoke it and had his pronunciation corrected into something more properly resembling a mop. "Do you want coffee or wine?" he said. "Nobody would turn a hair if you had wine."

"I do love drinking," she said. "I think it's the best. But it's a little early. I guess I'll have coffee." So they both did.

"Did a lot of people get hurt?" she said, indicating the best photograph, where the photographer had managed to show a pall of dust still rising.

"Amazingly enough, I believe no one," he said. "They saw the crack the night before and roped it off. That was in '03."

"Were you already in Italy then?"

"Oh no, no. I was a little boy in Boston."

"Do you think we're the same age? I'm not telling you mine, because I'm a lady."

"That makes it rather hard to know," he said. "Doesn't it?"

Their coffee arrived, and soon, her plate. It appeared to be small dumplings with tiny fish inside.

"It's funny stuff for breakfast," she said. "It's funny stuff anywhere." But she ate a couple without hesitation and made a moue indicating approval with reservation.

"What's it like?" he said.

"Not bad." Then, "What do you mean, 'What's it like?' You chose it for me."

"I hoped you'd tell me," he said. "I hardly know Venice at all."

"Ooh!" she said. "Ooh!" She hit the table with her fist, causing everything to rattle, including a bracelet he hadn't noticed yet. The girl, two old men finishing their pipes, and the cook looked up. "You're awful. And now you won't get one. Will you tell me about your trip?"

He thought a moment and said, "You'd never have tried them but for me. Admit it. Yes, I will. It won't be what you're expecting though. And I'm sorry if I barked at you last night."

She batted that away with the same hand.

He said, "You were right and you were wrong. I had to do it, and it was not a lark." *Which is why we are here,* but he did not say that.

She said, "While you tell me, could we walk up to the Palazzo Fortuny? I like to touch it once a day. He is my hero."

"Do you say a prayer?"

"You think you're funny."

She was a good listener. Past the front of San Stefano and then the Oratorio Dall' Annunciata, she walked close abreast to him, often with her face toward him. From the corner of his eye, he could see that men looked at her, that she was used to it, and he counted it a grace that she neither preened nor cringed. In the calle, she walked closer and was good at gliding between people. At the Fortuny palace, he was startled to see that she in fact took her glove off and felt the stone as though questioning it, but he still had her attention.

He ended about then, saying, "Lies and cheating do not go very well with death. And bullying is cheating. It was worse because of the horses. They tend to tell the truth. They are not as good at being apes as men." He left out only the part about the prowlers.

He thought it was perhaps because she was a big girl that there was a great deal of calm in her grace. He already knew she was not afraid to look at people. She stood before him still in the crowd and said, "I could have told you quite a lot of that, Alistair. I'm not going to tell you why that is yet, though I will. But I could have told you." And then, "I said it. I didn't really mean to, but I did. I said, 'Alistair.' Will I be a vulgar American girl if I go on?"

"No," he said.

"Will you walk me back, please? Papa is having some very grand people for lunch, and he likes me to be his hostess."

"Of course," he said. "That must be fun."

"Oh yes," she said. "Oh yes." And little more until the geraniums were in sight, shivering less terribly now. And said then, "Could we go and look at your new palazzo in the afternoon? I should like to see it."

"I don't usually have this much leisure. I have my tutor, and there's the horses, of course. But, yes, this afternoon I could. Yes. Let's."

"I am quite good with color, if you are still decorating. No, I am not quite good. I am very good indeed."

HE DECIDED THAT HE himself would go and see the palazzo now. He went up to his room to get a warmer coat and detained himself with a notebook while he tried to find an architecture for his thoughts of the morning, which had changed the weather of his life. Upon this looked briefly Miss Schrauler's, Victoria's, steady blue eyes. He gave it up for later and came back down. In the lobby, he came upon Miss Schrauler's, Victoria's, father attended by his fellow grandees, one could have said a bullfrog and three toads. Their charming hostess was still secluded, no doubt, until the hour of luncheon itself. Mr. Schrauler must once have had his daughter's coloring, more or less, and it was precisely that his skin was now perfectly white that made his neck, where rusty bristles lived, so much like a pig's. Alistair had never heard of Mendel, but it crossed his mind to wonder how one got a thoroughbred out of two plugs. He found a gondola and directed it to the Rio di Ca' Foscari. He had not had time to learn the *vaporetti* routes.

But he was glad of the gondola, for it was slow, and his eye needed much more time in Venice. The Rio di Ca' Foscari, with an entrance more funnel-like than most, enclosed him gently. He was learning that reflection is the Venetian mode, where Rome's is glory and Florence's, joy. As they came up to the palazzo, it pleased him, and he was happy it still did. In their last house, his life had passed through the frontiers of whole kingdoms. He wondered how many were left for here.

Inside, the place was coming to life. In the service quarters, in hideous Italian, and heavily Roman, Irish Kitty, his mother's nanny of years ago and now her personal servant, was haranguing a covey of Venetian servant girls who alternately quailed and giggled. The chef, a foxy fellow with sandy moustache (only cooks are allowed a moustache) pantomimed not listening. Further in and further up his mother's classical Italian (no Venetian here, thank you) descanted through its aspirations to draper and *maggiordomo*, who bowed to Alistair. His mother broke off with, "Oh, hello, Alistair. What are you up to? Over your trip? We'll be camping here tomorrow or the next," then descanted on about shades of rose.

He went up to his own quarters, which pleased him as they had at first. He had his own staircase beyond the *piano nobile*. He liked it that the electricity that had strayed into the palazzo stopped here. He had become fond of gas and candles. He had a bedroom with generous ceilings, a bathroom where things were big with clawed feet, and a study, which he supposed would double as a schoolroom here.

A maid ran in with linens, was all confused to find him, was calmed, and set about her work. To relieve her feelings, he went out onto the little balcony, not much use in the coming winter but nice to have. He could see that it was the agitation of the Grand Canal, squeezed by the funnel of the Rio di Ca' Foscari, that gave his mother's shadows on the ceiling their life. The maid signaled her departure with giggles.

This was best left to women. He went down. He would discover his new neighborhood a bit. He left the gondola for his mother but told the man that he would be coming back with a guest and that he would be needed to take them home. He would figure out how the vaporetti worked. He knew that one stopped right by the Gritti.

Therefore he came to the Gritti terrace from the vaporetto dock, saw Victoria, tall, her blue-grey anticipating the evening shadow that stole toward her, in her grand coat that made her neck look as young as a foal's, and looking the wrong way. Affection, building for some time in an unwatched room, suddenly poured upon him. *I haven't even been very nice to her,* he thought. He went up to her quietly, would have liked to throw his arm around her neck in amends but lightly touched her shoulder instead.

She turned, already smiling. "Alistair," she said. "One never knows where you are going to come from."

"One does seem to know roughly where you are going to be," he said.

"That might not always be true."

"Lets's get a gondola," he said. She put out her hand for his as they got in. On his, it was a pretty hand, sinews clean, fingers well tapered, and with just the last trace of a young girl's pudge.

The sun was low enough for color to seep back into the stone. The wind had dropped, and the gondola no longer went *slap-slap*. He sat her in the big double seat and stood by her shoulder. He let go of her hand, but, with his arm on hers, took pleasure in seeing her look around.

They passed the Ca' Rezzonico across the canal and began to angle toward that further side. "I know what canal it is," she said. "But I don't know which one it is." And, as they passed the side of the Ca' Foscari, "It's not the one with the fawn, is it?"

It was. The fawn was over the door above the watersteps, all, in this light, a mild marble with a faint wash of green, like a bush in earliest spring. "Look at the windows!"

"The windows are all mine."

"They're lovely windows."

He moved to get out.

"Your hand, if you please," said Victoria, and, though the step was easy, put some weight on it.

Their own gondola was gone. They might have passed his mother, probably with Kitty, going the opposite way. The house was locked. He remembered that he had a key, learned to jiggle it into the old iron, and let Victoria in. Doing so disconcerted him; then it occurred to him that he had never used a key in Italy except in the cause of love. Alistair's bed often knew true affection, but true affection, for pretty women who were unconnected with his friends usually led to thoughts of more, and this, with her, confused him. It was quiet inside. Well away in the kitchen, two Italian women seemed to be finishing up their business. He took her toward the best feature of the house, the grand staircase up to the piano nobile. Her coat came into her waist. He gently put his arm there and steered her to the best view.

"Oh gosh, Alistair," she said. "Oh my!"

One had to look up. He saw her delight first in the flush of her throat.

The staircase was Punch's, *Pulcinelli*, very late work by Gian Domenico Tiepolo. At the bottom, three fat old Punches had another in a rope sling and tossed him as though up the stairs. All are having a grand time, but the face of the tossed one, very awkwardly in the air, is of shy rapture. Further up, Punch, so overcome he prances, grabs with glee the breast of a girl in a ball gown, surely no better than she should be and disguised with a pointed nose. A Punch gently holds up a Punch baby to see the tumblers and knows the baby is as ugly as he. At the very top, as three Punches sprawl all anyhow in the grass after a racquet game, a tall sad Punch with a tall, sad dog looks out, over space, through the windows, to the sea.

"They are the most beautiful colors I have ever seen."

"It is Tiepolo." He had the idea that she had heard the name and that it meant nothing to her. Which hardly mattered since she was leaning against him, her eyes were shining, and her lips were a little open.

She was entirely right. The colors are gentle. The skin of the Punches, even the satyr, is weary. The eyes are malicious and kind. A patch of ochre or the leaf of a tree are exclamation points. The hussy's dress shouts to high heaven. And the countryside around is memory. He as well as felt his lips on hers, said to himself, *She's a lady, damn it,* and instead felt cold water on the back of his neck.

"They'd be incredibly difficult to work with," said Victoria, "But I'm going to try. I wonder if Mr. Fortuny ever saw them?"

"He has to have," he heard his own voice say. *You're allowed to show her you want her, even that you want her quite a lot.* He did kiss her. She turned so it was her cheek, but she did not take it quickly away, and their heads stayed close together.

"Maybe they're too difficult even for him. I'll show him." And showed him a flash in her eye and then a smile.

"Come up," he said. "There's one thing more."

She took his hand up the stairs and, looking more at the fresco than her step, needed it once for balance.

In the ceiling of the *sala,* a hawk tilted in the wind. Starlings escaped it, flying for the clouds. She put out her arms to reflect its wings, her head imperious like its own, and laughed.

"We don't get the late light," he said. "We're facing east. But look, those are my mother's."

"What are?"

"The waves." A heavy barge, perhaps, had gone past on the canal, and the shadows on the ceiling all came to life, as though clapping hands. "The windows are mine. And the waves are hers."

She smiled. "It's nice to have things just for you in a house," she said. She looked down at a heap of fabrics, all more or less rose, abandoned on a chaise longue. "Is she using any of these?" said Victoria.

"I guess so. She was fooling with them when I was here earlier."

"She shouldn't be, Alistair. They're none of them quite right." She shook her head quickly. "I'm certainly not going to argue with your mother. That would be absolutely terrifying. Could we go to your part? There must be one."

"Up," he said. He took her arm and brought her to the anteroom from which his stairs went up. The door was hidden in the painted orchard of the wall. He opened it for her. *This is not a good idea,* he thought. And *To hell with it.* The stairs were not very wide. "I'll lead," he said. Their footsteps were the only sound in the house, though a distant thump outside might have been the gondola coming back to its mooring.

"This is my study," he said. "I'm going to need to light the gas lamp soon."

"Gas?"

"There's no electricity in this part of the house."

"I remember that from when I was quite young. Is that the desk where you write poetry?"

"It will be. I haven't written a word here yet."

"Will you sit down as though you were writing? I'm going to think about colors."

He smiled. "If you want," he said.

"But hold your pen as though you're writing." She was silent a while.

He tried to think of one, just one for grace, line for her, and failed, of course.

She said, "I think that your desk should be dark. Which it is, being wood. So that's easy. So you look down into it, like water. When you look up straight in front of you, I think you should see blue, because blue reflects back to you and you're still thinking about what you just wrote. But if you back off a little and look this way, look at me," she was between him and the window, which was ecclesiastical in shape and looked straight across the canal to the white turrets of San Stefano, "I think you should see a blaze of gold, yellow, sun. Of course, I'll have to play with those colors, but do you think I'm a little right?"

She was absolutely right.

"I had no idea you were so clever," he said.

"I am with color," said Victoria. "Let's see the rest." She liked the bedroom's balcony. "Are we still facing east?"

"A little more north," he said. Which allowed the sun fall to float down San Stefano's campanile, blessing the stone where it was white.

"When that happens, I call it evening," said Victoria. "Let's go back in." And then, "It must be lovely light in the morning. I never mind being wakened by the sun."

Oh God, girl, why must you say that? he thought and saw his pillow with the sun on her sleeping hair, a smaller and lovelier sun, as gold.

It was a little dim inside, and he reached for a spill to light the gas mantle, but she reproved his arm. "It's nice like this. I love the ceiling." She backed across the room to see the whole space, rather a shadow in her blue-grey, and he heard the door click as she backed into it. She came back and stood in front of him. "Do you really like my clothes?" she said.

"Yes, really, I do." Though less than the movement of her bosom, the scent of lilac, and, the last of the light being on her face, her blue eyes.

"Would you take them off, please, now, and make love to me?"

She had spoken with such calm he could not believe he had heard her right, thought the words must have come out of himself, and felt dizzy. He opened his mouth. At which her face instantly became a frightened cat's.

"Don't you dare!" she said. "I will tell you. But not yet. I'm not a deluded fool. We both know you're not allowed to say no. There's nothing to say." She took both his hands in hers, raised them to the buttons at her throat, and held them against her. Her hands were steady. "But I don't know very much about this, Alistair." Her voice was calm again, and when he kissed her, she had a small, quiet smile.

Given her enthusiasm for wardrobe, there was a great deal to take off, much of it complicated. She was beautifully helpful, a parent on Christmas morning, whispering such as, "It's over here, Alistair," or guiding his hand and saying, "You've got to do it, but it goes a little left." When the last cover dropped off her breasts, he was enchanted by them and kissed them for their merit and her rapturously on the mouth for being such a clever girl. This, for she returned it, lost them some time, but when that was over, he took her hand and led her toward the bed. Though the rule apparently was that he entirely undress her, she did not seem to mind helping with his own.

She was, of course, a virgin, and the first he had knowingly come to. At the moment of her undoing, her own ruthlessness startled him, but although she cried out, it also took away any doubt that he was meant to be there; he was entranced with her and passionately finished. And then, when languor should have been, was appalled by the damage he had much too obviously done and had never dreamed of. In fact, he was frightened, but when Victoria said, "I'm a complete mess," he could not abide to see so noble a creature, so lovely a form within his arms so brought down, and said, "You're absolutely beautiful."

"I'm a horrible mess," she said.

Both, in fact, were completely right, but he put forward his own argument by bringing her head very gently to his chest and whispering in her ear, "If I can think you're beautiful, so can you. Just think it." It did work for him.

"OK," she said and quite soon took his hand, which he saw as a good sign.

"I hurt you," he said. "And I'm very sorry."

"I expected that," said Victoria. "Girls do know a few things. It's being a mess I don't like." Which, he being an idiot on the subject of bravery, affected him.

"Don't move," he said. "Not even a bit. I'll be hardly a moment." He got up, was overcome by the thought that she might get cold or come to more harm, very gently drew a sheet over her, was away barely longer than to come back with a new towel, took away the sheet, gave her the helpful towel, lay down beside her, and took her in his arms again.

"Thank you," she said. And then, "There's things I have to say, but can I be quiet for a bit?"

"You can do anything you want," said Alistair. "You're queen of tonight."

"Can I really be?"

"Absolutely. Tonight take on perfection and a woman's name. But I didn't write that."

"Is it poetry?

"Yes."

"I expect I should read it. It sounds encouraging in moments like this."

After a little while, she said, "You're most amazingly sweet and dear, Alistair. I hadn't seen that in you. Nobody's ever held me and been dear to me like this, so I had no reason to expect it all. I'm really rather happy."

At the top of an empty house in a creepy city with a male only my instincts know. He saw that she had put her womanhood in a risky and illicit place, and survived, and that this gave her heart.

"Hush," he said. And put his finger on her lips.

She kissed it and nibbled and then sat up so that she hung over him and he could look at her fine strong white shoulders and her breasts. "I'm over that," she said. "You did it, so it's stupid to be ashamed of it, and I asked you to, so it's a bit late for modesty. I'm a proper woman now and this is an inconvenience that doesn't happen again. Can I think that?"

"Yes," he said. He put his arms up under hers. "You really are gorgeous, and all creation should say thank you, but right now it has to be me."

"Oh, Alistair," she said. "I'm not a stupid girl who falls head over heels in love in three days or whatever. I'm a complete fake. My father's a vulgar rich gangster and a swine. I doubt if our name's even Schrauler. When you're a complete fake, it's nice to have real arms around you. The only thing real about me is what you're touching. You've got me all, Alistair."

He said, "Did your father sit around the kitchen in his undershirt?"

"How do you know that?"

"I saw a movie. But I could never work out where he kept his gun."

"In his pants, I think. Alistair, you're going to have me laughing, and that's not the idea."

This was easier than she had thought and a very great deal nicer. Alistair had been raised on his family's far bright morning, jolly centuries of predation: his ancestors, mailed and gilt, riding at the head of cattle whose stolen flanks glowed in the setting sun of the bogs of Antrim, of Gallic women weeping by the ships. His grandfather spoke of this without apology, and his mother with unconcealed enthusiasm. He couldn't care less what her father did. Victoria was touching chivalry, admiration, and delight.

He said, "Yesterday on the stairs you were angry with me."

"You said something that mattered to you, their master and being all they've got. Then you tried to patronize me. 'Just a lark!' 'Ha! I'll show him,' I said. I was frightened but I knew I would do it. Being frightened is what counts, isn't it?"

"Of course," he said. There was enough light left to let him look her slowly up and down, which he did for the first time and with delight, and saw her smile at his delight.

"To hell with modesty," said Victoria. "Listen, Alistair. Get this. I will be the greatest *couturiere* in Europe, Alistair. Nobody else will be able to make what I make, and my clothes will bring the women who wear them happy lives and dear lovers. Just like me. Is that crazy?" she said.

"Are you asking a poet?" said Alistair. "Of course not."

"For a poet," said Victoria, "all you seemed to notice about me was I was female."

"I didn't know all the rest, did I?" And then, "Victoria, darling, girls in your condition should not sleep alone. They deserve to wake up with arms around them." He demonstrated how this would be.

"I can't," she said, though she stretched at the idea of it and then kissed him softly on the mouth. "I just can't. In fact, dear, I think we had better start moving now. I'm going to need your bathroom. So let's up."

"Are you all right?" he said.

"It will probably hurt." She got up. "It does."

"I'm sorry," he said.

"It's not important. I don't think it takes very long to go away. Alistair, do you like being with me?"

"Truly I do."

"Then instead of being queen of today, can I be queen of a day when I feel better?"

"Of course," he said. "Any day."

"And you'll obey me?"

They were standing side by side in the dim light. At that, he laughed and threw his arms around her, arms under her breasts, and kissed her between them. "Do you know what I thought the end of our day on the mainland? I thought you might be bossy."

"You just wait," she said. "Is there a candle in the bathroom?"

"There's a candle right by the door and then there's gas. You just turn it and light it. It's easy."

When they had gotten her dressed again, she said, "Walk around me carefully, Alistair, and see that everything's all right. Can I trust you for that? I wouldn't mind looking like a brazen whore, but I really would not like to look stupid."

He walked around her, holding the candle. He found a bit of her blouse outside her skirt and patted it back. "You're much more of a hussy, I would say. There's lot of good to say about hussies. You're fine."

"Thank you," she said. "Alistair, how are we actually going to get home?"

"It's easy. We have a gondola. And a gondolier. I told him to wait. He will have. Gondoliers do."

"Don't you think he'll be rather shocked?"

"Being Venetian, if I weren't seeing off ladies, he'd probably think he'd come to a disorderly house."

This time they sat together with the rug over them. The wind was now slight but still out of the east and cold. When they turned the bend under the Ponte dell' Accademia, the dome of S. Maria della Salute rose like a dim moon down the canal. Above it, like a lofty lantern, was a cold bright light he had not seen. If S. Maria could be a moon, then its light could be a star. He squeezed Victoria's hand and pointed with his other to the light.

"Do you see that light? It's Venus. She's come up to welcome you. And quite right."

His dear lay back and laughed. "Well, dear lord," she said. "I'm having an affair with a poet in Venice, and Venus comes to see me home. How do you like that?"

"Very much," he said. But she suddenly stiffened. He knew exactly why.

"I hate the guns at night. They're worse than in the day. I hate to think of people dying at night."

"Grace and courage," he said. "They are the only things that balance death." And hugged her.

At the landing stage, he said, "Go in first. I'll be a while later. You look fine."

"Alistair," she said. "Would it be awful if I ended liking you really a great lot? It wasn't necessarily part of the plan. It seems to be happening, even though I don't know much about that either."

"It would be just great," he said.

"Read your mail," she said.

3

The next morning, Anna had news that Maggiore could be there late that day and remain for two. This, as Alistair expected, turned her starry-eyed and a bit vague, having not hoped for this so soon. It also made her hell-bent determined to get them all into the new house.

It was accomplished, with little help from Anna. Once, seeing her smiling amiably while all around scratched their heads and pulled and lifted, he muttered to her, "You're a disgrace, Mamma," getting a faintly embarrassed smile and an opening of her hands in reply, while he secretly believed that heaven must smile upon a move involving a happy woman. During one of the many dashes back to the Gritti—the gondolier's muscles must have bulged by day's end—he caught sight of his own angel, who sent him a smile that flew all the way across the room but which she did not herself follow, so he did not approach. At the palazzo, things just about fell into place.

Maggiore arrived, very grand in *divisa di colonello,* very weary and very worn, and made by all three older, but still able to say things about the new house that had Anna glowing with delight. The new chef produced a festal dinner, ostentatious and not too bad. The new maggiordomo found most of the serving things. The new parlor maid dropped them only in the pantry. Old Kitty and the old lady's maid dug out a dress Anna accepted as pretty enough. Alistair, of course, dined with his parents and tactfully left as the last of the tiramisu went down. This was after Anna had raised her glass to Maggiore for being at the beginning of the new house as well as the end of the old, and Maggiore had replied that he was with the two people he would most be with in the world. After he left, Alistair's parents would have to get on with their evening as best they could, Maggiore's official bedroom being, as Alistair knew, completely full of trunks. After a long walk, he was able to view his own room with affection, though glad enough he had not been there when the little maid came to make it back up. The bed was still scented with Victoria, though faintly.

The next morning he made a report to Maggiore. He told himself that was what it was, so began it formally, addressing him as *Mio Colonello* with a subaltern's quick half bow.

"Sit down, sit down, Alistair," said Maggiore. This was in the new morning room, a small Gothic nest on the piano nobile with a corner view of moored barges, bright reds and blues, down the *rio*, and right now a smell of bread as the baker's barge went past. His mother was in the room, in the grey taffeta morning gown he knew very well. She had listened to men talk of armies since girlhood.

Maggiore in due time said, "There is a new poster, Alistair, which you may not know, and which, when I think about it, can make me want to cry. It carries our flag, not the king's head, thank God. The message is, *"Mamma! Il Esercito Del Rey Ha Bisogno Del Tuo Figlio! Perche Nasconderlo?"* Mamma! The King's Army Needs Your Son. Why Hide Him? It speaks to a real problem. We need about three thousand men a day. Most have not come back or come back maimed. So the women hide them. Usually mothers, sometimes young wives, sometimes sweethearts, young women for whom I have intense respect. In haylofts. In quarries. In the woods. Somehow they feed them. So it is better if the conscription officers arrive without warning, because the poor women cannot hide them all the time, though usually the local authorities are told. Naturally, it all becomes a little brusque. I believe that that is what you saw outside Orvieto. Did you see the Carbinieri beat anyone? Did they appear to be checking papers?"

He was not reporting. He was looking to be told he had seen an outrage. He would not be told that. He took the expectant out of his tone and looked the other way from sentiment.

And Maggiore said, "I have some sympathy for the remount squads. Which you do not. We need horses and mules even faster than men, and the law for requisitioning them is stuck in the assembly while various interests argue over it. Horses and mules are actually valuable, unlike men."

Then, as he went on, Alistair thought, *I have never really looked at this man, he being Mamma's creature, courteous and correct, of course.* He had a sense, behind Maggiore's eyes, which were the color of river gravel, and pleasant, of an intelligence tracking to the left and right of his own narrative, testing it against more than one reality and rejecting the comforts either of sentiment or rote. *Mamma may have chosen better than I knew.*

How about the prowlers in the railroad yard? He had been in danger, he supposed. Traveling with horses, even a groom carries money. They broke into cars to steal boots. Would he have been in danger had not he and Manfredi practiced killing each other five days a week? If they had rushed him, he would have been hurt in the end, and if hurt, hurt badly. They had no leader and he had a sword, was the thing, tilted the balance. And was not the point. He had felt very little danger at the time, and his judgment was presumably better then than now. The point was they were broken. Of course, he had seen Maggiore's eyes before. They would have been his grandfather's as a much younger man. *She's fallen for her own father then, good God.* She listened, chin lifted, nostril very slightly flared, attention severe in the sense of coiled, eyes steady. His mother's bridal mode was charming, no doubt, and all right even if you happened to be her son, but as a wife she was pretty high grade, he'd say. He finished.

"They did not look like curs, Maggiore. They did not look like brigands either. They looked real men who had been sucked out. The ones who stole boots didn't look like thieves, exactly. They looked liked men who needed boots."

Maggiore said, "I'm sure you are right that they were deserters, Alistair." Then stopped and thought. "They may not have begun as deserters. Sometimes men on leave cannot get back on time. The trains are broken or something like that. Or maybe they leave it too late. Then they will be treated as deserters—there is no argument, no excuse—and put into punishment squads, which is almost sure death. Occasionally shot as an example. So they become real deserters. If they get home, they may survive, somebody may hide them. They were probably in that yard looking for a train. Meanwhile they have to live somehow. And walk." He stopped again, thought, and decided. "I am going to talk to you as I should not. Our men are kept in the line too long. The Austrians rotate their men two or thee times as fast as we. Leave is very irregular. When they get it, the soldiers are not treated as brave men. They are treated as something filthy that should not be seen. They are filthy. The are filthy and lousy and they smell. They are not allowed here, they are not allowed there. They can be arrested for asking for shelter, for water at a house. The military police treat them as criminals on the street. A private on leave, if he gets to his home, can be arrested for being seen with his fiancée. He may consort with his mother, his sister, or his wife. Otherwise, for women he is supposed to go to brothels."

He saw his mother shut her eyes. *"Cio c'e una schifezza, GianCarlo. Cosa facciamo? Prendiamo uomini e ne facciamo bestie?"* Which is filthy, GianCarlo. What are we doing? Taking men and making beasts?

He was not sure who the "we" was. He knew that all Maggiore had said was a gift to him. He considered before saying,"I was bred to war, Maggiore. I did not think to be dismayed. Why does so much about it seem wrong?"

"In the end, I am to report to you, Alistair?" But he smiled.

"I wish you would, sir."

Maggiore looked at his pen, tossed it so it turned twice in the air before falling on the notes with a clack, sat back, smiled again, lost three or four years of age on top of the several he had lost overnight, and spread his hands. "Alistair, Alistair, I could tell you the things I think of every day, which I bore your mother with, she being a soldier's daughter—the methods of training of the Italian army, the character of our general. But I am on two days' leave and with my lady"—at this, Anna smiled beautifully and did not know it—"and talking to a poet. And I am an officer not a philosopher. I will tell you three things I have thought of. Maybe you can join them up. I'm not sure I can."

The maggiordomo came in, bowed, and murmured to Anna. She raised her hand lightly to her men. *"Pranziamo, signori?"* she said.

Alistair said, "Mamma, I simply cannot lunch with you. I have got to go to see about my horses."

"Oh, Alistair!"

"Horses are horses, Anna. If he has to, he has to. Make them wait. I won't prose on. *Primus*, Alistair. We are of very similar family. We have a vast vocabulary from our fathers concerning war and battle and courage and arms. Is there anything in that vocabulary about men gassing each other like rats in cellars? It is not that gas kills so many anymore. The masks work, though they are beastly things. But I think that the gas left something in the heart, perhaps in the soul.

"*Secundus.* My father was born in 1835, so he was a little younger than you when the first railroads came. His father saw the first train at Turin and said to him, 'That machine will be the end of the gentleman.' *What a stupid remark,* my father thought. *What is wrong with a train?* And even I, Alistair, am too young to remember how miserable the old roads and the old carriages were. But I think about that remark and when I do, I think maybe we were not as strong as we thought.

"*Tertius.* Italy has always had conscription. In all our gallant little wars, peasants were dragged out of the fields. But they were usually following their lord, whom they knew, and it was usually a summer campaign, and they'd be back for harvest. There was some belonging in it. When it dragged on, it was horrible, always. When a girl makes love, it is usually a happy thing, even when she is not very sensible. Not so in a brothel. Why? Because things that should be done with a high heart should not be done as a slave. If Manfredi fights, and I'm sure if you do, it is for what you believe of yourselves, for honor, and then it can be a passionate thing. I have fought the wild Arabs, they are something on their horses, and there was a true glory of combat. I think a conscript army is a brothel.

"And, *quartus,* which was not in the list. The real mystery is that the Italian soldier fights magnificently, in impossible conditions, loyally, against a very skillful foe. That is the mystery I confront every day. I cannot unravel it. Maybe you can. Alistair, to your horses! Anna, I am all yours. Alistair, do not keep your ladies waiting, it is usually a bad idea." He rose and gave Anna his arm.

Outside, between the morning room and the dining room, Anna turned to Maggiore and said, "GianCarlo, how did we let this happen? The boy almost got killed."

Maggiore said, "Anna, young men usually almost get killed. The point is the 'almost.'" He squeezed her arm.

She spread her hands. "Really!" she said.

ALL THIS HUNG OVER Alistair's brow on the boat to Mestre, too slow, and where the Schrauler ditch had sprouted a coal dump greasy with mud. He finished the *panino* he had gotten from the kitchen for lunch. It pecked at him in the intervals of looking at a bad map and puzzling the car over country roads past Marghera to Malcontenta by the Brenta river. He looked at his watch. Daily riding would be out of the question. His formal tutorials were weekly now while Mr. Featherstonhaugh got on with his own writing, which seemed to be about a particularly homicidal British campaign in Africa. However, he still had just as much work to do. He would need time for Victoria. Please, surely he would. Would she wish, back to John Donne, to emulate that foolish fellow who went to sea but for to make him sick? No, she would not. She would be his dear thoroughbred, he was sure. And his poetry, now finding its legs strong under it, was finding new ways to pull at the bit.

But his heart smiled when he saw the stable. In the park of a great villa by the Brenta it sat, tile roofed with a high vault over the manege among chestnuts around a court. It smelled of hay and horses and piss, not stale. There was fine fluted ironwork on the wood, and fresh paint. The manege was serene as a church, raked powder smooth. Property of their neighbor the Duca di Foscari if the Foscaris still lived at the Ca' Foscari, which he didn't yet know. He thanked Pietro under his breath. About twenty horses. And, lord God, it might really be Palladio. He would ask.

He spoke to the head groom, whom he had met on the platform at Mestre. "A little rested, signore?" the man said. Alistair laughed, guessing what he had looked like. They determined together the decent thing to do about Roberto. He would get his wages and a little more, which would take him on the train and feed him properly. Alistair did not see him. He would make it home, with luck, to be conscripted with boys he knew.

In the grave and sinless company of his horses, who knew no irony, his puzzle cleared, and his mind stretched and smiled. He could only ride them a little time each, and in the manege. They were fine, a little soft from standing and low oats, but fine. He said to Pompey, "We made it, old boy," and thought that Pompey agreed. He said to the groom, "Back on hard feed now, please. Five kilos. Could they be put on the lounging rein and given a decent canter on the days I'm not here? It would help."

The groom said something that sounded like, *"Oo fashoo,"* which might be *"Lo facciamo"*—It shall be done.

At the palazzo, the new maggiordomo gave him a wafer in writing he did not know, and knew. It was in well-taught copperplate in a hand minutely childish at the edges, like her own. It said, "Tomorrow at eleven, at the mooring by the Ponte di Paglia, a boat, not ours, black stern. Embark! Victoria Regina."

Which was what he thought about through dinner, until sleep.

HE TOOK THE VAPORETTO to St. Mark's and walked. Thus, almost none of his way to the Ponte di Paglia coincided with Victoria's from the Gritti if she walked herself. Not Sir Gawain would so nicely honor a lady's command as he. Bridge of Sighs to the left, Ponte di Paglia to the right, and there the vessel lay, black-sterned upon the mere. Not Victoria's own fiery charger, but not bad. He walked the wharf to it. Its guardian stood aside, bade him aboard with the traditional bare word, ushered him into the little cabin, and, traditionally shut him in with a click.

He sat and wondered what the devil he thought. He had come to suspect a direct conduit, surely inconvenient, likely extremely dangerous, between his loins and his heart. The suspicion seemed well found. Victoria promised to get into and to be an extraordinary amount of trouble. Even apart from that, he increasingly liked her and was quite certain that he would learn to find rapture in her fair and noble flesh. He brought himself to order. What promised was a sentimental expedition with an extremely pretty girl, nothing to be despised. Or, of course, he might shortly be joined by the ogre, taken out into the lagoon, and drowned. With Victoria laughing and looking on? He did not believe that. With Victoria bound and with a dagger at her throat? There was certainly that.

Therefore the thing that could surprise him most was joy, joy at her ankles on the wharf, joy at the light movement of the boat under her step, joy as she opened the door, joy at her waist, lilac.

"Why, Mr. Stears," she said, "how exceedingly pleasant to come upon you here," and thought that so resoundingly funny that he laughed himself, and they quite chastely kissed. They sat down together, but he made her get up again and looked at her all over.

"Is that really all your own?" he said.

"Not the material, but the rest," she said.

The boat now going smartly astern, they fell over each other, which was not disagreeable at all.

He said, "It's even more amazing when you know just what's inside, how it works."

"Most girls don't have a clue what's inside," she said. "Or they have it all wrong."

What she wore was long and all one color, between lavender and blue except that the color drank the light, it was one of those cloths of hers, so the blue and the lavender lapped and flowed over each other, and sometimes a wand of silver magically appeared and died. It gave her shoulders a touch of frailty, which was attractive, swept with sweet gravity over her behind and rippled gently with the motion of her thighs. It was decorous, the neckline was high, and could make you melt right there in your tracks. It was the prettiest he had ever seen her. The tilt of her hat made her hair look like the setting sun.

"You have to begin with what's really there," she said, "your own or the woman's it's for. That's easy with another woman, but for yourself, you have to avoid wishful thinking, and that's what most girls can't do."

"Some girls don't have to," he said, and kissed her cheek.

"God was fairly kind," said Victoria, "but there are problems. I have shoulders like a stevedore. Or a Polish peasant."

"I love your shoulders."

"You're sweet." She put her hand on his. "Anyway, then you have to let your imagination go loose and think of shapes and colors that can come out of it. It's ridiculous to say dresses shouldn't be noticed. The question is, what do they say. When people say a dress sticks out, it's because it's saying the wrong thing. At my age, most dresses say, 'Choose me,' because that's what you mostly want. But who's me and who do I want to choose me? That's probably why I wear so many different sorts of dress. But, Alistair," they were seated side by side again, she took her hand off his and laid it on his thigh and looked at him, blue eyes under the hat's brim, "when I thought yesterday about today, I knew exactly who I wanted to be and exactly who I wanted to choose me. So here I am. We're going to Torcello. And we know exactly what we are going to do."

"You shouldn't say things like that. It could give someone a heart attack," he said. "And I don't know Torcello. I don't know any of the islands. And if you feel like you look, I'm in heaven."

"It has a restaurant on it, which is, I am happy to say, an inn. And I happen to have, on this vessel, a little portmanteau, for appearances. Your queen thinks of everything. I keep forgetting that part. You're my subject, aren't you? And yes, I do feel that way." And then, "Alistair, I'm going to start reading your poetry."

He said, "I really don't . . ."

"No, no, no, no, no! You're not getting away with that. It will not do. My dresses are my passion. Every time you see me, you see my clothes. Or very often you see my clothes. If you look at my clothes, I shall read your poetry, or I shall turn my face from you, and serve you right, and consider you a phoney. Anyway, you're my subject."

"OK," he said. And thought, *That was easy. I write the damn stuff to be read, and now it's time.* "I'm not as good now as I will be."

"Who is?"

All that settled, and leaving the cemetery island behind, they were in the open lagoon, though Murano was not far to port. Even in the confined water, there was a slight swell, not so unlike Penobscot Bay.

"We have a lovely sailing boat in Newport. I rather miss it," said Alistair.

"The boat you know is the first we've had."

"It's terrific. But completely different. A sailing boat feels faster."

"It couldn't!"

"Somehow it does. Shall we go out? It's pretty out."

"Sure," she said. "I didn't want just anybody on St. Mark's to see us go off together but, of course, it's fine here." They went out and stood behind the sailor. Murano was close enough that its houses reshuffled as they went by and its windows winked in the sun.

Victoria said, "You don't like America, do you?"

"That's not quite true," said Alistair. "I don't seem to belong there."

"When we were on the mainland, you were angry with me. I couldn't think what I'd done, except Ariosto maybe, and then I thought maybe it was because I was American. You do sound American, but not much."

This was true. His mother's and grandfather's accent, castle Irish, was English country house with somewhat softened vowels. In childhood he had taken on a hint of his mother's lady's maid's servant Irish and, from school, a juvenile beginning of Harvard. Both of these were nearly dead.

"You're an astoundingly smart girl," he said.

"But you're not angry anymore?"

"Now you're you." He lowered his face under the brim of her hat, where it was tilted the other way, and breathed the edge of her hair.

She took his hand. "It's pretty chilly," she said.

"We can go back in."

"No. We can squeeze together. Like this." There was a corner where they could comfortably do so. It is quite a long ride to Torcello. They said nothing but extremely commonplace things about ducks and Italian candy, but he began to feel that her flank belonged in his, and her shoulder blade, just below his arm. They entered a canal, quite overgrown along its banks and with some cottages here and there. It was their destination. She began to move about. He already knew that, just as colors flowed up and down her dress, so age flowed back and forth over her, from right behind she was a tall, grave young woman, but a sidestep that uncovered her throat and cheek uncovered something very young indeed. She was fully in lady mode when they arrived at the *locanda's* wharf, to which the porter hurried. There was their portmanteau; it was clear that the young couple had decided, probably at their breakfast table, that evening dress would not be required on so small an island; he, it could be, was the kind of young husband relaxed enough not to mind a trace of his young wife's scent on his shirts and underwear, so they had sensibly resolved that one case would suffice overnight for both. For the matter of that, anyone could see they were on their honeymoon.

"I've got to go and powder my nose, darling," said Victoria, pleased with such extremely grown-up vocabulary, "but then let's go straight in to lunch."

He waited for her a short time in the dining room. It had certainly been a farmhouse. He had heard a little of this place. Opened not long ago by one of the Venice hotels, on this the very oldest of the Venetian islands, the cradle of the great city itself, the first basilica was still there. Quite posh, they said. He was impressed by her choice.

She came in and they sat down. She put her head close to his and said, "Just so you understand, we are going to have a very civilized and grown-up lunch, both knowing what awaits upstairs and after. At least you obviously do, and I am optimistic that I do, much, much better than last time."

The waiter gave them a menu, short and handwritten.

"I shall, of course, decide what you are to have. What do you want?" asked Victoria.

"*Gnocci di bacala* and then *pesce spada in cartoccio*."

"What's that?" she said.

"Fish turned into clouds for small angels and then a very different fish in a paper bag with shrimp and herbs and things. It's all fish, but it's very good."

"Golly," she said. "I'll have that too. And Champagne. I just love to drink."

"Prosecco's marvelous, a lot like Champagne but from right around here, if your ladyship permits."

"OK," she said. "I do." So that was what they had.

It seemed to be his fate to have girls who chowed down, and he found this entirely endearing. On Victoria, as light flowed and age flowed, so also flowed the nature of an extremely healthy young animal and a creature of darker question.

Between the gnocchi and the swordfish, and as he began to have doubts about the lease on life of their bottle of wine, she said, "Obviously it's amazing luck for me that Pa has a dirty deal going here and not in Pittsburgh or Jersey City or somewhere. I know a little, little bit about how it happened. There's Italians in it on both sides, in Italy obviously and at home. And the Italians at home couldn't decide which one of them should be the manager over here because they all hate each other, so they had to pick a crook who wasn't Italian at all, and that was Pa."

"Of course," he said, though it was hardly clear, and Schrauler *pere* wore the costume of 2nd Murderer in his mind.

But crime in America was not her tack. "I know this is the most beautiful place in the world, and I'm nuts about beauty as you know, I really am. I try to look at all the paintings, and some of them are so lovely I can't stand it. But they're all jumbled up, and half of them are in dark corners, and mostly I don't know what they're about. If it's a battle, I don't know who I'm meant to root for, and if it's people, I don't know who they are. I know a few of the saints because of parochial school, and at Foxcroft they taught us some names, such as who painted your beautiful Punches, but I don't know anything about them. No more than about Ariosto, which was horribly embarrassing and I'll never do that to you again, Alistair. So maybe where I really do belong is Jersey City, you know, or Pittsburgh."

Confession of ignorance was thirsty work. The bottle succumbed. He ordered another and kept it a little further from Victoria.

"Oh, look," she said. "I've never had food inside a paper bag. Except at a baseball game, and that was peanuts and I bet this isn't."

"You open it gently with the point of your knife, honey," which seemed remarkably erotic under the circumstances. "I'll show you the museums. That's easy."

"You'll spend that sort of time with me?"

Oh yes, he would. He promised it, watching her lovely throat and the movement of her breath beneath her breast.

"Oh, Alistair," she said. "The other thing about Venice is you. But that's a subject for later, I guess. I have a little workroom now and a seamstress who works for me. I showed Pa that making dresses myself cost about a twentieth as much as getting them from Lanvin. Will you come and see it?"

"Does it smell of lilac?" he said. "Because you do."

"Then I expect it does," she said, primly.

He thought he shivered. He thought she saw. She touched his hand. "Oh, Alistair," she said again. And then, "Alistair, is it true your mother's having an affair with an Italian general?"

"Colonel," he said. "But she doesn't see it that way. As far as she's concerned, they're married. And that's about how I think about it now. I don't think there will be anyone else for her. I'm sure there was no one else when she was with my father. She's a very loyal woman. Of course she won't divorce."

"That's so romantic," said Victoria. "I guess at my age just an affair is a good place to start."

"I think at our age an affair is absolutely incredibly marvelous, especially when it's with you."

She considered this while the plates left. She gave a wistful look at the second bottle, which he pretended not to see.

"I think you will agree that I ordered excellently," she said. "Now I command that we have a dessert."

"Which one?"

"The frothy one."

He ordered zabaglione.

"Because it will be nice to kiss with," said Victoria.

So, when it came, they ate it rather respectfully. When she finished hers, she wiped the corner of her mouth, put her hand on his, and said, "And that's the end of lunch, Alistair."

On their way up the stairs, dark wood on stone, she turned to him, the zabaglione all fresh in her lovely mouth, and said, "Pa often brings crooks out here and I think sometimes women. I'm going to inveigle this bill into his. Can you imagine what a horrible puzzle it's going to be?"

He thought it appalling. It must have showed in his face, for she said, rather sharply, "I am the queen." And then took his hand, leaned to him, and said, as though they were two children sharing a toybox, "You can't believe how smart I am about things like that." He could think of nothing to say, standing with the key, his very own erotic symbol, in his other hand and right in front of their door.

Once in, she led him straight to the bed, sat down beside him, threw her arms around his neck, and hugged. They stayed a long time so. He felt the lovely familiarity of bodies, breath, and scent, which they drank in together as they tasted the last of the dear zabaglione on each other's tongues. She said, "Oh, Alistair," disengaged her head and neck a little way, and put his hand as before to the fastenings at her neck.

"It's going to be much easier this time, darling. Everything on top just opens down the front, and the rest isn't very difficult either."

It was so. He could lay her back and open her up so that her clothes lay like wings beside her, leaving only lacy clouds. She lifted her shoulders and then her hips to help him with these, they were discarded, he looked at all of her and most of all her smile with joy then kissed first her mouth and then most of the rest. She followed gentle pressure of his hands and rearranged herself. Her blond loins were like a beacon of sunshine. There was no calamity this time, and the next thing she said, beginning to soften into bird down beside him, was, "Alistair, Alistair, what a fantastic, amazing, colossal, fabulous improvement. I can see I'm going to start enjoying this a lot," then kissed his cheek, each eye, and for a long time his mouth. The neural pathway between his loins and his heart, however unique in his sex, was in tiptop form today. In this moment he adored her, and they lay together in a cloud of happiness, musk, and lilac.

Victoria next said, "Alistair, do you know incredible it is to be here just for each other, no other point in it, to be lying here making each other happy and enjoying the hell out of each other, nothing to be gotten out of it except you and me, and me being absolutely certain that you're going to be dear to me. Well, of course he does, Victoria, you little dolt. But from where I'm from, it's not so obvious. People aren't nice. I don't have any friends. They didn't think much of me at school. Pa doesn't have friends. Ma doesn't. There are people you can get things out of, so you scare them. One of those things might be sex, I guess. You have people who can help you get things out of people, so you bully them. Very occasionally there are people who can get things out of you, so you try and outfox them. The idea of being with someone just to enjoy them would seem completely batty. I don't care at all, Alistair, if you like me because I'm female and I've got what I have. I am female. That's me. But you're the first person who's ever just been sweet to me. So you're my first friend. There," she threw her splendid arm over him, snuggled closer, and said, "All of me for my first friend."

To Alistair's present dazed fondness, this seemed a cry from a wilderness of ashes. In his own life, almost everybody was there to be enjoyed, his friends, his friends' girls, his parents, certainly Mr. Featherstonhaugh were not only enjoyed by him but enjoyed each other, flying through the air like a flock of birds delighting in each other. He was filled with absolute woe for her and kissed her to console and assure. In the state they were in, any warm emotion was at a high risk of catching fire. His did. Of course, it spread to her. This time any reservation in her was gone. Her ardor would have startled him had he any attention left to be startled. It was not brief, she gave a long shudder, and they collapsed beside each other in a heap.

In due time, she said, "Alistair, is that going to happen again?"

"It will happen lots and lots of times. We'll make sure of it."

"Golly," she said. "What a week!"

He thought she slept. He watched the swallows begin to circle, surely over the canal. The billows and ridges of their bed began to send out exploratory shadows. He heard fishing boats drop their sails at mooring beyond the window. He ran the edge of his hand down her throat, between her breasts, and down her tummy.

Victoria said, "I wasn't asleep, but that would be a lovely way to wake up."

He said, "I know we have this room until morning."

"Don't think I haven't thought about it," she said. "We could get dressed and sit by the canal, and have a lovely dinner even dreamier than our lunch, and come back and be us again for hours. But I can't. I absolutely, not possible, no doubt about it, no matter how big a shame it is, can't."

"I think we have to start to go then," he said.

There was a washroom attached, not really to be expected in that time and place. It was simple, but it worked. The portmanteau held a dressing gown, which she did not need, some underwear, her hairbrush, comb, and sponge, and a large leather-bound Italian-German dictionary, for weight. He made do with what he had, though she lent him her hairbrush and comb. In her clothes, when she had them back on, she became his original blue-grey ghost, with a tendency to fade into evening light.

She said, "The other lovely thing is that Pa is giving another crook lunch with me as hostess next week, but this time it's out here. All the waiters will know that his lovely, virginal daughter has been fucking like a squirrel more or less just above his head. It's going to be so lovely for me. For the first time, I'll enjoy one of his lunches. Do you think the waiters will snigger? He wouldn't know what was wrong, but he'd know something was, and maybe one of his dirty little friends would put two and two together and laugh at him behind his back. Do you think they'll snigger?"

He said to himself, *Oh Christ!* He said to her, "I think they are trained not to."

Victoria said, "Would you walk around behind me, darling, and see that everything's all right?"

He did, rested his chin on her shoulder, and said, "I think your filial piety is excessive. I think you should think less of your father and more of you. I think this is obsessive and obsession is sin and sin is evil and evil leads to hurt. They must have mentioned that when they catechized you."

She stood still and said, "They also mentioned mortal sin, which turns out to be such a dreamy idea. I don't think you're a very good priest, Alistair." But she did not say it lightly. And, "If you hate something, you have to fight it. Don't pretend you don't understand that, Alistair, because you do. It's why I'm with you. Why it's you who's here. It's not obsessive. All I want is once to see him cry and then I'll never think about him again. I will be the greatest couturiere in Europe; my clothes will make the women who wear them beautiful and give them happy lives and sweet lovers, just like me. For the moment, all I've got is me. And maybe a little bit of you."

"Your modesty's not a fit weapon," he said.

"If all I've got is me," she said, "all of me is."

But she looked at his face and said, "But Alistair, you must believe this. Today was no trick. It was a brand new day, and you are my first and darling lover and my first and best friend. Kiss me again if you just believe that, and then we'll go down." He kissed her. "Thank you. I'm very glad of that. Am I all right behind?" she said.

"Your behind is beautiful."

"That is good too," she said.

They went down and sent the porter up for the case. Alistair explained to the manager that business called them back to the city, which was graciously accepted, considering that there was no telephone in the room and no carrier pigeon present. He managed to give his own address to send the bill to instead of the one she gave him, probably her workroom. She slept most of the way across the lagoon, her head on his shoulder and one hand in his lap. He listened to the inflections of breathing in her throat. Certain that madness was evil, he feared even its eye but could not think her mad. When they got back to the Serenissima, the fantastic domes and colors of St. Mark's were caught in the setting sun, the calles were shadowed, and the canals all black.

4

Though Anna's palazzo was very shortly to have a telephone and the Gritti had several, Alistair and Victoria never used them much, preferring gondolas and notes. Her one day of despotism was two days gone, but Victoria got splendid use out of her phrase, "Maybe we should . . ." to serve her bossiness, which made Alistair laugh. When he was handed a note, "Maybe we should meet in my sewing room since you've never seen it Calle Caotorto 23 2nd floor 11 o'clock your V," he crossed out the time, wrote 2 in its place, and underneath, "school work. Baci," and sent it back.

He was delighted to go there, did not think it girly or sissy at all. He liked to see things made, gunstock or boat strake. He was at this time fascinated by the idea of conception in art—why exactly do you begin Ann Karenin's story with Prince Oblomov and the nanny, how the devil do you even start to design a dress. And he found things to do with women jolly and warm. He was proud of her when he saw that the calle was a humble one and a tabby cat wandered her stair all as though she were a Venetian girl earning her bread, and, besides and anyway, he was in favor of Marie-Antoinette. He didn't knock. She was there with her seamstress model girl, which stopped neither of them from a warm kiss.

Indeed they made things there. It was a small, close room, though it lacked the conviction of a garret. It did smell of lilac, also of fair hair, and otherwise, he supposed, of cloth and what might be wax in thread. This was not Mme. Lanvin's workshop. Cloth was in bolts, not bales, and hung from hooks. A pair of shears kept close her small and smaller sisters, scissors. Small articles seemed finished. Collars? Cuffs? He knew as much about sewing as about childbirth. It was quite clear to him that difficult things were done here in order and with skill. His dear had attached herself to his side, looking at him look. He was proud of her and murmured to her cheek, "You're no fake, honey."

The girl was Lucia. Evidently she liked her young mistress. He thought she was a good sort of Italian girl. It was no trouble for him to be easy and pleasant with her. He did not even try not to be pleased at intercepting the glance of congratulation she sent Victoria. They were fooling with a dress on a form, long light-green velvet with embellishments a tone up from rose; it spoke of a cold spring day. Victoria beside him said, "Do you like it?"

It was about her size. He said, "Can you put it on?"

"I'd have to take this off," she said, touching what she wore, and looking, for Victoria, a little at a loss. Lucia shrugged—not at a loss at all, she reached up for Victoria's shoulders, whisked most of it off, revealed a good deal of lovely Victoria, slid the other on, and turned her mistress back to face her patent lover who had patently seen all this and more before. "Oh well," said Victoria and smoothed her hair. "Do you see?"

He almost really did. Spring was it, for sure. With a girl inside it, the green came to life like a young tree while the cool rose shivered. But the energy was vertical, he was sure his mother would have said of a figure, and the rose bits knocked that awry and took its strength. His own work was never right at first. You had to let it settle, go back to it.

"It's terrific," he said. "It's April." Which it was. He would find a way to make her think about it again.

She smiled happily. "We're going to look at paintings?"

"That's the plan," he said. She gave Lucia instructions, in limping Italian and fluent signs. They seemed perfectly understood, and he said nothing. She put on her coat. Lucia, smiling or grinning, waved them goodbye down the stairs.

He took them to San Rocco and Santa Maria dei Frari across the street. These were gospel paintings. She didn't need him here. Parochial school—his mistress the cutpurse's daughter, thank God, was Catholic—teaches all that perfectly well. He understood his role in front of Titian's *Assumption,* the altarpiece of Santa Maria. She took his arm as soon as they bowed and rose. He had seen her stand the same way on his own staircase with the *Pulcinelli.* Here again she had her head lifted up, and in this painting the angels exulting over the Virgin's head seem to press forward, exalted over the nave. The Punches' colors were ironic asides; here there was an angelic chorus of golds and deep reds. Her lips were open again and her throat flushed. Under the *Pulcinelli,* he had been beside himself in besotted sexual surmise. He could still be besotted, but she was his mistress now, on whose waist his arm might rest, and such thoughts could wait upon occasion. What was clear was that her immersion in the painting was too deep for safety, left her unguarded as a newborn, and that his place beside her was not pedagogue but knight. She tried to show him what she saw, took his hand and gestured with it at what must have been a conversation among the golds of the serafim and the gold of heaven's sun, but his vision was too coarse, he saw it only crudely, and she gently let his hand down. When she eventually swam back out of a painting, she shook herself—he came to wait for it—lightly but like a dog.

After San Rocco, when she had come back to the surface from Tintoretto's *Annunciation* and they were outside, dusk and fog had come and the lights wore haloes. She said, "That was so lovely, Alistair." And then, "Your house is quite close, isn't it? Shall we see each other tomorrow?"

"I think we're leaving out something we shouldn't leave out at all," he said.

"I'm very glad you said that, Alistair. I think exactly the same." She looked up at him seriously, though she didn't have to look up very far. "But I'd be shy in your house now. And my room is out of the question. And we can't live on Torcello. I suppose there's lots of hotels besides the Gritti. I'm going to feel a little awkward without luggage. Oh well."

Both looked at the pavement. Both said, like a proper duet just a half beat apart,

"My sewing room!"

"Your sewing room!"

Both, for their timing, laughed. She threw her arms around his neck so he rocked on his feet. "We can make it work perfectly," she said. "Why didn't I think?"

Alistair, thinking of the bolts like rich serpents, thought it would do amazingly.

They crossed the canal again in one of their hazes of quiet holding. Their own and the other gondoliers' calls through the fog flew like loons. Out of the gondola, in front of St. Mary of the Lily, he started left, but Victoria said, "Maybe we should go to Florian's and have hot chocolate first. There is no haste, Alistair."

He nodded. In St. Mark's, the fog was cold and solid and the lighted arcades were a universe to themselves.

Victoria sipped her frothy chocolate. "The nice thing about this is I'm going to keep being your hostess."

xxx

THE GUNS THAT HAD discomposed Victoria on her bridal night were late actions following the Ninth Battle of the Isonzo, a fight over the same country as the first eight. The couloir where the father of Rodolfo, his riding friend from Rome, had been killed was assaulted for the ninth time over the remains of its previous assailants, those of the original settlers, Rodolfo's father and his company, being by now largely atomized. They would not have known their couloir. The sparse vegetation they had tried to use for cover was now entirely gone, and the banks on which it had grown had been eaten back by shells, as though by rats. The mountain stream was now a muddy seep between craters in the brittle rock. These were now full of snow, and the cover they offered in the summer was not available for men, unless corpses, or for the numerous summer vipers. Italian gunnery had improved. Some support was given almost to the Austrian lines. The fatal battery had been suppressed. On this occasion, a second and a third company were deployed. After the destruction of the first two, the remains of the third actually breached the Austrian defenses, heartening the ghosts of earlier attackers. They were fighting uphill through snow with forty pounds of pack. Their breathing tore their lungs. Many loosened their gas masks for what relief that gave. An intelligent Austrian lieutenant guessed how it might be with them. Most were killed in the gas attack that followed. The rest were dispersed by a counterattack. Cold came early that year. After four days, the campaign was stood down, forward supply becoming impossible in heavy snow as frostbite, pneumonia, and typhus began to challenge Austrian arms as enemies. The pretty Isonzo valley had by now consumed some two hundred thousand Italians. It was by no means sated. When the same ground thawed in the spring, the Umbrian girl's young husband, the recruits in the street in Bologna, and the horses led past Alistair on the platform in the night would be there to take their places, those that were still left. In the intervening lull, Anna began to dare hope that Maggiore would be able to spend a proper Christmas with them at the palazzo.

xxx

ONLY A FEW HUNDRED yards separated San Stefano, still Alistair's favorite campo, from what was by any margin in the world his favorite sewing room, and from the ogre's cavern at the Gritti Palace. Within these bounds was the little eatery where he had ordered Victoria's breakfast, which they had an affection for now, regarding it as their beginning. Consequently, they were often about in this area. One chilly afternoon, they were going for a pastry in the Campo San Stefano when Victoria pointed to the baroque facade of a church—it was San Vitale—and said, "Have you ever been in there, Alistair?"

"No," he said.

"Let's take a look."

They did and were in the presence of an altarpiece with a beautiful horse.

"Who is he?" said Victoria as they rose but referring to the rider. He was a bearded man in armor, carrying a battle-ax in a garden where people walked around. The people looked like saints.

"It's got to be San Vitale," said Alistair. "He's a very early martyr. He was a general, I think, and Nero had him buried alive."

"Oh my," she said. And shivered, only a bit for show.

But it was the horse that mattered. It was a grey, and Alistair was sure it was a mare, though it was anatomically unclear, for she had that lovely head carriage of some mares, imperious and shy, between dowager and flirt, and the eye, serene and askance that could just as easily offer you a cucumber sandwich or scare you to death. He would have loved to have had her, and now, seeing Victoria look at her fully, thought she carried his fate.

And she did. For Victoria said, "I'd love to ride."

"You easily can," he said. "I can absolutely organize that." And having said it felt washed with relief. For she had fox hunted in Virginia, he had a photograph's absolute proof of that, and he had let it build inside his mind as a supernal feat, as though she had crossed Niagara Falls on a rope, and thence had to reckon that she might very well be a better rider than he. He had never in his life competed with a girl on his own turf, still less with a possibility of losing. He had never let the conversation go near his riding, and knew more clearly every day that this was abject cowardice and meanness of spirit on his part, and then of course had gotten into this so deep he could find no way out. And now this beautiful mare had taken it on herself.

"I don't see how, Alistair." They still whispered by reflex but had largely forgotten where they were.

"There's twenty horses at my stables. They're hardly ridden except by grooms. They're good horses that somebody doesn't use, and I think he's even my neighbor. I know I can get you one."

"I don't know how to ride, Alistair."

He looked at her.

"Yes, the photograph. I was on that horse for thirty seconds. A Negro was holding it. I was scared to death. It's only a photograph. Another fake. And then thinking about it, I was so ashamed I couldn't tell you."

"I'll teach you," he said. "Do say, 'Yes. I'd love to.'"

"Then, yes," she said. And touched his hand.

"I can't teach sidesaddle," he said. "It's going to have to be astride."

"I think we both know I've learned that, Alistair," she said and smiled. And stiffened. "Oh, Alistair, that was awful, awful, awful! We're in church. I'm so terribly, terribly sorry."

"It's all right, honey," he said. "But let's leave."

"I need to light a candle. And say some *Aves.* And some *mea culpas* too." She did all this and excused herself again. Alistair also lit one, as he often did, and only outside realized that the day had finally come when he had lit a candle to a horse.

From the ice cream parlor they could still see the church.

"This is going to need a bit of organizing," said Alistair.

"Our boat. Our car," said Victoria. Heaven appeased, she had her usual cheer again.

"Gosh," said Alistair, impressed. "Still, a bit of organizing."

"We're talking about me," said Victoria. "This is going to take more than a bit of clothes."

They celebrated with ice cream with chestnut mousse, which they had been delighted to discover was the very favorite of both.

When they got back to the Calle Caotorta, Lucia, good girl, had finished her work and tidied up. Victoria looked around the room and said, "I suppose a better girl than me would be terribly, terribly embarrassed."

The couch they had used, and had filled up considerably with cushions and cloth, had now been brought cleverly into its closest possible simulacrum of a bed, a pillow had been set, and on the pillow a bit of deep red taffeta had been cut into the semblance of a rose, placed in a way undecided between satire and romance.

"But she's been worried about me because I didn't have a boyfriend. She does. She tells me quite a lot, really, as best we can, so I suppose there's no reason to be embarrassed at all. I think it's sweet. She's a dear thing. I bet she'd bring us breakfast in bed if we only could."

Alistair had not much been listening, for Lucia's last work had been redoing the long green velvet dress. The almost rose had been moved. Now it flowed down the line of the hip and the whole thing dove into the vertical as happily as a seal, and April blew in the cold pale rose. It was just the kind of triumphant change he could imagine making to a line of his own. He was delighted and kissed the back of her neck

"That's even better," he said.

She followed his eye, and said, "Oh good. I think so too. But the color's so obvious, Alistair. I couldn't find the cloth I saw in my head." And then, "Undo me down the back, would you, darling. It's silly to have to do it when you're half lying down." He did, and she, now lacier, said, "But it's nice to be held first, especially when I've something to say to you." Cozily in his arms, she said, "Tomorrow's Pa's lunch for his crooks on Torcello."

He tensed then willed himself to hold her gently. "Don't go."

"I am going, Alistair."

"Why?"

"I could say it's none of your business."

"Except it is."

"Except it obviously is, because I'm telling you and it's very, very important you understand. It's not about sniggering waiters."

"That is something, I suppose. You still mustn't go."

"In fact, I don't give a damn about the waiters. I've told you a bit about what it's like, Alistair, and I got it wrong. I think better when I'm with you. So we're going to have this conversation where I've got you pinned by my female wiles. Let me finish, Alistair.

"When I got back from school in Virginia, I think Ma and Pa were both a little proud of me. They're awful, but they are my parents. At first, doing these things, I truly think Pa was showing me off. We're talking about me, dressing up. It was already my own clothes, mainly. Obviously they don't curse and swear and wave their pistols and whoop and holler at these things. They sit down at an expensive lunch and talk. They do horrible things and they make it dull. They steal and spoil and cheat, and it's so ordinary. They're hardly ever wrong. They know who can be bribed, or blackmailed, or scared. They just do it. I don't see they even enjoy it much. And then of course my father had to show he could make me do it. Because I was part of it, you see. It buys the Gritti. It buys this. So in a way it buys me you, Alistair. But when I think of me and you together there, I have a completely different world. Because, Alistair, when I said you were my first friend, I meant you're the first person I can be me with."

She put up her hand, for he had opened his mouth. "So you know what I'm going prove by going there? We're more than them."

He saw the vast, greasy ditch with its steam engines around the brim, and, as he often did now, the lines of army trucks, the recruits, the Umbrian girl. Ten thousand a month. The guns. He held her chin between his hands and said, "Victoria, I can use three things. A sword. A bridle. And a pen. One's a toy. One's a game. One may not be as much as that. Don't set me too high."

"Alistair, we're the wolves. Not them. We're free. Wolves are free. Nod if you agree." He did. Her hands engaged themselves at her shoulders, and he was looking at her breasts. "And these are ours too, Alistair. These are really, really ours because they're not much good unless we're both here. We have everything we need, wolf, in you and me."

He smiled. "I can't look sad with those, you know." He liked the way the palest rose turned to pink and then coral. "I think they're one of the best things you've done."

"And I'm very glad you do," she said. Certainly they kept them warm and content until, as always not very late, she had to be put back together, inspected for defects, and sent back into the Gritti.

THE NEXT EVENING AFTER dinner, Alistair lay on the sofa in his study, on his tummy, his heels wrapped around each other and his head propped up on his elbows. His legs were pleasantly tired from two horses. With him was Calypso, girl, goddess, and baggage, strong-armed by Hermes into letting Odysseus go, who was trying to do that, and to keep him with her, and to explain that letting him go was entirely her idea. It was a bit he loved and was too familiar for the Greek to be any bother.

There were footsteps running up the stairs, the door opened fast, and there was Victoria. She looked at his surprise.

"Oh my God," she said. "You don't want me."

He untangled himself as quickly as he could, went to her in the door, took her fingertips, then her hand, and finally both elbows, drew her in, and kissed her.

"Not so," he said.

She, as Victoria did, threw her arms around his neck and pushed him back a step. She was definitely in the room. She was definitely breathing. "Thank goodness!" she said. "Alistair, I'm yours. This is where I live now. I ran up all the stairs."

He steered her to the sofa. "All right," she said, "but only like this." She sat partly by and partly on him, securely attached.

"You went to Torcello," he said.

She took a breath, and her brow slightly furrowed. He smoothed it with a fingertip. "All my life," she said, "I have lived in an alien land. I cast myself into the sea, and as I was drowning, my foot found you."

"Was it horrid?" he said.

"He didn't snigger."

"Your father?"

"The old waiter. The one who brought us the zabaglione, as a matter of fact. All I was thinking about was us, and I was trying to remember everything. I was probably looking up the stairs. I couldn't see him and he smiled. But nicely. He didn't snigger."

He looked down at her again and wondered what flower was sweeter or purer than her face.

"That was nice of him," he said. *And should save him from some particularly unpleasant death.*

She said, "It doesn't do much just to say I'm better than those people, does it?"

"You are, though. By a lot."

"Not as much as if I earned it. Alistair, I did learn one thing from that lunch. We're going to be here a long time. Are you?"

"As long as there's a war, I think."

"This is what I want to do. I want to start selling my dresses to other women. Then I would actually start to have my own money. Then what we are wouldn't matter, because I'd just be me. That stuff about seeing my father cry is pretty stupid, really. I even think being a crook might be better than being a crooked general or a crooked priest."

"Well done," he said.

"I want to understand all the paintings in Venice. I know I can. I might even be able to write about them. Do you think I might?"

"If you were able to make me see what you wanted me to see at the Frari, I'd read you. It's long slow work, you know."

"That's colors having conversations. You don't see it in all paintings. Then I want to learn to ride extremely well. I don't quite know why that's important, but I think it is. A lot of it's you, of course."

"You'll be tired, sore, sometimes scared. You might get hurt, though you shouldn't and we'll try not. It's the company of horses that makes it worthwhile. You'd never find a horse at that kind of lunch. That's stupid, I know."

"Not a bit stupid," she said. "And the other parts don't scare me. I'm not scared of being scared. Really."

"I know that."

"And then I want to understand poetry. That's mainly you, Alistair, but I do want to know why it matters. It may never mean as much to me as shapes and colors. And better Italian. Golly, this is going to be a lot of work. I'm going to need a lot of you. Is that all right?"

"It's going to be my pride, my joy, and my delight," he said, feeling each word slip into its lock.

"That's so nice," said Victoria, and put her head on his knee. Then stood up. "Alistair, it's very late, and I want to try my new bedroom and our bed. And I never feel as safe as with you in bed, anyway." She stood with her back to him, her shoulders slightly hunched, which meant, *Undo me down the back, please.* He did.

It was their night of greatest delight. The music would have been a cello's. The wind would have been from the west. The scenery would have been a lake, with geese flying slowly across the moon. At his moment, he cried with the happiness that what he was dissolving into was her, herself.

Victoria said, "Do you think we'll manage the morning, somehow?"

"Somehow is the word," he said.

He said, "I'll tell you a story in the morning, about the first time we were together. But the sun has to be on your hair."

"That will be lovely."

He slept. He felt a hand cool on his forehead and a breast warm against his.

"Alistair, I've been thinking it may really be a terrible amount of row if I don't go home. Could we, darling?"

Sleep gave a reproachful look as she glided from the room. He could make out Victoria's face, breast, and the bundle of her under the white cover. He groped for a match, and being really and truly a nice boy, kissed her.

"Come on, honey," he said, pulled the covers down, and slapped her gently on the behind. "Let's get moving, baggage."

To her question, he said, "Our gondolier's left, I know. The vaporetti might be running still. We might possibly find a gondola."

They found cold. They started toward San Toma, away from the Gritti but to the vaporetto stop. Turning toward the Palazzo Corner, they could see the top of the campanile of St. Mark's playing hide and seek with low cloud, nervously.

Victoria said, "You were not in bed with a silly little twit, Alistair. I'm doing a lot of new things, and sometimes I have to try them on. Or pretend. Did I really think I could sleep all night there and have breakfast with your mother or something in the morning? Not really. Not quite. But it was lovely pretending it, and it had a lot to do with what we had an hour or so ago. And if you don't think that was worth taking your girl back across the canal, I'm disappointed. And I am not your baggage. And it is crude to smack a girl on her bare ass."

In this time of his youth, he liked to think anyway that women were the wild creation, that their girdles and visiting cards and teas were only the sheep's clothing that let them slip into the town, and he loved to run with them in their dark, native woods. He squeezed her hand. "Yes, you are. No, it isn't. But I wasn't cross, honey," he said.

"All right," said Victoria.

Soon they were under the bulk of Santa Maria dei Frari, to which Victoria waved. He put an arm around her dear shoulder. They got to San Toma, to the dock. The canal was black, and cold, and slapped with wind, and empty.

"I have horrid news," he said.

"I know," she said. "We'll walk.

Her shoes were hopeless. By the Academia bridge, she was limping. Since she tried not to show it, this wrung his heart. His former girls, he could have carried, he supposed. With Victoria, he was not so sure. From the top of the bridge, even the cross on Santa Maria della Salute flirted with the cloud, and Venus was having nothing to do with such a night.

"Almost there," she said, in their Campo San Stefano. "May I have my story?"

"Not until there's sun on your hair on my pillow," he said.

"We'll get there one day. Will I see you tomorrow?"

"Obviously. Probably the afternoon. Will you really be all right in there?"

"I'll think of something."

He brushed a little snow off her forelock.

"Kiss me here," she said. "I'll walk the rest alone. You can see the lights in the lobby."

He did and turned around into the dim calle. It was true that in Venice you were meant to slink like a cat.

The next morning, the snow was there. Alistair waited upon Mr. Featherstonhaugh in his study. He looked out at the aged city showing off—*look at me!*—one more and brand new fantasy. Venice, this Christmas, might have been thought to aim at some kind of Macy's parade. It was, in fact, barrage balloons against Austrian bombers, tethered by hawsers from some of the *campi,* great billowing things so that the domes of Venice seemed in some lights reflected not only from the lagoon below but from the sky above. He went back to his desk, Victoria's desk, for her colors had been followed to the letter. He thought it a small masterpiece. He needed this, for he was just now standing over the forge where the geometry of the aesthetic that would serve him most of his life was being fired, and he was even to some extent aware of this. He had fallen with delight upon some Italians just a little older than himself. Guiseppe Ungaretti:

Un'interra notte
Buttato vicino
A un compagno
Massacrato
Con la sua bocca
Digrignata
Volta al pleniluno . . .
(All of a night
Thrown beside
A companion
Massacred
His mouth
Snarling
At the full moon . . .) though the vowels are better in Italian.

A compression like a furnace flame, which thrilled him. Thrilled and then bored. He went back to it in some of the Tagliamento poems, where the matter was such that luxuriance of line was like stretching before one bathed in a sewer. Homer, Virgil, Dante, Tennyson were too deep in him to be thrown away. He sat more easily with Yeats, though in truth Ungaretti was not always to be that extreme. It had become clear to him that every thought worth realizing was the fulcrum between something small and plain (an unknown girl's face, Victoria's dear breasts) and something huge and shambling, filling the horizon. He was erudite and could contain the huge and shambling thing; mechanized war would be a case in point, on a map with received and rational perspective. He also believed that received perspective was as apt as not to be bosh and that the reality was as it appeared to him: stumbling, blind monsters. Sword, bridle, pen could also be a territory. His loyalty was always with the face, the breast, the horse. This was clear to him by now. The question was what tied the small thing to the great and yet is not seen.

He was tearing up poems at a great rate now, but not in darkness, for he knew where he was going, got closer most of the time, and Victoria's colors helped his spirit breathe. These thoughts would make a critic many years down time write, "the 20th Century observed from the 10th." Just now, it was observed from Victoria. Obviously, clever girl, she had put herself in his study and so in most of his life. But recklessness, which he loved, for it was the arch of life, became brighter yet in a frame so frail as Victoria's. He feared for her because she was what he could hold, and she directly faced the distant giants.

Mr. Featherstonhaugh stood in the window and rubbed his hands at the snow.

"Won't last," he said.

"No," said Alistair.

"How's Ausonius?"

"Some of his lines are good." At Alistair's request, they were reading Latin poets of the later Empire to learn how technique often admirable can end in forgettable poems.

"He's good with the slave girl in bed," said Alistair. "He seems to like her as well, you know. And that comes over without actually saying it. That's good. I admire it."

"And the rest?"

"You always think it's going to be better than it is. None of it matters."

"You're not repeating Gibbon?"

"No. It's what I think. The best of it is rehashed Virgil, anyway."

The tone of his lessons had changed. It would be easier now to call them conversations.

"You're supposed to say why," said Mr. Featherstonhaugh.

Alistair smiled as he sat back. "Try this," he said. "It may be old rope. In Homer, in Virgil, in Dante, there is the presence of fear. Not cowardice. Fear. Shakespeare too. Tennyson fakes it, I think, but it's there. Sir Gawain's terribly afraid. It's not in these people. Discouragement. Resignation. It's not enough. No edge to it. *'And after many a summer dies the duck,'* if you see what I mean. Maybe that's why it works with the girl. Girls are always a little scary, in the background, at least. Do you think I'm right?"

"I have no idea, Alistair. It's a perfectly valid thought. I would caution that it may be connected with your age. You are drawn to the precipitous. Which does not make it untrue. I'm going to give you something else to read. Castiglione. *Il Cortigiano. The Courtier.* It used to be the most-read book in Europe. I wonder what you'll make of it."

"I've heard of it. What should I make of it?"

"It's either a manual for dancing masters or as important as St. Francis. And I'll not tell you which I think. Alistair?"

"Yes," said Alistair.

"Even old warhorses hear the trumpets."

That seemed likely enough, so Alistair nodded.

"Turkey. Entered the war on the wrong side. A great mistake for a failing power. Gallipoli was a disaster for us, that Churchill puppy, but it will not save Turkey. She will lose her empire unless we lose the war. I myself would love to see Istanbul become Byzantium again, the throne of the King of the Greeks. I would love to hear Mass at the Hagia Sophia, thought it would not be in our rite. She will surely lose the Arab lands, her nominal sovereignty over Egypt, the Sudan. England will take them, of course, our empire among the Arabs. Those are the places I knew, Alistair. The tribes I knew. Sometimes still the men. I have had offers to put on harness again. That would mean leaving you."

He remembered the early days with Mr. Featherstonhaugh and Captain Pizorzky in Rome at the villa when they were buying his first horse. There was that amazing first lesson on the bloodiness of war in the kitchen with knives. There was the fun of Mr. Featherstonhaugh's new jacket, the lunches along with Manfredi and when he had made Serafina laugh. There was his unfailing courtesy and kindness, back before Maggiore, when Mr. Featherstonhaugh was the only man he had.

Alistair said with great sincerity, "I shall be very deeply sorry for that, sir. I wish you godspeed." In fact, he loved him.

"I will be very sorry to leave you, Alistair, and that is not said by rote. But there is little more I can do for you that you cannot do by yourself. Your classics are up to a good degree from Oxford, and you are barely seventeen. Your military history is close to Sandhurst standard. You know the literature of four languages well enough to find out the rest for yourself. Your writing is your own thing. You and the critics will test it, not I. You can barely count, but that's not your game. I have taught several young men, Alistair, and you are my great success."

Alistair looked at him steadily and said, "Thank you. You were my great good fortune."

"And I think that you are in peril, Alistair, and that it is not your fault." Mr. Featherstonhaugh saw that his pupil's eyes had not moved and hoped that he might just possibly not be wasting time.

"You have no loyalties except your affections and your appetites, and perhaps your hates, though you are not a good hater yet. You no longer have a country. Most things are easy for you. You are hard not to like, which may be your greatest danger of all. You will most likely never have to earn a living, that is, to learn anybody else's rules. You may become a disconnected and dangerous man, Alistair. You put me in mind of a young wild stallion. It's attractive while you're young, you hurt no one, and I am quite sure the mares think you're very nice. But you could become a nuisance. And then people will learn how not to like you, and you will not understand, and you will become bitter. You will learn to hate then, and then you will not understand another thing: that there exist people who will know how to bend you and use you very well. My old trade, and your grandfather's, is full of men like that. You do not deserve any of this, Alistair."

Who did not answer quickly but then said, "I submit to the discipline of my craft. It is a difficult craft and has great masters. They are my standard, though I may never reach them. That is not nothing."

"It is by no means nothing, Alistair. I did not call you a trifler. Only as a poet, you tend to be your own counsel, judge, and jury."

"I am not a lenient one."

"I did not say you were. But you are your own."

"There is something more nebulous but yet real," said Alistair. "I try to embody my family. Life not for ease but as a formal dance."

"I understand you as most people would not. It could become a fop's life, before a mirror. That would really be unworthy."

"Could but has not. What would you have me do?"

"What our faith tells you to do. Submit. Submit to something larger than yourself, the merit of which you cannot deny. With your father, that may have been the law, but I do not know him. With your grandfather, it was the service. For you, it would be the Church or the army. They are strangely similar. I do not see you as a priest, though there have been stranger ones than you. So the army. At least for a while."

"Whose particular army? And in everything I see, the more men form masses, the more beasts they become. My grandfather and Maggiore are the exceptions, I think. Our time has the plague, I think, and health is in isolation, a villa above the city. I would give my loyalty to a woman before an army."

"With exceptional self-indulgence, I am sure," said Mr. Featherstonhaugh. "Alistair, I am not even your conscience, just your mentor, and not that for long now. I will always think of you. I expect great things from you. But I do worry. Try to think of this from time to time. The word is *connect*."

"But the word from you yourself is *disconnect*, and I am sorrier than I can say," said Alistair, with a sad and sweet smile.

"Certainly not before Christmas. Alistair, we shall not forget each other. There are pens. There is the mail."

xxx

A CALL TO PIETRO Vendramin, his closest Venetian friend—though he painted, and marvelously, in Florence—gained him entry to the Ca' Foscari, six strokes of the gondolier's oar from his own, and to the duke. In the *salone*, he stopped with amazement and delight at a creche, the figures of which made one Serafina and he had loved in the via delle Virgini look like something you could win at a fair. There were camels, fierce Orientals with moustaches of ebony, earth-colored shepherds, cattle of polished walnut with ivory horns, silver filigree angels with sapphire eyes, and a baby of pearl held by a Madonna of pure gold in a deep blue dress. It was set not against a tree but a small altar, and when Alistair had bowed to it, he found that he had also very nearly bowed to a small old man with a pointed beard, smiling.

"Those are Venetian," said the duke. "It is not only the Neapolitans who do them. Ours are cleverer, I like to think. I know exactly who you are. I knew your grandfather when I was a younger man in Rome. You want a horse for a girl."

"Si, la sua grazia," said Alistair, using the exact translation of "Your Grace."

The duke smiled again. "We do not use that here. But thank you. It is quite elegant. Can she ride?"

"No, sir. But I will teach her."

"Can you?"

"Yes."

"That is what young Vendramin says. Your mother could ride. I remember her a little, at the hunt. It is agreeable suddenly to have her as a neighbor. I hope that I may call upon her one day."

Alistair bowed.

The duke said, "I do not want to sell a horse. I keep them for my nephew and his young bride. They are in France now, he is with the French Staff, but they will return. I do not want a beginner wrecking a mouth."

"A snaffle bit, my lord. Only that. And I shall not let that happen."

"Very well," said the duke. "A girl and a horse go well together. Pick which you want, and we will work out terms."

"Thank you, sir. I love your stables. It is happiness to be there."

"They are rather fine. My great-grandfather built them, so I can say that."

Victoria, for her part, was ordering cloth.

Christmas morning came with bells. The peals flew over the canal, the silver of St. Mark's, the great bell of San Polo striding forward, the bronze choirs of Santa Maria dei Frari, all the parishes in their different weights and verses. There had been another light snowfall in the night, a pretty sister to the cruel falls on the mountain front. With Christmas morning had come the sun, and the city is fresh and fragile. The boats on the canals wear Christmas ribbons. At a moment when the bells all flow into each other to unite, the city herself seems a single thing, a painted music box floating on the lagoon.

At Anna's palazzo, breakfast is slight, for luncheon will be grand. They assemble in the sala before Mass at San Toma, smaller than the great Santa Maria and lately become their church. They are a family well devised for ceremony, but today not all is entirely at ease. Maggiore is here for much less long than Anna had let herself believe. In his full dress uniform, his obvious exhaustion—the Ninth Isonzo has been a catastrophe—makes him austere and distinguished but not what his lady would wish to see. This house has no associations for them, though the *Pulcinelli* look on and wish them well. It is Mr. Featherstonhaugh's last day with them. Before

New Year, he will take the train for Milan, for Alexandria by London. Anna begins to marshal her family to the stairs. She is not quite as young as when we first knew her, she has lost some of her self-deprecating lightness, but she is a tall, grand, and beautiful woman. Though fretful about this and that this morning, she is generally content, for her man, though wearied, prizes and adores her, and it shows. As her hand is on the bannister, the water door opens and feet come running up the stairs. It is Victoria, breathless and almost late. She has been bidden to Christmas luncheon, and Alistair told her the time of Mass. She is lovely this morning again in rippling blue—Fortuny for Christmas!—and Maggiore and Mr. Featherstonhaugh smile and bow. Anna is a little taken aback, but Victoria is sweetly deferential and Anna can hardly look askance at a girl who has come for Mass. Alistair steps forward and gravely takes her arm. In fact, she cheers them all up. Kitty joins the end of the procession in her bombazine best.

Before luncheon, they gather again in the sala, and there is Champagne. They stand around the tree, a mountain fir more blue than green and smelling of the forest as the needles are warmed by the candle flames. Anna is disposed to be Protestant to this degree, and the presents are gathered under it. Anna has given Maggiore a beautiful saddle map case of Florentine leather with his arms in silver, to be the companion of the sandwich case he never rides without. Mr. Featherstonhaugh has for Alistair an eighteenth-century Italian printing of *The Odyssey* with particularly handsome typography in Greek. Alistair is admiring it and has already turned to the Calypso passage when Victoria takes him gently aside and gives him hers. It is a fountain pen, a German Pelikan, with a silver barrel, beautifully chased. He will use it the rest of his life and now, overwhelmed, takes advantage of the mistletoe, which the *Pulcinelli* have never seen before in their lives. He had great difficulty thinking what to give her—anything to wear would be absurd—and finally decided on pretty opera glasses to see paintings too far away in churches. He explains it, she is happy, and the mistletoe serves again.

Alistair has a Kodak box Brownie, and the sun through the Moorish windows is bright enough today for him to use it indoors. Anna and Maggiore could be minor royalty on the edge of history, imperious and fragile. By himself, Maggiore looks embarrassed, for he has just misunderstood the mistletoe and has kissed departing Mr. Featherstonhaugh formally on both cheeks. Victoria looks delectable even now, though it is odd for us to see a girl so young so grandly dressed by day. The tall sad *Pulcinello* poses at her shoulder. Alistair looks absurdly young and slight, though the preoccupation, as with the first sign of an enemy seen at the edge of the plain, is just on his face and will become more pronounced. He is tilted, Victoria being no hand with a camera.

They are not joined by anyone else, for this is Venice and they do not have their friends of Rome. Anna has done an Irish Christmas luncheon, scarcely anything of Italy, though the roast goose is perfumed with truffles. Maggiore, who met Christmas pudding the year before in Rome, opines that it was probably developed by Nero to smother Christians. It is brought in burning in brandy, and the box Brownie captures even this. An album has preserved these photographs; they are dark brown, but they can be seen.

After lunch, the children slip away and find a gondola in Christmas ribbons to take them to St. Mark's. They love hot chocolate at Florians, especially to drink it outside when it's cold and no one else sits in the arcade. Because it is cold and Christmas, Victoria wants brandy. She plays with her new opera glasses, looking at the mosaics on the basilica. He uses his new fountain pen to write her couplets in Italian on the back of a Florian's menu, which, though of nice heavy card, has not survived. Late afternoon found them at Calle Caotorta 23. What with Anna's Champagne and Florian's brandy, they were by then wrapped in other's arms and fast asleep. Though with questions of their own, they were probably the happiest of those at Anna's Christmas. They knew that they owned all but eternity, and courage, and pure hearts, and that no question remains closed to such light.

5

Victoria had her own orbits. If you tried to hurry her waist with your arm, its welcome turned ragged and then cold. When the time came actually to choose Victoria a horse, it was still winter, the Brenta was high, black, and foamed, water in furrows flashed in the low sun, rooks settled into trees as black as themselves, but there were shoots here and there. Alistair had spent time among the duke's horses. He excluded stallions, mares, and anything under eight. That left seven.

He rode them all. First he rode as himself and then as an ignorant rider. He rejected two firecrackers, one more that used the rider's hands to keep its head from scraping on the ground, and one whose canter seemed driven by steel wheels on bent axles. Having ridden his own two first, his thighs were now approaching pain, but sooner or later they would be where his dear's own thighs would be, and that encouraged them. He liked a bay with willing movement, a keen eye, and an air of conscience carried bright upon the brow like a Boy Scout's. There was a grey he could go with too. He left the last trial for his next ride. Walking to the Isotta, he saw that the first stirring of a furze bush was a green from Giovanni Bellini, a message from the new province of his world.

Victoria was in the world's great honeypot of painted color. He thought Venice a dark city. By winter, it is so, when its finest effect is the engraving of planes of grey against the sky of the lagoon. But Venice painted color and light. His mother's passion was her sculpture. Sculpture had been her excuse to leave a chilled marriage for Rome. There she had worked on it daily. But as a child of Rome, where she'd spent her happiest girlhood, her taste was entirely for Roman balance and mass, she sniffed at Venice as "paintbox stuff," and seemed to have great difficulty getting to work here. For his Victoria, it was heaven.

When Alistair does not ride or write, he goes first to the Calle Caotorta. Lucia exacts a chaste kiss before Victoria's warm one. She has become the sister of both, of both the elder, tolerant, but knows just what they're good for and what they're not. She does not like making britches for her mistress. It is, in itself, indecent, and simply dangerous in its intent. There is now a pile of art books and Venice guides. When Alistair arrives, Victoria leaves things to Lucia and sits on the floor with him under the window, with luck in the sun. They make a plan. Sometimes this had required a call to Pietro, whom Victoria badly wants to meet, to get them into peoples' houses. Just now, Victoria wants to look at all of Tintoretto in sequence, as painted. They did this with Bellini first. Long notes are written with the fountain pen before the opera glasses are carried off and used.

Their prize today is *The Miracle of St. Mark Freeing the Slave*, one of Tintoretto's earliest of great note. The glasses are taken carefully in their case but will not be much needed today since even in their time the painting has been moved to the Academia from its native hall. Today's rose skirt and jacket the sky blue of a fair winter day against his arm draw glances as she talks him across their Campo San Stefano. The hand that does not hold his arm has her broad notebook. Over the bridge is the Academia. They go straight to their goal.

Victoria says, "I'm a little foggy about this miracle, Alistair. Please?"

"It was a Christian slave. They found him praying, so of course they had to break his bones one by one and blind him, all the usual, but St. Mark appeared miraculously and smashed everything up and set him free."

"Golly. My kind of saint," said Victoria and nothing more for quite a while. She looks.

These colors make her nostrils flair. He knows she will look for families of colors calling to each other across the space. Gold shouts *Stop!* from the Evangelist's cloak in midair, clings to the soft shoulder of the girl with the babe, abases itself on the jailer stricken down, turns to fire on the exulting believer holding the shattered instruments of pain, fades into stone, and relaxes into the flesh of the naked, marveling slave. Red shouts from the corners, glows genial in the tunic of the saint. When she points with his hand so he can follow her eye, she is no longer tentative and vague but stabs the air. Her eyes are of a different species from his, but he is beginning to follow her, more or less. He loves to be led by her through a painting as he feels her breathing at his side. He could in a manner see the painting through her flesh. Where Titian's *Assumption* was a long, rapturous melody of Our Lady rising into majesty, this is a stone thrown at a beehive, and he feels it in her breath. She has given him no grand overview of her thoughts since they've been doing this. He supposes she will. Victoria gives her shake.

"Lunch," she said. "Where?"

Which he had considered. "Behind the Rialto? Fish?"

She thought. "Sure. And we can take the vaporetto. It's easy from here."

The restaurant was a place of white tiles, green stone basins for swimming fish, iron shelves carrying piles of crabs, a smell of iodine, and waiters in starched white aprons. Victoria was by far the most decorative object in the room. They came often, and she was a favorite of the waiters. They were almost the only non-Venetians.

"He's not very grown up," she said.

"It's a young man's painting. He wasn't much older than us."

The dock and the vaporetto had been noisy and full. These were almost their first words.

"He's mostly trying to amaze. The only thing he truly imagines is the girl with the baby. She's much more interested in her baby, so she's not knocked down like all the others. And he's much less grown up than young Bellini."

"His *Adoration*'s at San Rocco, right by San Toma. We could see it on the way back. It might be different. If you want to know, I think he's brilliant."

"I didn't say he wasn't talented," she said. "My boots should be here from Florence any day. Lucia's finished my britches, though it tore her heart."

"You'll have a horse tomorrow. Should have. It's down to two."

"Golly, Alistair," she said. "Is one of them a mare?"

"God no!" he said. "I wouldn't put you on one of you. Where are you going with this, Victoria?"

He meant the paintings, not horses, and had not directly asked before. She considered and leaned toward him.

"You remember me telling you on the boat to Torcello about designing a dress, how you let everything you know about it, who it's for, what season, possible colors boil around in your imagination? I'm right at the beginning of that now. You may be tired of me by the time I decide where I'm going. Let alone get there. Maybe nowhere. I don't suppose an honest to God couturiere really has to be an art critic."

She was a couturiere, for she had a customer now. All the family—that is, she, he, and Lucia—were intensely proud of this. It had come from one of the house visits, Pietro the key, to see a painting, a small Bellini. There, the young lady of the house, a cool Venetian, talked to them throughout and ended by ordering a dress. He suspected she meant it as a lark, these odd young Americans, though he never told Victoria that. She was in for a surprise. The dress was at its distant origins Kate Greenaway, the slim young shepherdess. Kate Greenaway had grown up, the bodice was closely fitted under the looser cloth, the collar only mimicked the demure, the skirt had closed in on the thighs, which moved it. Now it was for a shepherdess who could smoke a Balkan Sobranie and who kept something better than a lamb for pet. It was nearly ready.

The mussels arrived, the inviting shell always slightly suggestive. So did the wine, neatly collared by Victoria, who had developed reflexes. Alistair laughed. She looked in question then poured too much wine in both their glasses. "There's something else coming up," he said. "Manfredi, you know, has finished his induction phase. He's a full cadet tenente now. I'm allowed to go and see him, so I will. Other side of Turin. I'll be away four days."

Victoria ate several mussels, with increasing deliberation. "I could come too," she said.

Their eyes met. This hung between them, so enormous he could see all the sides of it, and its sides were very different. To have her beside him in the car would be extremely pleasant. To have her for two whole nights in a distant inn would be, in her own word, dreamy. To show her off to Manfredi would be highly gratifying. And he knew absolutely that he would rather have Manfredi to himself. He lacked the art to tell her this without hurt, would not hurt her, and disdained lies. So if she could come, obviously she would come. He breathed deep, and a mussel just missed its chance to take deadly revenge, though he was not aware of this.

"Gosh," he said.

"I'll work on it," said Victoria. "No promises."

ALISTAIR ALTERNATED HIS HORSES between manege and field. Today was Pompey's turn to ride out. The peasants had begun to sow. Some of them he now knew to greet, as in his earliest days on the Campagna, when a boy on his first real horse. The country was as different as could be. Flat black earth, ruled by furrow and planted tree line, stretched away purple under the slate sky, potted here and there by tangled bottoms holding deer and boar. He picked a path under poplars by the Brenta. It was high and angry with the snow melt of the lower hills. In this year of heavy falls, it would rise much higher, likely flood. The fishermen's rowboats of summer were pulled up into the trees and tied with withy. He whistled in surprise as a line of cranes flew across the field behind the poplars, *cantando lor lai*, singing their lays. The first back from Africa.

Riding back into the stables, he was pleased to see that junk had been piled precariously in the corner of a kind of gathering hall between the loose-boxes and the manege. He stopped to inspect it. It looked high and awful enough. He gave Pompey to his groom and mounted the grey, his second choice for Victoria, checking the girth a second time. He rode toward the manege into the hall. Two grooms with pitchforks sent the junk crashing down into the small, echoing space. The grey went wild-eyed, reared straight for the sky, nearly went over as a hind hoof slipped on stone, came down, spun, and bolted for the half-open gate to the manege, where he would have crushed his rider's knee. Alistair became himself again, turned him hard, and kept him turning between bit and spur until the steam had gone out of him and his drenched flanks had slowed. *Cross that one off!*

While saddles were changed and the thing was laboriously built up again, Alistair threw his arms around his Boy Scout bay. He said to him, "Do be good, old boy. I'd hate to have to start all this over again. You'll like her. She'll be the carrot fairy."

He was rewarded. The bay, not being dead, shied violently, spun but not viciously, stayed mostly on the ground, and needed only a few seconds of judicious riding to settle down again. This, the confined space, the slippery floor, the gate set as trap was as bad as it could possibly get and never would get. She'd be off and bruised but not torn. Bruised would happen.

He rode formally to the head groom, who was part of the audience like all the others. He brought the bay to a foursquare halt and said, deliberately grand, *"Questo e stato eletto il cavallo della mia donzella. Che riceva il migliore."* This is chosen as my maiden's horse. That he have the best.

The head groom saluted. "Si, signore."

Alistair gave money to all, this having been extra work.

THE NEXT DAY CAME. Victoria got out of the car, looked with pleased surprise at the gracious building and fair entrance, walked in with him, and was in an alien world. He should have thought of that. So, down the line of boxes, his affable chestnut reached out his head for carrots, and she shrank against his arm. In a stable, something always goes on. He realized that she listened to sounds he barely heard, the thumps of hooves, jingle of buckles, whinnies, farts. The smells, horse, bran, piss, the sudden high note of farrier's hot iron on hoof that were to him pure pleasure were to her startling and barbaric.

"Is that mine?" she said. Pompey stood in front of them, saddled, glossy, and tossing his head.

"That's my Pompey."

"So you're on him? He's awful big."

That was good, if it made her think hers small. This morning, he had first seen her in her whole outfit, boots, britches, coat, tie. He was enchanted. This might all have started as a lark. He knew now that Victoria was in a place where she had no guide but him, was carrying it through for him alone, and was afraid.

There was her horse. It was standing still, good man, and its ears were forward. He deployed his forces. He gave her his arm to the mounting block. For a moment he felt her fear of the huge, hot, breathing beast in front of her. He moved to help her. She saw, and, before he could, got on.

"Put your foot in the other stirrup, honey," he said. "And take the reins just so he knows you're there." She nodded solemnly. She did it. He took the mounting block away.

He rode by her side that day. On the raked footing of the manege, he led her into walking arabesques, which the floor recorded, so she got an idea of rein and leg. He talked at most half about riding. He listened carefully to her voice, out of which unease drained slowly, though faster than from her body.

Finally she said, "What's his name?" and he felt that the beginning's worst was over.

"I think it's Matteo," he said. "But you can change it. He's almost yours."

She thought through two arabesques. She said quietly, "I think I'd like him to be Ariosto, Alistair, and I think you know why. Can I do that?"

"It's a lovely name," he said. "Shall you and Ariosto trot a little? He'll tell you when to come up in the saddle, and you do, just a bit. You've got good strong legs. If you feel insecure, grab his mane. It doesn't hurt him. I'm beside you."

"Come along, Ariosto," she said. "Let's show him," and, very jiggly, with indeed a handful of mane and on a horse a little startled but nowhere near a panic, she did. With great happiness he was close beside her. He loved her courage and her optimism and her hard work that grace taught her to conceal.

He said, when he took her down at the end and kept his arm around her waist, "You're doing it, and trying to do it well. That's worth a hundred thinkings about it."

This was somewhat from Mr. Featherstonhaugh's Castiglione, his *Il Cortigiano*. It turned out to be a series of conversations that covered, at a quick reading, statecraft, horsemanship, how to buy a hat, and much else. The important thing seemed to be that they were about things one actually did, and had to do very well, as opposed to merely know about. He also liked it that the conversations were entirely unrehearsed. Being Alistair, he liked it even better that they were made to seem unrehearsed.

Her school had cheated her where she should have excelled, art. They had done better with poetry. Victoria had her own tastes, Browning, the schoolgirls' pash, of course, but he liked him too and worked up a bravura performance of "My Last Duchess." She liked some bits of Sir John Suckling and Richard Lovelace. In fact, she loved the swoony. To Alexander Pope, whom he had begun to think he had undervalued, she said, "No, no, Alistair, no use. I just hate him." But he made her read "The Rape of the Lock" one long dark afternoon, the book on the pillow, themselves propped over it. She admitted that, "And sleepless Lovers, just at Twelve, awake," was pretty funny and began to see each word given its proper stature, each ending with lifted eyebrow, frown, or smile. Somehow she had picked up some moderns. She liked James Elroy Flecker's Oriental halvah, and Swinburne, swooniest of all

Of his own poetry, she said, "It makes me think, Alistair, and it's very like you. But it doesn't have your smile, and I wish it did." Criticism he noted.

He pined for the war, which had tasted Manfredi, had caught the scent of Pietro, had swallowed old Mr. Featherstonhaugh, to take him, too, into their company. When it did, he would be between two unthinkables, like everybody else, of being killed with life unlived or of living it as a coward. If there were a girl in it, and there usually was, was there any formula he could grasp better than Lovelace's to Lucasta, *"I could not love thee, (Dear) so much, loved I not honor more"*? He had a letter from Mr. Featherstonhaugh from London, about to leave in a convoy for Alexandria. He wished he had Mr. Featherstonhaugh. Mr. Featherstonhaugh had been able to make him see what he was saying. There were, ready to his hand as a poet, toys that Homer and Lovelace and Suckling simply didn't have: poison gas, bombs from the air, machine guns, factories. If he made poems of what he actually thought about and did not retire to the poetry room and shut the door, he would be writing about men and women in precisely that world that had erupted like a toadstool almost in front of his face. This he precisely did not wish to do, except seen in the far distance as stumbling giants, for he feared madness and feared infection. Which might be the only things he had. Thank God for horses! Every time he touched the thought, he was more certain that only what you could yourself hold and touch was worthy to be loved or hated. *An intellectual hatred is the worst, So let her think opinions are accursed*—so said his master, William Butler Yeats. He was seeing a world being driven stark mad by abstraction.

In the car after their second day with horses, Victoria said, "Alistair, do you have any idea how much I hurt? This is much worse than that virginity stuff. The area concerned is incomparably greater."

"I lack the direct comparison."

"You should try it, Alistair, you really should. And maybe some childbirth one day."

"We'll do less tomorrow, honey."

"We will do more tomorrow until it goes away."

"Good girl," he said and squeezed her thigh in appreciation.

"Ow!" she said. "Florians will be nice." It was true that hot chocolate and anything that might follow was taken to a higher level by horses.

It started happily enough.

What she could not do was relax. Her balance was good, as he knew from gondolas and gangplanks. She had good muscles for a girl and capable legs, as he also knew (he knew every aspect of her better than anyone on earth). Before her behind was marked with any trace of saddle soap on her new britches, he had her out of the stirrups at the walk. She would have kind hands. Her excellent posture would give her a good seat by and by. Her leg, weight on the heel, stirrup on the ball of the foot, was steady for a beginner. For several days, they thought each other, teacher and pupil, immense. Now, modeling himself on his old teachers, he sat his own horse ramrod and pitiless at the center of the ring, entirely forgetting that she was not a boy of thirteen. She was as stiff as a board.

"You've got to breathe," he spoke. "How would you like it if your horse stopped breathing?"

She dutifully breathed, several times.

"Open your toes and waggle them," he spoke. "It worked for me. And breathe."

He tried to keep Captain Pizorsky's military whiplash out of his voice. Succeeded somewhat. She was a supple and pliant girl. He told her so in the car home. "Don't you know how beautifully you move? Just be like you are the rest of the time."

She looked at him between tears and anger. "You're not always yelling at me the rest of the time. And I wouldn't like you a bit if you did."

Oh God, he thought. He never yelled.

From then he rode back beside her as at first, so he barely raised his voice. He showed her the seated trot, which, done well and comfortably, makes the rider's hips as soft as a puppy dog. She looked like a wooden soldier.

The canter—he trusted Ariosto by now, her bridle work and balance was good enough to bring it off, and he was beside her—brought a fleeting smile of exhilaration to her face. Not much change otherwise. They were stuck. A rigid rider can't learn.

Whenever he fenced or rode or sailed, he had meter running like an underground river in his brain. He was barely aware of it. Today, for no reason whatever, it was a bit of "Ode to a Nightingale": *O, for a draught of vintage that hath been/ Cooled a long time in the deep-delved earth*" and so forth. She was still breathing a little from the canter.

Of a sudden, he said, "Recite!"

"Do what?" she said in the aggrieved voice that had miserably become their manner in the ring.

"Recite poetry. If you recite, you have to breathe. Poems have rhythms. Recite poetry."

"What poetry?" said, still with the same note.

He was impatient now but turned it into energy. "Anything you like. That Englishman you like. The one you learned. The one about the gates."

"Oh," she said. She said hesitantly to her saddle, *"I am the gate toward the sea: O sailor men pass out from me."* James Elroy Flecker's "Gates of Damascus."

He pointed straight up. "Not like that, honey. Look up. Tell it to the ceiling. Big voice!"

"Oh," she said but took deep breath, then,

I am the gate toward the sea: O sailor men pass out from me!

I hear you high on Lebanon singing the marvels of the sea.

"Walk!" he said and moved off. "Steady from your hips down. Move from your hips up. Keep going!"

The dragon-green, the luminous, the dark, the serpent-haunted sea,

The snow-besprinkled wine of earth, the white-and-blue-flower foaming sea.

"Trot!" he said. "Keep it up, honey!" And by God, it worked! She was starting to enjoy it, and her own dear voice rose clear, putting a hint of question at the end of each line.

Beyond the sea are towns with towers, carved with lions and lily flowers?

And not a soul in all those lonely streets to wile away the hours?

"Canter!" he said and put Pompey into a dressage hand-canter, which was show-off and meant to be. "Squeeze leg, take rein, don't let your heel come up!" He knew the next himself and joined her.

Beyond the towns, an isle where, bound, a naked giant bites the ground:

The shadow of a monstrous wing looms on his back: and still no sound.

They were half around the ring by now. She was flushed and going with her horse. He fell back a little, so she was on her own.

Beyond the bay in utmost West old Solomon the Jewish king?

Sits with his beard upon his breast and grips and guards his magic ring?

Ariosto was having himself a fine time, though behaving like the gent he was. He went a little further from her. She kept it up three times around the ring, and, when she pulled up on her own, she had shouted the last verse like a schoolboy.

Sell the rotten! Buy the ripe! Their heads are weak! Their pockets burn!

Aleppo men are mighty fools! Salaam Aleikum! Safe return!

"Damn, Alistair, that was fun!"

This chasm crossed, all her abilities came forward. He quickly had her going over cavalletti, puppy jumps. When Ariosto finally ran out at a cavalletto (her fault, not his) and she stayed on through with a little shriek, he knew they could safely ride out.

They were lucky in their first day. There was real spring in the sun, though it would not last yet. Daffodils were replacing crocuses in the woodsides and the hedges, wisteria showed in the woods, and early apple trees were in their wedding dresses. They trotted the path by the Brenta. The river, now in full alpine snowmelt, had the baleful energy of a trapped snake, but in backwaters they saw dace rise to mayflies. Reciting had been such a success that she kept it up, a little as a game and because she could still go stiff. She therefore had a growing repertoire of poetry of the more loose-limbed sort. "*Half a league, half a league, half a league onward . . .*" "*When the hounds of spring are on winter's traces/ The mother of months in meadow or plain . . .*" became part of their riding, and he even taught her his old love, "*Dry clashed his harness in the in the icy caves?/ And barren chasms, and all to left and right / The bare black cliff clanged round him? . . .*" which gained such a charge from a young woman's clear, soaring voice that it tingled the back of his neck. On the way back, she spotted a small tree trunk on the ground and pointed Ariosto at it, who changed into a canter. They both took it decently. "Oh, yi, yi!" said Victoria.

In the car back to the boat that day, she said, "Pa has another lunch tomorrow. He wants me."

Alistair looked at her bleakly.

"I'll go," she said. "It's a pill. If it's my rent for the car and the boat and Lucia and all, then it's my rent. It doesn't matter. I'll talk to the Italians, maybe. Pa can't really do that."

"And what about?" he said.

"Painting and horses, Alistair. Painting and horses. Won't they get a surprise! I'll have my own little salon right among the thieves. If he wants a hostess, he'll get a hostess. And you know what I'll be thinking about? Of when I'm deciding what Paris will wear for Christmas while I correct the proofs for my third book. Maybe this time in Italian. Do you like that?"

"I like it lot," he said. "Very much indeed." And took her hand.

"Some it's a bit of a reach. But Fiamma Corner's asked me for another dress, and she said don't be surprised if some of her friends do. I could be making money in a year. And there will always be people who know more about the paintings than I do, but I might be able to make people see them especially well. Do you think?"

He took her hand to his lips and kissed it. "Yes, I do think. I don't see any reason in the world why not."

"Will you be around to see that, Alistair, when we're both colossally important? I shouldn't ask that. It's not fair. But I know I'd like it. And you'll deserve to see it, because a lot of it will have been you."

He looked at her hand with great affection. The puppy fat had all left it by now, and it was an elegant young hand. He said, "I'm not very good with paintings and I couldn't design a napkin. You know that, Victoria."

"I do," she said. "I know it very well. But you made me matter. That's what matters." She put her head on his shoulder and his hand in hers under the coat, in her breast, and so they remained until Mestre.

Therefore when he went to see Manfredi and she really couldn't come, they said goodbye affectionately and it was not a terrible thing. He took a photograph of her with the box Brownie sitting outside at Florians, looking sophisticated, and got it developed for Manfredi.

xxx

After a jolly evening in the mess of the cavalry school at Pinerolo above Turin, he walked back through the village to his inn. Italian officers ate well. There was plenty of wine, no talk of war, for the rule was no shop at mess, and just enough tales of the place itself, like jumping a horse out of a tower for which it was famous, to make a guest's flesh creep. Manfredi was happy among his own—gentlemen and horsemen with the luminous, fierce, and melancholy faces of young Italian men. The evening could not have been better. Manfredi, though a prisoner of the mess in the evening, was his for some of the next morning and for lunch.

Alistair's room was small and clean with an eiderdown like a meringue and a washstand painted with flowers. Lice and rank sheets is often the way of the Italian hills, but in this house was a scent of Switzerland, in the wood polish and the brisk smell of the fires. He sat on the windowsill to take off his shoes and shirt. Beyond the village roofs, the moon showed leftover sheets of snow, torn at the edges.

Everything I am is what I'm not. Though Manfredi is still my closest friend, though all made me welcome, though much in them is like me. I am not Italian, though their faces are what I love. They are a month from battle, and I am not a soldier. My poetry is my strength, but it is a cobweb that tears. The imagination of Victoria's hair on the pillow, her warmth and scent within the eiderdown and the long night squeezed his heart. The eiderdown did smell of soap, though not of lilac.

This storm wrack hung over the daybreak, though it was sunny, and over breakfast of coffee and bread and cheese eaten in the parlor where one chair pushed forward a claim to have been just right for Victoria at her soup the night before.

"You see, it really is a tower," said Manfredi. An abandoned castle a little way from the school had walls and a tower on top of earthworks, at their edge. Against the bottom window, much like a door, soil had been packed against the earthworks, somewhat less than vertical, but steep. One would have climbed with hands and feet. It was about twenty feet high.

"The descent of Mombrone. But they don't tell you it's the bottom of the tower. It's a tradition, mainly."

A horse's front appeared in the window, seemed not to have been let in on the tradition, and rapidly withdrew. A few seconds later it reappeared, ridden furiously, gave the "let this cup pass" look horses are so good at, and slid over the edge. The rider went far back in the saddle. The horse kept its feet, achieved the bottom, and the officer sat back up and waved. Everybody clapped.

"Pretty good!" said Manfredi.

Quite soon another horse appeared, expressed similar doubts, was urged three times, and went. Alistair's thought that the rider's balance was wrong was probably right. The horse's quarters began to slide out. The horse rotated, lost it, the rider threw himself off uphill, and all ended in a heap at the bottom. Both got up. Just as many cheers.

"Not so good," said Manfredi. "Chaps do get hurt."

"It would concentrate one's mind," said Alistair.

"We only do it once. Civilians aren't allowed to. If you come back here as an American officer, you will have to. Cavalry officer, anyway."

Alistair said, "I don't see it happening."

"We all hope you do," said Manfredi. "God knows we need help."

They had not met extremely early, Manfredi being unable to.

"I owe you lunch," said Alistair.

"I was just thinking that," said Manfredi.

Alistair did not know this country, the Val D'Aosta, Maggiore's country, the heart of Savoia. It went in for stone. They went down a side street like a tunnel, through a narrow door through granite two feet thick, brushed their faces against overcoats bulging from a rack, and were in a small, low space with big, tall furniture and a sweet smell of last autumn's apples. Manfredi bowed to a table of officers, nodded to a table of cadets, and smiled at a serving girl with chestnut hair. They sat down at a table apart, between the fire and the open cellar door, whence the apples breathed.

"Well?" said Alistair. They were for the first time alone and at leisure.

"It's a pretty decent place. You saw the riding school. They say it's the biggest in the world."

"It's grand," said Alistair.

"They work us hard. I have two of my own horses and three government ones. We ride four a day. Quite a lot of jumping and rides up and down the mountains. They make you use short stirrups here. Can't tell you what it does to your thighs. Up and down all day on short stirrups."

Alistair laughed.

"What?" said Manfredi.

"I'm teaching a girl to ride," said Alistair. "She made a comment about her thighs."

"What?" said Manfredi.

"Too indelicate for your ears. What else?"

"Swordsmanship. Very little mounted. Do you remember when we tried that?"

"Oh yes," said Alistair

"They make us learn carbine from the saddle. We don't carry them, but the men do. Revolvers for us. And lectures, of course. I learned more from your old tutor."

"I miss him."

"Those were fun days. Do you have a girl now? For real?"

He passed Manfredi the photograph of Victoria at Florians.

"Victoria. She's American."

"Not bad at all," said Manfredi.

"That's the one I'm teaching to ride."

"That could be fun," said Manfredi. "I assume there's more. Being an officer and gentleman, I would die before I asked, of course."

"How's Helene?"

"She's very well. We write twice a week."

"One esteems your faithfulness."

The scent of sentiment might have drawn the chestnut-haired girl, who now stood very close to Manfredi, who looked up at her.

"Signori," she said correctly. *"Cosa le piacerebbe?"*

"Il Gramucco, cara. E poi, cosa c'e?" Gramucco, darling. And what's after that?

"Any truffles?" said Alistair.

And got a second's worth of hazel eyes.

"In *Marzo*?" A little laugh. In March? And to Manfredi, *"E anche romano?"*

"E colonello americano. E molto famoso," said Manfredi. *"E venuto a salvare Italia."* American colonel. Famous as hell. Come to save Italy.

Full dose of the hazel eyes for Alistair, and the smile as well. *"Oh, signore. La ringraziamo. Tutte."* We thank you, sir. All the girls. Hand on Manfredi's shoulder. *"Burlone!"* Joker!

But other customers had come in, and the officers' table was looking impatient. "The boar's pretty good." And, leaving, stirred the air around Manfredi's cheek by the rotation of her hip.

Alistair looked quizzically.

"Neither past nor present," said Manfredi. "There's always the future. But I think she may be part of the curriculum. Tell me about your trip with the horses. Tell me more than you wrote."

He listened carefully as Alistair told. Manfredi had changed very little, Alistair thought, but saw now around him, as it were, the vapor out of which a cloak of professionalism would form, and which was new. Of the prowlers by the train, he said, "Draw it." Alistair did so.

He said, "You were the full height of the car above them? No platform? Then you were in no danger, Alistair, not if you fought. The danger was you would not have fought. Not seriously. Units get wiped out in their first action because nobody really wants to kill."

The Grumello, a wine for men who scale cliffs and build with boulders, was set down by the chestnut hair, who put both palms on the table and gave each some hazel eye.

"Avete deciso, signori?"

She wore a dark red triangular scarf that lit up the chestnut, but there were pathways around it into the dress that easily paid for the less formal plural "avete."

Manfredi looked at Alistair, who shrugged.

"Boar for both. Comes with red cabbage. Truly, it's good."

Alistair said slowly, looking at bread crumbs, "I had a throat picked out, Manfredi. I can see that throat still, though I don't necessarily want to." Then looked up and addressed the rest to a stuffed marmot in a niche on the wall whose glass eyes looked to hold long thoughts.

"Not to kill necessarily. But if they had not fallen back then, then I would have."

"Then you were all right," said Manfredi. "No good thinking about it. Deserters is a problem I don't like."

"My mother's friend," said Alistair, using their formula for Maggiore, "says their mothers hide them. Or wives. Or when the recruiters come."

"They do," said Manfredi. "Funny when you think of our mothers. Our girls."

"I think," said Alistair, "that our mothers know it's our war and their mothers know their sons are the chorus. I should not say 'our.' I'm nothing here. But you know what I mean."

"I think you are right. And our job is to erase that in the men. Alistair, if you take being an officer seriously, you half become a nanny. It's all about other people. I hadn't known that. And I will not hear that stuff about you're nothing. You're us. You'd be here as soon as anyone else if you were Italian. Or French. Or English."

"Thank you," said Alistair. *You will be a fine officer. And are my best friend.* "This is a good wine. Never had it."

"Local. It's hard on our women. My mother knows how close I am to the war, and she hates it. Helene hates it too. But would she want me if I were less than her brothers? Not for long."

"No," said Alistair. "You're going to marry her, aren't you? I think you should."

"Yes. And she will. But I won't make her a widow. And it's not fair to lead men while thinking about making her a widow. So there's the war to finish. Meanwhile, I ought to be more faithful to her."

"I think you are faithful to her. In what matters. It's a situation I've never had to face. She has her codes and should have them. Meanwhile you have yours."

Manfredi very gently touched Victoria's photograph with a fingertip. "If you've never had that problem, you're lucky in her."

"I am very lucky," said Alistair. "I know I am lucky. She's pretty and talented and she was scared to ride but she did. And that's not the only thing. How's Aurora?"

"That's a good girl then, Alistair. Aurora went back to Rome. She said she couldn't understand anybody here, and the local girls smelled like goats, and the only thing she had to do was sleep with me and it got boring. I don't blame her a bit. It's Lizl now."

Their meal arrived, stoneware plates and bowls, knives with wooden handles, all by the grace of the chestnut girl, who hovered, was not much noticed, and looked ill-used.

"Aren't Lizls Austrians?"

Manfredi laughed. "She's Swiss. Or her grandparents were. Her father's a farmer. She's a perfectly good Italian girl. I've seen the farm. Switzerland's near here. Not Austria. I feel badly about Helene. And then I can feel angry with her for being so strict. And then I am ashamed for thinking that. Because it's not because she doesn't want to. I know that. She goes to Mass twice a week. She's very serious. And her mamma's always there. And then I get angry for being ashamed. It's ridiculous. With

Lizl I think about when Helene and I are married and everything's simple. If it is. It should be. And Lizl's nice. She's a dear girl. I'm grateful."

The officers' table stood up, three captains, inspected the cadet and his civilian friend, but politely, took their greatcoats off the rack, and left. Manfredi had put on a formal look.

"There's apples in this," said Alistair. "It's good." It was. Juniper pulled against the shriveled apples, and the wine sauce was stalwart.

"You probably came closer to fighting with a sabre than I ever will," said Manfredi. "But I would like to kill one enemy with a sabre. I may be the last Ferrara who ever does, and that is a very strange thought. We've been doing it a thousand years. Will my sons? I doubt it. At Solferino, which is only fifty years ago, my grandfather led a regiment that his father had raised himself. Peasants from our villages. Farmers. Local squires. Was that less efficient? Men leading men who had always followed them. Men being led by men they had always followed. I will be paid by the government to lead men whose Italian I barely understand who were pushed into trucks by men they had never seen. It is my job, if I can do it, to get my men to the point where my grandfather's started. Is that efficient?"

"No," said Alistair. "The change is not efficient. You can say that it is made inevitable by other changes that are more efficient. You can say it. But I am not sure I believe it. I think I know what happened. We used to do things and know things as they were. Your grandfather's soldier was called Carlo and he had seen him grow up and knew he was a bit dense and scared of bulls. He commanded a man. You command a ledger in the Carabinieris' book."

"You get the man back a bit as a junior officer. But yes," said Manfredi.

"And we fought with sabres so you could smell your enemy's breath. Now you set the sights for two hundred yards."

"Often."

"But that's the way of it. There aren't very many real things left. Riding a horse and making love to a girl, maybe. When you're not really there, there's no responsibility. Just pull the trigger."

"Just go to a bordello."

"That's the way of it."

"Solferino was a slaughterhouse," said Manfredi and also shook his head. "The old ways were not always kind. That's not the point, is it?"

Alistair looked up at the marmot. He felt the wood fire on his cheek, the excellent food and the wine, the presence of his surest friend. He felt both elder and junior to Manfredi.

"I think that we have lost form," he said. "I think that we are fragments without a center. We talk as though we were our grandfathers, but if we were German, we would torpedo a ship of women. Just pull the trigger. And then play Schubert. If you were artillery, you would fire gas canisters. And then read Leopardi. You do read Leopardi, Manfredi. Why would you stop? Command a machine gun nest, go to Mass, and go back to the machine guns. I think our forefathers could be one continuous thing, in the drawing room, on the battlefield, with our grandams, on their lands, at Mass. We can't. We're cut up. I see art moving away from life, war moving away from honor."

"Not always, Alistair."

"Not always either one. But that is the direction. The strings are breaking. I think they've been breaking for a hundred years. At first we didn't notice. And then we lied. And when the lies begin to run out, we can only shut our eyes. Can we get some more of this wine?"

"I think they have it in jugs," said Manfredi. When that had been managed, and the girl soothed and gotten rid of, he said, "On the other hand, Alistair, we're alive and we're here. And we have to be officers and husbands and fathers and take care of our land, or we're cowards." He raised his refilled glass. "This is turning into a very decent lunch, Alistair. Thank you."

"Yes, Prince Andrei," said Alistair. "You're very welcome. I'm sorry about the truffles. You are Prince Andrei, a bit. I'm Pierre a bit. I know you know the book. You said that kind of thing and did it too. But I think that's what a hundred years has done. I think Pierre has the word now. But I'm not really Pierre and I agree with you about the things we have to do. But everything's a choice now. A calculation and a choice. And every choice is momentous. For Prince Andrei, it wasn't."

"Such as pudding, since you're paying. They have an apple thing here. It's really strudel, so we can have treason for pudding. And I am beginning to learn, Alistair, that in battles the choices get made for you. How you react is yours, yes. But you don't frame the choices. We're not Mr Featherstonhaugh's Achilles. I tell you, we're nannies."

HE WENT BACK TO the mess that second evening. As he entered, he saw Manfredi with a group of cadets. They were somehow formal, as, he could say now, a group of young courtiers by Veronese, sculpted faces, grave but smiling, smiling specifically at him. He moved toward them, and they as quickly toward him. They parted to let Manfredi be next to him.

Manfredi said, "There is something important you should know, Alistair. The United States has declared war. Your country is in the war."

He received it as a bolt of joy. "I'm your ally, then." And looked at Manfredi and from face to face around them.

"Very nearly," said Manfredi. "Not quite. Your country declared war against the German Empire. Not the Austrian. But so much closer, Alistair. You will be."

The bolt of joy turned somewhat to lead. But there were hands shaking his and hands on his back. Manfredi kissed him on both cheeks, and said, "I am so happy to have told you." And then, "This calls for a revolting amount of good wine."

Everybody knew that declaring war just on the Hohenzollern emperor was a clerical error. Rustics in Washington, Alistair hazily thought, could hardly tell the difference between one empire and another. There would be American troops in Italy. He would join them, of course.

Manfredi, whose voice used quiet to speak over hilarity, bent his head across the table and said, "This is extraordinary, Alistair. How many Americans know us as you do? I've been there. And how many of those are young enough to fight?"

He nodded. This was a fact. His Americans, he knew, would be as bewildered as the horned cattle they had left behind. What he could offer was rare.

He bent back to Manfredi. "How many people love a country that isn't theirs and can fight for both at once?"

Manfredi thought then laughed. "A wife and a mistress who are best friends?"

Alistair laughed too. But the thought had held humility. He looked a little while at himself choosing to remain a lieutenant while assuming the duties of a brigadier, welding together the cavalries of America and Italy, or at the ambassador's sleeve, as well as all this a poet, whom the simple uniform became. He saw the pasteboard in this walking home with his footsteps for company in the deserted granite town. He could certainly be a battalion officer, attached to the Italians, keeping liaison with the Americans at their flank, switching language and thought under the falling ordnance, galloping the hundred yards between, the greater skill, the greater risk, and fitting. His soldier's cot did not need a girl that night, and he slept well. The morning light across his room's painted washstand found it still fitting. He rose in a joy, which was part of what Victoria felt, mussed and happy at the lightness of his return.

xxx

THERE WAS A WAY FROM the stables Alistair and Victoria had never taken, the other way, toward the lagoon. The day was joyous. One could have said that spring had won at last over the terrible winter of '17, for one is used to being wrong. They rode knee to knee. Their horses were friends. Pompey, become rather stately, had told Ariosto to be content with being junior horse, and there were no more quarrels. Alistair had been rapturously glad to see Victoria after four days, and she, surprised, flattered, and startled with skirts a garland around her neck—"Really, Alistair!"—had settled back into toasty happiness. She had orders from three girls at the pinnacle of Venice. *L'americana* was on the edge of being a fad. She and Lucia were half out their wits, so this ride was almost a stolen pleasure.

Their way went over a canal. The rice fields ended quickly, and the land was wild. It must have been a little higher, for the trees became beeches. The wind out of the west was enough to make a quiet chorus out of the upper branches, though they could not feel it on the ground. He stopped his horse in a clearing. There was a stream in it with wild irises. The shadows of castle clouds ran along it, big as elephants and quiet as cats. She turned to him in question. She had learned to be erect in the saddle. Her hair flared and fell between sun and shadow.

"I just wanted to look at you," he said.

"That's very much allowed, Alistair," she said and smiled.

Today's poem was: *"Come into the garden, Maud, / For the black bat, night, has flown. / Come into the garden, Maud, I am here at the gate alone . . ."* She didn't need it any more, not at just the trot, she barely had time to memorize them, but it was a game and she knew he loved it. She moved off. *"And the woodbine spices are wafted abroad, / And the musk from the rose has blown."*

The path entered under the boughs again but not for long. It came out of the beeches to the marsh, the lagoon a little way ahead. They sat their horses in the open, where the clouds voyaged out of the beeches over the water. At its center, La Serenissima flashed and paled in sun and shadow, while the magic city of balloons above it swelled and diminished with the light as though breathing. Alistair looked at the path ahead, which became potted and mired.

"I think this is as far as we can go," he said and led her back under the boughs, where the sun faded from her hair.

6

The summer of 1917 found Anna's family living in a farmhouse between Udine and Gorizia, a little way off the main road. The village nearby was Buttrio. From the farmhouse, the main road hung in the sky as a pall of dust raised by ambulances, gun caissons, staff cars, supply wagons, and marching men. The farmhouse rooms had been freshly whitewashed. Under the whitewash hid the smells of cows, and of the boiled bacon, boiled salt cod, and garlic of peasants' food. Outside the house, the air smelled of sweat of the unwashed, which had come to permeate the highway, when the wind was from the west, and, faintly, of corrupted flesh on the battlegrounds if it were from the east. Though that summer was hot, the rooms were cool, and full by day and night of the sound of guns, now about thirty kilometers away.

When Anna roams the corridors, some of which are trespassed on by fowls that breed faster than they are stewed, her face is often set. She removed to Venice because Maggiore could not be in Rome. She disliked Venice, aesthetically and socially. Then Maggiore could not be in Venice. In this regard, this farmhouse is her last card. When she accepted Maggiore as her lover, in her sitting room in Rome, she accepted him as the companion and apex of her life. Though manners may hide it, she is an intense woman.

Anna will do without maggiordomo or footmen, but not without a lady's maid. They live in fourteen rooms: Anna's and Maggiore's, Maggiore's official room used for dressing, Alistair's, a living room, a dining room, the kitchen, two writing rooms, Anna's studio, Kitty's room, the maid's, and one for Maggiore's batman when present. There was also a room for Maggiore's young staff officer, Tenente Angelo Castelnero. All of these rooms had been lived in by a family or so of peasants; the kitchen had fed about thirty, who ate in it too. Conscription having overtaken strictness and become hysterical, some of the local farm women, stringy and in black, did things for the family. Kitty now much resembles them, though with Irish elements of bog hag. A young man, back from the war with a peg leg, in principle keeps the fires in cold weather and waters the gardens in hot. Alistair's groom is shell-shocked but soothed by animals and gentle with them. Maggiore could quite often be here. Sometimes he came with the tenente, treated by Anna as a nephew and by Alistair as a tentative friend. Angelo had been at Pinerolo six months before Manfredi. Alistair and Angelo rode together when Angelo could.

This was their situation during the Tenth Battle of the Isonzo, one of the longest of them all. Anna's intention had been Udine. This pretty hill town, once Venetian, was now the military capital of Italy. Even the king was there. Anna had just proved that fair houses in Udine could be had neither for love, nor for money, nor even for both at once.

THE AREA OF MAGGIORE'S, or, as he was properly called, Colonel the Barone D'Issogne's, military duties was the sector east of Udine, from the small town of Uccea in the north to Gradisco in the south. During the Tenth Battle of the Isonzo, as during the First, the lines ranged along this swift and pebbly river where Schubert could have met his trout. In the north, the country is the high Dolomites, lower than the great Swiss Alps, but with slab-sided dark valleys where the eastern winter blows free. At places, the country relaxes into valleys running east and west, as around the pleasant small town of Caporetto, still not much damaged, where a horsemen jingling on a crisp winter day could feel himself a Napoleonic hussar. In the south, around Gorizia, the hills were lower but more sinister. This country is called "the Karsh." Its Slovene natives thought it of demons, not God. It is fractured limestone, full of caves and rifts. Both were dear to vipers. Bits of it had once been pretty, summer glades with deer and boar. The troops knew the Karsh as infernal in summer, blasted in winter, bare. Its potholes and rifts, useful for ambush or shelter, held drying bones or rotting bodies. It stank. The troops agreed with the Slavs. Alistair's friend Rodolfo's father's couloir is in this country and was assaulted five more times during the Tenth Isonzo.

Any point on this sector was about thirty kilometers from Udine. Maggiore went to and from the front by staff car, often very close by Anna's farm near Buttrio. At the front, he left the staff car as soon as he could. He carried a saddle. A horse was usually arranged for him, at whose sides Anna's sandwich case and the new map case kept Maggiore sentimental and useful company. He carried an old, stained duster. This hid the crimson panels, braid, and decorations of a high staff officer of the king's entourage. By horse, a military wagon, or even on foot, Colonel the Barone D'Issogne, dusty, rumpled, his hair in early grey, his bearing fatigued because he was so, became of that category described by Aquinas as "things that may be imagined, but yet do not exist"—a staff officer among lice and bullets, at the front.

What he saw was bitter. The trenches (the Italian word *trinc-e̱-e* jingles like a sleighbell and so sniggers) were less believable to the men who fought in them than to us, over whom they have brooded for a hundred years. Maggiore's fighting had been cavalry war against the wild Arabs, to which Sir Lancelot's might have seemed static. He had known fear, had nearly died of thirst, had heard of his son's death as a new lieutenant, and had nearly been shot to pieces with his company by tribesmen much more numerous and nearly as well armed.

Here he saw dissolution.

As on May 30, 1917. This was before the small mountain of Hermada, which dominates the Adriatic coast east of the Isonzo. At its top, the double eagle still flew. The sun of the Karsh was already like a flail. Maggiore struggled to breathe air his throat perceived as a cigar-shaped object made of shit, putrefaction, and smoke. Some fifty thousand Italians, thirty thousand Austro-Hungarians, and God only knew how many thousand horses lay dead or getting on with dying in ten square miles of warm slaughterhouse. The fall of Hermada, though not accomplished, was sure. The beginning of the road to Trieste, the object of the campaign, was promised, though the army seemed incapable of movement toward that infinitely distant goal. Some martial vigor remained. Two Sicilian regiments were reported to have run away. Out of the corner of his eye, Maggiore observed some summary executions connected with this being carried out by firing squads as blank-faced and trembling as their victims. The shots had the virtue of covering the calls, cries, or shrieks of the unrecoverable wounded. The report turned out to be untrue, after the executions. Two days before, in his other life, Maggiore had seen his lady actually stamp her foot in vexation at finding no house in Udine. He held before his eyes this memory of vigor, purpose, life, and, in his lady, beauty. Since this campaign was conducted by the Duke of Aosta, the king had trusted Maggiore to ensure that this tall, handsome, virile, popular, affable cousin took no advantage of its glories, His Majesty himself being destitute of all these qualities.

May 31. The army moved. It moved backward.

The enemy, overpowered and outnumbered two to one, counterattacked. This was unimagined, unprepared for, and at first not wholly perceived. The Austrians were not thrown in waves against Italian positions, as the Italian command would have done and done again the next hour and again the next, but driven like nails into the weak points between them. Units were surrounded before they were organized to fight. Far to the west of Hermada, the Verona Brigade retreated through a railroad tunnel, was trapped in it, and crawled out to surrender a day later, crazed with thirst and blinded by gassed air. The next tunnel disgorged another shattered battalion. The Puglia Brigade died, with its commander. This first attack, it turned out, was a feint. The enemy now drove south to the coastal road. With one colonel dead and the other captured, the Arezzo Brigade broke. The Italian forces and the Duke of Aosta himself waiting for the plum of Hermada to drop helpless to their hands were now five kilometers behind the disaster. Their best legs served to catch up with the retreat. The Italian army lay like a bloodied whale on the low coast of Monfalcone. One hundred twelve thousand of its men were casualties or captured. Austria stood secure in its bastion of Hermada.

June 3. Maggiore, dusty and shabby, left the improvised headquarters where a general staff fought a rear-guard action against shame while it struggled back up the slopes of conceit. He talked to officers and men where he found them, but for the most part, he thought. He was not a big unit commander, but he knew tactics when he saw them. What the Italian army had won by reckless spending of its greater weight over a week had been undone in two days by intelligence and skill. Respect for the Austrian officers was the only warmth left to him.

The Duke of Aosta, the warrior prince of the House of Savoia, and General Cadorno, commander under the king, resolved their few differences into a shared truth: the cause of the defeat was the cowardice of the Italian soldier.

And at that, it came to Maggiore that he was watching the destruction of the Italian army. He loved that army. He loathed his job.

xxx

GIACOMMO, GIACCO, WAS ALISTAIR'S groom. He put Vipero's reins, tended to a butter softness, into his master's hands. Vipero rested his muzzle on Giacco's shoulder. Once in the saddle, Alistair turned back to face his groom. Whatever shell shock was, it was as though Giacco's eyes had been skinned so that you could see inside. Alistair never looked at him very long, for what he saw put him in mind of a face within asking a terrible question—*the room is burning, where is the door?*—through glass too thick to hear. Move your eye and the outer face was mainly a scar like the surface of the moon.

"Due ore," he said. *"Forse un'ora e mezza. Ma gli serve del moto. Poi l'altro."* Two hours. Maybe one and a half. But he needs exercise. Then the other one.

"Si, signore." Giacco very gently wiped a corner of Vipero's nostril in farewell and looked bereft as the big head turned away. Vipero stopped and nodded to his groom, *Goodbye, and not to worry so much. I'll soon be back, you'll see.* Riding past the farmhouse, picking up a trot and driving chickens like a cloud, Alistair said to Vipero, "Which way, old boy, the river or the hill?" Whether river or hill, they would be beside the highway at the end.

He rode so that, after twice fording the summer threads of a shallow river, he came up onto the Gorizia highway about a mile and a half south and east of the farmhouse road. The fields on the side of traffic from the east were open. So late in the war in this region, they were poorly planted. With a little care he could ride as close to or far from the highway as he chose.

The military traffic was continuous but not as one convoy. It snored and gasped and sometimes cried out as motors strove to overtake mules and marching men. He avoided pods of broken equipment, guns, and gas launchers, on motor trucks and occasional groups of feltgrau prisoners. Both had Carabinieri attached. FIAT ambulances did him no good, being closed. The wagons full of wounded were what he wished to study. And here was one, long and slow, pulled by four mules out of a sea of dark myth, for the men in front, though heavily bandaged, were upright and alert, and behind were grey ghosts, silent, unmoving, faces closed in bandage, blind. They would be from the battle of the brittle Karsh, of limestone exploding into needles, erasing sight, which sometimes was restored.

He approached at a walk, and always with his horse lathered and dust on him. He thought of his rollicking, rocketing pursuit of the column on the via Flaminia. He thought of it now as an indecency, though he perfectly well remembered that everybody actually there had seen only a boy's merry pluck. After a tempestuous ride, both he and Vipero enjoyed their walk in the heat up to the road, and watching Vipero's fine shoulders roll back and forth cleared his mind. The disgrace of the via Flaminia was not a bit the gallop; it was the windy verse he had sat in those days and mooned for. He walked his horse slowly enough that traffic overtook him like a summer river, his wagon drifting to him.

"Eh, ragazzo. Mica tanto brutto quel cavalo." Nice horse. A corporal, older than a corporal should be, left shoulder, arm, and chest a bandaged mass, not clean. Leaning on the strakes of a wagon, bored enough to say something about any horse. Alistair's heel touched Vipero. Keep up! We're on stage.

A turned head, quick smile to the corporal, and nod.

"Fai palfreniere?" You the groom?

Now Alistair raised his eye in the mildest reproof. The "*non*" was almost silent but seen on the mouth.

A moment's alarm. An officer? Surely not.

Alistair had been shy to look at first, shyer to listen, seem to look, and speak. He also knew he had two duties, which were also rights: his birthright, arms, from which he was fenced out for this little time, and his bride, the art of poetry. If he could learn from these men as a future officer, he could as honorably use them as a study for verse. Don't lie. By look or gesture or word, don't lie.

A sharp man, a private, beside the corporal, greasy forelock mimicking the angle of a thin nose. His wound must be below the waist, for Alistair could not see it.

"Perche non combatti? Sei troppo ragazzo?" Why aren't you fighting? Still a boy?

Still a question, not a jeer yet but pointed. And still the familiar, the *tu*.

His own eye a little more austere now.

"Combattere non mi e' permesso. Sono americano."

Let that sink in.

"Ma saremo li. Saremo con voi. Saro' accorto di voi. Bisogna aspettare." But we'll be there. I'll be at your side. Have to wait.

Then, *"Cos'e'?"* What's it like?

If you could not in honor lie to the soldiers, then still less could you lie about them. Thus far, he found this understood in the packets of new poems that arrived once in a while from London and from what the censor hadn't noticed in Milan.

"Cos'e'?" Bandaged arm lifted to point at a hollow face, body sprawled on straw on the wagon strakes, lips and eyes registering strong pain at each slight jolt. *"Domandi li."* Ask there. But given as fair answer, not jeer, and the familiar gone. However suffering, the man he pointed at was not blind. The blind were not pointed at.

Alistair looked and asked, "Where were you? What happened?"

If you couldn't lie about the soldiers, they had to be in it. Their souls can wait, that's presumption, but footfall, rhythm of talk, shape of vowel, perhaps from that the shape of thought should be the spine to carry the poem. Thought enough to bring him to the road twice a day.

In front of Gorizia. Just the usual. Bullets and shells. Nothing special. A little whiff of gas. The edge of a jeer, *"Difesa!"* Defence!

What passed him here was Homer's people. Homer's people whether on foot, tired horse, sprawled in a wagon, or in a grey neat box, FIAT ambulance clattering along.

Nowhere, never, does Homer put a pretty dress on war. Hardly ever Virgil, lesser but still a god. Never Dante. And let us hear it from Mr. Featherstonhaugh in the old kitchen, his best teacher's best day. Take it best of all from Homer, Achilles's shield: Half of it showed the world at peace, half at war. And what of peace? Broad-chested cattle in the high grass, boys and girls jumping to grab grapes, reapers' meal of honeyed wine and meat, a boy's lyre played to break the heart, and girls' feet dancing, a rippling stream with reeds and wind to stir them. Eighty lines. And war? Slaughter's cloak slimy with human blood, a living man dragged by the heals, breathing men grappling others' corpses, dragging off the dead. Six lines. That's it.

"Da quanto tempo siete li?" How long have you been there? The roof of his mother's farmhouse showed to the right across the fields. Vipero sidestepped a

little to remind him. He could see an officer coming up the column. He would not have much longer, likely.

"Da quanto temp? Due anni." Two years.

With leave, surely?

And only now anger: Leave? A week looking for roof and bed. In the mud.

The officer arrived, not quite in condition, jowls a little plump, breathing from a trot. *"Chi sei? Che cosa fai qui?"* The familiar again, this time not friendly.

So Alistair, Tuscan at its coolest, eyebrow fully raised, "Exercising my horse. Our house is over there. You have gallant men." Give him the familiar back! And to the corporal, whip and head inclined in bow, *"Iddio con voi. Sono lieto di vi aver parlato."* God with you. I am glad to have talked with you.

He turned his horse slowly, though Vipero wanted this foolishness over with, and lunch, and walked him away. Away from the road, beyond appearance of flight, he took up a mild trot that would loosen Vipero more than heat him. As they neared, and at its sound, Giacco came out, almost running, almost stumbling on a stone. He put his arms around Vipero's warm neck in happiness and welcome. Vipero pushed his nose against Giacco's back, saying, *You see. I promised I'd be back. I don't tell lies.*

IT HAD BEEN THOUGHT Alistair would have spent time in Udine at the fine library of that lettered town, until his military situation had numbered off. Mr Featherstonhaugh had sent him a curriculum almost from the gangplank of his ship. Udine was close enough to ride a horse there had he wished. But Alistair very rarely went there. The place pullulated with rank. Turning from the Duomo square to the piazza where two giants beat out the hours with their hammers upon bells, the stroller could take fright at what might be a locomotive headlamp bearing down. It is three generals, rigid with medals, behind each a satellite, a major, less brassed but still divine. The light coruscates. But what now? The generals cower like chickens, back and bow. The majors skitter. In his powerful automobile, from the fairy palace above the giants, it is the king! Alistair in civvies felt himself a filthy eremite, a scurrying clerk, a bug in a book.

America was not allied with Italy. She had no military presence there. Alistair could have taken ship home and would probably have survived. Though still a few months too young, he could have enlisted by hook or crook, though not as officer. He would have been trained and sent presumably to northern France. Since his loyalty was to Italy, this had no point.

There existed, were rumoured to exist, probably existed a band or bands of Italians calling themselves the *Accesi*, the Ardent Ones. They fought beside or apart from the Italian army, savaging Austrian flanks, retaliating against believed Austrian sympathizers at the edges of the war. They were originated by, or inspired by, or loyal to the patriot poet prince D'Annunzio. Whenever Alistair went to Udine, he tried to find out more. If he did that, the scurrying clerk could be a disguise.

MANFREDI SAID, "DON'T BE a bloody idiot, Alistair. You don't want those people. They're gangsters. If they exist. I thought you loathed D'Annunzio."

"My opportunities," said Alistair, "are not broad."

This was at lunch in Udine. It turned out that young gentlemen of the cavalry, since there was rarely use for them, were often used as postmen by the general staff. Manfredi, trying extremely hard not to look intimidated, was here on such service. His uniform was cut by Caraceni of Rome but had no medals and only a nineteen-year-old's beard of braid. They had found a tin table on the corner of a cafe's terrace, wanted by no one more important them themselves.

"If your country's not in the war, you can't fight. No one thinks you're a coward. I wouldn't go to America to fight red Indians."

Manfredi was not often impatient, but today had worse. He got to it as the waiter, his deference all used up in service to the gods of war at other tables, dumped ice cream in front of these beggar children.

"Copenhagen," he ended it. "Copenhagen. Copenhagen. Eskimos!"

Helene's father was to be transferred, by now within the week, from Rome to Paris and then an embassy of his own, Denmark. This was splendid news for the parents and beastly for the young. Helene's letter—she had no way to telephone Manfredi—had eruptions of teardrops on its violet ink, even while it released, at this tin table, a tiny, mournful shade of the scent of her skin. Alistair shook his head.

"It's all my fault," said Manfredi. "If I hadn't been wallowing around with Lizl this would never have happened."

"I don't think the Quai D'Orsay's focused on Lizl," said Alistair. He thought. "Manfredi, is this going to make much difference? You've only seen her twice since you left Rome, and that was with her mother. They have mail in Copenhagen. Then after the war, you can marry her. You weren't going to do that until the war's over, anyway. Remember? That's what Lizl was all about."

And although Manfredi began, "Don't say Lizl!" Alistair was happy that it seemed to be what he wanted to hear, since he could say it without misgiving. "You are right, Alistair. It won't make much difference. I just hate to think of think of her miserable." He added, "It's a horrible thing for me to say, but I could be glad she's out of Italy. There's something wrong here."

He looked around, over military shoulders, the Piazza del Duomo, the pretty signoria, the palace, and the giants.

"I hate this place," he said. "It's where it all goes wrong."

Alistair nodded and hoped Manfredi knew more.

"A sergeant spat at me the other day. Infantry. Not so I could swear he did, of course. We school horses in the ring. They fight and die and live in shit. They call us 'pretty boys.' Do you know what it's like to work your heart out at Pinerolo, the traditions of the cavalry, and be spat at? If I could have sworn he did, I mightn't have had the heart to take him up. That's where it gets you."

"Cavalry waits. In modern war," said Alisair. "There's use for you. Or you wouldn't be there."

He was startled to see Manfredi frown then look at the decorated shoulders around, judging distance, close to furtive. Manfredi! "Do you have a map in your head, Alistair?" he said. "I think you do. We're stationed just east of a place called Caporetto. Not a bad place. There's some ground we can use there. If we cross the Isonzo, there's ten kilometers, straight line, of mountain passes up to twenty-three hundred meters. Then a plain. But the plain doesn't go anywhere. If we go down to Tolmino, twenty kilometers on our side, there's a plain we might be able to force entry to. And that goes nowhere too. There's flat country between Monfalcone and Trieste. We could dash down that. But cavalry can't take a city. Especially a military city. Do you see?"

Alistair nodded.

"So where's cavalry country?"

Alistair thought he knew now, but "Tell me," he said.

"Behind us. In Italy. We have fairly easy passes from Caporetto to the plain. The northern Italian plain. To the Tagliamento. To the Piave. To the Brenta. To Venice. The Austrians have the passes, too, but we'll move faster. We won't fight in the mountains. We'll meet them on the plain. They'll be a little disorganized, I think. No heavy guns. Few motors. The Italian cavalry!"

"Will it happen?" said Alistair, whose voice had followed Manfredi's into conspiracy, though he was not sure why. From his highway, he had his own belief.

"I think so. Our infantry's wearing out."

Alistair nodded.

"We outnumber them, but they're bleeding us. And that's why they spit, I think, truly. But to say it, Alistair, that's treason. Say it, Alistair, officer or man, and you could be shot."

"So then what?" And asked it sharply, to get an answer, for the cloak of authority was finally firm around Manfredi.

"Keep our horses fresh and iron hard. Beg the best feed. Change shoes before they wear out. Drill the men till they drop. Fast, accurate shooting from the saddle at maximum carbine range. Quick dismounts and remounts behind cover. Our company captain and my brother lieutenant are good men. We can't talk, but we think alike. Our battalion colonel can talk even less, but he lets us get on with it. The cavalry's ready, I think, in spite of all. We can save Italy." He seemed to uncoil, so that his shoulders were for the first time above those at the tables around, and smiled. "And that's what Ferraras are for. And what you're for if you can be there. How's your own girl? The pretty one you're teaching to ride, which I hope is indelicate. Do you see her out where you are?"

"I do. It's a little difficult." He shrugged. "Closer than Copenhagen. And I'm sorry about that, Manfredi."

"Things happen. I'm glad for you. I need to get back. The front's better than here, anyway. Do you think we need to tip that waiter?"

"No," said Alistair.

"No," said Manfredi. "Don't go with those gangsters. Even if you find them. They're not for you."

Alistair nodded.

"I went down the slide. Mombrone. We both stayed up."

Alistair grinned, gave Manfredi a thumb's up, and waved him away.

Nobody said "Good luck" these days.

xxx

DINNER AT THE FARMHOUSE was by candlelight since Anna had never dined otherwise. Other light was oil, the farmhouse having no gas and certainly no electricity. Kitty served. Kitty, Assunta the lady's maid, and the batman had their own table in the corner of the kitchen where they were served by a drifting population of farm women. Maggiore, on duty at Udine that day, was there. Anna's dress for dinner is a fine shawl but over her working smock. Anna, who had barely seen the inside of a studio in Venice, is working hard here. She had modeled one of the farm women, entranced to be paid to sit still, and a gawky little stick-child of a girl. She is pleased with her new work on Tomasso, the amputee factotum. What she is doing now is the foundation of the best she will ever make, and she knows it, though not clearly. She would like to work with shell-shocked Giacco, but like her son, she can't quite face him. On being served soup by Kitty, she sees clay in her fingernail and the crease of her palm. "I do apologize," she says and briefly leaves the table. The rest of the meal is another assault on the chickens, with some sausage, polenta, and onions.

After dinner, the mild light of an oil lamp shines on her auburn hair, and the shawl, its decoration barely visible, is curiously strict and New England for Anna. She reads in Italian to Maggiore. She reads German army tactical and training manuals, obtained by the British, translated into English, and made available to Allied staffs, though they are not much read and not at all in Italy. It is lucky she is a soldier's daughter. Even so, she must often say, "I don't know the Italian for this, Gianfranco. I'll have to paraphrase." She does. He nods and says, "Thank you, Anna." Some of the material is in French, which he reads easily.

Alistair listens for a time, though the lamplight folds his parents into a privacy almost as solid as their room. He went out on the porch. There were quiet noises from the stable, a whinny almost buried in the throat. He thought that Giacco slept with his horses, though there was a loft for him there. He found it prying to ask. The guns were close. In the clearest air, you could see their flashes on the hillside, which came long before their sound. Even barrages were heard as a swarm of knocks rather than as a long roar. One tended not to listen by now.

In the night, Victoria, whom his body wanted, was close, the same darkness doing for Friuli and the Serenissima. In fact she was not far, far enough to have made her damp-eyed when Alistair's family removed, but no worse than that. Even then, the road from Udine to Venice was not too bad. It was ninety kilometers. The Schraulers seemed to have no problem with wartime gas, though it had lately become precious. She had had fun learning to drive. The way she clapped on her goggles with both arms over a smile seemed to move a car forward five meters all by itself. In fact the road was cluttered with convoys, in thrall to military police, and the threat of the Austrian air force on that flat and vital highway was mostly mythical, but it darkened the air. She could not telephone her coming. She had come twice. He had not been easy when she took the road home. His mother, he knew, dreaded her as a young woman who could neither be married by her son nor given to the fishmonger's boy at the worst, but seemed to like her, brusquely but cheerfully, for herself. They were left tactfully alone.

The night covered Victoria and Venice and surely covered Helene. Compared to the scores of thousands crawling in trenches, dying on the Karsh with no water to ease their ebbing blood, shitting no doubt in terror in the last breath before the charge, hollowed out like Giacco, they were so far all strangely safe: Manfredi to his own shame, Maggiore certainly at risk of stray bullets and shells but not much aimed at, himself cocooned in his nation's inanition, the girls for sure, thank God. The conscripted were in hell, the knighthood, doing fine. The night also covered—not in the plain speaking of the guns, not in the silent wistful thought of sleeping girl, but between sound and thought—the notice of a cataract. He knew he heard it. He saw it in Manfredi and Maggiore, saw it possibly in his mother, soldier's daughter and soldier's mate. It was a sound that made you seek stillness and pressed down on talk not for purpose. Care, perhaps, would save you. He did not question that he was Victoria's knight and she his lady, and he would have taken no other even were there other to take. She still rode. He made her take a groom. She had sold more dresses. Ceremonies protect. The cataract should surely spare her.

When Colonel the Barone D'Issogne now rode his missions of inspection, he rode no longer alone but with a companion whose bodily shape he did not know, except as a distillation of his lady's voice, reading to him from the papers of Fritz von Lossberg. So apparent, and largely pleasant, was this company of an officer and gentleman like himself, though an enemy, that when he had occasion to take a glass of wine in the field, he would say, "Mein Freund, zu Ihnen." Because this was much of the German Maggiore knew, it was often von Lossberg's papers that Anna read to him from the purloined English with the lamplight in her hair at night.

Major von Lossberg's innovations did not overwhelm the intellect. Adjustments to existing armies with existing weapons cannot do that. He served as staff officer on the Flanders front. He was Maggiore's age. He was just recently a colonel. He was of Maggiore's sort of family. Just like Maggiore, he often stole forth among the men and in the mud where, had Maggiore only known it, he wore a stained cloak to hide his glory. His thoughts could be reduced to a postcard. The primary point of decision should be the battalion, not the army group: this reduced the time for orders to reply to information from ten hours to two and enabled rotation of battalions as units so that the enemy constantly faced fresh troops. The greater weight of the army should be held in sheltered rear positions: thus, as soon as an enemy attack began, as ever, to lose cohesion, a flood of fresh and well-ordered men could be unleashed on it. At an attack, forward troops should vacate their trenches, taking their machine-weapons with them, and disperse into shell holes and excavations, all higgledy-piggledy, which any aerial reconnaissance would have reported as smilingly empty: thus each of these snuggeries was at a different range for the enemy's artillery, and the enemy tide would not meet a struggling line but be absorbed into a hornets' nest, shot at from every side. Attacks should not begin in waves, to be mown down in waves, but with infiltration by stealthy small bands that would concentrate on taking out machine gun posts, preferably from the side where they were rarely protected. These thoughts were quickly welcomed, tried, and adopted by the generals Luddendorf, Falkenhayn, and Hindenburg and turned the German and then the Austrian armies into lethal machines that handily mastered Allied offensives with one-third the casualties. They were also strangely humane. General Luddendorf proudly wrote, "Now the German soldier is no longer told, 'Here you stand and here you die.' He is told, 'Here is where you begin, and here is where you use your head.'" For the Italians, General Cadorno found the first maxim more befitting a soldier and much more easily understood.

Maggiore reflected upon the disaster at Hermada. He put the theory against the facts, and they fit. From this, he deduced that the Italian army, as now led, would be fed in detail into a maw made to devour it, with little indigestion. The army, Maggiore saw, was envenomed with suspicion, inertia, and fear, and shot the messenger as easily as it shook hands. By 1917, the state of the sentient classes in Italy was that of extremely bright men and women fallen into an experiment by torture masters whose simian intelligence was no more vexing than their narcotic predictability. This went for all the Allied powers, but in Italy, the material under subjection was more volatile. The shadows were full of the wing beats of forbidden thoughts, the light ones of lieutenants like Manfredi very common, those of staff colonels, very rare. The lieutenants knew to keep quiet. But Maggiore was a staff colonel of the king, and it began to occur to him that he could save both his own honor and perhaps the Italian army.

Much of the trouble flowed from its commander under the king, General Luigi Cadorno. The army had known Maggiore since he was seventeen, never knowing ill of him. His family and General Cadorno's, both Savoian, were distantly linked. The general had served with Maggiore's father as a young man. Maggiore reckoned that by reckless spending of this capital of goodwill, he might do his duty and still come through. He intended to bring up pointedly to his senior officers, most of whom were in some degree friends, his lessons from Major von Lossberg, demonstrate that these lessons were precisely what their enemies had followed each time they whipped his own army, and contrast their intelligence with . . . he would not quite say *bloody stupidity.*

For her part, Anna took the Isotta with a tank of what gas they had and went off. Anna came back with a large package and a smile that was merry but too reckless for anyone to want to light a match nearby. She fended Kitty off the package and went into her room. She came out in a long grey uniform tunic. She carried a cap. When she put it on, it was handsome, in a spectral way.

"I am going to drive an ambulance," she said.

7

In night air, this season chill again, Alistair, no coat by choice, sat in a porch corner, arms wrapping his chest. The farmhouse showed two dim lights. Tonight it held just the servants and himself. Maggiore was at the front. His mother, at the monastery, the *kloster*, which had become a military hospital, whence and whither the grey ambulances ran, lion-hearted mice.

His horses must be ridden gently now. Good feed was scarce, just hay. The horseshoes were ill made. The horses' dusty muscles fading. He wrote by the hour, sat over paper, catching words like moths. He was assembling the figures of what would become the Tagliamento poems, though the blow to set them moving was still withheld. It was good work—he knew this. Gasoline was all but gone. He had an old motorcycle. He rode it badly. The danger in doing that, as vacant minded as shells, pleased him. He had learned from the wounded that life, love, the children of your loins, the poems of your brain were all at the will of a fool playing roulette. He was always dusty now.

All of this lay stretched over an anger that had nowhere to go but back at his own face. In the black days after Serafina's loss, his mother's actions had held some taint of frivolity, then of cowardice, for his anger to stick to. But it was unfit to have toward a heroine. Anna had arranged the ambulance behind their backs, the American Red Cross, herself almost the only female driver. She had used the embassy, flickering back, as though by changing her gloves, into the virtuous Mrs. Lionel Stears of Boston. He felt she made him, with no ill will, a coward. But his passport proved him too young. And an ambulance was not a warrior's way. There was that. In this chill and dark, he could have wept for Victoria's warmth, and willed her away. The guns were bright tonight. It was the Eleventh Battle of the Isonzo this time.

ON THE BROKEN STONE of the Karsh, Anna knelt by a fallen man. The ambulance was twenty meters behind her. She had driven it there when the barrage seemed for a time to waver. The hill continued up into scrub oak. The top was still held by Austria but might yet fall, being assaulted on three sides—thus the wavering of the barrage. The higher slopes had new snow, but here in the hollow it was warm. Two stretcher-bearers, American boys, came up. Anna shakes her head. They are shocked, protest. They are both very young. She shakes her head again. When she opened the tunic to see the wound, she saw the guts spilled out, white, on the whole, complicated, giving off a rising pool of smell because perforated and steaming. They looked like nothing at all to do with a human being. She very gently put the shirt back, a barrier partly against flies, more against the man's own eyes. "You can only hurt him more," she said in English. "Leave us." Then, "Morphine?" The boy shook his head and shrugged. By pure chance, there were not many terribly wounded here, a quick look around showed her that she was not absolutely needed elsewhere, and she had time to be a little decent. The cicadas, recovering their hearing after the barrage, started up again. She was only a driver, nothing fancy, but one had to help. The wounded man moved his hand toward her, and she took it. He looked up and said quite clearly, *"Muoio,"* I'm dying, as though at an unexpected bill.

"Viene il dottore," said Anna. There was no doctor out here. Her hand was gripped more strongly.

"Mi fa male"—it hurts.

"Il dottore ti dara' qual'cosa di bene," said Anna. Horses and foxhunting had made her gentle and adept with large hurt things. Men and horses seemed about the same. The barrage gave indications of flowing back toward them. The cicadas thought so. One of the stretcher-bearers came running back and said, "We got to go, Mrs. Stears." He was no weakling, just sensible, and always found her proper coffee when they got a rest.

"You can drive, Dennis," she said. "Run along. Come back when you can." He looked at her, imploring. "Run along," she said.

But by the time the barrage really came back, the man was dead, which was a relief, for she had not been looking forward much to staying, truth to tell. It was quite often quick like that, if only you didn't try to be too kind and move them. It was very simple theater, repeated over and over.

But it was hard, hard work, laborers' work, and the most cruelly hurt did keep stealing out from behind curtains in her brain. She and her boys are overdriven; this is to be the great offensive, prodigal of life. Red Cross boys from Ann Arbor, Cambridge, and Long Island are fraying fast. Some got hurt, the boy from Ann Arbor quite badly. For the first time, Anna looks drawn. This does not diminish her as a woman. Where she is drawn, the cracks show some fire beneath. Danger leapt over by courage is sensual, in Anna quite strongly so. She feels that she feeds Maggiore with this, and that he needs it. They are together at the farmhouse perhaps one night in five, one or both usually leaving before dawn. Maggiore's heart is looking ragged. She sees furtive, weasel fears she can't see the face of and that frighten her truly. So Anna hums like a dynamo and feeds bolts of energy to her inamorato by night, calming herself and bucking him up. Her son, whom she adores, is quite wrong to think that she is careless of what she has done to him. She knows absolutely and is intensely sorry. People do suffer. That she knows.

THERE WAS A LIBRARIAN at the Palazzo Bartolini, young but purblind, honorably not serving, and an acolyte of D'Annunzio, so in shame of his situation. Alistair became aware of his shadow one day between himself and the window and saw his black sleeve by his own arm. He whispered a contact, if Alistair still had interest in the Accesi. Alistair nodded, with not even a library whisper.

xxx

THE DOOR OF THE eating house in the small via Pelliccerie was recessed and dim. Inside, it was not really dark, but it was a bright cold day outside. Alistair could see little but the serving counter and the range fire. The "*Salve,* Alistair!" came from a booth, and Alistair was standing in it before he saw Rodolfo. He supposed he was seeing an unexpected friend and supposed he was glad. "Unexpected" was quite sure. He had last seen Rodolfo in Rome. They rode together, for Rodolfo's parents lived in the villa where he kept his horses. Alistair had reasons, none of which he could explain, for a mixed opinion of Rodolfo. His father's death, in almost the first battle of the war, seemed to have coarsened him, which Alistair found hard to understand; it seemed to have taken out of Rodolfo most of what was best and to have changed it to opinions. Rodolfo was also his friend.

"Well," he said. "Am I looking for you, Rodolfo?"

"Yes, you are," said Rodolfo.

Alistair sat down.

Rodolfo threw an arm around his shoulder. "Old friend," he said, "would you die for Italy?"

Before even an offered glass? thought Alistair.

"Rather live," he said. "But yes. How are your horses? How's your mother?"

"It's our question," said Rodolfo. "No time for all that now."

Alistair, who could see now, looked at Rodolfo in full. He was in second lieutenant's uniform, with indications of staff, not front. He had, after all, been afraid of Vipero. *Which is not fair of me,* thought Alistair.

"Are you running this thing?" he said. All of this was in Italian.

"I'm hardly more important than you. When your name came up, then . . . Are you still an American citizen?"

"Yes," said Alistair. "You're army."

"The army can't do everything," said Rodolfo. "Not everything to avenge my father."

That would certainly be true of staff, thought Alistair, who had absorbed his stepfather's opinions. He said carefully, for this was a friend, "Rodolfo, when your companions do these things, whatever they are, you're with them, I take it. Fighting. There. With them."

"Of course I am," said Rodolfo. "Are you with us?"

"I know nothing of you," said Alistair.

"That's as it should be. We don't chatter. We are of steel. You should be glad. When you're with us, you'll know what you need to know. Just like me. And you do know me. Are you?"

Which Alistair very little heard. He sat much as alone, with his arms sheltering his chest as on the farmhouse porch. He was not aware of this. He thought the message ill carried, the warrant dangerous to give, the consequences set about with mines and traps, the path through it to be set by the unwise, and he perhaps alone to follow it.

"Yes," he said. And knew at least that the night sky would not now crush him.

Rodolfo said, "Put your hand on your heart and say, 'Italy.'"

"I said, 'Yes,'" said Alistair.

"You commit yourself to what is ordered of you?"

"Of course," said Alistair.

Rodolfo smiled and settled his shoulders against the corner of the booth, stretching his arms against the sides. "We shall have a hero's lunch. The Ardent welcome you."

"Have the Ardent a way to find me?" said Alistair. The waiter's face approached like a full moon in the dusk.

"They will," said Rodolfo.

"Then good day, Rodolfo," said Alistair. "When they will, they will." He rose and walked away, troubling the moon in its orbit. He took a moment to find the door, and, it opened, blinked in the light. He did not feel exhilarated. He felt that like everybody else, he now wore a harness, whether good or bad. It occurred to him that Rodolfo would be called "good-looking" now. Just that. He walked two blocks to where his motorcycle was propped up. Like him, it was flavored with dust and gasoline.

Riding, not well, through the traffic, he caught a glimpse through the window of a grand establishment of his stepfather in dress uniform with two of even higher rank. There was nothing odd in this. Udine was ridiculously small for its present use. One could have tripped over the king. His stepfather's expression looked emphatic. His listeners' indignant or even angry. Alistair did not try to be seen.

He was at his desk. He heard, over the woodfire in his study, the sound of the Schrauler Packard. His heart rose, found chains around it, and rose anyway.

Victoria parked beside the Isotta, which was now in dust sheets. She looked tired, looked harried, unusual in a sturdy girl. She got out and took both his hands but didn't kiss.

"Convoys," she said. "Police. I was pulled over. I guess I look Austrian. Luckily we have letters from the prime minister. I need a bathroom and a long glass of water. In that order. I brought these." She pointed at boots and britches.

"Well done," he said.

"I'm a sweaty mess," she said. "I don't know how when it's not hot. The police upset me." She was sweaty, but he kissed her anyway.

"Mmm," she said. "Thanks, Alistair. Bathroom."

He carried the boots and britches. "There's no one here," he said.

"That's nice."

On the way through the main room, he said to Kitty, "Miss Victoria is dusty from her journey. Would you bring her towels and a sponge? And a girl with water for the basin?"

"Yes, Mr. Alistair."

They went into his bedroom to dress, and he poked up the fire. After drying herself, she sat for a long time on the bed in a turkish towel, but the time came when he passed her the boot hooks, and then they were ready.

He put her on Pompey. Another of the farm's peasants had come back. He could not exert himself, because of gassed lungs, and was followed around by his wife, a young rag doll in black, but he proudly held Victoria's stirrup while Giacco held the head. Alistair ministered to her arm on the mounting block. Victoria prettily thanked all for the unneeded, herself being a decent rider now. Pompey just possibly understood that what he carried was precious, or, more likely, lacked energy. Anyway, was a lamb. Vipero, who understood the *bella figura*, just wanted to be handsome, ill fed or not.

"You should send them back with me, poor things," said Victoria. "Ariosto and I would take good care of them. The duke still has feed. I guess dukes do. They like you there, you know. They told me how you tried the horses for me at the end. Which I shall not forget. Which no female ever would forget. I think Pompey likes me."

Now in midday, it had turned from cold to warm. They unbuttoned their coats. They rode slowly for the horses, trotted only briefly, on the flat. He tried to phrase his situation with the Accesi, a word he could not bring himself to speak, and his fury at his mother's magnificence, but could not phrase it, did not speak, though the proper course of all his thoughts was to Victoria, and they strained at the dam. She talked of Jacobo Bassano, her favorite of the moment, which would pass.

"He has the most lovely architecture, Alistair. You know how in Tintorretto everything buzzed. You can sit in front of Bassano and just feel calm. But it's not much fun without you, Alistair. You remember our lovely lunches? Now I just have a sandwich with Lucia, bless her." His topographical puzzle was how to avoid the highway, which was most of the rest he wanted to talk about, and would contaminate her, he felt. They could not avoid a particular draw where the wind funneled the smell of rotting meat from the front, a touch of dirty honey on the tongue, though the guns were desultory. The Eleventh Battle of the Isonzo had been put away, in disgrace like the rest; the Twelfth was not quite begun. She did see the highway from a distance, and the wagons. She said, "Are those wounded?"

"Mostly," he said.

"Poor boys."

Back at the farmhouse, dismounted, she said, "Now we need a nice long nap together, Alistair. But maybe a plate to keep us happy. And a bottle, of course." It was not chicken they carried into the bedroom, thank God, but the excellent prosciutto of Friuli and a bottle of merlot.

He saw the light begin to draw in its skirts and kept his arms around her head against his chest until it might be too dark to go. But she was awake and said, "I'm afraid I've got to begin to leave, my darling."

He said, "No, you don't. You mustn't drive back this late. We've never had a night together, not once. Even if someone turned up, they wouldn't eat you."

"I know that, Alistair. I'm not shy of your mother anymore. We're just two women. Her colonel. You. There can't be much difference. But I still have to go, darling. You know I do."

They walked to the Packard with his arm around her side. He kissed her. She opened the door and sat sideways in the driver's seat. "Sit beside me, Alistair. I'm going to talk." He did, and closely, though the geometry was uncomfortable.

She said, "I lied that I couldn't stay here. Could have, but won't. It's horrible here. Everyone's half dead. Your horses are dying, Alistair. It even smells bad. You're getting peculiar, my dear, even for you. I think your parents have forgotten you. Venice is so close. Get in the car, here and now, and come with me. We'll get an apartment. It's easy now. I pulled you into bed once, and I can pull you into a car. You'll write. I'll make dresses. We'll go and look at lovely paintings and have nice meals and make love. We'll be together every night. Go in there, Alistair, and get the pen I gave you, and your writing tablet. Your passport might be a good idea. We can send for the rest when we're there. You can borrow my toothbrush, what's the difference? Do it now, and come back, and get in beside me. Here. Now. I am all the girl you need."

He heard her as a breeze of pure air onto his heart. He saw himself doing that simple thing, coming back, shutting the door, and being beside her in the scent of lilac. The guardian skeleton of his honor, the more commanding since he despised what it had offered as means, looked at him with contempt.

"I can't," he said.

She leaned against him so he felt all the length of her body. She said, "I knew that wouldn't work. But I had to try. Think of it until I see you again. Which I will, obviously. Think of what's here then think of me. I'm pretty confident. I don't give up. I'm not asking you to marry me. I'll go on at the Gritti, officially. I'm going now. I love you, Alistair. Think until next time."

She got up and swung into the seat. He kissed her, held her, and buried his lips in her neck, then pulled back, and she shut the door. She started the engine, and drove off without delay. All the words he needed to say fused into two, and he wanted to yell them after her: "Be careful!" But, other than the manageable hazards of the road, he could not think of what.

On a morning when the new skin of snow on the neighboring hill and the sweet-smelling flames in his grate competed to make Alistair's desk warm and bright, Fausto of the peg leg came in. Alistair looked up to nod and smile on this fair morning, expecting a basket of wood. Fausto instead proceeded to his desk and stood close in front of him, breathing importantly, smelling of young peasant, something between bacon and saddlecloth, not unpleasant. He put his cap behind his back for the greater respect and handed Alistair an envelope, sealed. Alistair had no doubt whom it was from. He slit it along the line where Fausto's thumb had left not dirt but only grit. The Accesi would call for him for duty at dusk two days from now.

He nodded to Fausto, adding, *"Mi servi del legno"* Need some wood, and because he was never sure when he was understood in this province of Italy, also pointed to the fire. Into which, when Fausto had closed the door, he dropped the letter. Not the worst means of communication. The messenger did not have to come into the house. The peasants were illiterate, which took care of prying eyes, and regarded letters as bolts from a malign god, which ensured diligence. It occurred to him that he should make a vigil by his sword. His sword was Manfredi's, and his second thought was that it was impertinent to press it into this service.

His mother was in the house. It was her "day off," in Anna's mouth only in Cockney, "Me dy orf," the joke being that she was employed, a joke somewhat fuzzy to Maggiore. They met in the dining room for luncheon. There was still the elation of snow and crisp flames. His new situation released him from being in rage with her; but even when he was, sulks were not their mode. He kissed her on the forehead and sat down.

She said, "Kitty says your girl was here. Victoria."

"Kitty can normally be relied on for the truth," he said. "And you, for your part, have the name right."

Kitty advanced with a platter. It was chicken. He added, "Mamma, does this vile animal have to be here? Victoria and I found some perfectly decent prosciutto. There must be bread."

"What a brilliant idea!" said Anna. She waved the platter into oblivion. "The Italian ham, Kitty. Sliced thin. Have one of the Italian girls do it. And bread."

"Yes, my lady."

"Did you two have time to find some cheese?"

"No."

To her son. "Alistair, Alistair, look at 'em that age, they get pregnant. Kiss 'em, they have twins. Do be careful. Obviously you are." Kitty was deaf when not directly addressed.

"I like her a very great deal, you know," said Alistair.

"Oh, so do I. Honest girl. Doesn't simper or curtsey or make me feel like Queen Victoria at all. Very refreshing. It's terribly hard luck to have the wrong parents. Especially for a girl, I think. You simply cannot marry a hoodlum's daughter, Alistair. You probably think you have the wrong parents yourself, of course."

"We all married hoodlums' daughters," said Alistair. "We were hoodlums. Hoodlums with coats of arms."

"Long ago," said his mother.

"I don't really have the wrong parents," said Alistair. "My stepfather's not too bad."

She looked at him with the cocked head, like a fencer's, that was the sign of her caring, and said, "That's a very sweet word to use, Alistair. Thank you. I'm worried about him. He's making enemies. Not good in a war."

He saw then that her life as it was now was consuming her, sharpening her into a blade that was becoming dangerously thin. One did not discuss the peril she put herself in. He spoke to her more carefully than he had done since the day of *Lusitania,* now distant.

"Whatever he thinks he has to do, he'll manage it. Rely on that, Mamma. You know I'm right. You know him."

"He's more than worried. He's in danger. As only I would know. Maybe your girl would know of you. And I would have to ask her why. And it frightens me."

xxx

TO WAIT FOR HIS masters, Alistair sat on a stone wall a little down the farm lane. Deepening dusk brightened the ragged snow and the headlamps on the highway, fast and sparse at night. He would have liked the stones to reflect his thoughts. Every sentiment, once it had begun to speak, chimed in to the strutting and declaiming he chiefly feared. His elders were away again. Given his habit of the porch at night, his absence would surely be unnoticed. His preparation was warm clothes. He did not know who he was about to be. *They're late,* he thought acidly. The thought was for his own superiority. He erased it as he could. They were scarcely late at all.

And with that, they came. A Cyclops eye turned from the highway and bent its beam on him. That only. By its light, by its sound, a motorcycle. The headlamp bathed his wall. He stood, stepped forward. A motorcycle with sidecar. The driver turned his goggles to him and braked hard, sigh of tire plowing gravel. The driver pulled his goggles up. Alistair, who now recognized a corporal of Maggiore's small detachment, turned taut with rage and near the heat of tears at the knowledge that the man he thought of as father, admired, and loved dabbled in the pasteboard and greasepaint he was forced to choose himself.

The man said, *"Signore, venga subito!"* He groped and found a pair of goggles, which he held out to Alistair. In the dark, they looked like handcuffs.

Alistair said nothing.

Now the windy password. *"La signora baronessa e' gravamente ferita."* The baroness is badly hurt.

Alistair had not been taught the right reply to this. He said thinly, *"E chi sarebbe quella baronessa?"* And who might that baroness be?

Maggiore's personal troops, over-awed by Anna on rare encounters, referred to their baron colonel's lady as *la baronessa.* Alistair knew nothing of this. The man leaned out of the saddle to hold the goggles closer. He shook them to make them prettier as he said, *"Ma signore, la baronessa, la sua madre. Venga subito!"* Your mother! Come quickly!

So Alistair got in the sidecar.

Granata, the man said before the engine started. Means grenade, mortar, or shell. *You don't throw a grenade at a woman,* thought Alistair, *so must be shell. "La sua condiizione?"* Alive. Which meant she was alive when he left. Knew not much more. Don't talk. Go.

Thirty minutes to the kloster. So that's when the man left. But this was Maggiore's man, not from the Red Cross. So how long had that taken? Roulette played by a fool. Maggiore knew, obviously. Was there? She alone? All the doctors knew her. Cividale del Friuli, the one town, did not hold them at night, straight through. When the summits of Mt. Matajur and Mt. Stol flip places around a bend, you're halfway, she'd said. But which the hell was which? He'd noted previously with interest that the kloster, Poleva, was pretty close to Manfredi's place, Caporetto. Why kloster in Italy? Austrians built it, didn't they? All looks Austrian here, the villages. Is she still alive? A shell? What, what, what if she's dead? Tall, cool walls of the kloster under the night sky, and spire, Counter Reformation. Cloister full of vehicles and bodies on pallets. Are they dead? Is she? Or barely alive, worse? Roulette played by a fool. Dear God, a shell! Which way?

The way was into the basilica, where electric light glared on staff moving between, touching, bending over still bodies, the pillars rose in into the dark above, and the altar candles surveyed all, unblinking. It must have been a reception point, for pallets were carried in from the cloister. Chapels served as booths, some half closed by screens. From one such rose Maggiore as Alistair turned to seek, grey-green coat slit for the saddle, boots, spurs, medals, eyes grave and steady. Angelo the tenente rose beside him. Quickly, Maggiore took Alistair by the shoulder.

"Vive. Vivrebbe. Ma e' grave. E non mi e' permesso restare. Vieni." She's alive. Should live. But bad. And I cannot stay. Come.

A creeping barrage covering an enemy tactical advance. The ambulance had driven too close while the barrage walked on its fingers toward them. Wounded to be cleared from its path. A shell striking a fallen stone wall nearby, fragments. Anna at the wheel struck on shoulder, upper arm, disintegrating them, and chest, ribs yet uncounted. In that state she had turned the ambulance with her other arm and driven it a mile to a rear post. When the door was opened, she fell out. While help arrived, the walking wounded in the ambulance formed an honor guard around her. Maggiore pushed Alistair gently toward the screen. Angelo put his arm on Alistair's shoulder.

"Poverina. Poverino. Che terribile!" he said. Poor her. Poor you. It's terrible. He stayed behind as they went in.

Maggiore said, "Awake, but morphine, thank God."

A doctor bent over her, and Anna said to him, *"Non sono una gallina a essere disguinta, imbecile,"* I'm not a fowl to be disjointed, fool, but touched his wrist with her well fingers, as to a friend. Her voice would not obey her will and spoke in her idiom, flatly and abstract.

The doctor explained, gangrene, the great foe, very difficult to stop when lodged. Much better get rid of the arm now.

"Sona una donna, idiota." I'm a woman, fool. The fingers again, more lingering now, a prayer.

The doctor reached toward the hand of the mutilated arm. Alistair was close enough to see a cloud of fear pass through his mother's eyes, but the hand was taken very gently. Then the doctor pressed hard on the nail of the index finger, and watched the nail as he might have a thermometer.

"D'accordo," he said. All right. If your luck holds. Then Alistair was at the bed.

"Oh, hello, Alistair," she said. He stood over her, bent, and kissed her forehead. She was white and clammy, hardly a surprise, over that her auburn hair almost a shocking wig. The day of the *Lusitania*, pale and sick, Maggiore's letter creased beneath her body. But Maggiore was here for now, thank God. A tube was taped into her good arm. Blood, as he guessed. He looked into the doctor's eyes and saw intelligence and friendship.

Anna said, "It's nice you can be here. See, they shoved me by chance into the Lady Chapel." He looked up and saw indeed that it seemed to be the Virgin's chapel, where the candle burned. The Church served mercy but had not forgotten grace. "We always got on, She and I. It's nice," said Anna, but vaguely.

Maggiore touched his shoulder, and he withdrew with him a few steps.

He said, "I cannot stay. Overdue already."

He went back to Anna and kissed her. "I have to go."

Anna smiled, slightly, and touched his wrist. "I know. Thank you, love." (Her eyes touched Alistair). For him too.

They went through the screens, Alistair giving his mother a glance to promise return. She was in the best of hands, said his stepfather. The hospital is well run and the doctors know and honor her. Alistair nodded. Maggiore turned to face him, putting his hands on Alistair's shoulders.

"I'm leaving. The reins are in your hands." Adding, as he had never said before, "Dear son."

Alistair bowed to accept both, said, *"Veglio."* I will keep the watch. Maggiore picked up from a bench his stained field cloak, threw it about his shoulders, extinguished himself, and passed beyond the light.

The tenente lingered. This time he took Alistair's arm. *"Una donna magnifica. Alistair, stai bene? Puoi mantenerti?"* You OK? Can you handle it?

"Looks like I have to."

"Bravo." They would be back as soon as they could. They thought an attack was coming. Some thought it might be big.

The doctor said, "Remarkable woman. No common sense."

Alistair nodded—yes, a family trait.

She should survive the wound. The lung was not perforated. Internal bleeding was absent or ceased. The shock, it seemed, had been survived. The danger was infection. That danger was great. She added to it by refusing amputation. The helpful amputation, being concrete when the rest was not, was quite clear to

Alistair's eyes and made him shudder. They would keep her in this hospital. She was among friends, and for such as her, the road was hellish. They would move her to a better space tomorrow.

"Now she needs sleep, and that I can do. You too. No beds, but find a place."

He went back to her, watched another injection, which she seemed barely to notice, held her hand until she fell asleep.

Which he would not, could not at first. He wandered, feeling like the ghost of himself on Vipero by the road, at pains to be not in the way. The wounded were much as he knew them, though the freshly in great pain were not. The merely sick, he knew less well.

In that thicket coiled a new snake, its face not yet clearly seen. Pneumonia in winter, diseases of lice, fleas, foul water were household demons, common as wounds. The new was a respiratory horror, beginning as influenza but reeling past it into fiery fever, organs going into a parody of their proper function or shutting down, mucus rising as a flood. Austrian troops perhaps had caught it further east. If caught, one died. Youth, it seemed, was no defense, but bait. One drowned in one's own lungs. He saw a young corporal die so, was warned away. At that, remembering his watch, he went back to his mother's space. There, faithless and futile, late at night, he slept.

He was wakened by guns, much, much closer than at the farm. They were not a noise in the night; the night was the guns. He watched his mother. She, well drugged, slept on, though the Virgin's candle trembled. He went beyond the screen. Men rose up on pallets, the Day of Judgment. Through windows, he could see the gun flashes, white pencils in the night. Austrian guns.

That storm passed. Italian guns took it up still well before dawn and fell silent, too, before the light. Judgment deferred, bodies slumped back on their pallets. A nun came in. His mother opened her eyes. In the slack white face, under the messed-up hair that went on yelling its good health, they opened as the eyes of a confused, frightened, and older woman, went transparent for a time, and came back as Anna's. They found Alistair.

"This is a rum go," said Anna.

Alistair, who thought a lot about bravery, knew he was seeing the real thing. He returned her look, walked over, bent, and kissed her forehead this time in salute.

"The good thing is you're in the right place," he said. "You're family here. Makes a huge difference. They know what they're doing here." And know what? To what end? He had no clue. He was purely terrified.

Anna said to the nurse, *"Il dottore e' nei paraggi?"* Is the doctor about, at all? making it a social query.

"She needs the doctor," said Alistair, making it a plea.

"He'll come when he can," said the nurse, making sufferers equal.

"The thing is," said Anna to Alistair quietly, "before they get going, I could do with some more pain stuff. It's what woke me, rather."

He touched her hand where it lay on the bed rail, and felt it rigid.

"Hang on, Mamma," he said, "I can make that happen." As, that time, he could.

AT EIGHT, THE AUSTRIAN guns began again. Rumor—and the Italian word *rumore,* sound, talk for its own sake, does just as well—began to run. These guns were more impetuous, terrific, but focused on maybe two chosen points. Rumore: a band of Italian mohawks had descended on a handful of Slovene villages within the border. This was a topic of the neighborhood. Farmhouses had been burned, animals killed, men beaten, a couple shot who fought back, a girl or two raped, which this war was not used to. One granted that the Slovenes might have welcomed the Austrians had they come, but they had been impeccable so far, even having sons and brothers in the Italian army. Meanwhile, outside rumore, trucks and some ambulances were seen to assemble in the cloister.

Alistair knew what men without officers meant. And men without rifles was worse. And officers without men was worst of all. Some men were wounded and helped by others; that, in its own way, was good, he'd say. Some wanted food. And then some demanded it. It was now said that the exhausted Italian army had been assaulted not only by fresh Austrian divisions but by the German Empire too. Twenty divisions of it, some said.

The doctor said, "Signora, the line has been broken. Anna, you know exactly how close the line is." He was unshaven, and why not, and there were patches of blood here and there on his coat. His eyes were level, and why not, since Italians break no more easily than any other men. Behind the screen were heavy sounds of moving, and some orders, now and then. Guns came from here and there in quick boiling bursts. Machine guns were mixed in now.

The doctor said, "I am evacuating the lightly wounded, who will fight again. The rest I am leaving to our enemies, who are not animals, and have doctors too. You two neutral civilians have nothing to fear from them at all. They will care for a hurt American lady. You should stay."

Anna spoke to Alistair. "I'll never see him again. Not through all this war. And then who knows."

Alistair nodded.

She said to the doctor. "I'm going with you. We're going with you. I'm going with the Italians."

"A terrible decision. I promise nothing. The road will be dreadful for you. Worse than you think."

"Sono la donna d'un ufficiere italiano." I am the lady of an Italian officer.

"I know." He would at least be going with them.

"That would be most agreeable," said Anna. She said to Alistair, "Am I a fool?"

He thought. "I don't think so," he said. "You'd know."

"I'm glad I raised a man to lean on," she said.

"It's going to be hard for you. I do think that."

"I suppose so," said Anna. "But, Alistair, it's not far to Udine. It's where GianCarlo's bound to cast up after all this. When I get sorted out, he'll get us back to the farm. It's worth it for sure."

He nodded. That seemed true. He saw with warm pleasure his horses, his books, Victoria for their anniversary not many days away. He touched her dear pen against his chest.

ANNA'S STRETCHER WAS CARRIED to the cloister. The basilica was a little less full. The empty spaces looked less like deliverance than missing teeth. Alistair walked behind, beside the doctor, who said, "Why did I pinch her finger?"

"Because if she could not feel it, the arm must be dead."

"Not bad. But no. Circulation. If the nail turns rose again after it is pinched, there is blood flow, the flesh is alive, and may heal. If next time it does not, I amputate. Not fun on the road. Why did you not ask me? Watch and ask now. Then help. I can't have useless freight."

I didn't ask because I am afraid of all answers here, thought Alistair. "I will," he said.

When the bearers went up the short steps to the cloister, Anna looked in fierce concentration at nothing at all.

The doctor watched her, and said, "Unfortunately, this is nothing. Steel springs and bad roads are much worse than steps. And she has had her last heavy dose of morphine. We can't keep it up."

In the cloister were ten FIAT ambulances and two trucks. On each truck, a red cross had been daubed in paint that still looked bloody. Anna was handed up into the rear of the lead truck. By the rear truck was a section of infantry at ease, who stood like twelve tired butcher's ponies. The light in the cloister made their faces grey. Their *sottotenente* moved like a fox terrier. The dry, cold weather that had creased Alistair's face as recently as the sidecar ride was gone, and rain fell steadily.

The doctor said, "I can't give her privacy, but I'll be in that truck. The Red Cross boys will be in and out. She'll know them. And it's where you'll be." He saw Alistair looking at the infantry. "They're not for fighting the Austrians," he said. "I am in command of this convoy, incidentally." Alistair nodded. The doctor was a medical major. The other doctor, who had authorized the morphine in the morning, leant against the truck, seemed to use its engine heat as a blanket and the hood for a pillow, rested one foot on the running board, and looked at the ground. He raised his head as the major moved toward him. The rain was on his cheeks.

WHAT THE TRUCK CARRIED made its rattles and thumps fill the inside with smells of gauze, carbolic, spirit, soap, a fleeting trace of chloroform, a bitter drop of morphine, all sharp and sweet. It was full. His mother had a kind of room, between bales of dressings, and her pallet was set on blankets piled thick, for kindness. Kindness as could be; he sat close, where she could see him, but looked at her little even when she took his hand, for suffering needs its privacy. There were indeed Red Cross American boys, whom she knew, and nuns. These were a shifting crew. The convoy stopped often and they ran errands up and down the line. When they got back in, the Red Cross slickers glistened and the nuns in wool turned by stages into wet dogs. The doctor major sat with the driver in the front. Alistair could see slices of the world, front and side. A good deal of time had passed. The early November dusk was falling. The headlamps were pale yellow on the road.

Therefore he saw the first flowers of fire far off to the north, not the white flash of guns, but burning. He saw the major turn his head. The road was still orderly. They stopped for groups of men, wagons, trucks, and overtook them, but all seemed bound together by a shared concussion and easily under command. Wounded were held up into their light like unwanted babies, and once in a while were taken on. Alistair did not think things so terribly bad. They moved forward, though not fast. A third of the road was behind them. There were nurses and doctors and supplies to hand. His mother got no worse. It seemed to him likely enough, the way things were, that you would one day have to pay for love in pain and danger. And so one would. To convey his mother to her love, who was his stepfather, and whose mild authority he embraced, might be the last office he performed to honor his childhood. The fires bloomed a little brighter to the north. All this lasted to the Natisone bridge.

Which announced itself as streaks of rain on the windshield turning to white fire, were smeared by the wipers, and resolved into searchlights trained on the bridge with lakes of darkness in between. There was a roadblock here. This was Carabinieri country. Their hats looked like black stones on their heads when they passed through the searchlight beams. The lesser road from the kloster joined the highway from Caporetto. To their right and behind them was a solid line of head-lamps and wagon lights with a press of men between. The Carabinieri ran in and out of the highway pulling men aside, opening truck doors, manhandling drivers. Their lair was the shadow by the road where they pulled their victims. Alistair saw a man roughly handled and saw it was a captain in great fear. The Natisone, essentially a torrent, had risen quickly. The searchlights caught its wake against the bridge pilings. What the Carabinieri did made little difference. The weight of traffic was too great, wheels and men rolled past them, they picked at its sides like blowflies on a cow. They did stop one line of wagons on the highway just to the convoy's right. Their own driver slammed the gear, the truck jerked forward, Anna moaned, the convoy closed up, and they were all on the bridge. Alistair looked back out of the truck into the changed angles of light and saw, where the black bank plunged down, a man who looked like the scared captain kneeling in the mud and looking into bright light. As the white search beams fell behind them, the red fire in the north climbed brighter. The captain facing the light popped his mouth open, jerked sideways, and fell over.

They were in a continuous press of traffic, held to the pace of mules, though increasingly there were wagons with splintered wheels and poles apparently pushed to the side by trucks. The foot traffic eddied around them. There were pulses of men under command, rifles and packs sharp in the headlamps. The rifles were glassy in the rain, like the slickers of some officers. These kept the highway's edge. Beyond them, there was a hoard. If you kept your eye on it, you could see a steady sideways progress into the dimmer light, into the dusk, into the dark like beetles, into the fields. The army was melting in the rain. Alistair touched his mother's hand to promise return and went up into the cab behind the major. The major had drawn his sidearm and held it in his lap. Alistair knew that he must hear choices, must make decisions to carve independence for him and his. So there really was a cataract, and they were in it. They passed through Cividale del Fruili. There were more Carabinieri here, but in the gaps between them the house doors opened and families crept sideways out and joined the retreat with burdens on their heads. The Natisone was to the left now. They could see it through sidestreets, black with silver waves.

The river strayed away. Outside the town, a road joined to the left ahead. As they came up to it, the major and the driver spoke urgently and seemed to disagree, though Alistair could not quite hear the words. There were the wipers, and now the rain was roaring on the roof. The major put his hand on the wheel, a movement of authority. The driver opened the window, rain blew in, and he made large gestures to the convoy behind. They turned onto the new road, and as each ambulance came up to it, its wheels turned sharply left. Alistair pushed his head forward and knew the major could see him. He could smell his breath, on which there was tobacco. The major glanced at him and pointed his finger at the northern glow, the point of its crescent even with them now and nearer.

The major said, "That way is Udine. Udine is gone or going. We are headed south. The Tagliamento. There is a bridge at Latisana. They might stop them there."

Alistair went back to the rear of the truck. His mother's eyes were shut, though he doubted she was sleeping. She would know soon. Don't insult her. He touched her wrist. "Mamma," he said.

She opened her eyes at once. She said, as though having said it over and over inside herself, "Udine? Are we nearly there?"

He touched her forehead for fever, found none, went on, "Not there. *Andiamo al Talgliamento. A Latisana.*"

"Dear God," she said. "And what is to become of us?"

He had seen only as he spoke exactly where they were. To the left passed the country road to Buttrio, their farmhouse, horses, home. The truck did not turn. That he did not tell her. Behind them, not many miles away, a fountain of flame burst up into the rain. An ammunition dump or fuel. Something like that. He did not exactly sleep. He dozed. Each time he found sleep, he found the captain in the mud, dragged away in fear, sinking to his knees while his eyes pulled him like a rope toward the glaring lights, then popping his mouth and jerking to the side over and over, as though that one military skill had been all his training.

THE SODDEN DAWN BROUGHT a beautiful thing: a unit of the Italian army, brigade strength, halted by the road. Anna, always happy with armies, broadly smiled, and smiled yet more when a Red Cross boy, Dennis, her old friend, brought something much nicer than coffee, a syringe.

"My new best friend," she said.

And the excellent convoy quickly sprouted tents. They were out of the hills, the fields were nearly oozing, but never mind. Anna was lifted down. Soothed by morphine, she could walk a little with support and had some dignity for her needs. Her dressings were changed. It was done by a nun, brutal, quick, and kind. The younger doctor watched. Alistair did not, knew his mother was close to screaming, thought she'd do better to, and knew as well that she'd take hurt flesh over hurt pride. He found Dennis's arm on his shoulder.

Dennis said, "The good thing is that what comes off with the dressing is dead tissue, nothing else. The bad thing, morphine doesn't do much for nerve endings. So we let the nuns do it. They're tougher. I'd say the doctor thinks she's doing pretty well."

Anna was exhausted and silent. Alistair went out.

It was not a brigade. It was fragments of brigades. It had no precise commander. It was held together by good sense. It had no orders. Telephones were down, the radio hardly used, orders might come by motorcycle if anyone knew where it was. It would fight the enemy if it knew where that was. It didn't. It had kept a very few guns, and their wheels were sinking into the grass. It had a row of wagons, mules with their nosebags on, and a command tent whose sagging roof pissed water like a horse. In the middle of these it had a young officer whose back he thought he knew, knew he knew, and it sent his heart tumbling like an acrobat. For it was Angelo's back, Maggiore's tenente, and where Angelo was Maggiore must surely be, and Alistair had not known until that moment how forlorn and tired and terrified he was. Angelo turned and saw him, and looked at him like a ghost fleeing the dawn, but that was the expression of the Italian army just now, and Alistair found himself close to tears. He walked faster toward Angelo than Angelo to him, so they met outside the pissing tent.

Angelo said, "I had heard about the ambulances. About to look for you." He took Alistair's arm, rather hard, looked away, and said, *"E la madre?"*

"No worse. Better, maybe a little. Where's the colonel?"

Angelo studied the tent. Alistair realized then that Angelo had not once looked him in the face. "Let's go in. Nobody there," Angelo said.

Angelo took him in. Outside it smelled of mules and rain, inside of mold. Angelo now turned straight toward him. "My colonel is dead," he said.

Alistair said absolutely nothing. The remark made no sense. It was his mother who was in the valley of death, and hadn't he just said she seemed better?

Angelo said, "He was shot."

Alistair heard himself say, "How?"

Angelo now took his arm and leaned toward him so that their faces almost touched. "He was not shot by the enemy, Alistair."

Alistair tried very hard to navigate. "By his men?"

"No. I have seen that happen. Not to my colonel. By the battle police."

The captain in the mud burst out of Alistair's brain, caught him, and began to pull him under. He said, "No. No." He found that he was holding Angelo like a girl and was held.

When they pulled apart, Angelo said, "They were shooting officers without their troops. It was one of the last orders from headquarters. He was a colonel. He should have had a regiment. We all know he had fifteen men, and hardly any of them were there. They were Calabrians. Southerners. They hate the Savoians. They hate the palace staff even more, probably." Angelo hung his head.

Alistair said, "They didn't shoot you," realized it sounded like an accusation, which it wasn't even minutely, and touched Angelo's arm. "Angelo," he said.

"I ran," said Angelo. "You cannot imagine the confusion. I wasn't very important. I suppose I'm still running. I have to find headquarters. And the king. The king, Alistair. We don't know where they are. We think they got out of Udine in time. I didn't actually see him die. But there's no doubt. They made them kneel. They all knelt. But he wouldn't. So they—"

"No," said Alistair. "No. No. No. What I can't see, I can't tell her. I have to tell her he's dead. She'll hear somehow."

They were sitting on the edge of a map table by now. Neither could quite get up and move away. Angelo said, "Alistair, shall I tell her? She was always so decent to me. I'd do that for her."

"I don't think you're a good liar, Angelo. She'll accept that he's dead, in her own way. Not the other. Not for ages. Thank you, Angelo, but that's for me."

"I have to stay until I find where to go. I'm not scared of talking to the king. He knows who I am. He knows my family. And it's the last of my duty, isn't it? *Il telefono e rotto. Nessuno risponde.*" The telephone is broken. No one answers.

They knew they had said goodbye. Alistair nodded. "Good luck, Angelo."

They walked out of the tent. Just before they turned their separate ways, Angelo said, "Alistair. They shot quite a lot of officers. I don't mean hundreds, obviously, but quite a lot. I saw and I heard. I don't think they shot any other colonel."

Alistair nodded again, again said, "Thank you, Angelo," and turned away.

He saw everything leave his mother's face as though it had sunk to the bottom of a lake and left her features bobbing on the surface. At length, she said quietly, "Soldiers die, and women who love them know it. I do not have to ask if he died with honor. I do not have to fear for his soul. He was an upright and gentle man. I am just so unhappy that I have been left. It shouldn't have happened. A few feet closer with that thing, and none of this would matter. I do not think that God fumbles, and I do not know what I have done that he should play with me."

He was wretchedly sorry for her. Her feelings were intense and true to the bone. That they should fall on one maimed, in great pain, and part of a miserable caravan of the afflicted creeping through a land in mourning surely scoured the basement of woe. He could still barely speak to her. What she grieved for had form, therefore comely even when terrible, a soldier dying for his duty. What he knew and lied about was treachery, form turned against itself, a soldier murdered by his own. He had seen that treachery on the bridge over the Natisone and had believed it a single anomaly, a septic point of panic where the wise and decent purpose of the convoy was the rule.

The convoy did not break down. Nor did what passed for a brigade. No official advice arrived, nor orders, but it became clear that king and command were at Pordenone, beyond the Tagliamento, safe and somewhat functional. Angelo, a ghost at cockcrow become again an officer, acquired a car, a corporal, and a private and set off. Dispersed soldiers straggling in—in this eddy, at least the broken army was reforming—brought news that the main enemy was still to the north, moving quickly west. The brigade took it upon itself to form a rearguard screen, a move of generosity become gallantry that, repeated a thousand times by whole divisions, by lost companies, by corporals left with two privates in a ditch, in fact saved Italy. The maggiore dottore, whom by now Alistair respected absolutely, resolved to continue southwest to Latisana. He came to see Anna when she was taken back into the truck, before they moved. Her dressings, changed eight hours earlier, could wait. He gave her a light dose of morphine. Standing by her, he said, "Anna, you are doing rather well." He sat down beside her, took her good hand, and said, "And, signora, I am intensely sorry," though precisely what he knew Alistair was not sure. Anna, in whom the beauty of form would survive most things, summoned from wherever enough light into her eye to gravely clasp his hand and gave him a lady's thanks. The maggiore dottore gave Alistair, no nurse, the honor of helping to read the maps. It was a country of obscure and tangled roads. Thought and care were needed.

Thought and care, the vault over Nothing. All flight is into Nothing. Nothing's atoms change back into a grange with a mossy wall, a hill with a crooked oak and a boulder shaped like an ox, a table with a family round it by the action of a heel turning at bay, by intent, by resolve, by courage. The convoy had these. It headlamps looked Nothing in the face. A farmhouse emptied is Nothing, its animals stray into Nothing, its people flee and beg as ghosts. Their headlamps lit and overtook the backs of ghosts and their lumpy burdens, ghosts sleeping by the road. Odysseus, Sacker of Cities, knew this before Odysseus the Wanderer ever met the dead. Alistair wondered whether reflection by itself would ward off Nothing. He'd put his money on map reading.

The distances were negligible. From the kloster to the brigade was forty-five kilometers. Latisana, in a straight line, was not much further. The maggiore dottore decreed no towns, no railroad lines, no main roads. Alistair sat with a flashlight in the cab behind the major. He peered through the windshield. His eyes moved behind the wipers, placing the thread of country roads over the lines on the maps. The rain was slackening slowly. The signposts were down for the war, though the old mile-stones, overlooked, remained. He was good at this and gave it everything. He had a headache, which barely counted. Once he got it wrong and the convoy went back, like a snake turning in a pipe. No one blamed him. In another part of his mind, the captain in the mud's whey face in the searchlights quickened with his stepfather's blood and the captain joined the Umbrian girl as consort. Just before dawn, one of the ambulances began to blink its lights. The convoy stopped. The maggiore dottore got out, came shortly back, took surgical masks and gloves out of stores, and returned to the ambulance. When he came back, he said nothing.

In the dawn it became clear that they, traveling southwest, had bisected the route of an Austrian force, not a heavy one, advancing northwest, perhaps from Malfalcone toward Codroipo. There had been fighting. They smelled it on the west wind long before the light, villages smouldering in the rain. Slaughtered animals littered the fields around, smelling yet too faintly to overcome the sodden ash, and butchered for food, it was clear, hurriedly but not wantonly. The carcasses showed bones like diagrams. The humans who had stayed looked at their smoking barns like spirits of the newly dead. The ghosts driven down the road stopped to beg and soon would take. In between villages, the convoy stopped again. Both doctors put on masks and went into the same ambulance. This was odd. The convoy, though merciful, carried not very badly wounded men, mostly officers and NCOs, who could be expected to stand and fight again. Alistair supposed a wound had gone bad, requiring that the kind of amputation threatened for his mother at the kloster. When the major came back he gave him a look that meant he would like to know. The major closed his face and shook his head. There was now an infantryman posted on the ambulance before and the ambulance behind.

Anna was now sitting up, at least had a pile of blankets pushed behind her back. After the next dressing change, which she met with a bitter, bleak endurance more unnerving than the first, the young doctor said to her, *"Bravo!"* and smiled. This could have been for two things at once, but he muttered to Alistair, "Without a foul up, should be OK. She's lucky." Her body was pulling her spirit up from oblivion by the scruff of its neck, and her spirit had to make do. Alistair knew of himself that he was so far on the distant side of tired that sorrow, sympathy, and dread were part of one lead weight that pulled at his eyes. If you threw a great deal of pain on top of this, he guessed that his mother was in a like state. It might be for the best, right now.

His imitation of a respectful subaltern could be so good he almost convinced himself. The convoy stopped again, the doctors armored up, went into the afflicted ambulance, came out, took off masks and gloves, and talked apart. The younger rolled up the gauzes fastidiously, looked at loss, and threw it into the running ditch. The major came back to the cab. The sergeant driver was out checking oil, water, and tires. Since Alistair now cared very little what he said, he said, "What's up?"

He was looked at without enthusiasm but then with reflection. "It might be easier if there could be discussion in this cab. Wait for my driver. He's a sensible fellow."

He said, "A lieutenant in that ambulance has become infected with a virulent flu. His fever is insupportable. He will probably die. The nurse, she is a nun, became worried before daylight. The condition has advanced very quickly. The flu is similar to some recently seen at the hospital. Whether it is one disease or several similar, we do not know. Its effects appear variable, but at the state this patient has reached, it kills. The others in the ambulance are in grave danger. Whether they are doomed, I simply do not know. We do not know the incubation period. I suppose we have an experiment in hand now. The others have been told that the masks I distributed are purely precautionary. The nun at least knows that this is a lie. She is a brave woman, as they usually are. The ambulance is in quarantine. That is all I can say. It is all I know. Now I have a question. It is much easier. Where are we?"

Alistair said, "The next water will be the Stella. It is the last before the Tagliamento. The village after it will be Droloassa." He showed the major on the map.

The major said, "How long?"

Alistair looked at the driver. He said, "Ninety minutes as we have gone?" The driver nodded.

The major nodded. He motioned the driver forward. Before the gear was in, he said quietly, "As far as I suppose, you are not in much danger. I thank you for not asking."

The major could have added that the disease, at this time, put one in mind of an inexperienced artiste trying an insanely audacious act. Its contagiousness had no one approach it without a mask, and often it seemed unable to pass itself to a mewling babe. It appalled by the merciless expedition of its murders, and it had become clear that one could catch it and have no worse than a bad week. It killed through atrocious fevers and by turning the lungs into a lake. This phase it seemed to relish and linger over. Why it liked the young, God knew, perhaps. It was not widespread. It liked barracks and trenches and such. It had also gained some foothold in Venice. But Venice was so good at that.

The major said none of this. Alistair thought that dissolution was now within, as well as without.

THERE WAS A NICE SURPRISE: the Tagliamento. He had been over it between Venice and Udine, a skein of rivulets in a stony basin. He didn't see that it would stop a fox. Now, from very near the bridge, he saw it wide with the rains, lead-colored, and savage, heaping itself on the bridge pilings, roaring beneath. Its river god had slapped Italia on the shoulder. "Don't worry, old girl," the river god had said.

That was the nice surprise. When he had imagined the crossing, it had been like unto Jordan's, the afflicted stripping off their stained apparel, braces and crutches cartwheeling in the air, milk and honey on barrows. The encampment on its banks, new but sodden, the infirmary seeming its most squalid suburb, disappointed but did not shock him. The Way We Live Now. From close by the eastern bank, it took them three hours to attain it. The order to withdraw beyond the river had not quite gone out yet. The humanity had seemed to rise out of the ground to immerse them as the roads converged on the bridge, therefore was not under organized commands but made of broken units partially controlled, bands of deserters, miscontrolled, and the poor countryside in motion, rained on for a day and more, hungry, apparitions who yet begged, relieved themselves, and stank. The lieutenant was dead. Those in his ambulance were quite well and very likely lethal. His mother had a fever, exhaustion and misery most likely, but dangerous in her state. He thought they would lose their major here. The streets were mud. His eyes were too tired to rise much above it. Sometimes he promised them that if they rose, they would apprehend Victoria—lilac, warm, and somewhere. Sometimes they saw her, and sometimes the captain in the mud.

THE RAIN FELL FOR two more days. The Tagliamento spread its chest and squeezed its shoulders against the banks. The bridge pilings shrank. The river god smirked like an innkeeper at a wedding. There were puddles on the floors of the tents which, when stepped on awkwardly, poured into the mud outside. Army units, all bearing wounded, jammed the eastern bank back into the countryside. Though with inadequate transport and harried by the Italian cavalry, the Austro-Germans broke successively the Torre line, fully occupying Udine, the half-formed Stella line, and occupied San Daniele del Fruili and Codroipo. Tents grew like mushrooms. Mushrooms grew in tents. The military police set up, not in the festive mode of the Natisone bridge but in closed tents, small malignant cells. There were trials. There were executions. Italy was angry. Alistair spent all the time he could keep his eyes open pulling at the sleeves of the doctors they still knew, tiring the last loyalties of the American Red Cross, standing in kitchen tents to get a bowl of macaroni, a mug of hot tea, and bring it back. Anna's fever relented. He could see no way to get them out of here. It was said that Venice might easily fall. He was increasingly happy.

He knew his happiness monstrous, which sharpened it. His Italy gutted, his family murdered or bereft, cut them from the earth and moved them into the rule of art. The figures stored in his imagination began to move. He looked, motioned them this way or that, looked, moved his hand again. His books were gone, might be found one day. His horses were gone, he knew. Austrian officers might ride them if they were very lucky horses. They might pull wagons. They would die. They had been the friends of every weather of his life. He mourned them bleakly. He mourned that he must know them to lack souls. Phrases began to cover their memory like amber. He wrote nothing yet. He had Victoria's pen safe against his heart. All paper was soggy, except the maps, which sweated. He was not worried much about Victoria. If Venice fell, Mr. Schrauler might lose money, or might not. She would be fine. They would both be fine. They were in this but not of it. They looked. They were the wolves, she had been right, for sure the foxes. There would be a hole on the hill for his vixen and he to look down at the ruin below, noses quivering, each other's scent in their fur.

ON THE FIRST OF November, the bridges over the Tagliamento were dynamited from the Carnic Alps to the sea. This cut off five thousand Italian heroes, who for days had held off entire Austro-German divisions on Mt. Ragogna, a betrayal supporting the essential truth of poetry, Ragogna being a full rhyme to *vergogna,* shame. The rain immediately ceased. A dry, scouring wind set up out of the east, turning waterlogged tents into cold storage. The Austro-Germans were now on the far bank. The Italian army had lately lost two hundred thousand as prisoners, close to the same as deserters or stragglers, scores of thousands killed and wounded, and eighteen hundred guns. The Tagliamento is a big mountain stream, no more. The bridges began to stretch their legs. The river god became hard to find. Seven days before, the grey-faced shades of the Italian army's exhausted trance had been sent running by a real enemy vastly reinforced and led with genius. In that time, Alistair had seen cowardice among the Italians only in mouseholes here and there; his admiration grew through every disastrous day, his highest for the army doctors. His mother needed care but was out of any obvious danger. After the next retreat, which was certain, he thought that he could cut them free.

THE ORDER TO FALL back beyond the Piave River came November 4. This retreat was less dire than the first because expected. Two army corps acted as nursemaids. It was not raining. Their old convoy, nurses, and doctor major were still a unit. His mother's pain had lessened greatly on the tenth day after her wound, apparently according to some schedule, because this caused no surprise. She was handled very gently, nonetheless. "Her body is loosening its defenses," the major said. "There is a danger of hemorrhages now. But it doesn't last long. She is our success, I think." And very briefly smiled.

The infected ambulance had of course been detached. Four of the six in it had sickened, the nun among them. There was now a circle of quarantine for them to join. The disease had enjoyed the disorder and the rain. It seemed clearer about its ambitions. Surgical masks were becoming prizes.

It was cold. They moved through a country in settled despair, Giulia now, real Italy, with disbelief at its betrayal as the army went past, hard-eyed, and awaiting conquest the next day. He had barely been able to wash, never to bathe, had no change of clothes since the motorcycle sidecar in another life. He woke up one morning certain he had fleas and praying he had no lice. His mother's morphine had been stopped. Its merciful fog had lifted from her eyes, which were hard, quick moving, and clear. He knew that he had either to hope that she never in her life learned how

Maggiore died or tell her something now. The truck's bales of supplies had been largely used. Their semblance of a habitation had been stripped. He spoke as quietly as he could above the engine and the wheels. He ended, "One thing I can tell you because Angelo told me. He never kneeled. Maggiore never kneeled."

"Of course not," she said. She looked down a long time and he saw no movement in her face. Then, "It is no worse, Alistair. I am not even quite surprised, though I am appalled. Of course, there are things I know that you do not. I was his wife. There was no mistake. He was murdered. He was fighting his own people out of loyalty to them. It is the bravest thing of all. You did right to tell me, Alistair."

She was silent again but now looking at him. He was near to taking her hand, but she raised hers, though softly, to hold him off. She said, quite steadily, "I thought I knew what my life would be, Alistair. What it would be in all that mattered. Now I'll have to start again, with less, of course. It happens, Alistair. I'm not singled out. The wounded, the ones I picked up before all this, they're very clear in my mind, and some I sketched. I think it's time to do something with them. Modeling, of course. I can't just stop living. Is that terrible?"

"Never, Mamma," he said.

"I forbade you to do that once. I should like to have his body buried properly," she said. "And I should write to his daughter. I wonder if she even knows. Could you help me with some of that, Alistair? As though you hadn't all through, dear God."

"Of course," he said.

AND NOW, BEYOND THE Piave, one could nearly think their caravan had seen the Jordan passed. They were in another military slum of tents, only less sodden than before. He stood in the kitchen line with two hopeful bowls. Though Anna might be honored by the doctors who knew her and a comrade of the Red Cross, they were beggars here, and it was getting worse. But there were mountains to the north again, fine-lined and white on a November afternoon. The spires of a city rose between them. There were proper settlements even by the camp where he had found a prosperous farmhouse, paid to have a bath heated up, and had found new clothes and thrown away the old, all of which should have made him feel better than he did. They were going to get bowls of stew that seemed pretty good, and he could barely look at it. But their way out was sure. Any skilled physician could serve his mother now. There was no disorder here. The disbanded had come in, disappeared, or been rounded up. The fleeing countryside had been refused the bridges, and ghosts cannot cross water. Looking down at the Piave, he found it serious and deep. He came before the cooks and was served. He kept his face from the gravy's steam. His bowels, not happy for some days, had begun to mutiny. Riding so long in the truck had made his bones ache. Venice was not very far and stood yet unconquered. He saw Victoria's face smiling down on the canal as when they first had talked and smiled himself, for their anniversary was close. He moved beyond the kitchen range reluctantly, for it was surprisingly cold and he had found himself shivering, which he rarely did.

He thought that the night was interrupted by storms, the kind with clouds lit up like crimson ashes. When they woke him, the night was still but must have been very cold, for he was shivering worse, and his pallet was wet with sweat. Getting up to find another blanket made him shake as though flying apart, but he found a thick one that smelled of horse and so comforted him, until it became Pompey and Vipero and he wept. When he seemed to wake up, his eyes were gummed, but he was able to open them. His thoughts could not hold steady but flickered back and forth around the point that he must be quite sick, which confused him because he was never sick, that his breath hurt, and that he had fouled his bed. It was the last that drove him up, horrified.

He was probably in his mother's space to tell her that he should go to sick call, probably. He was still wrapped in the horse blanket. When he went in he saw that the Red Cross boy, Dennis, her old friend from the battlefields, was there. They were talking, he interrupted, they turned their heads to him in a morning's welcome, looked at him, and still looked. He moved toward them, but Dennis moved more quickly, putting himself between his mother and he, and said, "Alistair. Come with me!" He was delighted to have a simple instruction. His mother's mouth fell open. He thought he should assure her that she would not be shot and fall sideways but then doubted that she thought so herself.

He followed Dennis and even caught up with him and walked beside him. Dennis turned his face a little from him, which made Alistair extremely concerned that he might smell unpleasant. They went through passages he knew and past stains on the canvas he knew. He welcomed even the distant warmth of the range as they passed the kitchen, almost threw up at the smell of food, and his bowels stabbed at him, for spite. They turned right and past canvas walls that smelled of carbolic and through a flap in a tent whence that smell issued. Here it was new canvass and brightly lit. The light blazed on white-robed figures caught steady, motionless. They turned their heads at him. But they had no faces. Dennis spoke some explanation of him. He wanted to correct the Italian, but then forgot what had been said. His eye caught one of the lights directly and stabbed him like a gimlet. One of the faceless paced toward him, came to him, took him by the arm, sat him on a trolley, and put a thermometer in his mouth. He sensed a woman. The lack of face must be a surgical mask, he realized. The eyes read the thermometer. Her arm smoothed him out on the trolley. He felt cool linen drawn gently over his forehead and over his eyes against the light. As the light withdrew, he saw that Dennis was gone. H realized where he was.

Part by part his body loathed him and promised him death. Of this was made time. His bowels fluttered like a dying fish. His lungs tricked him by becoming wood but met nails at the top of every breath. He was wrapped in a blanket and drenched, though the linen on his forehead from time to time slid off and came back cool. His throat betrayed him with syrup that his lungs of wood could not draw breath through. The gimlet of his eye did not dull but grew and filled his brain. The thought squeezed up in his brain, *"Muoio."* I'm dying. He shied from it as from an unjustly presented bill, remembered that he thought in English, and thought, "I'm dying," which had a completely different sound. He felt disappointment in a terrible stab and terror at what the passage all the way through death would be. He did not know this, but the priest who had been watching him by his shoulder began to raise his hand, then lowered it, and slightly shook his head. He despaired of even trying to breath and breathed more easily.

8

Anna, in whom terror still lay as a band of ice between throat and gut, looked at the pencil rendering of her son on the hospital bed. The doctor said, "He's just weak. He's not sick anymore, Mrs. Stears." He said it in English, for he was so; he was part of the new succor, come from England, France, and even America to stricken Italy, eight allied divisions coming behind them. He went on, "There is no fever. The illness is beaten. It was a very close call, I'm told, but it does not come back. That much we do know. Men die at this stage, but they were sick before the fever ever took them. Fleas, lice, malnutrition. None of that applies to your son. He's a lucky young man. I am truly not worried, Mrs Stears." She raised her head and nodded to him. The same manners kept within her the question she asked with every breath: *Have you ever wondered how much one woman can lose so quickly*?

Alistair was quite aware of the nurse and even lifted his head to watch her. The nurse said, "Oh, hello, Alistair. They said you might be here. It's Cynthia."

He thought his time for hallucination was past. Perhaps it was not. He really looked at her. He remembered her. He remembered her throat when she balanced and looked up. He remembered that but nothing else.

"From Manfredi's yacht. Do you remember? Years ago. We called each other Miss and Mister then."

Oh, it was sails, then. "Good God," he said.

"Everybody's doing this stuff now, so I thought I should. It's not so bad when you get used to it."

She spoke holding his bedpan, so he supposed she was right. He remembered something of importance. "You had brothers," he said. "How are they?"

"Both dead," said Cynthia. "Passchendaele and Malines. I'm all that's left, like most of us."

"I'm sorry," he said. He knew that you could not say any of the things human beings used to say. They all implied meaning.

"How's Manfredi? Do you know?"

"He was alive two weeks ago," said Alistair.

Cynthia gestured happily with the bedpan. "I'm so glad," she said. "He seemed to be your friend. Really. And they say you're not going to die."

"That's very nice of them," said Alistair.

"Don't," she said. "We can't all just die. We just can't. I expect I'll see you later. Goodbye, Alistair."

"Goodbye, Cynthia."

He wasn't depressed by her. They all lived under death now. It had arrived over them all like a November sky. It did not listen to questions. He believed Manfredi was alive. He looked at his bed with dislike. He looked up at the weather of their life, on whose cloud the light brought by a girl he barely knew flickered and did not quite go out. Death had sticky fingers and defiled. To himself, he smelled of the grave.

He was at least right about Manfredi. Just like Alistair, Manfredi lay on an iron-framed cot. He was in greater pain than Alistair but better spirits. He had learned that he would get up as a captain and probably a decorated one. He held in his hand a wafer from Helene in far-off Copenhagen. It was only a telegram and so did not carry her scent, but it began, "My darling, dearest hero," and went on from there. Granted some prejudice, Helene was right.

The Italian cavalry did not quite save Italy, but some of it did very good work. Between the collapse at Caporetto and the Piave line, the war became suddenly and briefly a fight of small units, sudden authority, and frantic speed. Manfredi found himself with seventy-three men. Out of a wooded draw, screaming like Comanches, they first threw themselves on an Austrian transport and destroyed supplies worth far more just now than men. The same day, though with casualties, they damaged three guns and killed the gunners. After a night shivering by their horses in the pines, they held back an Austrian unit near Forame long enough for two Italian companies to cross the Manna River and dynamite the bridge. Water cresting on their saddles, they forded the river themselves. By now, their horses were shaking, their numbers much reduced. In an unimportant skirmish, Manfredi was hit badly in the thigh. With great luck, he and three more fallen were attached to an Italian ambulance train, and, like Anna and Alistair, brought to safety. His was no gallant flesh wound. Infection could have killed him. He would never walk far with ease again. But it would take no day from his life nor cast one cloud over Helene's nights. And Helene, in far-off Copenhagen, knew her chosen a hero, and never to fight again.

THE ITALIAN ARMY, HOWEVER affectionate and long-suffering, threw them out at last, to relief on all sides. There was a spa outside Treviso, so not far away. Anna needing a great deal of directed exercise for her arm, and Alistair being convalescent, it was thought a good place for them.

In happier days, it had pursued fashion, wistfully. Lofty halls were set about with ormolu blackamoors whose uplifted torcheres illuminated the skin conditions of leather sofas and billiard tables whose greens endured the droughts of August. Long corridors had sculptures of Italian medical worthies, remembered only here. These corridors echoed discreetly with the taps of canes of injured officers and the passing sound, like a social kiss, of rubber tires on bathchairs. Anna was attended by a Finnish female whose small mouth in ample jowls was lit up by a sunny smile, entirely unconvincing. Her sessions were extremely painful. Long immersions of her arm in hot, salty, radioactive water helped a bit, Anna had to say. This happened in the Sala di Benessere Marie Curie.

Venice was whole, had never been touched, was nearly safe. In the highlands around the Monte Grappa, Italians still fought desperately to keep the Austro-Germans from the plain. That could go either way. But if the enemy reached the plain, it was no longer clear that he could go where he pleased. Italy's scattered were returning to the colors every day. The English and French divisions were battle trained. Munitions were being made and were pouring through the ports.

The enemy's supply line was long. Alistair could certainly travel now. The way to Venice was open. For Venice, read Victoria.

He did not go. He did not write. If Victoria had been with him all along, she would have kept this winter from him, and his arm would lay warm around her. If Victoria had been with him all along, she would very likely be in her grave. He did not know how to go to her. In his worst moments he thought she would not recognize him, after a moment of joy would turn away as though he had dropped a clumsy mask. He did not fear for her in Venice. She would fear for him, but moderately. She knew where he was when the damn had burst, would know that he must have been carried away. He was a civilian, and his nationality still protected him. He might be in Vienna, but he'd come back when he could. Only the strangest accident could have overtaken him. Victoria didn't dwell on the worst.

He found an alcove in one of the corridors with a desk and chairs and a blackamoor to light the desk. He made it his own property. Canes tapped as they passed behind his back. He wrote most of the day, and the rest walked by a little lake where there were winter willows. The figures in his poem were as clear as woodcuts, but they moved as feebly as Aeneas and Odysseus had seen the dead. When he got tired of them, he thought of Victoria. He thought one day, *When I can bring to mind the exact flush on her neck after love and its exact texture and its scent, I will be ready for her, and she will know me.*

Mail came, Anna having had the idea of telling the post office where they were. To the credit of both the Austrians and the Italians, mail came forwarded out of a different life and a different rule, quite fresh, since the farmhouse at Buttrio had been less than a month before. An old letter from Lionel Stears had been sent first to Venice. Anna carried it unopened for two days, but gently, and did not hide it. Eight lines from Manfredi, tearing a crack in the November sky, gave a military hospital in Bergamo as address, said everything was fine except a stupid leg, where was he—surely not on that damn farm? And write! He answered it before lunch. The next morning, the waiter needed to push twice at the distant kitchen door, limped over a very great part of the floor toward them, turned at right angles to take an admiral his ham, did so, stood quite still to ponder where he was, let the tray tilt frighteningly, was distracted by a raised finger in a remote province of the room, seemed surprised to remember them, approached so they heard the teaspoons shiver by the cups, and set down a tray with toast and coffee and a letter that reached up and tore the November sky apart. Victoria took one loopy page to be worried, proprietorial, bossy, indignant, and fond at once. Alistair knew two things there and then. He had only to tell Victoria exactly what had happened, give her time to read it, and go to Venice. And that the first would be the most difficult thing he had written yet.

He wrote the letter during the three days they took to bury Maggiore, a car and driver to the Val D'Aosta. Colonel the Baron GianCarlo d'Issogne would lie with his fathers until spring under the Val D'Aosta snow. The difficulties with the body had been brief. Such friends as Prince Moro helped. The funeral would be private. Anna knew it as an honor extended in grace to her that she would be there. The body awaited in a sealed casket. There would be military honors after all, one bugler, three riflemen. There was no suggestion that the casket or anything about it would be opened, ever.

Anna had looked at her son with her most limpid eyes. "I should do more," she said.

He gave no sign back.

"I am one foreign woman," she said. "It would become my life. And I think it would fret GianCarlo's spirit more than heal it."

He nodded. He thought that GianCarlo's being shot by the wrong uniform had importance but limited weight. He had not thought that with Angelo at the brigade, but he thought it now. He believed that his stepfather had done everything he could for his own case by not kneeling, whatever not kneeling meant in a particular time and place, which in his stepfather's instance had meant just that, not kneeling.

An hour in the car took them from the war zone for the first time since Venice. A little longer and they were beyond the sound of guns, then beyond the possibility of guns, for the first time since Rome. Lombardy lay in hard winter. Farm courts and campaniles stood brick square on black earth. Life kept to the dooryards of houses and barns, feeding cattle, tending fires. Disaster had no evident lodgment here. The girl with the basket of eggs coming back to the house, she half ran, cold pushing at the small of her back and the crimson shawl around her breast flying loose, had no shadow reaching toward her. They were beyond the country of the plague. The plague could shift its borders silently, swiftly, and at any time it chose. Since he had no idea that it moved by divine grace, this was close to heresy, but it was what he thought.

At Maggiore's manor, which she knew every angle of and had never seen, Anna walked toward his daughter as tall as to an execution. Italian women are not always kind. But Maggiore's daughter knew what weapons she carried and kept them sheathed. She seemed curious about Anna, which she hid well, but was grave and gracious and had her father's eyes. The two women stood together, very far apart. The little boy, in stiff new black, looked round-eyed at the estate that now was his. The echoes of the bugle wavered on the hills, and the rifle shots came back like stones. The car started them back across Italy to the spa. Both knew that they would not be there long. Alistair wondered if his mother would join them in Venice.

When all was said and done, what he wrote to Victoria was at a far reach but a discernible one, from what he had said to her in the gondola to the distant guns bearing her home when Venus lit the way. Late in 1917, he had no thought that the war had less than a year to run—in Italy, one battle. Very likely that a Fourth Age had been decreed, that the Age of Lead he had been born to had been withdrawn and an Age of Blood given them, so the war would go on until its origins were long forgotten. He himself would recover fully in time to be of age to die legitimately, go into somebody's army, and be killed. To think otherwise was to pluck at fates's sleeve and beg for coppers. One didn't do it.

He wrote entirely happily. He put down what had happened to them. It excused all silence, so that was that. He did not need to say how lucky he had been. The flu was known and feared now; in Venice, the traditional dance hall of plagues, known well. Victoria, respectful of love, would understand all about his mother. Writing to a woman, there seemed no edge in saying what he easily saw. His mother had a second bereavement, less easily owned to: an unquestioned beauty since girlhood, she now was flawed.

Then the joy. There wasn't much future, but there was certainly them. What her own letter had begun, the journey had fulfilled. The bones of the willows by the lake had colors in the afternoon sun that moved and followed the light, and when they broke the surface of the lake, it dimpled. The girl running with the eggs was beautiful, and if a shadow came one day behind her, it came in its own day, not this. The bugle and the shots rolled around the mountains, came back in farewell, and any mockery you heard was your own, because the sounds were pure. He had been given a resurrection, but no future. With the future fallen in, sunlight could pour into the room, though it would not last. What cannot have time can have only form. Form is art, and art is joy. So, writing now, my dear, we have to earn it. Not much we haven't done before: Titian, poetry, love. And Vipero will forgive me if I get another horse. We can't take for granted. Do you understand? She would. Trace the veins behind your hand, hear the tone behind your voice, drink what your eyes see in Titian's gold, know everything your body tells in love, and you to me, for me, in that completion something stands not needing time. And time, let us admit, my dear, is the air it cannot breathe. Will you? Yes, she would. All he had feared for her when they lived among solid shapes, she flying out over a precipice on a beam of thought, was right for just this age without time, she was bred for this, she'd come to him without flinching, with a swoop and cry. He finished his letter. His eye lifted to read it back. Not this one time, he told his eye, this is the invitation, not the dance. Just send it. He folded away the letter; the crease ran through his thumb. On the envelope, he wrote her name and Calle Caotorta, a last kiss. The atoms of the desk, the blackamoor, the torchere drifted back in place. He rang a bell and listened for the signature of the place, halting feet. When he put the letter in the proffered tray, he'd go outside. The sun would just be touching the willows.

THERE IS NO DOUBT from the first stanzas that the Tagliamento 'Cycle'—a word that Alistair Stears never used himself—are poems of the First World War. He had been composing them for a year, and they were not finished until late that winter, but if he had been able to go to his desk in pyjamas the next morning, he would have. As it was, the waiter became worried about him and bore aloft down the corridors a trilling and chirping of eager spoons which turned into coffee for Alistair and toast. But the smile the waiter got, some of which went all the way to his poor feet, was gratitude. Not so much for toast but the artist's gratitude for when elements for a long time stony begin to move with little urging. There was gratitude to Victoria for existing, in which there was a bracing dose of sex. A good thing, for someone virtually a corpse two weeks before.

This is the energy of Tagliamento, which survived into much darker weather. As he gave it a shape, there appeared in the far distance a thought of Vulcan's shield for Achilles, the mirror of peace and war. We visit landscapes, definite, but with the

Celtic quality of changing color and form, or smoke, or fire, in which figures, rather like Vulcan's, seem to go about their business, to be themselves and whole, then change as the landscape changes into archetypes of disaster: the murdered officer, the Umbrian girl. If they end demonic, it seems by no wish of theirs. Changed by what? In Tagliamento, what is missing is as striking as what is there. There is no No Man's Land, that dark entrail of the poems of the war. There is no anonymous dread foe. When Austrians appear, they, too, are menaced as the land itself by stumbling monsters too blind even to tell them apart. A journal as of war, it could be as well a journal of weather or of plague. The enemy is not human. To a Catholic, other choices appeared.

In sound, in form, in tone, Tagliamento is quite unlike Brooks, Blunden, Sasoon, the English canon. The lines are quick and allusive, concealing emotion like the brush strokes of the Japanese. The thing is sometimes gone past before it is seen; what began as blue has ended as scarlet.

WHILE THESE POEMS were being accomplished, Anna and her son dined together, coincided sometimes at breakfast, passed each other by accident during the day. They were the closest of friends. Mother and child was over since her wound. She gathered that Alistair intended to be in Venice, whether she went or not. Her own thoughts were long, tentative, necessarily sad. She felt that she had to deal with a new self she was barely acquainted with.

Since service at dinner was inordinately slow, as though they were the only passengers on an ocean liner, they did not think it rude to bring letters to the table. Anna always had several, most from Rome, some from Boston, a few from Venice. The other rule at dinner was to keep each other's spirits up, not difficult for Alistair in just these days.

She put down a letter from Boston. The gilt at the bottom of their soup bowls glistened additionally with a film of consommé, now entirely cold.

"They are locking everybody up over there," she said. "Especially Italians. One expected better of a Virginian somehow. Don't they all ride to hounds?" She meant President Wilson.

This was not one of Alistair's interests. "Do you suppose the service here is to encourage digestion or to wean one entirely from the thought of food?"

"Given what it is when it comes, the latter," she said. "Look, it may be coming now." The kitchen door was making motions, like the wing of an injured bird. "But I have time for a letter, I should think." She picked up one from Venice, with a beautiful Italian stamp, a lily. The waiter this time pushed a trolley, and the spoons behaved. He was quite close when she seemed to find a ghost in the letter, looked shocked, looked at Alistair, and put it down. Gnocchi was on the trolley, leaden, he knew. He saw her expression; she often came upon memories of Maggiore in letters. He tried to walk very softly around them, for he was deeply sorry for her.

"The gentleman in the bathchair is trying to become close, I think," he said. "Yesterday he looked at me, and just now I swear he nodded his head."

"Oh yes," she said.

It turned out that they talked of Mr. Conrad, the English Pole, whom they had both begun to read, and liked, and swapped his books. The eventual guinea fowl was much better than one might have thought, and they did have the wine, a nice Barolo. In the long calm before dessert, the bathchair was taken away. In a far province, the Admiral of Ham deboned his bird with vigor.

Anna said, "I can't do this, Alistair." She picked up the letter from Venice in long fingers like scissors. The pretty stamp showed on top of them. "Alistair, I have to give this to you. This paragraph." She heard in herself her old tone to the wounded, amended it, sat up straighter, and so did her voice. "I have no preamble worth the giving." She held out the letter. "I am most terribly sorry." He unfolded it.

"Poor Victoria," she said.

He knew her last breath, for it had been his, but one. When his throat had relented, hers had tightened. He knew the terror of that, when the mind had given up everything else. Before the mind gave up, he knew the shame at the body's mutiny. He walked most of the night, though dressed for dinner, and tried to sit against a tree, but it was too cold.

The letter was from an American in Venice asking about the lay of things in Rome. He added, "Rather curious man Schrauler, who lives at the Gritti. One must feel sorry for him. His daughter caught the flu and died, of course. Quite a lot of us went to the funeral. The first of us, but it seems Venice may not be healthy, and I should like to ask . . ." So the seed of this was very small—a cough on a vaporetto, the breath next to hers before a painting. It was clear from the date that he had sent a letter to a corpse.

He went into Anna's room the next morning.

"Can we get out of here before we both go mad?" he said.

"I do have a thought," said Anna.

He did not stop working. This was not heroism. The poem that had come to life in those four days of sun was evidently the only thing he owned himself and perhaps Victoria's last possession. It was merely a fact that his would have been the last face she thought of. He tried to remember how late into that dark Victoria had stayed with him. He could not remember, but thought it was quite close before the end. Perhaps he had pulled her in.

Anna's choice was good: Stresa, the very edge of Italy, almost Switzerland, the Grand Hotel des Isles Borromées, overlooking the toy island and the toy lake.

"For I take it we are going home," said Anna. "And you'll go to Harvard."

"Right now I need to go to Rome," he said. "But that is not difficult." She nodded.

"I need to talk to Eminence," he said. This was their name for the cardinal he had met the very first days in Rome, the most astonishing of all the astonishing things for a young Boston boy. He had learned, as astonishment simply climbed its ladder, that the cardinal had literally been his grandfather's savior once. And now, four years later, Alistair's own master, apparently his taskmaster for some unseen time to come, and very nearly his confessor.

"Eminence is a friend but not the only priest," said Anna.

"He is the only Eminence," said Alistair.

"I suppose I shall not stop you," said Anna. And sighed.

There was almost no sense of the war here. Their rooms looked out over the lake, and the Italian naval launch was patently a toy. There was an American bar at the hotel, dark wood and ice and bottles. He had last seen such a thing at the Gritti. He was sure he should have foreseen her peril, had known it his last sight of her, had heard the cataract and thought she was safe. At the bar and at dinner were a young American and his wife or girl, pregnant he thought and English he was sure. He was certain the American had been in the war. He wanted badly to talk to them. He felt less lonely with them in the room. That first night he saw no way to do so graciously. He looked for them in the morning, but they had left. The hotel was unsettled. A boat belonging to the barman had been stolen in the night. There were police around. But he liked to think of the man and his girl and their baby. All the day after that he spent on the train through Milan to Rome. At Milan, walking to the Rome Express, he walked past the platform of the train to Venice. He had no desire to see her grave there and knew that he never would. The train was full of Carabinieri.

So, climbing into a Pullman of the Parigi-Roma express, warm and rich with cigar, he found himself now again as though he had left his skin behind, as in those old days, the uprooted Boston boy for whom everything in Rome was frightening, delicious, and utterly strange. *And why not?* He thought. *I was a poet then.*

His mother had said, "Dress for a palace, Alistair. We are going to see a man of great importance to us. A prince of the Church. It will be a lovely drive, in our lovely carriage."

She wore, he saw, a veil the color of mist with breaths of smoke. Through the mist, but only in certain lights, flew across her temple the ghost of a small swan.

Around the great window, an exultation of larks flew in frieze. Beyond it were flat-topped pines and bits of the road they had driven up, rather dusted by furiously overtaking motors, where it crossed the side of small hills lined with vines. An hour's drive below, the city of Rome and the dome of St. Peter's received the October morning light. From before the window, in a chair that denied it was a throne, Juan August Cardinal Galisteo said to Alistair's mother, "But I remember you better than that, my child. I remember you quite well."

The eyes rested on Anna's face in its veil like autumn mist, and Alistair wondered if they could see the swan. He could hardly expect his mother to flirt with a cardinal.

"The day of the first fox hunt, when your father let me bless the dear hounds." At the let me, *Anna perceptibly bowed in her chair, and the autumn mist registered a smile inside.*

"You wore a blue habit. You rode a grey, a dappled grey, in an English bit. You rode him very prettily, although he was overexcited by all the other horses. To tell the truth, you were the most noticeable person there. They would not let you follow the hounds that day. I thought it nonsense. Young people rarely come to much harm on a hunt. Your horse would have quieted down."

Indeed the room, the villa, were full of horses. It was as though a manege had broken into a church. Between the crucifixes and the pious paintings and even a memento mori *were crowded canvasses of horses, defiant and alone, flowing down race courses, wild-eyed, kind-eyed, supporting officers of cavalry, in the midst of packs of hounds falling on snarling game.*

Anna said, "My father charges me to carry to your Eminence his deepest gratitude and respect. He says that the kindness you did him in his hour of need is beyond repayment." Which should have sounded like a book, Alistair thought, except it sounded like a song as his mother and the Italian words played together.

Even Galisteo savored their warmth. "We must defend our children in the northern lands. Especially in England. Especially in England's Ireland. Your father's service to us was exemplary, given his loyalty to his own service, which I respected entirely. That end to it should not have happened. And his grandson is here." He turned to Alistair and looked at him entirely without haste, as one would look at a horse or a vase. One was expected to recognize authority. One was not expected to recognize pain. There was pain behind those eyes, and it rose and fell like an uneven flame. Alistair saw it and almost flinched.

But, after all, only a platitude was offered. "And how do you like Rome, my son?"

He would have answered easily, platitude for platitude, but the pain had startled him, and he heard himself say, "I do not think I know it, sir. I have seen only the surface, like a painting. I do not know it, your Eminence."

He was looked at again, until the eyebrows rose a very little, and he did not know if that were for show. The cardinal turned back to his mother. "And his grandson is here," he said.

His mother said, "He is my son before he is his grandfather's grandson."

"Of course." The cardinal's hand rinsed anything otherwise from the air. A little more sharply, "You have remained in the faith, my child? I know you married outside it." More sharply still, "For some reason."

"Yes, your Eminence. My son also. That entirely." The sharpness had been parried. "There is no question of that."

The conversation afterwards did not have much for him: his mother's enthusiasm for her art, her hopes for it, her sitation (a woman's, so nebulous) with the American Academy of Rome, her need for a confessor—all quite a different life from the pretty young girl on a horse at the hunt, but the cardinal seemed to know about it already. He imagined there were things unsaid because of him. One noticed much that one was not encouraged to cogitate. His problem was manners: how to be fascinated by all those horses and not gawk. Then a matter far easier to be appallingly rude about than horses. Legs.

The cardinal's legs were richly covered, but, and one could not look, there seemed almost nothing inside the cover. What there was did not seem to be, one could not look, the right shape. There were no feet. The throne, if it was one, was not high, but no feet were on the floor. None above it. The covering was not long enough, one could not look, for legs and feet.

So the pain, a dark imp, was out there, and could be seen, like a demon driven forth in an old painting. But how, what? It was a story his grandfather must know. A terrible riding accident? Did cardinals hunt? The horses, memories of a different day? His mother must know.

The eyes were back on him. He was still examined, but this time there was interest, there might have been humor, and, he did believe, friendship.

The cardinal said, "I am your host in Rome. Your mother also is, of course, but I say this to you. I am a remnant of a rather old Rome, and you are very young. My house is yours, also my library. I am told that you are studious, and that you ride as well as your mother rode. There is no better balance. I shall be disappointed if I do not see you."

Alistair bowed and began to speak, but the bow and the speech were returned to him, unopened.

"I think you know that you have heard echoes this morning of stories you did not know. I leave it to your mother to tell you the substance, as she sees fit. What I want you most truly to understand is that your grandfather was my friend. Your grandfather could see. That is what made him so good at what he did. What he really did, though that also as yet is for your mother. You will come back here, please. You will come here to study or to talk, or for council, or even for my worn out old memories. I do not leave this villa."

And now Alistair bowed with pleasure and grace and said that it was his honor to comply. He was almost stopped in the midst of saying it by the certainty, He saw me see the imp.

And now, in the Pullman, and considering even a cigar for himself, though it would have been his first, he let himself remember the first telling—his mother not very willing—of his grandfather's story. It was necessarily theirs, too, in point simply of family. In the years that he had known it, reinforced by every meeting with his master, the cardinal, he had come to think that the story of the cardinal and his grandfather had an architecture that had to do with him, and that his master held it jealously. He held the scene back until the dome of Parma's cathedral rolled from left to right on country as flat as a billiard table.

Back in the landau, within the forest of orange trees that immediately surrounded the villa, his mother said, "That was an order. To me. His Eminence deals in them. Can you imagine what these oranges are in bloom, or fruit. I do not have to, for I have seen them." She said, "And I think he is right, Alistair. What I am about to tell you is not known in Boston, as I believe. But it is still known here, a little, and usually inaccurately. You know that your grandfather was military attache in Rome. That was my girlhood and a very great part of why we are here."

He nodded and allowed himself a frown, to show there was more, surely.

"And what you know is right, but not entirely right. Your grandfather was in charge of British secret intelligence for southeastern Europe. Italy. Austria-Hungary. The Balkans. Turkey. Rome was convenient and safe for him. Apparently he was very good at what he did, of which I of course knew nothing then and very little now. And then he retired, as is normal. He retired a little early, for Ireland was going through one of the many convulsions the English visit on us, and he felt his position called him to Irish politics. He was allied with Mr. Parnell, who was an old friend. I imagine you have heard of him. He does not matter very much anymore, and he is dead.

And then nothing. And then, "Eminence really is a part of the old Rome. Which I knew, but only as it ended. You would be very foolish not to take up his . . . kind offer. He is the head of Vatican intelligence, as is no secret at all. It is undoubtedly the most efficient such service in the world. Your grandfather most certainly knew him very well, quite outside of horses. Part of your grandfather's effectiveness in this part of the world was that he is Catholic, very unusual in a British official of that kind. Do they really have to overtake so rudely?" For the landau was clearly in the way, now on this main road, and motors were gnashing their gears, and striving past, and cutting in not nicely at all. "I suppose my pretty carriage is part of the old Rome too."

He watched her fingers. She said, "The Irish church turned against Mr. Parnell. I will not bore you with why. There are times when I do not admire our church. Your grandfather turned to Rome, for Dublin will bow to Rome, surely. Of course, he turned to Cardinal Galisteo, his friend and to an extent colleague. Galisteo asked him questions, the answers to which he knew from the British service. He answered. Dublin did not change its mind, or Rome did not try hard enough. The British heard of your grandfather's indiscretion, which was not, which was never, ever, Alistair, faithless or treacherous. No matter. To the English it was a crime and a serious one. There was a warrant for his arrest. Galisteo got word of it. He warned, and he helped. Your grandfather fled. That is the only word. A fishing boat to Spain, and then a steamer, La Coruna *to Boston. And that is why I met your father. And that is you, my darling son. And that is Cardinal Galisteo. For good or ill. And, yes, I think your grandfather was his friend. Do you understand?"*

He said, "I think so, Mamma." And realized that, now, he could have amended his first answer to the cardinal just a little bit.

Even in Rome, the air was cool and fresh after the Pullman and increased his wish, theological as much as bodily, that he had not found a cigar. The air was gentle, as is common before Christmas. For the first time, Galisteo received him in a chair by the open window. A robe hung more casually than usual over his cheated, twisted legs. Alistair made obeisance, although to his friend. Even the room had become his friend. It was the first great room Alistair had known beyond their own palazzo in the days in Rome. And Mr. Featherstonhaugh might be his tutor on earth, but the cardinal was his higher one.

At Alistair's full obeisance, touching one knee to the ground, the cardinal smiled and moved his hand toward his head but did not quite touch it, then motioned him to the chair set near. In the garden below them, the orange trees bore fruit.

"They are rather extravagant people," said Galisteo, passing the same hand through the air above them, "but it seems churlish to ignore them. They go to so much trouble." And indeed, saying *look at me* out of the leaves, the oranges were preposterously gorgeous.

Though this time with his back to the room of painted horses, Alistair felt them just as present. This time, he understood them. However posed, they were horses, never a circus act for long, and as horses they comforted him and filled him, as though he could smell and hear them feed. When he left the villa, after an obeisance more formal for being to a friend, he felt that a curtain had dropped behind him, easy to cross but muffling the past.

xxx

He drank wine with his mother in her sitting room before dinner the next day. It was nearly dark. The lake and the sky and the fir trees on the mountains were one and the same slate so that by the window, one could seem to float. A Champagne bottle in a cooler between them anchored it all. It was not festive, but it was civilized.

"Not Harvard," he said. "West Point. I have decided."

"That is not odd in your family," said Anna. She spoke levelly, but he heard her take a sharp breath. "In you, though, it seems a little odd. And sudden."

"The thought is not," he said. "The solution may be. I do not need Harvard. Harvard and I would bicker. West Point is American and has something to teach me. And a civilian is nothing now. And an officer always has a trade. West Point or the navy, one."

She said, "There were ships' commanders in your family. But that was really a long time ago. When the Danes were our enemy. We've been soldiers since." She gave that up. "You have decided. Immediately after seeing Eminence. So it's a penance."

"Not a penance," he said.

"You do not owe a penance because your girl died, Alistair. I could say that if anyone owes a penance, it's Someone Else. I could say it very easily because I've thought it for myself, but it is blasphemy, so I won't say it." All the terrace lights went on of a sudden. They were no longer floating in space but in a hotel room. She threw her head back at the change and said, "West Point, as I understand it, is not easy to get into. Your father has no contacts there. The president of Harvard would write for you, I imagine."

"Cardinal O'Connor will give his full support. That is sure."

She said, "You went to Galisteo in grief and confusion over a girl, and he snapped you up and gave you marching orders."

Alistair smiled, sat up straighter, changed which leg was crossed over which, offered her wine, and poured for himself. The smile was for the offered wine and did not linger.

"When Victoria was alive," he said, "I was going into the war as a common soldier when the time came, expecting death. Eminence told me not to waste myself. That was the only order. He pointed out that profligacy is a sin. So far, I would think you would agree, Mamma."

She breathed out with a sound, like a smoker. "So far, yes. There's always a 'so far' with Galisteo."

"He also told me that the Tyrone service to our faith goes back a very long way. Elizabeth and Essex, even. You never told me that."

She spoke now with little inflection and a straight eye, as though looking at Galisteo over a sword blade.

"Not wishing to glorify it. Your ancestors were fighting a naked and all but heathen conqueror. With what they had. As with the Danes. You have nothing to do with that."

"'America,'" he said. "Yes, I'm quoting, 'is a nascent empire and all its power is Protestant. To that degree it is England carried over. The Catholic nobility and gentry must be nurtured in the one as in the other. And never wasted.' With West Point, if I live through this war, I could have value. I'm my grandfather's grandson, just in a different place. And, after all, Manfredi's lived through it. Almost for sure." He smiled, and this smile stayed.

"Galisteo," she said, "never said anything really stupid in his life. That's the trouble. Are you going to give up writing?"

"Oh no," he said. "That was never thought of. There is also value there. That is taken for granted. He said I should I finish what I'm doing first. He said that anyway I still look awful and no army would take me. He even had a priest bring me a mirror. He's right. I hadn't noticed. He said I probably hadn't looked in a mirror made by Benvenuto Cellini before. He spoke of the spring. We can stay here. And that way you don't have to sail in the winter, Mamma."

She looked up in piety. "Dear God," she said, "to think of absolutely everything. And be a prince of the Church. And live on top of orange trees. What hath God wrought? How lovely it must be."

"Actually, I was the one who thought of the winter sailing, Mamma," said Alistair.

"Sweet babe," she said. She got up, swinging her legs out of the chair, and smoothed her long dress over her hips. At such times she stood often with her elbows out and her hands on her waist, but the bad arm now hung stiff.

"Shall we go down to dinner?" she said. "I think it's safe. I don't think there's anything really awful left to happen. Right this minute."

He finished his Champagne, nodded, and got up himself. "It's not the spa," he said, "is it, thank God? We can *have omble chevalier* here. Or hare again. It was a lovely mirror. Horses, obviously."

"I don't really mind West Point," she said. "I don't mind that."

MANFREDI SAID, "NOT THE girl at Florian's, Alistair?"

Alistair nodded.

Manfredi said, "Oh, that's awful, Alistair." He looked down and slightly sideways at the bandaging and splinting of his knee. He seemed to have a made a habit of sitting with his crutch beside him, his hand extended up to its pad, so he looked to be about to rocket up like a pheasant at any moment. Now he slowly lowered his hand to Alistair's shoulder. "A girl like that. That's as bad as anything I've heard. And you liked her a lot."

Alistair nodded again.

"What's to say?" said Manfredi. "People go. I heard about you, but only after you came through, thank God. I'd never have heard about her. We used to think people were here forever. Now you look around and they're gone. I'm so sorry."

They sat in silence a while. Manfredi's hand crept back up the crutch. They were in a sort of reading room of the officers' hospital near Bergamo. Through the window was a slice of lake, beeches and pines, and then the white Alps. There was a carpet and a wall of bookshelves with scrolled sides, and reading desks here and there in corners. They were not alone in the room, but they might as well have been. Manfredi's legs were cotton pants and bandages, but on top of that he wore a military jacket unbuttoned with a captain's bars and the ribbon of an Ufficiale del Ordine Militare di Savoia, which was even better than Alistair had hoped for him. He was in a deep leather chair, which would take him some trouble to get out of.

Manfredi said, "I did kill one man with my sword, Alistair. He was a gunner." He looked down. "A rifle may be cleaner. But I am glad that I have done it, once. I promised you . . ."

Alistair shook his head. "I'm going home for a little while. Though it's funny to call it 'home.' Our officers' school at West Point. I'll get in somehow. I'm going to fight in our army with a commission. It seems the only thing to do. So I'll have my own sword. But thank you, Manfredi."

"Keep my sword for now," said Manfredi. "It's a continuity. I like to think of an Italian sword at West Point. Bring it back when you come back to Italy."

"Well then," said Alistair.

Manfredi still had the deep tan of Alpine military exercises. Pain and stress had given his face shadows. He had moved along from Bronzino to Caravaggio.

"It is the right thing to do," said Manfredi. "A well-trained officer is what to be in this war, for yourself and everybody else. You'll be better trained than I was. I'm not sure I bow to the Anglo-Saxon armies. I don't think they could have done what our men did. But West Point and Sandhurst are serious. Well done, Alistair. You'll be a good officer. And you're in the war now." This was true. Today was December 12, and the United States had declared war on Austria-Hungary December 7. "So you can come back here as an officer."

"I'd like to think so. But I don't. I don't think we're going to fight here. Probably France. France I'm almost sure. But I'm not going until the spring."

"The spring?" said Manfredi. He smiled so his teeth showed then erased the smile and touched a finger to his mouth. He moved slightly closer to his friend. "Alistair," he said, "is it all right if I talk about Helene? After . . . ?"

"Oh yes," said Alistair. And said it freely, for he loved now to find that there were points of light here and there in the world.

"It looks like they're not invaliding me out," said Manfredi. "They say I'm going to get a little boy staff appointment with the Duke of Aosta. He's a friend of my father's, I expect is why." Alistair was fairly sure that the staff appointment would reflect Manfredi's age, yes, but also his obvious ability, his recent battle record, and his rank. "But I'm not going to be leading troops in the field ever again, that's clear as hell. So I thought, and I decided I could marry Helene now, and she said yes, and it's going to be at her parents' chateau in the spring because there doesn't seem to be the time there used to be anymore."

"That's fantastic," said Alistair. He did not know how much he smiled. "She's a terrific girl and she adores you."

Manfredi looked modest. "What I was coming to, Alistair, if it's still all right to ask, is would you be my best man? You'll have to stay until April 14. That's when they have daffodils at her parents' place. She wants daffodils."

There were daffodils. They were the first flowers he had noticed that year. A sitting room was added to his bedroom, and he wrote most of the day through the winter. He made himself take a walk of two hours each afternoon, up from the lake, to where snow indeed crunched under his boots. When the fall was fresh, his legs sank into it with a whisper and left his pants with a dust that turned sodden in the village. From time to time in his life, he would pin a medal to a poet whose work had just proved true. He did so to Keats one dark afternoon for "St. Agnes Eve":

St. Agnes Eve—Ah, bitter chill it was,
The owl for all his feathers was a-cold,
The hare limped trembling through the frozen grass,
And silent was the flock in wooly fold,

having seen a hare so, and, passing a hut, smelled sheep and heard only the faintest sound of breath and one soft stamp. The lights were on along the lake when he turned back.

When his tray for lunch was brought one day, a thick brown envelope was on it addressed in an unknown hand and with a stamp he recognized as English. There were three letters he had written to Mr. Featherstonhaugh, so long ago that they still had lived in Venice. With them was a letter to him. Mr Featherstonhaugh had never reached Alexandria. His ship had been torpedoed in the Bay of Biscay. He was not among the saved. Alistair read his own earliest letter. It was still much about late Latin poets. He and Victoria had discovered the Byzantine paintings of the church of Santi Maria e Donato on Burano island. She had brought a picnic that day, he recollected. Mr. Featherstonhaugh must have died in sight of Trafalgar, the letter said. It was from his brother, who appeared to be a priest in England. *He was fond of you, and spoke of you when I last saw him. Sorry this has all taken so long.*

His application to West Point seemed to progress. It was well supported. Cardinal O'Connor was most helpful.

The manuscript of Tagliamento was sent off to London and New York on March 27.

The flu that had made him its childhood playmate grew and began to kill more than the war. He was apparently one of the safest on earth in this regard; he could bowl his hoop over the plague pits, picnic in the hospitals.

The Austrian army attempted a breakout from its winter position and failed.

He became friends of the hotel staff. The barman told him in the end that the young American had been fleeing the Italian military police and had escaped with the girl up the lake to Switzerland. That was the whole story of the boat. *So there was one they hadn't got,* thought Alistair.

So, daffodils, and Helene was a very pretty bride, to make the heart smile or weep. Manfredi, in uniform of course, seemed very slightly awkward in France. His mother and the marchesa embraced, long ago girlfriends in Rome. He caught a glimpse of Manfredi's little sister, Ottavia, the gargoyle of Capri. She would not be a real little girl much longer. She must have recognized him, for she waved at him across a room.

The honeymoon was to be in Lisbon. He embraced Manfredi at the end. In that moment, as their cheeks parted and they shook hands, he realized that Manfredi was gone, that he could no longer see him, that Manfredi came out of a dark place, out of a cave of monsters, whence he himself had escaped only two days before with a filling of his lungs he had not understood, and where he would never, ever go again.

April or no, Cherbourg had leaden sky, which descended to the sea. Walking on the promenade, not warmly enough dressed, he saw the mist seem to thicken and then divide and sharpen, and realized that he saw two Royal Naval destroyers that sailed briefly into the land of the living and then sank back. He thought that might reassure his mother, who certainly still thought secretly of the *Lusitania,* and went back to the *Normandie* to tell her. They already had their staterooms. They would sail in a few hours. He had decided he might like France. It might be Europe, but it was certainly not Italy.

He did not see much of it. He stood at the stern as they sailed, but the sky swallowed Cherbourg almost before they passed the breaker.

His lost Serafina is not recognizable in the Stears canon, unless she is everywhere. There is no doubt that Victoria is in Tagliamento. She concludes it. A creature we have not felt before is there at the end, with a motion that is new, soaring between darkness and light. It is not clear that she settles on one or the other. She does not heal. But what is left seems to have its own being again, to live with as it can.

It was, after all, written with her pen.

PART II

9

Chestnut leaves slippery on the sidewalk of the Rue de Sevres. Chestnuts roasting on the corner of the Boulevard St. Germain, odorous bright hearth in the united grey of walls, sky, and street. Chestnut the skirt of Alistair Stears's camel coat hastening to Alistair's townhouse in the Rue de Furstemburg, to Alistair's lady, Nancy, to Alistair's promise to take her to the flower show. His watercolorist's delight. Rain past, rain future, rain not present. Happiness of chestnuts pushed aside by paper damp at the edges from the newspaper stand at Mabilon. Woe on Wall Street. Nineteen twenty-nine, all's wrong with the world. Committee meeting thoughts bilious as Paris news in Alistair's head: another prize for Ford Maddox Ford, politic, but not what he had wished.

He's late. He opens the front door, lacquered sea-green set in clean grey stone, and sees her coat and handbag in the hall. Nancy is at once on the stairs. Anger is quite beyond her, to be irritable a mighty task, but she is the littlest bit miffed, and her light fair hair, blue eyes, and Amherst cheeks light up the room but do not warm it.

"It's only that's it's not that long before it closes," is her greeting, but, quickly down the stairs, she puts her arm in his. His lips to those cheeks bring linden blossom to his nose.

"I did order the car," she says, and Denis the driver, peaked cap and boots, brings it before they are through the door.

Out of the conservatory came a throng. In went late drips and drabs, like them. "Really, Alistair!" said Nancy, for her incandescent rage. Inside it is warm, of course, forced flowers, and still quite full. Conservatory architecture, the dusk already black above the lights inside, but merriment in the cast-iron work, somewhat like the Metro. The evening had the delight of the artificial done well, ladies ably dressed, Champagne on trays, waiters who knew how to give the trays a semblance of lazy flight. The conversation was content and mannered. The smells of the flowers themselves, a chorus and no solo, dispersed in the general air of ladies. Their roots and earth added a base note ignored, like civet in a floral scent, of dark and want. It was a treat for Nancy. Most of her work was portraits of children, for which she had acclaim. Her joy was a sparse Cape Cod meadow, wild flowers spinsterish but with supple spines and bright eyes that her brush understood. The far other end of the spectrum was here, peonies, violets, paperwhites wistful for Christmas, orchids, all forced—the point, of course—by regimes of heat and light. She brought no colors, but a sketch pad. He liked to watch her work, but just then they were approached by friends, he American, she French, Max and Chantal, a couple. A plan for dinner was made. Nancy never shifted her eyes and held a smile that said, *You're interrupting me, but I can manage*. The Brasserie Flo, then, not Heinegger's, just a trace of the slum, another scent of earth, fit frame for two women each with most of the bonds of wife but still the woodland scent of mistress.

When they came out, it was dark. The pearl of the edge of clouds in city light sailed off to the east above them, but it was surely a break only, not the end. They went home to dress, the flower show being a daytime event, though they had arrived late. The house on Place Furstembourg was ample. His bathroom had dark wood and brass, *style Monsieur*. He showered and thought of walking in on hers, Lalique lights and swans engraved in the corners of the mirror, chance of a dropped towel, kiss a toothpaste mouth, thought better. Nancy did not much like such goings on, more endured them with a smile. They were on time at Flo.

Not a frivolous dinner. Max Peters, long upper lip between cheeks becoming broad, figure still with the poise of tennis but going stout, eyes one might say puffy but still a wise retriever's, was on the board of the magazine Alistair half owned. Much of America's best writing was done in Paris, so why not publish here, and not New York? Their magazine's big fish this quarter was Conrad Aiken. The pleasure of that fact was reflected in oysters and Chablis. They were, however—the last oyster shell dropped rattling in the ice—a little short on material. If they could have Alistair's last? No. Why? If the point is to publish in Paris, why send his work to New York?

To publish in your own magazine is like crochet work. Said it before. Won't do it.

Max Peters leaned to him. "Translation, Alistair," he said. "I wish you would. Italian. French. Latin. You and Ezra are the erudite ones. No one can do a line like you. I wish you would. If you did, could we have that?"

Nancy smiled at Max, for she agreed.

Thought and smile touched his heart, small chilly points.

He smiled. "Translation is a little different. Maybe," he said.

He brushed the bill toward himself. Max and Chantal did not have much. They walked from the table. His coat was offered to his shoulders. The fairer of two women put her arm in his.

As much as anything in their waking life, he loved to watch her in the night.

Though cool as a primrose, Nancy was affectionate in her way and generally slept against him. Raised in the Berkshires, sent off to a school of chill and Cream of Wheat, she could barely feel any cold—against him, none. He could freely pull the sheet down. He supposed a man could live as a constant entity, a bridge support against which the water foamed or trickled. In a woman, he was sure that would be close to death. He loved the changes in women, their daily re-makings, but loved most the ones secret even to themselves. She was painting a child here tomorrow. She would breakfast in her smock. From studio to drawing room to love to sleep seemed to him a handsome and harmonious order of changes. When her nostrils whinnied gently, he squeezed her tummy for it, in salutation, but also gently, not to wake her. Her skin was as smooth and firm as their Pratese sheet, the only thing of Italy in the house.

The child she painted liked a flopsy hat. She painted on the top floor, in summer looking down upon a lawn of plane trees where they had built a skylight. The child's nanny would be in the servants' parlor. Were there a Mummy, she would be put in the morning room, for gravity of neither nurse nor mother was allowed to weight the face she painted. Nancy would be in sky-blue smock. Cut flowers would be around. Purity becomes a painter of babes. He, as ogre, was sent to his office.

Which he walked to down the Rue des Saints Peres, with its wrought iron balconies now changed to magic sugar by the morning's freezing fog. The light fog pleased him this morning. It kept joy and fear close into him, as when his thighs had closed around Vipero's saddle in the very early days, or on the few in his military service when he had gone forward into threat. There waited for him, their last day of reading, the galleys of his next to be published work. As on those older days, he observed. The street began to stretch its shoulders for the day. Fresh sawdust, bright as sunlight in the fog, poured from the shovel of a waiter as Breton fisherman by a brasserie door. The waiter's hands were Breton blue from cold, and salt and iodine came from the oyster barrel he spread the sawdust around. Max Peters could not know that, wisps and shades aside, the path beyond these galleys was empty. Tail straight up walked the stationer's cat, twice around his doorsteps. If Alistair Stears had abdicated, it was to his own honor, to no mob.

As his office drew near, he thought of his writing desk, dark wood, Limousin oak more than a century old. Over its grain, pencils floated on their octagonal shades, but no pen, for his Pelikan was always with him. There was a single framed watercolor, wild grasses in seed, almost sere but with a lingering green wash. It came from Nancy's thinnest brush. He thought it the best thing she had ever done and had claimed it the moment it was dry. Nearer was his writing pad, half full of lines and arrows and loops. Nearest of all, a pile of galley proofs.

He allowed galleys one hour a day. He was rigorous. West Point had led him to where grief and dissolution had already pushed, toward himself as the perfect professional. His sanity had survived and some of his heart. Craft had become to him like an emplacement wall as shelter. He read these poems with as much care as when he first had set them in line. They were nearly living their own lives now. For this brief time, he could still massage a joint that seemed stiff, resolve a doubt within. He searched and did not find. They stood at the far end of a progress he had followed for eight years. Like little sea shells, they were perfect. Tagliamento ended here in geometry engraved in obsidian. The voice was spare. Silence lay beyond.

He heard this silence with the joy of a cold, clear dawn. The expiation of Tagliamento was complete. He had tamed the shamamic language through which he had woven blood and love into patterns of his own devising, not theirs. The exultation in blood and pain, thus waste, thus sin, was repented of. He had written now in perfect form nothing but the poor bare truth.

The poems would take away with them the last light he had to give. He had known that long before they came back to him in this form. He had written them nursing what he had known to be a dying light with skill that the light in morning had neither known nor asked for. He read with perfect contentment. He felt cold. He indeed this one morning had not turned the gas stove up. He was this morning stripped of the warm overcoat of language he had worn since youth. He needed warmth. He would like coffee. Maybe brandy and a human voice. He rose. He put Victoria's Pelikan back in his pocket and sustained suddenly the thought that it, her shade, might come to scorn him now. He put on his mere material coat of camel, put the galleys in a careful pile for Mlle Prudence to mail, and left.

Human voice—talk about the races at Auteil, therefore about horses, therefore he listened—warmed him no longer than his coffee lasted. He liked better, admiring care, the shoo-shoo of the barman's cloth on the counter's zinc and the silver glow that followed it. He drank half his brandy. He went back out of the cafe onto the Rue Lobineau.

He went to the Pont Neuf. Dry, golden October being long past, the Seine was high and the stern of the Ile de la Cite seemed to dash forward through the waves. He loved a busy river. If he had nothing else left, he had skill, consummate skill, skill like a well-trained footman, clothes still neat, to knock at doors until it found a worthy master. The busier wind pulled at the skirts of the camel coat, the gold of the leaves of weeks ago. He was glanced at there, mainly by women, who saw a containment one could perhaps unwrap, with fingertips. He was aware of this, and a very quiet laughter rose inside him, moving his lips, as though the fingertips had had effect. Lonely nobility by the Seine was a toy that Alistair, after all, could play with.

ONE MORNING, DARKER AND Christmas still not glimmering, he left his office for the Jardins de Luxembourg. In the gardens, the grass was brown, creepers like old ropes, leaves a slime on the paths, but there were still the shapes of noble trees and mighty carp in the ponds. He stood to watch them. He felt the air raw on his face and set against it the warmth and scent of food of the Closerie de Lilas twelve minutes away. *Brandade,* in this cold weather, soufflé of salt cod.

He loved bravery in women. So he had one first-rate reason for being involved with Sylvia Beach's bookstore, and that was Sylvia Beach. That the nose under those brave eyes could bring to mind a misplaced parsnip and that the hands were made to hold onto a bun until the slim wrist snapped made him only more admiring. Red light on the Closerie de Lilas's dark wood and brass made his back smile with warmth after its cold walk. He sat turned slightly sideways. The luncheon had turned out to be about her ways of lending money to poor writers. There was her own accountant, who was French in a suit much like an umbrella case and squashed, at the trouser ankles, by the mark of bicycle clips. There was her American banker from the Paris branch, whose ex-patriotism had liberated him into a loose tweed coat and who could have used the accountant as a walking stick. There was a man who seemed to represent Mr. Joyce, for some reason, a Mr. Beckett. Alistair loved the master and honored the man. The brandade on Alistair's plate had been reduced to shallow lines of mush, elliptical, for he had played with them.

The banker enlarged himself from chest to cheeks, as though to sum up. He summed up.

"Just a little more method, Sylvia. See what you've got before you lend. Let Monsieur Clochod see it first. Be sure what they can really pay. Send them round to me; we're good at that. We know it's all about the Great American Novel, Sylvia. Just a little method. Not so off the cuff." He caught sight of his own graciousness and beamed. M. Clochod pursed his lips. Mr. Beckett went on looking at the floor and now sighed. Alistair saw the slate in the back of Sylvia Beach's eyes harden a little and rejoiced.

"But it does work rather nicely off the cuff," she said, looking at her own as though she had never seen it. "And they almost always pay it back, the poor dears." And she turned to Alistair.

"Of course," he said. And since he was the largest shareholder after the lady, that was that, more or less.

Pouilly-Fuisse rewarded chivalry. It was 1924, just the age for now—with a straight spine of manners and a golden heart, much like Miss Beach. Her generosity flowed up and down dim stairways across Paris, allowing poor American writers with pure ambition and scratchy skins to write of a world whose decay Alistair found unstoppable because the abscess was in its heart. A decade before, at the spa outside Brescia, he had imagined that the Age of Lead, his birthright, had been changed behind his back for the Age of Blood. He had been merely petulant about that, he thought now. The Age of Blood promised its own end in death, quite decent of it. Remove death, and the prospect was hideous. The busy ambitions in the smelly stairways would likely go on writing forever in a world every year cruder and more just. They made a coarse guffaw out of even his efforts, or Mr. Joyces's, or M. Proust's, or Conrad Aiken's. He did not care if Miss Beach lent them a dime. He did like her eyes. He hoped she was not paying for lunch.

A note from Mr. Beckett told him that Mr. Joyce thought it a long time between drinks. Perhaps he would join Mr. Joyce and his family at the Maison Prunier two evenings later. The note had been sent as a pneumatique, so replying was not only a joy, but, to Alistair, fun. Yes. Of course.

Mr. Joyce liked light. Liked light that made raven the headwaiter's coat and made soup plates cast the shadows of crescent moons upon the snowy cloth. Mrs. Joyce beside Alistair said that JJ had loved Nancy's sketch. It was so dear of her.

Nancy had done a scrawl for Mr. Joyce, just the angle of his hat, his cane, done large so he could see it.

Alistair said, *"Il capello non?"* The hat.

Yes, she said, but especially the walking stick.

He sat when he could by Mrs. Joyce, who seemed always pleased. He thought that she found him nearly as correct as her husband, and thus pretty decent, for a writer. He looked, however, toward Nancy with affection warmed by a little pride.

"E' carina, Signor Stears. Carina." She's a darling, Mr. Stears.

"Si," he said. Their Trieste Italian carried a note of Friuli and caressed his spine, a blade held lightly. He spoke Italian here in Paris only with the Joyces. To left and right, raven sleeves took up the soup plates. It was quite a grand place, as Mr. Joyce preferred.

Nancy sat by Miss Lucia Joyce, her contemporary and almost her friend. The Joyces had invited another guest, thus assuring Alistair that he would not have to pay for all the dinner. He was M. Larbaud, who owned the Vichy Spa, and Barbanooth the poet, on one chair, which sufficed also for Mr. Joyce's translator into French.

Nancy was telling M. Larbaud in French something about a perfect translation of Edward Lear . . . *"Une cuilière peu commune . . ."*

"Et l'anglais, Madame?" said M. Larbaud. What is it in English?

"A runcible spoon," said Nancy. "'They dined on mince and slices of quince which they ate with a runcible spoon.'" She elaborated, "You see, it's double. *'Runcible'* in English is '*peu commune*,' but the word is *peu commune* itself. I love it."

M. Larbaud said an appreciative round "Oh!" His mouth was well shaped for it.

None of this was as odd as it seems. The Joyces, except Lucia, had poor French and spoke Italian among themselves as much as English. M. Larbaud, or even Barbanooth, spoke almost everything. Nancy spoke no Italian. Flattered by such company, she was showing off her French, and why not, since it was excellent. Alistair liked to think that Mr. Joyce understood all human thought whatsoever, as a god should.

"Still, the very best thing has to be, *'En parlant des revolutions, a la guillotine!'*" said the god and bent his eye on Alistair with head cocked and a small smile. One could see the ghost of Nancy's hat on him. She really had got it right.

"Can anyone give me the English reference of that, I wonder?"

In silence, the soles endured their quartering.

"Oh," said Nancy. "It's the White Queen. Isn't it the White Queen? It's 'The world revolves on its axis' isn't it? And 'Speaking of axes, off with his head!' It's the French *Through the Looking-Glass*. Revolutions and guillotines for them, isn't it, not axes and Tudors. How clever of him!"

"A very admirable transference," said Mr. Joyce. "I would like to have done it myself." He saluted Nancy with the fingers that cushioned his cheek. "You are a clever watercolorist, Mrs. Stears," he said.

Mrs. Joyce beside him asked, "Staying for Christmas? Or the mountains?"

Nancy liked to ski. They had been to Davos twice for Christmas. He didn't really know. She had been a success and would be a happy girl tonight.

AT THE WINDOW OF a bistro, on the Rue Jacob near where she bought her paints, Alistair saw Nancy looking over into the window of Debauve et Gallais, the chocolatier whence he sometimes carried her a little box. It had burst out in gold now: a star wrapped so it glittered, Mary in golden gown inside a chocolate stable, a milk chocolate cow with golden horns, chocolate coins in sacks, and a lovely wise man lit up in crimson robe, golden turban, and a hawk-nose bitter chocolate face.

"I see children every day, and it doesn't 'specially make me think about making one. But I can miss them at Christmas," said Nancy, who was twenty-eight.

So Alistair decided they would go skiing after all.

They had left it late. The best hotels in Davos were full. He thought, *Zermatt,* and thought it again, and over this pleasant memory no claw reached out to scratch. He had been there, a child with his mother, before the last war. And it was a Catholic village, with a church porch where your responses could smoke on the air if the nave were full and a Virgin blessing an ice ax for the climbers. They had rooms at the Mont-Cervin. The first full night, they remembered how sweet skiing, and wine, and trusting arms can make a pillow.

Her body was young and healthy. She didn't get up much at night. But that night she woke him. There was a full moon over the snow, which her shoulder had kept out of his eye, but when she rose she let it in, a torrent. She left the room, but was soon back and went to the shutter to close it. Something caught her interest. She checked and turned her head. He heard hoofbeats and a sleigh's rasp, a shout perhaps drunken, another voice in warning. She was alarmed and pulled the shutter wider. Her shoulders drew back and deepened the crease in her spine. She bent forward. There was a jangle of harness, the hoofbeats thudded to a halt, the sleigh bells crashed and stopped. A voice in anger. She half turned on her right hip, her buttocks were awry, and the moon seized upon her breast. More voices, placating, boozy. What she saw now she thought funny. She bent forward, becoming Curiosity, and then all of a sudden became Modesty, with one arm to cover her breast. The voices seeped away, harness chimed, the hoofbeats picked up. Modesty became Exultation—was the street now empty?—and stretched her arms up the shutter, letting the chill bathe her body and looking out on the village and the hills, ivory nymph with golden loins. She shivered suddenly and clutched her arms around her chest, becoming Borea, and pushed the shutter to.

All night, in his sleepless brain, Nancy flickered and changed, as once, also in the moonlight long ago, a girl in Rome had shown him her art as model. Serafina. At breakfast he was all kim-kam. The coffee brought early to their room curdled in his throat. Waking up, he had looked over Nancy's sleeping head to a very old thought.

Do them, then, get on with it and do them. "*Them*" was Ovid's *Metamorphoses.* That got him up. But by breakfast the savor was gone. He gave a stupid answer to the ski-room servant asking what wax he wanted for the day. There was a shadow over him, an oath betrayed that he could not remember having sworn.

This was Christmas Eve. He went to late Mass so they could ski on Christmas. Having changed for dinner first, he was almost late, ran on the street, and found himself in the same place on the church porch as he'd sat with his mother fourteen years before. He thought of her with fondness and regret, as an old best friend he knew only by letters now. She lived alone in a manor farm house in the Berkshires, an old Stears holding. It was spacious and light, though her letters from it had a summer evening's electricity, crackly and edgy. When he'd last seen it, she had brought what she could of Italy to the gardens, but what she did or thought there now was hard for him to say. Kitty still ran her household.

All of this he held up in his head until communion rail, when he had to drop it and face his prayer for the souls of Manfredi's bride, Helene, and their firstborn who died with her a year after the wedding with the daffodils. With this came the recollection of Manfredi's voice on the telephone, and his own reply that as they were not close kin, there was no possibility of military leave, and he could not come. Manfredi's reply of course, of course had understood. He rarely entered this last cave of the dark valley.

Going back, he passed the Virgin blessing the ice ax, stopped a moment, and asked Her, please, to do something about them all, went out on the street into cold and lights and bells, and, with the sensation of pulling himself up by his hair, became the pleasant consort that Nancy, absolutely, deserved.

So Christmas had little time for Ovid, who tagged along anyway. Skiing to rhythms of verse was an old game for Alistair. Remembered lines got into the tempo of the new skiing, the christie turn, choppier now that Swinburne's loopy Telemarks had been in the past. He skied to Hexameters.

He could do the *Metamorphoses.* The labor would be terrific. He was not scared of that. It would need plateaus of time. He seemed to have it. The translation of a Roman poet would be seen by the world as the fit next step for a poet whose early passion had turned into glass. He couldn't have cared less.

He nearly didn't do it. Back in Paris, he was busy with nothing. He answered a letter from his editor about the last poems. He contemplated a play and knew absolutely that he wouldn't write it. He proposed a new literary prize, which was agreed as a good idea. He settled a grievance between Sylvia Beach and M. Gide. This took another lunch at Closerie de Lilas.

To finish it took a horse. Of course. After the event, when he had recognized that sequence, Alistair laughed aloud, for he had met someone coming around a corner and recognized himself.

He rode on Thursdays. For two weeks after New Year the frost was as iron. The first hunt of the 1930s was three weeks after Christmas. So he drove out in the Bugatti. The grey Paris bridges flowed away into little towns of squares and lycées, for the horrible broken tooth *banlieu* did not exist. Soon he was on main roads with poplars. He turned toward a village. The bare fields held their breath in winter. The smell of the woods was tart and lean.

Moss, stone, and leaves was the smell of the chateau's skin, and, walking around the corner from his car, of the stable. His riding boots hugged his ankles as town shoes did not. Colonel Rohan de Breteuil was there with his grooms, still in his stable jacket. Coffee joined stable on Alistair's nose. The colonel's bright blue eyes in cheeks never slovenly and never quite shaved and colored the old brick of wine and wind found him. Alistair went over and placed his smoother hand into the rougher. The colonel clapped his shoulder and pushed at him a mug. His nose had had it right, cognac in the coffee. The colonel said, *"On va du cote des Saurentours"*—a neighboring estate, the draw.

Alistair had a roan gelding and a bay. Today was the roan's. The horse was saddled but not bridled, haltered in the cross ties. He examined him as he approached. Boromeo had a way of standing with his off fore tentative, like a girl at a puddle, which he knew by now was not lameness. He watched the bridle put on, with space between the throatlash and the throat, the curb relaxed. He kept his eye on the colonel, for he considered himself still a guest and would mount when the colonel did. And so they mounted, and he ducked his head under the stable arch, telling himself yet again he did not need to. He smelled loam, leaf, and mow with a contentment that skipped right over Paris and drew from his whole life. They picked up a trot. His spine and legs felt for tightness in Boromeo's gait, found none. His hands caressed neck and rein. He and the colonel spoke little and liked each other the more.

The meet was at another small chateau, just a little grander. He bowed to the master, nodded to the huntsman, touched the offered hand and honored the presence of a gallant old lady sidesaddle on a grey. An Orleans-bred hound that had a liking for him jumped up to touch his boot. His horse sidestepped. He growled at the hound pleasantly, "Hold up there, Blancadrins!" before the whipper-in's ire could be incurred. He watched with pleasure the hound's fine muscles flowing down the back, heavier than a foxhound's, the kind eye, the strong head, for the hounds were also family.

And they were off. They found soon, in a spinney of oak entangled with laurel. He had a sight of the antlers and the tan flank stretched long in flight as they plunged into the next wood. The hounds stretched, too, and shot off like a flight of arrows, belling truly, for only a French pack has the music of a church bell.

It was a long run. The roan was warmed by the trot. He let him go. They galloped forest avenues, were forced into deep woods, which the French do not like. He found himself stymied by a thicket, lost ground. He was alone. He broke all the French rules and flew a ditch to catch up. In these deeper woods, the hunt was showing an edge. He did not swerve but bent low in the saddle for an overhanging bough and still felt it cuff his back. He caught up with the colonel, whose charge he was. They were at the front. All at a full gallop, the huntsman's horn fretted the shoulder of his coat, the hounds were sustained by passion, their tongues lathered. Around a turn, the stag was in full sight again and now close, and now Alistair saw the flanks wracked like bellows, heard the breath or fancied so, saw the breast convulse at each stretched bound. He felt a moment of sorrow, but the stag was worth his salt, turned aside for a high dense cover that would give a hound trouble, and leapt.

And was weak. Or slipped. And fell. And up again in a second, the hounds not quite closed yet. But the hindquarters faltered through one breath that Alistair did really hear, like iron on rock. And then the hounds were there.

It is rare that hounds tear down the stag. In modern hunting, the hounds bring the stag to bay, the huntsman dismounts, wades through his pack, and cuts the throat with a razor knife. There is not much fuss. Maybe the stag knows it is the better way. Alistair, not a very old hand in this, had never seen it otherwise.

He saw his Blancadrins leap first. Blancadrins's shoulders hurled him to the deer, Blancadrins's lips stretched back, a face of fangs. They slashed, shut, and shook, he saw the flesh torn from the shoulder, the blood well out. There was a sound he had not heard before. The stag screamed. The huntsman was standing in his saddle, one foot drawn half back to dismount, did not, the situation beyond control. Anglante came next, and Robert le Diable from Limousin. The stag half rose a moment. Le Diable had too deep bit in and was pulled up by his jaws still shaking flesh, but Anglante stripped meat from a white rib. Olivier flew at the throat, and a bubbling got into the stag's scream. Rugier of Burgundy, slower but heavy of shoulder and of head, broke in and hung to the belly. The stag still fought. He was on one flank now but curled and with his head and antlers raised, as though arising in the dawn. His foreleg lashed out. The sharp hoof grazed Blancadrins down the side. Blancadrins turned in rage and dove into the throat. Alistair saw the long muzzle, crimson now, deep into the stag and digging. That was the stag's last move. It twitched. The thick tongue stuck out of the lips, was seized. The head and shoulders fell. Was meat. The huntsman and the whips descended like Olympians now, boots and whips. Hounds yelped. Order got restored, though hounds still crouched and moaned at the blood. Alistair found that Colonel de Breteuil was by his side, shorter than he. "*Voit pas toujours, hein? Autrefois.*" Muttering, Don't see that every day. Once upon a time. Blancadrins, not much hurt, seemed to shake himself into order. Over now. Some of the hounds were collecting near the huntsman's horse. Blancadrins joined them. His eye by chance met Alistair's. *Not bad, eh, friend?* the kind eye said. The stag was not too badly cut up. The cooks would have no problem.

And Ovid's Prince Acteon, changed into a stag for no crime, his own dear hounds closing on him for the kill, cries out,

Acteon ego sum, dominum cognoscite vestrum! I am Acteon! Know your master!

But,

This is the *Metamorphoses. Verbo animo desunt: resonat latratibus aether.*

He has no human voice. And the air is full of howls. The hounds tear their once master down. The hounds are named. The wounds are counted. And a poet speaks to a poet.

The day after the hunt, Alistair took from the shelf the Ovid he had translated for Mr. Featherstonhaugh in the schoolroom in Rome, and knew his next work had begun.

He fell upon Ovid, a boy with a new girl. Now line by line. Its long threads soared and dipped between creature and universe. One tale. A doubting boy bolsters his courage by asking proof of his father's love. Alistair understands this easily. He supposes he'd love to be a father, understands the foolish promise that ends with his son up on his hottest hunter, shut your eyes. But this father, who has dimmed his own light for his dear son's eyes, is the Sun. Imagine the terror in that stable yard, the boy's hands on the reins of heaven, the sudden fear in them the last the father sees. The chariot is too light. It bounces. The horses feel fear in the reins, as they do, they do. Applause for Ovid's telling of the horrors of the heaths of heaven, the constellations alive and vicious, the scorpion's tail, the snake, all control lost, the sun unbridled, the chariot plunging, the earth on fire, the rivers boiling, fish poaching in the sea. Jove stops it with a thunderbolt. Boy's dead. And not halfway through yet. Jove goes out to survey his singed estates, sees a girl, follows her into a pretty wood, grass and plashy streams, how sweet the grass when the tunic's off her back. Alistair certainly sees it, though he's angered by rape. The girl gets pregnant, of course. Works for Diana the Huntress, who throws her out, slut, just as they do. It's a boy. Juno, jealous bitch, has been waiting only for the poor parturition on bare earth to change the girl into a beast, as it happens the dearest, most timorous, modest she-bear in the world. The boy grows up a gentleman, of course, must take up hunting. One day he meets Mamma, who, gentle, loving soul, looks on him with longing eyes; to the boy, eyes looking at a plate of soup. He throws a spear. Jove has had enough. He lifts the poor creature into the sky, the constellation of the Bear. From a boy's loneliness, the sun debauched, the world ablaze, a girl raped, a son born, and the Arctic stars are fixed, that never set. One tale among scores.

From the first, he and language were on honeymoon again. Where he had to get to was a given now, not an existential query. All he had to solve was how, at least ignoring for a while whether a translation is a reflected wraith or stands on its own weight. All of English stood to serve him. The light he lived in was changing. He noted this one day and realized that he was happy. He was becoming absorbed in the landscape of *Metamorphoses*, which shimmers like the dawn of *A Midsummer Night's Dream*. It is strange that it should. Lust here is brutal. Revenge is bloody-fanged. The gods, after moments of bare decency, happily revert to vicious children. Romantic love, when she shyly shows her face, turns insatiable and usually for father, or brother, or brute beast. But Ovid's style, glancing mercury, looks at these monstrosities as at a fly in a meringue. *How horrid!* it says and quickly passes on. It would have been pure Grand Guignol done by Virgil.

The shimmering landscape was Italy or a world made Italian. Apollo's palace would have done for the Barberinis, gone insane. Coreggio could have done his ceilings. The way to the underworld is down the road from Mantova. Arethusa flees through Liguria, he is sure, its hills and streams; and then Diana turns her, bleeding feet and failing strength, into a fountain. So the officer kneeling in the mud is never shot but turns into a willow weeping over the Natisone; the Umbrian girl rises up as a crane and flies over the Carabinieri and far away. And a girl dying of the plague in Venice? Something. She liked colors. A rainbow.

He was tired of France.

His manuscript grew, still very fragmentary, and pencil lines telemarked all over the pages. He admitted it: he was homesick. He would have loved the scent of wax on an Italian floor, a basket of fruit in the sun, the strong soap, clean sweat, and healthy girl on an Italian maid. The watchful monster tore each with its claws.

The thought grew in him and became fond and fanciful, that Nancy's glancing blue eyes, her spotless skin, her crispness, her Americaness could interpose themselves between the monster and himself. It was a known weakness in monsters that they sickened when not believed in. Nancy wouldn't believe a bit. Do a watercolor of the monster, really make him drop his tail. He could go back into the dark valley carrying his girl as a shield, maybe.

Nancy said, "Back to Massachusetts, Alistair?"

"Massachusetts was never home," said Alistair.

"That would be Italy, then," said Nancy. She slowly turned the stem of her Champagne flute, making the trace of her lipstick orbit the rim. It was not always Champagne before dinner, since they spent quite a lot anyway. This evening it was Blanc du Limousin, suggestive of the old Prosecco from Venice, actually.

"Very hard for me to get commissions there," she said. "I'm a success here."

"They have children in Italy," said Alistair. "Likewise paint."

"You have to be talked about to get commissions. It's not just being able to do it. Nancy Havelock is a name in Paris now."

They sat before dinner in the drawing room, which was on the second floor, with a double window overlooking the miniature square. Rain drove into the grove of plane trees at the center. The street lamps had just come on, and each cobblestone in the street was now an island in a narrow sea. The plane trees had advanced into earliest leaf. During a little sun, Nancy had done a watercolor of one offshoot of a bough, with great attention to leaf. It was propped on the windowsill. Alistair pointed to it.

"What they definitely have in Italy is plants and herbs, which is what you really like to paint, my dear. We won't need the commission money. It's a lot cheaper there."

"That's easy for you to say," she said. "We're both foreigners here, Alistair. And I've been here longer, so I even taught you things, back when. I don't think you're a foreigner in Italy. And I'll be one so much. I don't speak Italian. I won't be able to run the house, or shop, or have any friends, or go to a bookshop, or even read a paper, or do anything. Will I just sit in the flowerbed?"

He had thought of none of this, since the enterprise was mythic, and myths don't have those details. Her thought of her carefully now, but it was as though through the wrong end of a telescope.

He said, "If you learned French, you can learn Italian." But he felt now that absolute justice was required, and added, "It's a little more difficult. The grammar."

"I was taught French. I was taught Italian, too, but I forgot it all. We have to go down to dinner when we're called. There's a soufflé, I think. I asked for one. Not that it makes much difference, usually, what I ask for. It's so pretty here. We've made it so pretty."

Their cook made fresh potato chips every evening. Nancy ate few, thinking of her waist, which was in a dark blue satin sheath this evening. Right now, she ate them one by one, but broke each into four bits.

She said, "I don't think Italy's a country. Not for you. I think it's a girl or something."

Which shocked him, and he said, "There's no girl, Nancy."

"I didn't mean that. Girl's probably wrong, anyway. You've never asked me to marry you. Just to take me into the dark, now."

"Would you?" he said.

She seemed to notice her revolving flute, and arrested it. Alistair poured her some more wine with the beginning of a grand gesture and at once arrested that, as pasteboard.

"I have no idea," she said. "I'm very happy with you," she said, seeking the companionship of the sofa cushions. "I'm very fond of you. You're much the most important man ever in my life. I don't think I want a baby. They seem to use up all the air. Paint doesn't. I could live without you. I don't think I want to. Thinking about whether I'd marry you seems to use up a lot of air too. I don't seem to have much. Do you want to go a great deal?"

"I have no delight left in being here," he said. "Except, of course, in you. And I do not like doors I hesitate to open."

She took breath to speak, but footsteps on the stairs presaged Paul, their maitre d'hotel, in the door, and Paul in the door presaged dinner announced. She cut the chain at its first link, rose at the footsteps, smiled quickly, said, "A higher power calls," and took his arm.

At the end of dinner, he rose and approached her chair, often to take her hand. But she stayed him with her palm. Her shoulders and arms were the lightest place in the room.

"Alistair," she said. "My reputation here will not die overnight. I'll come with you. You'll be there, so it will be fun in one way or another. I said that I could live without you. I said it perhaps because I know very well that you could live without me. A time will come, and I am not setting months, when I will either stay or go. And if I go, you will either stay or come."

He bowed. He said, "Thank you," and now did take her hand.

He freely admitted that Nancy knew more about how things actually worked than he. She started studying the *Paris Herald*, the American paper in which many properties of the kind Americans bought and took were listed. They dismissed sequentially a portentous cube outside Rapallo, what appeared to be Miss Haversham's wedding cake at Salso Maggiore spa, and a place "suitable for conversion to hotel or school" lost in the Venetian swamps.

"Here's one outside Lucca," she said one evening. There was rain on the western wind again, for that was the season in Paris, and no one was about on the small street.

"Lucca's nowhere near Rome," he said.

"In case you actually don't know, Alistair," she said, "it is quite near Florence. This could be fun. It has an old canal running through the grounds and statuary in the gardens. And stables for you."

"What?" he said. He took the paper from her and looked where her relinquishing finger pointed. The word "canal" was spelled out among, "vlla, gdns, prime cond, and 8 b'rms.

"It belongs to a man called Marchese. No, he is a marchese. Marchese Ugolino-Ferrara." She looked up. "Don't I know that name from somewhere?"

He looked at the paper, and his watch, went to the telephone, and dialed. A servant answered. *"Il signore marchese,"* said Alistair, adding, *"Chiamo del' estero."* Calling from abroad.

But the man was perhaps more steward than valet and asked his business.

Alistair supplied it. "Tell the signore marchese that I am returning him his sword."

PART III

10

Nancy's leaving hung in the air behind his chair.

He said very quietly, "When?" Then turned and said, "May I say, 'Why?' I will say, 'I wish not.'"

"It has to be soon," she said. "I can't be with you and not with you. I can't live here, Alistair. Do I have to say why? Italy's rotten. Tomorrow."

"You don't have to say. You do have to know," he said.

"I do know."

He drove her to Florence in the evening, to Stazione Santa Maria Novella, to put her in a sleeping car of the Parigi Express. As she climbed into the car at the whistle, the last thing she took with her was the skirt end of her traveling dress. He watched it play with a late spring breeze that had gamboled all the way from the Apennines to the tracks of Santa Maria Novella and now caught the scent of linden, stretched it thin, and bore it away. He waited, unmoving. He heard steam fill pistons. He waited. The cars began to move. She did not wave from a window, which would be unlike Nancy. They had said goodbye carefully and well. The cars picked up the music of the rail. The last car passed him. It drew a veil behind it that dimmed the light. Its own red and baleful eye receded. He turned back into the station.

In the waiting room, Otone Resai's landscapes, still clean and fresh, greeted the eye: lakes and mountains, vines and roads. Nancy had even liked them and liked their painter too. By the station door was a clutch of Blackshirts, pale and pimply, which black will do. Just so it was. Nancy had none of the richness of his delight in Italy, but it did put out shoots. Each time it did, a fasces rolled over it. Thus, the parade they had blundered into the first day, a poster of the Duce filling the side of a cathedral, loudspeakers to shake walls. For him, the distastefulness was balanced by the honor paid to the Bersaglieri, Italy's most gallant division, just back from Libya. For him, but not for her. And as for the odd old vagrant, the very likeness of Ezra Pound, uniformed and in his old medals, who infested the government offices of Lucca to get justice for his dead son's family. To him, a figure of quirky magnificence. To her, a victim of tyranny, no more.

He could have gone with her. No, he could not have. American Paris had soured in his mind even since his lunch with Sylvia. He saw midwestern farm boys drunk by day on what it pleased them to call the "Boul' Mich.'" Literary France did not speak to him from its pursed lips and was chill.

The Blackshirts, though not always their party, were a boil on Italy, a sore, a venereal ulcer, an embarrassment, and surely in the blood. Nancy could not look past it. He could blame her for that. A thinness in the blood, a spinster's pallor. He would blame her. He missed her so that his eyes were dim. She had stayed a year.

He found his car. He pushed it into the late afternoon traffic. He took the western valley to Lucca toward the house he foresaw as dark, and toward his Muse, who had driven off her rival and waited for him with hungry eye.

THROUGH HIS WINDOW, MANFREDI'S garden in winter, most trees bare, was barely scratched by the canal. Beyond, the land of his rented estate rose held up by brown ropes of vine, then the Apennines, pines, streaks of snow on rock, then the white brow of Monte Prano blowing cold upon him. There was a fire in the room. In his present work, his mind shone light upon images reflected from myth, browsed by others, a quarry for Europe's storytelling. He was happily in love with them, the girls, the sparkling sea, the fell herbs, the harebrained young warriors, the chimeras, and the bloody deaths. They were becoming his own. His Latin grew ever better tuned. He knew that while his art followed Ovid, it was working in secret on its own next need.

Another voice that he heard behind his work now came through denser stuff. It carried with it the witchcraft of its Cyrillic script—"runes," he called them, though they weren't—on paper poor as thin gruel. For, as well as his own Ovid, he had a mission now from Cardinal Galisteo to rescue the work of a Catholic poet in Stalin's Russia, a poet who was assumed to be doomed. With it came the guardian of each leaf: it was already translated into journeyman Latin on paper from the poorhouse down the street, by a scratchy pen. It was brought to him from time to time by a priest from Lucca close to the Bishop. Each envelope bore Galisteo's private seal on a wrapping rich as cream. Nancy had pretended to avoid it physically, claiming that it had been breathed on by the pope and could turn a Protestant mistress into a green frog.

He read it from the Latin, of course, as though seeing through a grimy pane into a dark hut. In happier days, his poet had been published openly, was even passably translated into French—a side window, giving clearer light. He loved these poems, loved this voice behind him. Erudition was its arch, Ovid, Dante, Time, but erudition's soaring mass was entirely inlaid with joyous reality, a horse's breath, the scent of split beech, a hut warm and odorous with sheep, the cold of anvil in winter yard. Did Russia have wooden cathedrals with woodcut walls? He had no idea. Now it did. He felt the movement, too, though one could not entirely trust the French. He felt a railroad station full of people, anxious, alert, the glances of intelligence and love, the train's whistle compelling looks at baggage, what could be left behind, what too precious. Love and choice, which men and women could breathe. He saw Moscow, 1921.

In the murk he looked into now, he could not see the movement; but he could see the faces. They had changed. The tyranny implicit in 1921 stood simian and unafraid a decade later. The ill chances that had tested intelligence and love in 1921 had become too insolent to question now. They were certainly too brutish to oppose. Love and choice had dwindled to a tragic enfolding in each others' arms, or flight, or at its lonely summit the croak of defiance at the firing squad. He handled a new page with Latin lightly. It had issued from the plague. Moscow, 1933.

He could not translate it.

Some of it he didn't understand. And Alistair, who had never had to write with fear of consequence, had to wonder how much was simply disguise. Was that how one wrote in Russia now? But this much was clear: his Russian poet, long imprisoned, was now in far exile. Writing was forbidden, publication beyond fantasy, publication abroad, a crime to stretch the eye. These poems were written—imagination could decide—by night and candle end, behind the stair, in a sometime hencoop with dried up droppings, and on paper got, how? The Latin translator was a priest, not one busy with altar guilds and Easter flowers but just another hollow convict dropped out of prison to starve in some desert. So, a priest nonetheless and always though hell's suburbs spread around him. Which they had. A recurring image was famine. Alistair did not think it was metaphorical. He gathered, the Ukraine. Wolf-jawed famine loped the steppe in policeman's boots, devoured the granary, the pig, the hen, sucked the poor cow dry. Seven dead in one hut. Life lingers in an infant born to a near skeleton, sucking the breast shriveled and finally cold. The pig's child looks on hungrily. Beefy police will shovel them all out one day.

The Church must bear witness to Satan's crimes. So these black poems did. But Satan is a bore. Far more often his poet showed Dante's power of angels conquering hell. Galisteo was right. They were Heaven's trust. Galisteo claimed this in a letter where the familiar handwriting was loosening like uncombed hair. Galisteo was fading from him.

The poems were also Heaven's man traps. The style was personal. If published in Russian, a false name would never do. Some weevil professor would find his way even to the apes of the OGPU to say that the poet was their very own country guest. The style was personal. The poet by now was Alistair's friend. Tighten the screw. He loved him. Publication in translation under a foreign name would be safe enough, he thought. Bad translation is an insult.

His muse and he kept house together. He had not been altogether alone with her since Tagliamento in the shadow of Victoria's death. Clasped fast to him, her embrace unrelenting when he walked in the olive woods or lay in bed in the early morning light, she had a glitter in her eye he had not quite taken notice of. Walking back with her from the darkening woods, he wondered if he did not see her skull beneath her skin. He missed Nancy's light and sense, opened her letters like shutters to the sun, answered with care, and avoided company to lie with his mistress from the stars. Nancy found commissions. Her craft was better than ever. She had found a pleasant flat off the Rue de la Seine where she looked down at the new tomatoes on a green grocer's stall. She was content. "What do you mean, Alistair, have I fallen in love yet in Paris? I am in love with you. It's sad."

xxx

NOT FAR FROM SANTA Croce, amid the dark eaves and narrow streets where he had once looked in vain for another ghost of love, his lost Serafina, he sat at lunch with his easily found Rodolfo, who had a whole new persona to offer him, right there at the table.

Not the Grand Hotel, here. The Palazzo Vecchio, never to be trifled with and now the bastion of fascist power in Florence, pointed its tower at the street, and the street kept its head down. Rodolfo raised his hand, and the waiters rose on their toes. Still it was a cheerful little place. One hoped what was to come would equal the tomato and bread soup. Given the extraordinary compliment Rodolfo was paying him, Alistair decided that entertaining him here was an embrace of brotherly love.

He replied and kept all sting from his voice, "I'm not a fascist, Rodolfo."

"Am I, Alistair?" he said, and let it hang, then answered, "Of course I am, if you like. I have accepted the discipline, the chain of command. Which, remember, I don't ask of you. You are the citizen of a great power. You have your own loyalties, which we intensely respect. We want what you are, not what we can make of you. Am I so different from you in what I think? I don't know. We might like you to tell us."

For if he were to accept, yes, he would be inscribed, very rare for a foreigner and no bad thing, which office seemed to include, in majestic nebulosity, something of *censor mores*, a higher consciousness at the party's command, something of ambassador from and to the world of letters and something of ambassador to thoughtful America. The first, Alistair believed, most likely meant nothing. In the second, he would be joining a couple of good poets, a few admirable essayists, and even his own new friend Curzio Malaparte or Erik Suckert, as one preferred. The last seemed unnecessary, given that Mussolini was the most admired foreign statesman in America, the darling of the *New York Times*.

He answered as carefully as before, letting any scorn whatsoever in his eye fall upon the brown wine jug with the face of a plump young girl.

"You can look at a Blackshirt without feeling queasy, Rodolfo, or I suppose you can. You don't mind the braying and thumping that's coming over this country, photographs as big as alps, loudspeakers to rattle the cups three streets away. Bawling sentiments to bore a concierge. You do think differently. You must. And aren't you all socialists? Your man boasts about it."

"Circus stuff, Alistair. Circus stuff." The soup bowl went away. The waiter crouched a little more to Rodolfo than to Alistair. Rodolfo took out a long cigarette, looked at it, and put it away.

"Italians are used to a lot of circus," said Rodolfo. "All of that impresses the little people while we get on with the important things. Which could be . . ." and now he smiled easily, "running the countryside intelligently for the first time since the Romans, getting rid of malaria—which is a nasty thing, Alistair—treating the Church with the respect it deserves, giving the people something to do other than emigrate in rags." Rodolfo tossed these up like balls. Alistair knew a great sack more was underneath the table, but Rodolfo shrugged, seemed to get bored with his riches, and stopped. He said quietly, "Should we spare you the loud speakers and stop all that? And the fact is, we would like to be better and to see how." The cigarette came out again, but a rabbit in mushrooms beat it to the table. "And that's where you can perhaps help us."

Rodolfo was the son of a real, well-born, and gallant Italian officer. He had noble relations. His education was good. He was as far as he could be from the mongrels the party did most often throw up. Manfredi, whose dealings, as a great landowner, with the party were necessarily frequent, had said, "One might not love him, but you can't excommunicate a fellow because he holds office in a party most Italians admire." In spite of what had happened to them all, Alistair could still wince at the cruelty to Rodolfo of his father's death. He supposed he would do no harm by taking up his offer at all. He relished the tidbits—delicious morsels, no labor in the kitchen, no mess and blood of ribs and tongue, God knew no party card—it would surely allow him to pass on to Simon. For Simon Cartwright, his old fencing friend and son of the American first secretary in Rome, had become, he had to guess, some kind of spy, and he, Alistair, had somehow become one of his ears. Simon would love this. He just didn't want his name on it.

"Come fall," Alistair said deliberately, "are you going to have any useful gun dogs?"

And Rodolfo shrugged, smiled a little dismissively, but let himself be led away on that scent.

"From England," he began. "A setter bitch."

11

Alistair's study window faced the Apennines and Monte Pranno. His breakfast table faced down to Lucca, where lions on churches with birthday cake towers sometimes dozed on niches but just as often fought snakes, or eagles, or each other. As though the villa had been an artillery post, he could see over the walls, into the Piazza del Duomo, and down the principle street connecting that with the north gate of the wall. He could see much of the road up toward the villa, what was not pushed aside by billows of the valley, all rippling with grey olives. Consequently, he could follow Monsignore Kirchner on his bicycle.

A real artilleryman, with field glasses, could certainly have seen a black monsignore bug pop from the chapter courtyard, cross the square, quite soon burrow under the wall, and vanish and reappear, now a bug with a hat, among the bends of the road. Alistair never noticed him until he rounded the bend with the short Our Lady tabernacle and the tall Roman pine, and again when he could see the soutane agitated by the pumping thighs beneath. This agitation would pass straight to him, for the monsignore meant a poem was coming to him from Russia.

He had never asked whether the bicycle was mortification, healthy exercise, or fun. The soutane left no doubt that it was sweat. He liked the monsignore—blue eyed, from Bolzano. The butler too observed him, did not announce the obvious, and brought unbidden another coffee cup, brioche, and plate. The monsignore dismounted and leaned his bicycle against a stone seat beside the drive. The butler stepped quickly away and returned with a second tray, a bottle of water and a glass. The monsignore walked formally toward Alistair and stood before him. He brought a packet from his soutane. It bore Galisteo's seal. He presented it with both hands as though it might have been a chalice. Alistair so took it.

"Good ride?" said Alistair.

"Hot even early now," said Kirchner. He drained the glass, refilled it, smiled thanks to the butler. Alistair motioned him to sit and eat.

"But I need the exercise," said Kirchner. He cut his brioche in half precisely and smiled at the apricot jam inside. "I saw three deer on the way. A young stag beginning antlers and two does. They all looked healthy. You should have a good season."

"There were acorns last year and no late chill. It was a good winter for the fawns. God was kind to them."

"And thus no doubt to you," said Kirchner, and smiled.

"The chapter will not be forgotten."

"No boar," said Kirchner.

"I hear them at night though," said Alistair.

The monsignore did not delay. He drank down his coffee. He looked at Alistair, who nodded. Alistair very carefully cleaned the edge of his knife on the napkin, took up the packet, and pressed the knife-edge against the seal. It split. Some jagged fragments of hard wax fell on the tablecloth and made sharp small shadows in the sun. He opened the packet and found less than he looked for, three sheets of sickly paper only.

Alistair had no idea how far into Galisteo's circle Kirchner stood. He had no idea whether he was allowed to do what he was doing. To mistrust him would be merely absurd. He knew that he had been an Austrian army chaplain in the old war, when Bolzano was Bosen, and respected his common sense. Kirchner's learning was in early Christian hymns and verse, Latin and Greek, but his knowledge of the pagan poets and the Italians was excellent. Alistair thought his voice in Latin better than his own. He handed him a single sheet. Kirchner took it, cradled it in his hand so it stood straight, focused his eye, and read to the young Tuscan morning.

Alistair's attention twisted at its edge. He was hearing Latin, but the matter of the poem was Greek. The morning darkened. He was hearing of a Cyclops, one-eyed ogre. Homer's Cyclops? No. "Our Kremlin Cyclops." *Oh God, sweet Mary!* he thought, Stalin, the master, the horror, all but named. He began to see: the poem rests on a tripod above Homer's, with the monster filthy drunk on the floor "as wine came spurting, flooding up from his gullet with chunks of human flesh, he vomited, blind drunk." So, a domestic detail from Stalin's dacha. And the end: Odysseus, until then called "No One," shouts out his name to the monster over the wake of his good black ship escaping not to the morning of the world but to the cave's night.

The Kremlin is the cave. The cave is the Kremlin. Behind the one stupid eye, the monster busied himself with cunning, greedy of his cheeses, neat with his branding irons and pails, exact in the pens to progress the lambs to slaughter. The poem was not long. The woodcut delicacy was there. It was a book where all may read; Marx would approve. It was written for one's hangman.

He was appalled.

The monsignore said, "There is one more line. It does not seem part of the poem. It does not seem that it is in the Russian." He read, "This present work has been shared with others."

He wished that Kirchner had not read it. He could not ask for advice. He wished that he only had read the last line. He wished he could swear Kirchner to secrecy. He could not. He felt Kirchner's blue eyes upon him, looked past them, and they moved aside.

Kirchner nonetheless said, "He knows that he would not have lived." The Italian verbs made "anyway" unneeded. With one's head in the lion's mouth, how not, thought Alistair, and then said it, silence being ungracious. Kirchner nodded. He made to rise. He is also an officer, thought Alistair, with thanks. Standing, they shook hands.

"I shall pray," said Kirchner. Which one would assume.

"Also for the priest." Alistair nodded.

"For more material help, you can find me. Though I would not know what."

"Thank you," said Alistair. He watched Kirchner retrieve the bicycle, suddenly with the fussy gestures of one who wants not to intrude. He watched him ride off, the soutane no doubt to cool and dry in the downhill breeze. He did not sit down. When the bicycle was gone, he walked slowly in the driveway's formal circle. Nancy's rosemary had opened its blue eyes this season, and its look was returned by some kind of cornflower, he had never known the name, between the shade trees, two small blues terrific in the grey and gold of Italian summer. The villa made its gentle morning sounds of grooming. Evil could make a universe upside down, where the uncorrupted were not quite annihilated, they never seemed to be, but were placed at angles from which they could not touch. These days he dressed and breakfasted in riding boots (Nancy had never liked much horse in the house). He left the circle and turned toward the stables. There could be no thought of his own work this morning. He had Solferino saddled, his wise-mannered bay.

The cave, the lion's mouth. Was he already dead? In fact, he doubted it. He had the impression that things happened in sudden jolts Over There, but that the end was not quick. In the lion's mouth, you were given time to get used to a view of teeth. The mouth might even loosen. Maybe you'd sing a different song before it closed again. And presumably those "others" with whom the poem had been "shared" were men to trust, just as surely as one at least would prove a traitor. There was probably some time.

An avenue of grass, still springy though the ground beneath was hard, flanked a hill and overshadowed his canal, his nymph. Solferino gathered himself for the canter, which they had long agreed on here, and jolted Alistair, who had forgotten where he was. He set himself and at the first stride knew one thing: that Odysseus had triumphed again. He set himself deep in the saddle, shortened the reins, and gave Solferino a surprise at least as big, pushing him hard so his forehand lightened, his hocks stretched, and they flew the hill toward the Tuscan sky. What you do with a friend's triumph is celebrate. If the triumph cost his life, you lift the sky before you mourn. Larks fired out in front of Solferino's hooves, and once a covey of quail, good man, no swerve. To last as long as his poet had lasted was almost a joke, he guessed. They had the poems all here, forever safe, the poet's own hand, the Russian runes, the last huzzah. They breasted the top of the hill. Solferino checked, quite right, but he'd have none of that today and pushed him harder than before into a downhill romp, and, to hell with it, gave him rein. To contain the vaunt to the executioner, and to the overlord himself, in the geometry of Homer, pick up the threads of three thousand years, *au fin du rondel, je touche,* Cyrano couldn't have done it. They were plunging down now, Solferino frankly disorganized, not the safest thing for man or beast. He had to look to his seat. The ground tipped steeper for a short way, and they were in trouble, but Solferino steadied. In the safe sweet Tuscan morning, you had to raise a responding glass, somehow. The canal was near again. They were by it. Solferino came decisively to a walk, expecting no argument and getting none, and breathed deep rumination about what they had just done. Sixteen years before, Alistair had seen the officer in the mud die. He should not have. It's indecent. You should not see the very end. The charge is enough, not the final dying, the prison dawn, the prisoner too sick and shivering to face the rifles. The triumph was in the bag, all his poet's. Now it was for Alistair to get him out. He had long rehearsed this.

He had not the faintest, the foggiest, the feeblest idea of how.

HE GAVE SOLFERINO BACK to the stable. He patted him distantly. Then he in was in the house by the telephone, still in boots. He called the number at the Paris embassy that would yield up Simon in due time. He never thought of such a thing with Rome. If he was wanted, Rome would get him. All this was effortless, for he had thought of it before, and put its value on it, which was light. He put Galisteo's packet in a drawer and locked it. He guessed that he was here with time, for a while. Time walked around the room, found a chair it liked, sat down, and crossed its legs.

HE FOUND SIMON AT a sidewalk table near Santo Spirito. The train must have been on time. The Palazzo Pitti filled up the side street's view. Simon's spectacles looked down at the *Paris Tribune*, the angle of his chin being precisely complement to the V of his buttoned collar. He looked up at Alistair's shadow then rose. They shook hands, warmly, for whatever the matter, it was a pleasure to see Simon. Simon folded the *Tribune*.

"What's '*strozzapreti*'?" said Simon.

"It's for strangling priests. In case you need to, after lunch. Sinister country, Italy. It's a kind of *gnocchi*, Simon."

"Oh, yes, of course," said Simon. "I saw Nancy in Paris."

Alistair said nothing.

"At an opening. A new Spaniard. Called Miró. She was there with some French. Not with anybody special, I would say."

Alistair said the needed, "She was well?"

"I'd say so. Standing there with that little smile and seeing more than anybody else. At a painting. I didn't want to interrupt, but I did. I told her I'd be seeing you."

Alistair studied the menu. There were mussels but unwise in hot weather.

"Simon?" said Alistair.

"She sent you her love. You shouldn't have let her go, Alistair."

"Simon?" said Alistair.

"All that's for later," said Simon. "Not here. We'll take a walk."

There were two businessmen, one jowly, one bristly. There was an American couple like skinny chickens, faces of obstinate innocence, a Baedeker, and sensible shoes. There were three bored waiters. And a few flies. As secret agents, Alistair thought they amounted to not much, but it was Simon's occasion.

"How's Manfredi?" said Simon.

"Athenian." Manfredi had for some reason turned his estate into a literary weekend, and Alistair, as *eminence noire,* had of course attended as houseguest of Manfredi and his rather nice new peasant mistress.

"Talk sense, Alistair," said Simon. "First, the Soviet Union is not an enemy. The new administration respects the Soviet experiment. Not to follow blindly, of course, but respect. They have abolished hunger and unemployment. Most of it."

Alistair did not reply but merely braced against this gale. He did direct one new pinpoint of hatred against his own capitol, his own Roosevelt.

"And then, of course, it is a foreign country, with its own government, its own laws. And its own army. I expect you thought of that."

"There are men trained in abduction and such skills. I know there are. It is the proper response to tyranny. Defter force. The rapier over the club."

The gardens are nearly vertical, as Alistair had discovered long ago. Alistair noted that Simon was breathing hard and that his spectacles had smudges of mist. This pleased him. Where they were smelled of bay leaf. Far above them, they could see the peak of a fountain jet.

"They exist. They usually make a botch of it. I came a long way to see you, Alistair."

"I know it is a long time on the train. Thank you. That you came."

"I came on an airplane. Not to talk about vaudeville." Simon pointed his index finger at a stone bench between two obelisks of laurel and changed direction. From here, one could hear children up at the fountain. Simon sat.

They were, whatever, two old friends on a park bench. The couple from the restaurant came out of the Pitti and admired the roses. One could see the Baedeker lifted.

"Rapier," said Simon. "You liked the sabre better, at Palazzo Colonna. But we can stay with the rapier. He will be snuffed out, Alistair, and you can do nothing about it. You've seen the lovely light, and now you see the dark. You've always understood me. Now I think you're ready to see." He slowly raised his hand, and his index finger hopped, skipped, and jabbed the Pitti Palace and the towers of the Palazzo Vecchio and the Bargello. He said, "The world belongs to governments now. It always did, but now it really does. The war changed all that. If you can put four million men in trenches, you can do anything. People have to fit in. I don't mean you have to be a robot. You have to find out how much room you have and use it well. That is art, Alistair. It has to be possible. Your man got it wrong. How long have you admired stupidity?"

"It is not stupidity to show your hangman for what he is. To say that is stupidity."

"The rapier, Alistair. Very right to be angry. You may like your man, but you're not like him. Don't flatter yourself. You're not angry; you're affronted. You do not like to fail. You cannot see yourself as one of the weak. You don't even like to touch them."

Better than being one, Alistair thought, but did not say.

WHAT SIMON SAID NEXT Alistair did not much hear, for a line had come to him, derived though not descriptive of the children's voices from above, the notion of some infinitely gentle, infinitely suffering thing. He felt the rebellion, nausea of the soul, the lines had brought since he first spoke them aloud and then the need to cry for pardon for feeling so. He looked at Simon. In their old days fencing, when Simon pulled off his mask he was surprised each time to see his stern enemy too sober, too studious, too mild for a sword.

He said, "Your point, Simon?"

"You're one of us," said Simon.

He thought. "No. You run in packs."

Simon nodded once and said nothing.

"You came here, and in an airplane, Simon, to give me no help at all, and in a bad hour. Do I assume you want mine?"

"As you know. Do I have to say it all again? But now, Alistair, you have seen, surely? You want ours. Run in a pack a little. Earn the right to be heard. Earn the right to hear. The good shepherd of the baitfish."

Alistair said nothing. He tasted the thought and showed it quietly to Galisteo.

"It's your nature, Alistair. When you had a real life, when Nancy was here, you two fed half the half-artists in Tuscany. Always a welcome at Villa Pace ed Abbondanza. Now you're letting it go, of course, *noli me tangere,* there's only me. But it's there. What's a chieftain for? Our Italian contacts stink, which is why I'm here. There will be more of that. Here, Spain, Hungary, Germany I wouldn't doubt. And then where? Forget Russia, that's beyond the forest and over the hill." He looked up suddenly.

The Americans had made good time up the hill and now stood close to them, lifting the Baedeker to the Pitti's complacent bulk. They conferred, faces cheek by cheek above the book. Alistair suddenly liked them. Simon raised his hand for silence. The two heads frowned, read, nodded in unison. Not a bead of sweat on either brow. They turned and strode off uphill to the unseen children.

"For God's sake," said Alistair. "Why did we lunch on the sidewalk, then? Someone must have seen us."

"I hope so. Guessing's good. Look at me for a change, Alistair." Simon put his hand between them and turned it so his fingers hovered over the stone. He struck down the little finger. "You shouldn't exist, but you do." The children must have finished a game. Their voices rose in laughter. "You're in two worlds. You know them." The second finger struck. "You know perfectly well how good your contacts are, how easily they'll grow." Third finger. "We need them in Italy. We need them badly. But you're not a patriot, you're not for countries, and you're the devil to pay." And now the index. "We can pay you with help to help people who can barely pay you back. Alistair, the knight of the artists. I could sweeten the deal by promising there'll be no help for you if it ever comes. And it might. This will start safe, but that may change. I'm not sure I can do that. I'll just try. How does it sound?"

It was the apex of a sweet ridge. He felt his feet on it. He looked down, as he did now at the Duomo and the Arno, at high estate used nobly. The laughter came again. He heeded it.

"You can give me no help now. In a great matter. How can I know you ever will?"

The hand turned sideways. The fingers furled. Only the thumb remained to strike. It struck.

Simon said, "Because you can forget all that, Alistair. You'll do it because you want to. You want to be the subtlest of us all."

He tried to say, "That is almost an insult." He said instead, "Of course," and said it lightly.

"You were an excellent officer. We know you can love a service. This one is closer to your heart than keeping the Philippines safe for the navy. You wrote poems then, as I happen to know. See us the same way. We are loyal. Our arm is long. We are sure."

He turned back toward the bench and felt affection for that face of spectacles and lowered glance, whose smile at his good reason would be also his own. But when he drew breath to speak, he felt the breath ungrateful in his throat.

"I'm sorry, Simon," he said. "I can't."

12

A pumice sky scraped the hills for two days of lingering winter. It rubbed out the memory of Christmas in Umbria: a shooting party all mounted, Manfredi and Alistair the only really accomplished shots that way, the dinner party their guns had furnished, and two domestic days with Manfredi and Claudia and their little boy. Her son was to be raised a gentleman, Claudia's great Christmas present, first Latin lesson in its time (for a thousand years a young gentleman's first step out of the herd) and put up on a pony (whose stirrup was the second step). Her happiness was the last and warmest coal to fade.

He walked back from the stable the next morning in the sun that followed the grey. There were suddenly irises. They grew in the stone of the south wall of the drive. No one had given them a thought since last spring. They were as small as Nancy's brushes. He remembered that it looked as though she painted irises with an iris. The brush had borrowed in turn the pigments of the flowers, kingfisher blue with speckles of sunset, coral with calligraphy of gold, sky wrapped in butter. Their bigger cousins followed quickly, and, now he looked, were swollen. There was a whole bank of them between the lawn and the first plantation of olives. The large never equaled the small, a stage curtain against a paperweight, but they were still enough to savor in the best late light. With the end of the iris came the olive blossom, white, small, and intricate as frost flakes and nearly as quickly gone.

In the best late light, it was too cold to sit outside, but a high window of the drawing room gave onto the bank of iris. Waves of darkness had pounded the winter: each day's fading light, the greater dark of his bed, the more fiery darkness when he closed his eyes. Some of this must have shown in his face. His cook had persuaded him to drink tisane in the afternoon. This he did, but now looking at the irises like a bowl of claret, he found humor at this imitation of himself growing old.

The darkness was passing behind his shoulder. His Ovid was with its publishers. It had come upon him gradually and completely as daybreak that it was the first big and difficult thing he had accomplished altogether by his own terms since Tagliamento. He was surprised by himself. He felt the well-being that follows illness. So feeling, he knew that the illness had grown for years and had been the distemper, come to the point of separation, between himself and poetry, the breath of his lungs, the blood of his veins, whose loss would be the soul's death. They were back together again, warm on one pillow. The Russian poems were at another publisher. He could look at them now and believe that he had fairly and carefully done the little of the little part he had been asked to do: recognize them and bring them to sanctuary. The vanity that had made the poet also his proper ward dropped off his shoulder, for he no longer needed it. The poet might still be alive, somehow, in a camp. They published accordingly under false name, which veiled the cry "Odysseus!" but left the purpose plain. The translation had been better than he expected. The translator had come to meet him in Paris. He and Alistair spent four days on the sounds and textures of Russian words. He knew the language no better than before but saw the figures within it less dimmed by fog. Each Paris evening he had spent with Nancy, long dinners at their old places. They walked the Rue de Furstemberg holding hands. He thought her new portraits had passed beyond graceful possessions to be very nearly equal to her blade of sedge. She was the closest companion he had on earth who was not ghost or spirit. The apparatus between them was defective and would not reconnect.

HIS PRESENT WRITING WAS a littered shelf. He began poems, worked on others, closed some up and forbade further tinkering. He worked without any ordered schedule. The stables had their schedule, which he obeyed. His cook had hers, which he did not. He walked a good deal and took the shelf with him. So, scrambling up a muddy bank, mud being the stuff of spring, when the path dipped to a brook that fed the canal, he nearly fell over three lines of a possible somber start, put them up on the shelf, and took down in payment a difficult middle. At the top of the bank, he saw smoke, never there before, from the chimney of the only other considerable building on the property. It was a bungled place, begun as a pavilion with pediment then cobbled, grossly inconvenient he was sure, but not a peasant's or a servant's house and not part of his lease. It was a good way from the villa, but still Manfredi could have warned him. It was a good way, and he had to turn around now. This was Wednesday, the day of the last poem out of Russia, and he and Monsignore Kirchner lit a candle together in the cathedral where St. Martin divides his cloak with a beggar and the lions sleep all day long.

He saw the interloper from the saddle the next day but one. He and Boromeo were beside a wood and in the rain, which Boromeo cogitated while he steamed. Alistair had the impression of a slight young man in a long coat and hat like a rain cloud. It was surely worn for the weather, but with a suggestion of Tennyson if you wanted to be nasty. Tennyson was deep in the wood. Alistair knew the brambles in his face and britches slapped by dripping bushes if he went in there. He turned away. Boromeo sighed. So did he. It was not the only annoyance. On Friday the Junior School had half day, and the Junior Militia paraded. Or did target practice. Their rifles worked. Ocean swells of oratory poured from loudspeakers when the wind set right and could have sucked the uniformed tinies to their deaths in deep inanity. Once he had found a storm trooper lost and crying in the bracken. The Duce had gone to Berlin last year and had been impressed.

The Russian galleys arrived. They called for close work, all the day long. They called for a three-page telegram to the translator in English and transcribed Russian dictated to a Tuscan rustic at the railroad station. He should have driven in. He had a moment of desolation as startling as a falling chandelier, for he knew that the poems were leaving him, and Galisteo too.

The next day brought perfect spring, Tiepolo spring, spring as a young girl dancing to a breeze, throwing bouquets of rain and sun. So attractive, he even considered that as a line, and thanked God it couldn't scan. He rode Solferino that morning, got soaked twice, and came back gleaming like a knight in the sun. He took a rare holiday, never touched his desk, and set out after lunch on foot. Young quail and deer were his study. This kept him in the olive groves and the woods. Quail liked the olives—they had room to fly there and the hawks did not—especially near uncut wild grasses near the forest's edge. He knew where in the woods it pleased the deer to lie.

The winter that had buffeted him had not been as kind as the one preceding Kirchner's visit, Nancy's last, but it had not been dreadful. There were young birds, he could hear their voices in the grass, and, without probing hard, he saw young deer among the older. He turned by a tree he knew well, a pomegranate in the woods still with a few hard red Christmas balls, toward a deeper draw he judged might still be too wet. The path turned again, and there, he didn't believe it, stood Tennyson, long coat, slouch hat, poet's hair, looking up at a tree. He was immediately furious. An interloper should not walk these paths.

He said, correct and stiff to Tennyson's back, "Can I help you?"

Tennyson turned. Hair much like Manfredi's framed the face, which studied him. "But you already do," she said. "Every single month. I'm the other half of your landlord. That would be Manfredi's sister." She changed into English. "I'm meant to know you somehow. Don't think I do."

He walked closer. "Then you're Little Ottavia!" he said.

"Well, maybe I do, then."

"Long time ago," he said. "We came to Capri on the boat. Helene was there. An English girl and an American. You'd read about a man who cut his wrists in the tub. You went on about it, and your nanny took you away. We talked the next morning."

She closed most of the distance between them. "That was you? Yes, of course it was! You were such a love that day. I've never forgotten any of it."

"Alistair. Stears," he said.

"My brother really is a hound, you know. He should have prepped me on all this. He just told me to call on you. I would have, sooner or later. I saw you on your horse. The famous poet. I remember it all. You'd just lost a girl then. Do you make a habit of that?"

"It seems that I do," said Alistair.

"To lose one might be cause for condolence. To lose two merely argues unforgivable absent-mindedness. Oscar Wilde said that."

"He said something remotely similar. I thought you lived in Germany."

"Germany stopped being fun. It got nasty. Probably will get even nastier, I'd say."

She walked all the way to him and took both his hands in hers just long enough for him to feel warmth. She said, "It's awfully nice to find you again. I used to wonder when you'd come back."

"We went to Venice. My mother was in love with a colonel. We went to Udine. It was very, very complicated. There was Caporetto."

"I saw you at Manfredi's wedding, but I couldn't get close to you. I was just a little girl still. I'm an old woman now, twenty-six. When I came back from Germany, I stayed in Umbria for a while, being very grand, but Manfredi and I don't really get on under each other's feet. So we remembered this hovel. I don't have any money, you see, except half your rent. Do you know he's got a girl there?"

"Yes," said Alistair.

"She's a dear little thing. Do you know they had a baby?"

"Probably she had it, mainly," said Alistair. "And he's not quite a baby now, unless she's had another. I like her too. I was there for Christmas."

"Of course. You were there for Christmas, weren't you? I'm very, very glad about her," said Ottavia. "It was horrible, horrible, horrible for him about Helene."

Her hair and face became abruptly darker. He perceived that the sun had blown away. A dark cloud was over them, and the wind had begun to rain. There being few leaves yet, it found them at once.

He said, "We're going to get wet."

"I don't really care." She indicated her coat and hat. "I found these hanging in my hovel. They smell a bit. Cow, I think. I expect you were going to see if there were any deer down there. There aren't. It's a swamp."

He said, "I thought it might be." And then, "Would you come for dinner?"

"Out of my pigsty? I'd love to. I mean I'd love to anyway, of course." She said, "I suppose you're 'Alistair' to me now. What did I call you last time? Nanny called all of you, 'His Lordship's guests.'"

He laughed with her. "That could be stilted," he said. "For a whole dinner. 'Alistair' is good. But she was English."

"But she was English," said Ottavia. "Still, we're not, and I shouldn't suppose we want actually to drown, do we?" The rain, led astray by the general intemperance of the day, had gone hysterical. "If you're going in, we can walk together as far as the pomegranate, and then I go a different way."

At the pomegranate, he watched her into the wood, Tennyson received back into tossing boughs and the veil of rain, the horns of elfland faintly blowing.

SHE CAME NOT IN the stained duster but a spring overcoat, which revealed a dinner dress, dark blue and, here in the country, elegant. She asked to change out of her walking shoes. He realized that he had seen no new car on the place, but it was quite a long walk in the dusk that still came early. His butler bowed to her deeply, and said, "Marchesina Ottavia," but seemed in no way surprised.

In the dining room, the Galilean planets looked down on a perfectly strange young woman he had seen once as a child before any of the big things had happened.

She said, "Is Concetta still the cook?" Yes, she was, and she said, "Not bad. Not very good with game." She said, "It's odd to be here again, and with you . . ." she seemed to try it out, "Alistair." Whenever her shoulders sank, she sat very straight again, as though reminding herself to do so. The candles and the firelight chased each other across her shoulders and her breast. Her dress was cut a little low. Dragoons of untouchability stood sentry around her, and he looked away.

"I spent a lot of time here. After I met you. In my teens."

"I thought it was always rented," he said.

"No, no. Not always. We've had this place much longer than Umbria. My great-grandfather bought Umbria after they turned the grand duke out in Florence, and he decided to be anti-Tuscan. No place for a gentleman. Eighteen sixty."

He said, because he didn't know, and the conversation led there, "Before that, Ferrara, I suppose?"

"Not for ages. We come from a second son, back in the Renaissance. That's why we're only Ugolino-Ferraras, not real Estes, and poor Manfredi is only a marchese and not a duke. But the pig who hung his duchesses on the wall, that is us, yes."

"He hung one only, surely? Not a whole gallery. Still . . ."

"Still. So this place is almost home. Then, someone speaks to me, rather bolshily, in the wood, and God knows it's you. And here I am having dinner with you in my own house."

Now through the pantry door came Concetta from the kitchen, roasted rather rare, and curtsied. "I've made your guinea fowl for you, Marchesina and the *torta di mele* too."

He was not, thought Alistair, directing this evening but turning in its orbit.

Ottavia said kind things about the *pappardelle* and asked about Concetta's children. One was off in Libya. When Concetta left, Ottavia said, "I have to keep reminding myself that I was just a little brat you met on the beach a thousand years ago. And now, of course, I'm rather different. Is this strange, for you, Alistair?"

He could not, he realized at once, lie to that straight nose and grave, unguarded mouth.

"It wasn't in the wood," he said. "Now, yes. It is strange." He tried, "You trail things behind you I can't quite see." He tried again, "You're bookends, and I can't see the books between."

"For me, it's much easier. Odd, yes. Not strange. Because you've always been with me. When I didn't recognize you, it's because I had it in my head you'd look the same. To me, you were a man then. But I suppose you weren't."

"A very spoiled boy," he said. "And very, very dramatic." *I should be asking myself if she's sane.* But he didn't.

"I read Tagliamento here, the first time, when I was twelve."

"You really did?" he said.

"Of course we all did. We were so terribly, terribly proud of you. Even Mummy, because she knew yours, you know. I remember the parcel arriving from New York."

"I remember mailing it," he said.

"Mummy wouldn't let me read it. 'Unsuitable.' So I read it with Helene. She was like a very, very young aunt to me. I loved her, Alistair. But my English was much, much better than hers, so in the end I translated most of it to her."

The dragoon guard allowed her to be looked at, and he did look at her. When she forgot, her head sank a little down, and the fire and candles were in her hair.

"You translated Tagliamento into French?"

"That's what Helene spoke, really. Her Italian never got very good. She did try."

Ottavia raised her head and looked at him as though weighing him. "Who was she, Alistair? The girl I was such a smarty little brat about on the beach?"

"She was my mother's model. A young artist's model. So we were around each other in the house a lot. It was probably inevitable and quite unimportant. But I loved her very much."

"So that is the girl in Tagliamento?"

"You mean the country girl with the Carabinieri? No, no. I only saw her once, from a train. In Umbria, actually, but I moved her."

"No, Alistair. I mean the one who is the whole end of the poem. She's never named or even mentioned. But she's there. I always wanted to call her the redemption, but that's not quite right. I didn't see her at first, but it changes all the motion of the poem, the blood. It becomes a woman's."

"She died," he said. "In the war. Of the flu. In Venice. She died before Helene." And because even with his back to the fire he had shivered, said, "Who are you, Ottavia? What do you do?"

"Nothing much here," she said. "I read. Mostly German. Was Schiller, now Goethe. In Germany I did a little writing for a small newspaper in Wurzburg. And went on hunts and to dances and so forth, which is what I was supposed to do. Not with the same people, of course. The newspaper got bombed and burned. The people who did it came to power last year. Nobody in the family knows anything about that, Alistair, so don't let on, please."

Over a sort of pound cake, haunted by *vin santo* and an intense, incorporeal presence of apple, she said, "How old were you on Capri?"

He said, "Sixteen."

"Yes. That would have been about Manfredi. I was eight. Now I'm twenty-six. So you're thirty-four."

"It's easy with me," he said. "If it's '34, I'm thirty-six. You take the year, plus two."

"It isn't even much difference. On Capri, you seemed a different species."

"That does happen," he said. And then, "Is Tagliamento all you've read? Of mine?"

That lifted her head even more. "Of course not. I've read it all. Everything. Really, Alistair!"

"Did you like the last ones? The ones from Paris?"

"Not as much," she said. "They worried me a little."

"I'm so glad, Ottavia," he said.

She asked to be shown around her house. "I haven't been more than through the front door in years."

She said, "You've got a nice place for breakfast now. It used to be just terrace when it was warm and the dining room when it was cold. I like that."

She said, "Your desk is beautiful. Now I know where you write. It suits you, Alistair."

She said, "You're sleeping in my bedroom!" And he must have looked abashed, for she said. "It's perfectly all right. You could hardly have known. And anyway, you're allowed to."

He drove her home. It turned out to be not entirely. The pavilion, the hovel, did not share the driveway of the villa. The car could drive a track but not for the last three hundred yards, except in dry summer. They walked. All the clouds had blown away, but the wind was still nervous and quite cold. The quarter moon was low in the sky. He had not brought a flashlight, not knowing the need. They walked hand in hand. He thought of boar in the dark but dismissed it, thinking them not dangerous. At her door, she presented her face to be kissed. He did so and found that his lips sank a little bit into her cheek. She smelled a little bit like pear.

"Good night, Alistair," she said.

He worked the next day on the most unruly of his children, a poem begun well, an end with a shape visible but cut off at the knees, a middle all murk where creatures bumped into your thigh unseen. He worked at his desk. His desk suited him. When he recognized the forms he meant, they did not attract words, or attracted words that repelled the ones he was already sure of. Pear, he thought her cheek, but found it hard precisely to recall the scent of pear. He was not stuck, he knew, because in the end he never finally was, but this was thicker mud than usual. He left his lunch on its tray. Chasing phantoms made his brain as dark as the dark they lived in. He bathed with a headache. He came down for his drink before dinner and saw the evening ahead under the Galilean planets which moved on, though fixed, and himself fixed, though alive. He looked out and saw his car in the dusk and his butler opening its door for Ottavia. He looked behind him into the dining room, and saw his table had been set for two. His spirits jumped up, set off after the Galilean planets, and lapped them.

She had put on the dog. She thanked Girolamo, and thanked him again by trailing her arm behind her as she turned for the steps. Alistair opened the door, and she said, "Good evening, Alistair," nicely. Her evening shoes seemed to flow down her legs as she unlaced the walkers. Bent double, she said, "How kind of me to let me come," sotto voce, and sotto voce laughed.

If he were back with the eight-year-old, *look at me,* he could welcome her. Her coat once off, her dress showed no sleeves, shoulders, and a neckline that dived like a swallow and soared up at modesty—all, he supposed bravely done amongst cold water, tin cup, and old dog leash for clothesline, the kind of austerities the hovel must impose.

But then, straight up, serious, and looking in his eye, she said, "Is this all right, Alistair? Am I interrupting? I wouldn't do that. I can go home."

It was the eye and mouth he could not lie to. Therefore he said, "You were invited. I just did not mention it. You were clever to know," and touched her shoulder so lightly the dragoon did no more than frown.

"That's nice," she said.

He assented to Girolamo, who took away his whisky and poured two glasses of Champagne.

Still winter enough, still fire enough, for chicken broth with tortellini in it. China he had not seen since the first evening with Manfredi had reappeared.

"Don't think I have anything against young men and dances," she said. "I don't. Or young men and shooting, especially when they let me shoot. I love attention. I start off enthusiastic. Because I'm flattered. Then comes the day I can't do another word. Say or listen. I'd rather put my head in a hole. So I'm the nastiest kind of flirt, as is well known. And an old maid, of course."

"Women have incredibly complicated lives, I think. Mine have been mostly nymphs lately. Or went to nymph finishing school, if not."

"I really look forward to reading that," she said. "My Latin was never very good. Can I read the manuscript?"

"The manuscript is away. Galleys soon."

"Oh good."

Concetta came in, escorting a duck. They found that they had been leaning toward each other and straightened up. The duck was introduced, briefly, then, "There were green peas in the garden, Marchesina Ottavia, and new mint."

"Oh, well done," said Ottavia. "That is clever."

"It was the gardener who brought them in," said Concetta to the dish.

"Then well done, both of you," said Ottavia. "You do spoil us."

It was the first time he had seen the young chatelaine, he noted, for there had still been charade when she got out of the car. Not far to reach for, the chatelaine, bred in the bone, why not, but he did now see that she had a wardrobe of selves to pull out one by one. Concetta and Girolamo withdrawn, the planets looked at them and gave no advice.

"German poetry," he said. "I know very little of it. Tell me."

"Goethe can put on an Italian face. But that's what it is, a put-on face. He loved Italy though. Leopardi is a little close to the Germans. No, that's not true, but there are Germans who paint a bit as Leopardi wrote. Hoderlin. This is no good, Alistair. I have to say what I was trying say."

He bowed now to her straightest and coolest presence.

She said, "Are you an only child, Alistair? I think you are."

"Really, yes," he said. "I had a younger brother, but he died very, very young. I have no memory of him."

She nodded, as though to show condolence her visiting card. "I had an older sister. Between myself and Donato. Do you know Donato?"

"Only at the wedding."

"He's always with the army. He's in Libya now. She didn't die very, very young. She died at convent school. Of meningitis. Several of the girls did. It was awful. That was a little before you knew us."

And had vaguely known the fact. He waited.

"I think it had the opposite effect," she said. "It made you the only child. It made me The Sister. I wasn't quite Ottavia any more. I was part of a troupe, and I had a role. So I had to be more and more Ottavia. Me. Myself. To show. That was the little brat you met on Capri."

He looked entirely at her face. "But I liked the little brat. I tried to ransom you from your nanny, but Manfredi wouldn't have it. I looked for you in the morning."

Her face softened into a smile, and her chin dropped a little. She said, "I love Manfredi. But we fight. He loves me, too, but he doesn't approve of me a bit." The chin recovered itself. "Donato is the perfect officer. He'll be a major soon, and he's very young. Manfredi's the perfect marchese. Don't you think? And I'm . . ."

"Perfect marcheses have marchesas, and if one breaks down they get another one."

Her shoulders dropped this time, too, and seemed to curve a little toward him. "Because he can feel the cold. That's why I love him. Helene almost killed him. He can feel the cold and he needs his Claudia to warm him. I love him for both. I even love her. And you understand, of course. You would." She had her wardrobe back at fingertip now and changed back easily into princess. "*Mais revenons a nos moutons, que tu ne vois pas encore.* May I call you *tu,* Alistair?"

"Don't be silly," he said.

"Thank you. So, Alistair, there I was, a bad little child not much use for anything, and you came with my glamorous brother all wrapped in dark romance clouds, which I hardly understood at all. And you talked to me. No, that was easy. You listened to me before you talked. Even after I was a rude, silly little baby. And you were glad to see me in the morning. Then you sailed away, *mein schoner Lohengrin,* you sailed away, and I thought, next time I can talk to him about anything. Then I thought, all I was was stupid and rude and I've made him angry and he thinks I'm nothing, and he'll never come back. And you never came back."

"Dear God," said Alistair. "I was a boy."

"No, you weren't, and you know it. Maybe you were about some things. You never came back, but your books did, and people started talking about you. I read the books. And there you were again. Then I had the idea that if I understood the books better than anyone, it would be just like having you to talk to. And I did. I could flesh it out a bit, because I knew real things about you every now and then. I knew you were a soldier, with your horse and your sword. And you were on a tropical island. Were there beautiful women with bare breasts on the beach?"

"Oh yes," he said. "They were American nurses. Bare breasts more after the beach than actually on, though."

"So I was almost right. I asked you about the girl in Tagliamento, but you'd never answer until now. I had to guess. Then I heard you were in Paris. I knew all about that by then. So I knew you were with Fitzgerald and Gertrude Stein in a straw boating hat on the Seine . . ."

"Ottavia," he said. "What a horrid imagination!"

"Or very like that, I'm sure." She sat straight again and let her silence turn the page.

She said, "I'm not the brat. You know that, don't you?"

"I know it absolutely, Ottavia."

"I talked to you mainly about me. When I started writing myself, you turned away. I thought I wasn't good enough."

"I can't know that," he said.

"None of this is exactly the point," she said. She went on, "And now, when I'm thrown out of Germany, more or less, and I don't have anything to do, and no money except a ridiculous little bit of rent because Manfredi gives you my house for almost nothing, I find out you're here, when I see you in the wood, I mean, you're real, and we talk, and we're almost the same age. And you're sleeping in my bed. It's perfectly all right. So, Alistair, my being here this evening is not quite as casual as you may have thought. And I do not go under false pretenses. And I do not have to come again."

He touched only the back of her hand with his fingertips. The dragoon still clanked his spur. Alistair said, "You should talk to Concetta about tomorrow night. She shouldn't have to go on guessing."

She said, "Oh, thank you, Alistair." But the smile followed the words and seemed to spread upward from her feet. In this, she leant a little more toward him. His eye fell upon her breasts, and the dusk in her dress beside them. She saw it, and her eye brightened before her smile. For an instant, she bent another millimeter. The brave sergeant of dragoons wiped a tear from his eye and turned his face away. She sat up quite straight again.

They were both pleased to notice that their plates contained a crisp brown swelling of duck, and peas with shiny little faces, which were going to pout if not paid attention to. She ate seriously. He was glad to see it. He distrusted girls who didn't.

They didn't say much while Girolamo changed their plates. She was tall and straight again but seemed lighter than before.

Primly she said, "It's healthy to have lunch too. Everyone says that."

"I don't take long over it," he said.

"Oh, Alistair," she said. "You couldn't. You mustn't. You have far too much to do. It can be as short as you like. I'll bring a book."

A NIGHT OF CATECHISM still left his head clear in the morning. A year and more in a house with no woman's footfall to hear nor scent to breathe was not his way. And was not the point. His military years had been extraordinarily pure—not as penance, exactly, but still with the belief that his soul and Victoria's could benefit by chastity.

He did not hear the car, but when he came down for lunch, she was in a deep chair by the fire, from which she disentangled herself in time with his approach. There was a pile of books beside her. She wore a long wool skirt the color of the darkest iris, a high-necked pullover like mist, and pearls. She kissed his cheek. He touched her waist. She had the smooth, lithe look of a winter woodland animal. Pear, clear and lithe as well, he had ascertained in their evening's goodnight kiss. But away from the fire, the room was chilly, and her pelt did not look that stout.

"Are you warm enough?" he said.

"You should try the hovel. The heating's sick and the wood's damp."

"Do you make this stuff up?" he said.

"Not all that much of it. It does get cold."

Both laughed much more than that was worth. Girolamo brought very small glasses of vermouth. He did not usually drink at lunch.

She brought a book to the table. "Sooner or later you will be lost in thought. Did you have a good morning? Am I allowed to ask?"

"Yes and yes. That's not Schiller."

"You can't read Schiller all the time. It's Hugo von Hoffmansthal. *Jedermann.* People know him best for his words to opera, but he's very good." He was learning to hear her changes of thought in her silences.

She said, "Alistair, people always act as though Manfredi and I were Italian with a tiny bit of German. We're not. Mummy's a Kraut. Grandfather was one of those Germans who liked Italy—Venice Lido in summer and Posilipo in winter, for him. So she's spoken Italian all her life. My uncle too. But he had to go to military school and all that, and he turned back into German. Mummy married Daddy and became Italian. I'm half German, Alistair."

He absorbed that merely. He had known it if he had thought about it. He said, "I want you to read a Russian. So I can talk to you about it. In English. I wasn't the translator. I was the nanny. You don't have to wait for galleys. It's right here."

"I will," she said. "But I want to read your Ovid."

Lunch was not much: venison *bresaolo,* bread, and lettuce salad. His new boar prosciutto was still too young, but the bresaolo seemed all right.

"I suppose you shot this," Ottavia said.

"Yes."

"I'm not really such an awful shot myself."

"What would 'such an awful shot' be though? Your friends all dead and the stag running free?"

"Clever, clever," said Ottavia in a tone he liked.

Girolamo came back in. He left slices of blood orange with some Cointreau.

"Good for Sicily," said Ottavia. Giralamo left. She said, "Alistair, did you and your lady sleep in my bedroom?"

"No," he said. "Rather small."

"It's not so very small, if you're fond of each other. Which, obviously . . . But I expect you slept in Mummy and Daddy's room. Much grander."

"More Olympian," he said.

She laughed, startlingly. "It would be stupid of me to mind. You didn't know. And I suppose she never heard of me?"

He thought. He said, "She would have heard your name spoken, but it was to Manfredi. I never told her the Capri story."

"It's nice my name was mentioned occasionally, somehow. Alistair, she's not coming back, is she? She's not on vacation or something? I don't think so."

He would have hated to lie into those eyes. He said, "I know exactly where she is. We're very good friends. She is never coming back."

She said to that, "Very good friends can only be good. The other would be sad. I think I'd be disappointed in you."

He said, "You will find the Russian amazing. He's tremendous. He's wonderful. He's amazingly brave. You must read him. Because I need to talk about him. He's better than I am. I said that."

"I'll read him by the fire. I suppose I might believe you. Doubt it. Alistair, can I have a bathroom here? It's rather rancid bathing at the hovel. I brought some evening clothes."

"You can have the Olympian one," he said, and this time they both laughed.

He supposed a well-brought-up young lady, in a house not very warm, would have worn this evening's dress to seduce. She came down after him. Kissing her welcome, he disturbed her shawl and breathed her body, the pear bathed and fresh. He would have held her longer but for Girolamo's entering with Champagne. Her manner entirely negated this. Her lips were affectionate and composed. He realized his error. He was treating time as though it were normal time and not the time that prevailed here. Instead of going through the breakfast room, and the morning room, pausing at the billiard table in the smoking room, the astronomical dining room, they had just walked across the hall. Seduction was long behind them. Her body was one of things they had between them when it came time to stretch out a hand. At table, he pushed in her chair. Her body expected this and knew how to accommodate him. What they had now, a gift, was time.

"I began your Russian," she said. "He is quite wonderful. I love the day yawning like a caesura. Who is he? It doesn't say."

"The caesura's quite early. When you've finished. I'll tell you then. I promise."

"I think I know what you need to talk about. Already. But not quite. I will, Alistair. We have time."

So she gave him the story of her Germany: with prologue of her uncle's place, a hare bleeding into the snow and her pride at her shot, the year's first strawberries in thick cream at a dance—she liked the young man for a while, the train to Berlin, a really fancy restaurant, her first opera *Die Entfurung Aus Dem Serail* great fun, looking through the door of a cabaret at a nude girl, *Ottavia!*, smell of linden if you sat outside after dinner in late spring, finally allowed the car, big BMW, meeting some young intellectuals, by accident even Jews, the little newspaper up a side street in Wurzburg their town, herself trying out writing, romping into print.

"I had a little dog, a little English dog, a Sealyham. This was in Umbria. He went off one day. I found him in a corner of the garden where there were tall lilies several days later. I was very young. He was asleep. I put my hand on him. He was all full of maggots and blowflies. Even then I thought how many there were, and how strong they were, how very strong. And where had they come from? When they bombed the newspaper, that's what I thought. So many. So strong. From where? And now they're the government. They can be anywhere. Germany, Russia, here, France, communists, fascists. It all just names. All they need is opportunity, a little dead dog. Something dead. Maybe dying. I'm not sure if you know that. It's us and it's them. That's why we need to know each other."

He was not sure how much danger she'd been in.

"I was never there at the paper, Alistair. They had no idea who I really was. I'd just have been propaganda. I made up a name, Elfriede von Morgenstern . . ."

He winced.

"Yes, awful wasn't it? And the 'von' was just stupid. I mainly wrote about sex. It was the kind of paper that likes a girl writing about sex, intellectually. They wouldn't let me near politics. Politics for the boys, sex for the girl was how it was. I supplemented my knowledge. Uncle's library had a pornographic part, which of course I found. I think it was his father's. English and French, mainly. It was rather cozy reading that stuff. But I had to theory it up for my paper. They were respectable socialist intellectuals, not milord roue's. I wrote about caning as the paradigm of the capitalist's relation to his workers. That was a happy stroke."

"As one might say," he said.

"Ha! An English source, of course. *Les anglais etaient le plus douteux,* Alistair. So there were at least six reasons why Aunt and Uncle couldn't know a thing. Mainly, Uncle might have been drawn into it somehow if I had gotten into trouble, which would have been very unfair. I certainly wasn't there when it was bombed. I actually don't think anybody knows anything about me, by name. But I can't go back."

Girolamo knew them by now, how long they took. He had cracked the door several times and now came in.

"Is this a little what you want to talk about?" said Ottavia.

"Yes," he said.

Ottavia had chosen this dinner. It was risotto with dried porcini, and now it was beef from Valdichiana braised for hours in Barolo and leeks and parsnips. He admired a girl for wanting this and said so.

"Concetta's better with risotto than most Tuscans. And I like this stuff in the winter. And it's what Tuscans know. They're not very good with soufflés and crab."

And at the end, zabaglione. He adored it. He had it very rarely.

"I had to talk Concetta through that. She's not very Venetian. But we deserve it, Alistair. It was the only thing."

He scented it, and looked at it lying like a mist in the bowl. He had a sudden vision of Victoria with her zabaglione on Torcello. This time without grief.

He said, "It's a lovely idea, Ottavia."

When he took her home, there was a bright moon, almost half. At the final walk, he took a revolver from the car. It glittered in the moon. Of boar, he had realized that the sows would now be with their piglets and could possibly be quite dangerous if surprised in the night. Ottavia, certainly, could not be harmed.

Ottavia said, "That's fantastically becoming." She held his other hand. She said, "I have seen them. They never come anywhere close."

"So long as they see you," he said.

They kissed goodnight long and comfortably. They were even beginning to know each other's contours.

"Goodnight, my Alistair," said Ottavia.

One day he awoke to rain, waking later in the dim light. Rain sang in the gutters, ran over the tiles. Spring rain is good for Tuscan grass and woods, which the hunter and the horseman knew.

No sun made the house more chill. The fires were heaped higher. He breakfasted with the lamps on and the warmth pleasant at his back. He felt that rain reflected his thoughts back to him and made good workdays. In his study, the fire's flames gave life to the lamplight.

The door opened behind his back. Ottavia's voice said, "May I come and read? Will I bother you? Of course I'll shut up."

He turned his head and smiled without rising. "You may," he said. "You will not bother me. Yes, you will shut up." She came over and put her arm around his shoulder and laid her cheek beside his. Then chose a chair a little behind his left shoulder and quite near the fire.

He had his direction this morning: a poem, actually already good, containing two separate thoughts, which could be seen as colors. His task was to make these two ribbons better merge into and withdraw from each other. He worked well and with pleasure. Floating over this, quite separate, he liked the turn of Ottavia's pages, from time to time the scratching of her pen and the sound of her thighs seeking an ever better nest. She knew how to use a chair, Ottavia. Einsteinian gravity silently held their presences together and apart. He saw no reason why he should ever wish to be away from her. At the proper time, they went down to lunch, which, given the day, she had ordered warmed by *agnolotti* in a chicken broth.

Before dinner, they had a longer Champagne hour than usual, by the fire. The rain still filled the world. He wound up the gramophone and played them a cello sonata by Brahms. Though a windup one, the machine was good and the sound was deep. They did not talk over it.

At the end of the evening, he walked with her to the door. Opened, it showed rain like crystal in the house lights, showed waterfalls on the steps. Little worms of chill ran over the threshold and onto their feet. He shut it again. She put her head on his shoulder.

She said, "You weren't seriously thinking of that? Really, Alistair!" He felt her take two slow breaths. She said quietly, "I want my own room. And my own bed. And, of course, my own Alistair. It's time." She kissed him on the lips.

He kissed her back much harder and almost raised her from the floor. He relaxed his arms for fear of hurting her. He was able to say, "I could never have asked you. Do you see? I could never have asked. You."

Her head was back on his shoulder. "I began to understand. I was beginning to wonder what was going on, and then I knew. But it's time, Alistair. Don't we like each other better and better all the time?" She moved her head so she could see his face.

"Oh yes, Ottavia. Oh yes."

"I think we're going to like each other even better in a very little while," she said, and took his hand. They went back down the corridor and through the hall.

Seduction being already far behind them in the time that prevailed here, so was any possible awkwardness. He was first in the bed, she having gone to her toilette. She came back in a dressing gown and turned off the lamps. The fire, though low, still gave light. She stood beside the bed and close to him. She let slip the gown. The firelight worshiped her flesh; the prospect was as fair as one could want. But it was cold. He held up the blanket. She accepted it and got in.

He woke still to the sound of rain and the scent of her hair. The rain closed around them like a comfortable room. He lay with all this in delight.

The rain changed its nature. It became a cold drench, dissolving comfort, laying baseness bare. Lain with a trusting young woman, rutted on his friend's sister, betrayed the memories of a child, exploited his loneliness and hers, used her faith in his art. He was completely unused to such thoughts. He had trusted in love for joy all his life. He dared not move an arm. He dreaded her awaking and her sight of what he saw in himself.

At the bottom of this wreckage, a spark lit, spread, raced upward, and filled all. He was flooded with happiness. He put his arm more closely around her. He waited until her breathing suggested wakefulness. He kissed her ear and whispered into it, "Ottavia, will you marry me?"

"Yes, I will," she said. She moved the leftover millimeter into him. "What a lovely good morning!" Then, "Can we just lie here and think about it?"

"Yes," he said.

Then shortly, "I want a huge big wedding. Really put on the dog. Pretend we're Estes again. Can we?"

"Yes," he said. "We can. But that takes time. I want to marry you tomorrow."

She thought about that and lifted her head a little. "So we can stay like this? I think I understand. Because I'm me? I said, 'I'm yours.' So you can marry me. But a big wedding, too, please."

"Absolutely," he said. "I know a monsignore here. He's a friend. He'll marry us."

"That would be Kirchner? I know him too. He's nice. When he first came, he was still completely Austrian. Manfredi said we had to treat him with great respect because the Austrians had had a fine army and their chaplains were very brave." Her nose was still in the pillow, and her voice was snuffly.

"Manfredi was right." He laid his mouth for a while upon her topmost vertebra and breathed her skin.

"Alistair, we can't get married tomorrow. It's Sunday."

"Then we'll go to Mass and talk to Kirchner afterwards. Monday."

They were quiet a little while. Then, "Alistair, isn't there some kind of waiting period?"

"I think we can manage it. Kirchner will help. We might have to talk to the bishop."

"Ah," said Ottavia.

She said, "Isn't it going to be a little embarrassingly obvious what the hurry is? I can keep a straight face with Kirchner; he's a friend. But the bishop?"

"The hurry goes straight to the heart and soul of marriage. It is a reasonable and Catholic hurry."

"All right," she said.

She turned over to face him and laced her arms around his back. "I need to know your arrangements," she said, "since they're my responsibility now. Do the housemaids come up here early?"

"Not till I'm down. I doubt the stove's lit yet."

"Ah," she said. "Noted. Does someone sneak in here early and make up the fire?"

"I don't have that done."

She ran her hands up to his shoulders, and all the way down his arms, and took his hands and placed them on her breasts.

"I'd like some more of my husband then," she said.

BREAKFAST GAVE HIM THE savor of the future, ceremony to become accustomed, if your mind turned to Yeats. Ottavia talked to the two housemaids about the terrible weather last night, and please to attend to her parents' room and bathroom, which she had been obliged to use. At the edge of the sky, the end of the rain showed mother-of-pearl.

"I think that little Lucia girl has the makings of a lady's maid," said Ottavia in English. We'll see."

"I have to call my mother," said Alistair.

"I obviously have to call Manfredi."

"If I book the call now, it should go through this evening. Her lunch, more or less."

"I'm going to tell Mummy I'm engaged. She can get started on the big wedding. I'm going to keep quiet there about the little one unless it gets awkward later."

"Probably wise," he said.

"We won't have much trouble there. Everybody knows I've waited ages too long to marry, and she's always liked you, and she'll think you're a good catch."

"Manfredi can get here on Monday, can't he?"

"I don't see why not." And lowered her voice. Pointlessly, what with the English. "Alistair, don't think you're going to get me out of my own bed just because we can't get married until Monday. We'll just have to think of some other excuse. Boars, do you think?"

"Dangerous animals," he said.

THEY WERE MARRIED ON the Monday, in the Cathedral of St. Martin at Lucca, in the chapel where pretty Ilaria sleeps down the centuries with her little dog, at the altar under Ghirlandaio's Madonna.

They did not have to see the bishop. Monsignore Kirchner managed it and did it. Kirchner, whose business with Alistair had been exalted but gloomy throughout, took this as the happiest of inventions, even though, as he said, "It had truly never crossed my mind." He was a careful priest and gave them instruction in their new state, in German to Ottavia.

Anna Stears was annoyed to be disturbed by the telephone as she sat down to lunch in the grey Berkshires then went immediately into transports of delight. Alistair told her of the engagement, of the wedding, and also of the confidential wedding. Even across the telephone, he had the impression of objects whizzing past by telekinesis into a trunk marked, "Italy." Would she stay a little when she came? "Oh, I don't know, Alistair not above a decade or two, I should think." Before she could get the telephone down, he heard a shout of "Kitty!"

There was a difficulty with Manfredi, he being with an Italian agricultural delegation in Berlin, all the meetings arranged for the first part of the week. One forgot that he was deputy minister for that now. He could be with them later in the week. He had the impression Manfredi had asked, "Couldn't they defer?" His sister had gone into German the second part of the conversation, which he had never understood his friend to speak. He thought she said, "Oh, Manfredi, don't be so slow."

The witnesses, Shakespearian, were Girolamo and Concetta, deeply flattered, sworn to secrecy, and absolutely guaranteed to tell all the staff and all the villages nearby that the signore and the marchesina were truly, Catholically married. If they found anything risible in the young people's haste, it was subsumed, through Ottavia's artful planting, by the thought of the colossal scale of the revelries to come and their own dignified place in them.

Ottavia did not attempt white for this. She wore a dress of pearl-grey, modest and pretty, with one of the last miniature irises pinned at her breast. She told the monsignore that it was the favorite chapel of them both, which she had known for at least twenty minutes.

Kirchner said, "Thank you, my dear. It's not only for you." He pointed to Ilaria, whose dress was much the same grey as Ottavia's, though a little busier around the throat in the fashion of 1409. "One gets fond of her. One likes to brighten up her day. She was married here, too, you know." He gestured toward the door. "I don't think that's much in her line."

"That" was a nun who stood at a booth by the chapel door selling portraits on some kind of Bakelite, not cheap, of the Duce on his white horse. Though high and rather handsome, the nun carried the penance of a shocking squint so that she seemed to look as much at the spirits of the middle air as at her customers when she closed each transaction by bathing the portrait in holy water.

Alistair thought the Duce's stirrup one hole too short and his seat too backward, but this thought was not new.

Kirchner made the third at their wedding breakfast, obviously not advertised as such, at the restaurant on the square facing Garibaldi and the opera house. They had the prawns that came from the coast opposite Elba, suckling pig, tiny new spring artichokes in a casserole, and a great deal of Champagne. Warm sun fell on him through the window, and the bubbles rose into it. The sun fell on two fair islands the winter waves had left behind, his Ovid and the Russian. He felt a hollowness, but it was much more sweet than cruel. His youth had left, he thought. He no longer much wanted it and would have given it to Ottavia if he could. In the sun, their future could ripen like a peach against the wall.

They would happily have kept to her bedroom, but the choice was not theirs. Her parents' grand bed was scattered with irises and the earliest rose buds. The effect was of an overturned wheelbarrow, but the intent was kind.

"I suppose we're Mummy and Daddy now," said Ottavia.

"I hope we will be, Ottavia," said Alistair.

Ottavia looked at him seriously. "Oh, my dear," she said. "We've talked about so much we've forgotten things. Of course we'll be a mummy and daddy unless we can't. I even promised Kirchner. It just takes a little time. And a girl shouldn't be too pregnant at her own wedding. We could start trying a month before, though."

They spoke mostly in English, in which they had privacy, obviously a great deal in Italian, and sometimes in French. Until late and evil times, never in German. Alistair's was terrible.

Alistair never asked Manfredi, and Manfredi never volunteered, whether Ottavia could have known that Alistair was at the villa. It would have spoiled the story. His loyalty was to Ottavia. And he loved stories.

13

Manfredi arrived with a surprise: Claudia in a pretty traveling dress, with arm around a brand new pigskin case. Holding Alistair and Ottavia both in the highest possible regard, she kissed everybody twice. Manfredi said from the open double door, "I'm sure we can get you out of this somehow, Alistair. She's a horrid little thing when you get to know her," came forward, and kissed his sister with his arm around his friend. Girolamo tried simultaneously to bow to his real master and coax the pigskin from Claudia's grip. There followed a moment of uncertainty.

"Let's have glass of wine," said Ottavia. It was late in the afternoon. "The drawing room." There were a few steps leading out of the hall. Manfredi had trouble with them and put out his hand to Claudia's forearm, which was by his side. Ottavia said to Girolamo, *"Sciampagne."*

Ottavia spoke to Alistair in an upstairs corridor. He said, "We're in dinner jacket, no?"

"Yes," she said. "I'm not going to dress much, though. I bet he's given Claudia something to put in that case. I'm damned if I'm going to compete."

At dinner, Ottavia said, "So. Berlin?"

"Busier," said Manfredi. "I think they have their confidence back."

"The truth, Manfredi. You have eyes."

"If I were against them, I'd be uncomfortable," he held her eye, but he said it quietly.

"I don't know why the hell you do this, Manfredi. Why do you want to be one of this stupid government's little deputy ministers sucking up to Nazis? You're the Marchese Ugolino-Ferrara, for Christ's sake. You're a military hero. You're a cavalry hero. The only thing they can promote you to is God. You're just lending them your name. Which is mine too. And I resent it."

She was suddenly almost shouting, as Alistair realized. And was completely startled.

"I thought you were Mrs. Alistair Stears these days," said Manfredi.

"And I am proud of it."

"As you should be," said Manfredi.

"But she's not," said Alistair. He looked at them both. "She's the Lady Ottavia Stears. Your nanny had it right, back then. She was always the Lady Ottavia, and now she's the Lady Ottavia Stears. In England or in Ireland. And since the United States is a joint dominion of the two, there also."

"That's rather nice," said Ottavia.

"I forgot to tell you," said Alistair. He realized that Claudia could not have understood a word and murmured it to her in Italian.

Claudia thought this was terrific. She looked at Ottavia and said, *"Che bel titolo, Ottavia!"* She looked shyly. Claudia was indeed ritzy tonight, in russet apple and low cut. Ottavia looked handsome and sleek but somehow windblown, as though advertising evenings at a safari camp. The porters might have lost some of the trunks. Claudia had come down happy with herself, taken one look at Ottavia, whom she revered, and realized all of her mistake.

Ottavia said, "Really, Manfredi, my dear, sweet brother, why are you doing this?"

"It's not a landowner's party, our government. They're town people. There are very few landowners near the top. There is Prince Torlonia, whose plan for Italian agriculture is for him to own all of it he doesn't already. Which isn't much. They had some good ideas in the beginning, but they were engineer's ideas. They don't understand the land, and they don't understand the peasants. The local governments do stupid things, and the peasants get angry. Then the party stalwarts get angry and it turns sour."

"Oh yes. The party stalwarts," said Ottavia. "So good for the castor oil trade."

"By accepting an office, I get some influence. I can get a word in. They're not all bad people. They do not like being seen in the wrong. That may be the most dangerous thing about them. If you show them the better way in time, they're often happy to do it. I have thought about this, Ottavia. If you're a marchese, sometimes you have to use it. It can be a duty."

Ottavia raised her arms in a long, tired gesture. Alistair watched the flow within his wife's underarm. She said, "I don't know everything, Manfredi. I just think I do. You're my older brother. Maybe you're right. Please don't start hanging around Berlin. It's beastly place. You know it is."

For himself, Alistair thought his brother-in-law's—dear God, so he was!—attitude sober and generous, similar to his own delicate maneuvers, like the placing and shifting of spillikens, between Simon Cartwright and Rodolfo. This was now a part, though a small one, of his life. Of which he had not yet told Ottavia.

Fish was dismissed, veal invoked. Manfredi said, "When are you two going to have the real wedding?"

"Theologically, we just had it," said Alistair. "We are man and wife, Manfredi. You can't be more married than that."

"Like being more pregnant," said Ottavia.

Manfredi missed a breath. "Ottavia! You're not?"

"Don't be silly, Manfredi. It wasn't that sort of wedding. We haven't had time, hardly. We need good weather. Not April. It rains too much. Mid-May. It's lovely then. Not later. I want to get on with this. I do fully intend to be pregnant, Manfredi. You're going to have nieces and nephews."

"That will be lovely for Eduardo," said Claudia. "And we want to give him a brother or sister."

Girolamo and red wine came in, closing the issue of issue. Alistair felt that, even absent degrees of being married, he had very quickly become extremely so.

"Do you want to have it here or Umbria? Mummy will agree to either."

"Here. And Alistair agrees," said Ottavia. "It's where we're going to live, at least to start with. And we love it here. And Umbria gets dry as soon as the sun comes out. Lucca's much prettier. The cathedral too."

"I agree, as it happens," said Manfredi. "That's what we'll tell Mummy. I take it you're living at the pavilion, for her."

"Yes," said Ottavia.

"I bet she'll find out about the whole thing."

"I'm only buying time before the row. We're doing nothing wrong. I'm twenty-six. She must have found out about you two, Manfredi. She's not stark blind."

"She doesn't like it. And I'm a boy."

"I only want her to commit to a big wedding before the balloon goes up."

NOW THAT PASSION HAD blown the doors wide open, their bodies were learning to be friends. Their bodies loved these nights of blankets, and most when Alistair and Ottavia, their masters, were asleep. Then his thigh became the rest for her sleeping arm, her smooth haunch a warming pan for his tummy on chillier nights, his hand between her thighs brought release to her shoulders and deeper, sweeter sleep. When a single oxcart, with its symphony around it, came early to the back of the house and let loose a rumble of wood for the fires, or the tractor cleared its throat at the barn of Pozzo Nuovo, and Alistair and Ottavia ventured back to their bodies, they were usually surprised to find them so tangled up, and listened comfortably until crockery and servants had gone on long enough for master and mistress to get up, dress, and go down. Even this reluctant spring, the blankets went away one by one. Came a morning when Ottavia could stand by the window without shivering very much. She looked out at a pergola being built on the lawn as part of the apparatus of the wedding. It was pretty nearly done. There was a month and three days to go. She came back and sat on Alistair's edge of the bed and laid her hand gently on his groin.

"Alistair," she said. "We can start a baby tonight. It's time."

This was worth a celebration. They went into Lucca, called on Ilaria in their chapel, and stood by her, holding hands. The nun gave them an outraged squint and sold another Duce. They went to their restaurant and sat at their table. Elba had sent its prawns again. Ezra Pound and his medals and his boots and his furious hair were back again. He explained him to her, and his name.

"I've heard of this," said Ottavia.

Ezra's estate must have fallen. He was followed today by Young Fascisti in their uniforms. They shrilled at him from behind. "Old freak!" and "Your son was just a traitor!" It had to be said that they held rank, except to pick up small stones from time to time and throw them, not really viciously. Their older leader, who might have been fourteen, smiled with quiet pride when his troupe barely quailed as Ezra turned and faced them, though he faced them with scalding eye.

"This may not end well," said Ottavia.

That night, she said, "This is terribly exciting, Alistair. A baby! I feel completely virginal."

They had thought that, constraint removed, her womb would receive him as happily as the rest of her. In fact, her womb thought it should have been consulted, did not know this fellow, and was not much impressed. This annoyed Ottavia, who took it personally, more than it annoyed Alistair, for he felt in these many nights that he nurtured in his arms a vessel, above a mere girl. He was happy in this new estate. Shifting colors of earth and magic was where he lived best and where he had held Ovid's hand so happily.

They managed it somehow. On the first day that year that was positively warm, Ottavia patted the stone seat beside her in the rose garden and summoned him. "Darling, news from me. Something's not happening that should be happening. I think we've done it." She was bundled off to the doctor the next day.

The Lady Ottavia Stears went to her formal wedding pregnant, which gave her a feeling of accomplishment, but only by a week, which gave her a feeling of virtue.

xxx

HE SAW HIS FATHER, whom he had not seen at all for seven years, and who suddenly knew he had not seen plain since boyhood. He turned to Pietro Vendramin, his old friend in Venice and now acclaimed painter in Paris, and said, "Do you have to be our age to see your parents?"

Which was answered instead by Manfredi in full dress cavalry regimentals with the Order of Savoy polished up as bright as his spurs, who said, "Yes."

For what Alistair saw in his father now was a light figure whose face age had made into an intelligent horse's, slightly smiling at its own top hat, at the vestments and uniforms around him, and maybe at the villa, the cypresses, the olives, the stone caryatids holding up the steps, Catholic Italy in a tableau. In that moment, before his father was reached by the ambassador, a man whom Alistair would have liked better did he not call him "Son" saw the Yankee Protestant he had never bothered to see and divined in him an amusement, never hidden and never seen, not only at his wife's antics, but at his son's.

Anna, on the other hand, had been there three days, following a week with old friends in Rome. The winds of the Berkshires had scraped some flesh and color off her cheeks. Life among the natives had sharpened her imperiousness, but her eye was still luminous, and kind upon Ottavia. The three of them stayed close, when the bride could, and by the second evening, Ottavia, who had been ready to sit at the feet of Anna the legend, liked Anna the woman very well. This changed to delight when Anna asked to have opened the mysterious crate that had preceded her. It contained the bust of Alistair she had started for Cardinal Galisteo, on the stairs in the palazzo, in another age, in Rome. It was not quite finished still, but there was Alistair the boy, the shirt still lifting from his shoulder, face amused and severe, a present for the bride. "Oh mamam!" cried Ottavia in the French fashion, for so she called Anna. And then collected herself, for she had been dying for this opportunity. "Looks remarkably spiritual to have gotten me pregnant so fast, don't you think?" So now someone knew.

"You clever girl!" said Anna. "How wonderful! Thank you!" Kisses, of course, though none for Alistair, who had done a great deal of work, he thought.

He had other fathers, including himself, he supposed, a father now. Two were dead: Mr. Featherstonhaugh and Maggiore. Cardinal Galisteo, absent of course, was present in his own way. A cleric had come with a letter and a box from him. And Monsignore Kirchner, not old enough in years, had become a father ecclesiastically. He came now from the house, greeted Manfredi as old friend, met Pietro, and said to Alistair, "Your bride considers herself neglected and abused. You should go to her."

Alistair answered to his smile, "Father, I obey," excused himself, and went to where Ottavia and the marchesa were running out of hands to shake. He took Ottavia into the sitting room where they had heard Brahms in the rain and where he had breathed her body through her shawl. He sat Ottavia beside him, took Galisteo's letter from his pocket, and yet once again broke the familiar seal. The writing was Galisteo's, now very hard to read:

> My son, many years ago, you were a beam of youth into a life already old. For this I love you. You did what was asked of you faithfully. They who come after me know this. More may be asked. For this, my thanks. You will hear no more from me. They say my time is short, and I believe them. Such as remains is for prayer. I ask you for your prayers, my son. Dante knew that I would have need of them.

He put the letter in Ottavia's hand. He took the box and broke the seal, slowly, for the last time. Inside was a silver box bearing Galisteo's arms. In the box, he found a missal and with bare belief saw it was in half uncial script, illuminated, certainly Irish, certainly old, eighth century perhaps, its corners were set with ruby, a gift for a prince. He put it in Ottavia's hand, which softened to receive it, and said, "When he was a little boy, he was playing in the courtyard on the cobblestones outside a palace they had in the country. In Spain. It had been raining, and the cobblestones were slippery. His parents' carriage was there waiting. The coachman had had too much wine and was half asleep. Something startled the horses. That's what happened to his legs. He told me he cursed God for twenty years. For making him live. He told me that after the girl from Tagliamento died."

Ottavia put the missal back in the box and closed it. She took his hand. "We have all the time in the world, Alistair," she said. "Now we have the guests."

Ottavia's wedding had become muscle-bound, almost by accident. The American ambassador had accepted because his literary wife held Alistair's name high in American esteem, because of an Italian noble family, but mainly because of the promise of his old Harvard friend, the judge, who he had not had a drink with in twenty-seven years. The German ambassador knew that the bride's family in attendance included several names from the Old Army, now become suddenly again the New Army, and that this bride was marrying an American, and that the American ambassador would be there. So he came. The Italian foreign secretary, Count Ciano, in those days picking Italian allies like a girl with a dance card, divined that the two ambassadors were converging upon an Italian noble family whose relationship with the party was only adequate, not avid. He did Ottavia the honor of bringing his own bride, the blushing Etta Mussolini, looking startlingly Wagnerian. Hearing of all this, a bored Savoia princess remembered that she had once been presented with Ottavia when they were girls, and, at this kindest season of the year, bestowed the gift of herself.

All this put some strain on the receiving family. The marchesa dealt with it energetically, mostly in German, and Manfredi, gravely, in Italian. Claudia could be seen here and there, but whether as employee of some sort, or guest, or stray absolutely no one could have told. For two lovely days, Alistair had hoped that the whole Joyce family would turn up. They did not, but Conrad Aiken came, who had been touring in Naples. Ezra Pound (the real one, this time) had written from his new Italian castle that he did not have time to come, which they endured somehow, for they had not invited him. Simon Cartwright, also not invited, came from nowhere, was everywhere, was welcomed, and finally greeted Alistair, "I am impressed, Alistair. I am very impressed."

Well he might be. So was the provincial fascista, enough to detail the junior militia as parking guards. It was easy to see that the German ambassador's silver Mercedes and Count Ciano's special Alfa-Romeo were the cars to guard. Ottavia had said, "Don't let the little thugs inside the gate." The little thugs were paid in chocolate.

"I have to go and drool over the Savoia," now said Ottavia.

They touched hands as she rose. He supposed the ambassadors were his next duty. His hand lay on the silver box, but he did not open it. He felt the missal flow inside, for it was one stream from beginning to end. Its knots became serpents coiled, became the heads of birds becoming the ears of saints, the fangs of demons, its crucifixes probed roots into the hills to drain the venom of dragons and breathe it as incense through nails become flowers. He felt it spread over space and time and knew how long he would spend with it lying in its web. He rose and put the box among the presents.

He shut the door and went back to the garden. He saw Ottavia's wedding dress moving in communion with the princess toward the white dining tables on the terrace and changed his plan. He would capture Etta Mussolini Ciano, leaving Ciano to the marchesa. He walked along the cypresses toward her, saw his father, noted that his mother was there too. And then stopped and blinked, for they were holding hands.

LATE THAT EVENING, WHEN the sky in dusk held swallows and the dark lawn, the glow worms, tired Concetta brought a tray of wedding food out to the terrace.

Alistair and Ottavia, the three of them, were to go to the house on Capri on the yacht *Famagusta* but not this very day. Of the remnant, the marchesa had gone to lie down; Manfredi and Claudia had gone off somewhere. Anna and Ottavia, well shawled, and Alistair sat at a table where stray flowers lay around, escaped from their arrangements.

Ottavia said, "There is so much that is beautiful around Rome if you don't like the city anymore. But you know that."

For they had heard a good deal from Anna of changed Rome, the new street breaking open Bramante's St. Peter's like an egg and spilling its light, Palazzo Venezia turned into a nuisance, the buffoon on the balcony, black shirts under hobbledehoys' pimpled faces, their lovely palazzo turned into flats.

"Yes," said Anna. "I did." There were open bottles of Champagne still in their ice. Alistair held one that was almost full.

"And of course there is Venice."

"There was Venice," said Anna.

"The point," said Ottavia, "in this new Italy we have, is to be like us. Near enough to one of the great cities to use it as you wish but not to have your nose rubbed in it when you don't. It just needs thought. And of course we'll always want to have you here. You and your grandchildren."

"You are a dear," said Anna.

But Ottavia did not know her well enough to see that the straight spine and the oblique and downbent glance meant that weather was gathering within those eyes. He did, and held the bottle still, and watched her. There was some light still on the women's faces.

Anna said, "Your father is lonely and is growing a little old. He has asked me to go back to Boston with him. I have said I would." Grammatically, she spoke to him and even lifted her eye to him a moment. She might as well be addressing Time.

"He is a lovely man, you know. He was incredibly decent to us all those years ago. And I am tired of living on my hill. I am growing spinsterish and spiteful there. I belong to Maggiore, Alistair, and I always will, but he has been dead so long. I think that he would want me to do this. I have asked him, but it is not very clear. I am tired of having no man to think about. I'm afraid your mother was never much use without them."

It was Ottavia who spoke and said quietly, "Do you love him?" Anna turned to her fully, and there Alistair saw that in their attitudes the two women balanced each other and that age was the movement between.

"I don't know," said Anna. And then, "It shouldn't be very difficult, I suppose. I did once, you know." And then, "It is a proper question from a bride. I would like to know that you love my son."

"I do," said Ottavia, "but then I always did."

"I have heard something of that. We do things oddly in this family, it would seem."

Alistair poured them wine but with a gesture not of supply but of salute, rose, and went a little way into the dusk, now near dark. He not known that he had invited Time as their chief guest. The mold of his life lay broken behind him. Without his mother's betrayal of his father's bed, his life would have none of the shape he knew at all. Without Galisteo's urging, he supposed he would lie among the Flanders graves. This had been with him since he put Galisteo's letter into Ottavia's hand and had been cloud racing with sunshine across a wedding day.

He saw Galisteo now at his end, smashed in his beginning by the Holy Spirit into a service he would not have given whole. He finally understood all those horses. They weren't the dream toys of an injured squire at all. They were the form in flesh by which the Spirit trampled him, and he had clasped them to himself, obedience and dare in the same wild reckoning, to trust an impulsiveness only less than the Spirit's own. They had carried him, master of the Church's darkest ways, through the sharpest briars of good and evil, and now at the end of that wilderness delivered him to judgment. In his last gift, which was his last instruction, the Celtic church sent its dragons and its lilies to bind them all, their griefs, accidents, mis-turns, and joys into the color of poetry, if a poem could hold it.

14

The wedding presents joined their lives. Anna's Alistair-on-the-Stairs was with them at breakfast in every season, where it could be amused by the valley and the canal, severely. Alistair's father, the wry Yankee in the cypresses becoming delicacy and grace, gave the Fragonard off his own wall, remembering how it had captured his son when his son had been young, and his own, and unsure, and dreamy. Grandest, though displayed only in the office of a Lucca lawyer and there in light that struggled through grimy panes, was Manfredi's gift of his half of the estate, jointly to Ottavia and Alistair. So they owned the Galilean planets, and their bed, and the boar, and the irises; in fact, they owned most that they could see in between Lucca's spires and Monte Prano's head. Alistair, who had ridden and hunted and named this country, had never owned land. To have title to this seemed to him as vast and encompassing as Galisteo's missal in its box.

The end of the wedding closed the gate. Behind it, hours found their places, becoming ceremonies. No matter how deep he was in his own work, he wanted her taking her seat at her desk each morning. He liked the small grace with which she drew the chair under her thighs, supporting the belly that slowly grew.

A desk had joined his writing table. He heard her pen only until about the late morning time when the rake began on the gravel outside the window. She always said, *"Liebchen,"* quietly and barely looked up. When he could, he went over and sat to face her. She read him passages of German, so he could hear the sound. Her Italian was pleasant to the ear, but her German vowels were like bells. Then came a tangle of English translation, different word orders, idioms, tones, the work of her burrowing pen. That was what they talked over, sometimes on through lunch. They were translating Johann Wolfgang von Goethe's *Italian Journey* into English. Rather slowly.

"Pregnancy goes faster," said Ottavia to her belly, which was causing her unease.

"A soufflé," he suggested.

"Idiot," she replied.

In fact, her pregnancy seemed to go well. Thus, after breakfast, before writing, they still rode together, for now.

In September, when the olives began to stretch their skins and the earth smelled like an animal after it rained, the Jews of Germany lost their citizenship.

"Now it can't go back," said Ottavia. "He's closed the door."

Her remark had no context. They were breathing now precisely that scent of earth, for there had been rain overnight and high sun now, and of their horses. They were taking a long ride around the fields and the peasant farms, agreed to be Ottavia's last ride, she nearly four months pregnant. Alistair would not let the horses from a walk. They had heard the news the day before. He grasped the subject.

"In the mind's eye," she said, "a mob beating and setting fire is much more frightening. It is very frightening. Muscles and men's sweat and distorted faces and lamplight and clubs. But it could have ended. Could have been an ugly rash. Never thought so, but it could have. He did kill off most of the Brownshirts last year by that lake. Not this. It's done. It can only go on. Get worse. Not just for them."

Her hands moved to Solferino's shaking of his bit; he shook it during quiet conversations to keep up his part.

Ottavia rode astride. Alistair loved the turn of her shoulder toward him and the definition of her chin when she thought. "Yes," he said. "Done in calm is worse."

"I loved Germany," said Ottavia. "I was happy there. We have to do our Goethe awfully, awfully well, Alistair. It may be the only thing that's left. Maybe you should do 'Faust.' I can't."

"And I won't," he said. "Spare me."

"And Nuremberg's a nice city. That's the kind of thing I always think of. Was nice. Isn't that absolutely terrible pruning, Alistair?" Gesture now of her whip, which served for little else.

It was. The olives they had ridden through had been pruned in spring so that their boughs were spare against the sky, as though painted by a Chinese artist. A hard labor. Here there were rows of trees like mops. Their estate was a stepchild, though not quite abused. It had been the family's secondary landholding since the fall of the archduchy seventy years before. Alistair had looked on it with a hunter's eye and a fabulist's. Ottavia, whose grandfather had had their peasants' grandfathers as serfs, took a cooler view.

Alistair said, "Those are Maffei's trees. He's old. It's now too difficult for him—the army took his three sons. They're not meant to, but they did. 'Meant to' doesn't always work these days. Probably someone doesn't like him. We'll have to get him some help."

"Guzzi's got all his sons," said Ottavia. "Because of their ghastly squints. Simone Guzzi."

"That might be the way," said Alistair. "Though he won't like it."

They had had to become farmers.

"Italy's the other shoe," said Ottavia. "One waits. For it to drop. It's nearly ready."

Solferino shook his bit heavily. He was a monarchist horse of steady opinions.

Alistair looked away. "I'll talk to Guzzi about his sons," he said. He rode nearer to the trees. On the Chinese trees, Klee had done the olives, but there were not many here.

"He's about lost this harvest," said Alistair.

"Hitler's Italian journey," said Ottavia.

The estate, like all nearby, was run on the method of the *mezzadria,* very similar, as Alistair neither knew nor would have cared, to the sharecropping of the American South. It engendered between peasant and master a balance of respect, suspicion, dependence, envy, consideration, and muttered curse.

The *fattore* was honest. The land was sensibly worked. The peasants' houses were decent, just. Very little had been spent for ages. Thus the boar ranged in tribes, the woods were deep, the deer found food, and old walls grew wild roses where the stones fell out. Thus Ovid had enjoyed his stay. The tractor at Pozzo Nuovo that stirred them in the morning had no friends. The fields were full of the prints and dung of the grey Maremma oxen whose silhouettes, mighty as aurochs', moved on the skylines and drugged time. The Maremmas were a holdover even here, but what came in behind them were the white Chiana oxen, the Chianini, pretty as girls and kind enough for a child to lead them. Sickles caught the sun. Short saws and crooked ladders tamed the olive trees. Peasant wives carried a loaf and a jug into the field. Robert Browning would have been perfectly at home on a country jaunt. Ariosto, liking the fantastic, would have played with the tractor.

But they had read just enough to know that their estate was a fossil, left behind a left-behind region, and would never do more than support itself, however dear Manfredi had been. In October they visited him in Umbria. He received them in the room with the apes and peacocks, a good deal more collected than they, who were hot and dusty from their drive. Beady glasses of iced water looked lovely on a silver tray. Manfredi was by the secretaire with a photograph of brother Donato and some other officers being received by the king on the breakout of the brand new war against Abyssinia. It had been building for months. Donato and his Bersaglieri had been posted from Libya to Eritrea in readiness. Of all the officers present, Donato looked keenest. Bowing as he was to His Majesty, he looked like a sabre. Manfredi, by contrast, drew himself straighter at the image of the king.

"I know it's very nice for Donato," said Ottavia and clearly meant that. "Probably not so nice for the natives."

"It's their turn," said Manfredi. "The British and the French just forgot about them somehow. And Donato needs a war. He's only had skirmishes in Libya. An officer without a battle isn't quite all there."

"I know all of that. Oddly enough. It's changed, Manfredi. Our brother doesn't belong there. We can't touch things anymore. They make us dirty. Oh, hullo."

The last, coolly, was to Claudia who had come in and made what might have been the beginning of a curtsey to her. Claudia was learning to dress: her swings between bandbox and servant were much less extreme. Today she looked flowing and cool, and, right now, much more put together than they were.

Alistair said to Manfredi, "I need birds. I want to bring in Hungarians. I'd like to have grouse as well the quail. Can you let me have some chicks?" Hungarian grouse are grouse with most of the size of a pheasant.

"A happy topic," said Manfredi.

They had lunch in what was usually the breakfast room. It had frescoes, disconcertingly enough, of their own view down over Lucca.

"Where are you going to put your German?" said Manfredi.

"He's Jewish, obviously," said Ottavia. "In the room over the herbarium. Away from us."

"I don't think you say, 'Where are you going to put your Jew?' It doesn't sound nice."

Claudia had given the table and the sideboard a quick and cool appraisal. Now she nodded to the butler to proceed and herself paid attention.

"What I do not entirely understand, Ottavia, sister dear," said Manfredi, "is why you're bringing him here. I thought you had reservations. About here. I assume he's one of the bolshies you met at that paper in Wurtzburg. I do know a few things about you, you know. Here and there."

"He's not staying with us. He's on his way to France. It's easier for him to leave Germany for Italy and easier to get into France from Italy. Safer. He's thought about it. Obviously. Yes, Manfredi, we'll be just like Germany here but not yet. We're streaks ahead of them in castor oil already, nobody can take that from us, and I am sure we are catching up in rubber truncheons. There'll be a drumbeat about Jews in the papers first. Filthy yids. Stealing from Italians. Then Musso can seem to be supporting the Italian people. He's a coward, basically. Actually, he's a servant. So is Hitler. But Hitler's the more insolent servant, and Mussolini's the bigger coward. *Voila, allors*."

Manfredi looked quickly around the room. The first course had been easily served, being only celeri remoulade , and there were no servants. Manfredi said quietly, "I believe you may be entirely right, Ottavia."

Ottavia followed the glance. She said, "Oh Christ, Manfredi, we haven't come to that, have we?"

"I prefer to think not," said Manfredi.

THEY REINSTITUTED THE MANOR court at Pace ed Abbondanza. It was not quite forgotten here, for Ottavia's father had kept it in his youth. Twice a month, Alistair and Ottavia sat at the head of the dining table, all trace of conviviality removed from the room for a day, and heard the disputes and claims of their tenantry. Peasants turned their hats in their hands as they spoke accusations before only muttered to hedges or their own families. Those who were shy to speak had themselves represented by, and perhaps paid, the forester, whose saliva, together with the slight deformity of a lip, gave his voice an unceasing force of innocence and hurt. After Alistair and Ottavia conferred, with their heads close together, Ottavia quietly gave the judgment, as she carried the blood of the Ferraras, though a woman. If there were objections, Alistair invoked logic, as a man. Not since the fall of the archduchy, already seventy years before, had any of this had the slightest weight in law. Any of those judged could have shrugged a shoulder and gone to the police. But, in fact, the *contadini* preferred Ferrara justice, for it was comprehensible, measured, and utterly clean. The fascist authorities objected angrily to these pretenses, from which they were excluded, and were ignored. Nothing happened. This was just as Ottavia had hoped. In a present she saw as a filling swamp of brutality brought lower by farce, she raised up the old forms in its face. That the father of her child was poet and horseman, mannered and kind, made her naps, which became more frequent, sweet.

The father of her child was up for these demanding roles, for his muse had deserted him. November came. The olives were pressed. The estate made enough profit to buy Ottavia a beautiful peignoir from Burano for her new figure and Alistair a twenty-eight-gauge shotgun from England, very nice for quail. The peasant Mattei helped his neighbor Guzzi with some carpentry. It was agreed, with a glass of wine, that one of Guzzi's squinting sons would help prune next spring. It rained hard for days. Monte Prano emerged from the darkness with its first coat of snow.

Alistair gave his evenings to worms in olives and oxen, the mechanics of drought. He gave a lot of his day to the anatomy of his time.

About his Italy, he had been an innocent. His ghosts, and how many others', a deep rustling cellar of them, had laughed at being dared, and dripped poison, were dripping it still. From Paris, it had all looked noble Roman. As soon as the actors for these gallant tableaus came on stage, they showed buboes, chins, bellies, snouts, and fell irresistibly into obscene and vicious pranks. The eagles were only buzzards. And how do you salute that? Transcendence was his matter, the high narrow ridge. The honor of life was in its ceremonies. His wife grasped this as instinctively as he. Though they would have been surprised to hear it, Alistair and Ottavia lived behind their gates in a daily dance of courtesy and custom and arm around the waist for grace.

He couldn't eat lament all day. He couldn't not write. He poked away among Italy's piles of rubble and found oddities of chance and person he could turn into perfect engravings. They were as good as anybody could have made them, and, he assumed, as boring. He addressed himself as "Robert" for "Browning." He was back in Paris, at the end. His essays began now. He kept them short and almost as concentrated as sonnets.

Ottavia, remarkably handsome pregnant and always his gracious dear, ceased to write every morning and sometimes kept her room. He ate lunch alone some days. One grey and defeated day, he got fed up and drove into Lucca. The choice of inns was not great, so he ate his lunch at the one on the big square, where they knew him, where he and Nancy had once been used to go, and where Ottavia and he and Father Kirchner had had their real wedding lunch. When he came out, it had begun to rain.

The plane trees were stark and bare against the public buildings on the other side. No one seemed to walk that side. One of the plane trees, just outside the door of the pension office, had a burden. He went a little closer. The burden was their Ezra Pound. His tray of medals had been broken and thrown onto the street. He leant against the trunk and sobbed from a bloody face. His nice army britches and the boots he shined were fouled and stinking with his shit. An official in one of the new uniforms sat behind a closed window above him. He was drinking a coffee.

At the villa, they kept the gates shut. And pretended not to see them. Their child would be born behind them.

15

Once more the storm was howling, and, half-hid under the cradle lid and covering, his child slept on. The cradle had come from Umbria. On it had been paired the shields of Ferarra and Tyrone, hawk and lily, wolfhound and harp. Ottavia had been brought to bed in a February storm. Snow touched Boromeo's fetlocks in the hollows. The doctor had arrived before the heavy snow, was theirs to keep for now, though with little, given it was a safe birth, to do. The wolfhound came with the wind through the woods, broke into wild harp at windows and doors. For an hour, he had walked Boromeo and felt the warmth of horse, though stung by snow. Boromeo, with a lunge that had a shudder in it, climbed the bank onto the drive. Alistair turned his head, which snow needles stung, toward the gate unseen in the last light. Twilight darkened the great gloom in his mind.

He had heard his child's voice and had held him for a moment before Concetta took him and laid him in the cradle while his wife slept. The new nanny tucked him in, taking office. All was safe in fire warmth and flicker. A being ridiculously small, of course, to be snuffed by wind or war, defenseless before future years blown on a loudspeaker's bellows or bugle and drum. Out of this thought had come a sight he had no preparation for whatsoever: his father's quiet square house where time ticked on untroubled pendulums, and his own nursery above Louisburg Square. From this thought, that he had made his life out of dark dreams in a distant place, and that all his son would know of custom and of quiet was just such a failing spark in his father's head. Ottavia would soon wake. He could not let her see what might be in his face. So he had gone to the antechamber and given Girolamo orders for his groom. He rode in a shooting jacket and trousers stuffed into boots.

He'd school him in courtesy. Courtesy reigned in all the minds that he had loved, and prospered little in the winds that blew now. Courtesy, which held courage from bombast, honor from the strut, governed the cyprus, was the warmth in Ariosto's lines, glowed in Maggiore's last leave-taking at the kloster, inhabited Manfredi's sword, stood guard above the cradle in the paired shields. The lights of the villa now stood out clear. Very soon there would be dark as well as snow and wind, making the whole enterprise even more harebrained than Boromeo thought it now, as he willingly picked up a trot for home. At least he had given his child a mother who knew nothing of these thoughts but would wake to them herself. He'd have a house where all's accustomed, ceremonious. He could not roll back the dark beyond the gate. He was far from home. He feared for his son. The dark closed behind his back and made it shiver though the snow was at his throat. He knew it out of nothing: he must not raise his son now and here.

When Simon came in October, the cradle had been put away. Simon did pretty well. Giovanni seemed to like his round spectacles. Simon's eyes, mild and inquiring, looked through the sights of his buttoned collar down to the small face. Ottavia thought that very decent in a bachelor. It was understood that any other woman in Italy would be absent from this conversation. It was also understood that Ottavia would stay. When Simon was announced she buttoned her blouse from nursing.

Simon said, "It's Abyssinia drove him into Hitler's arms."

"Which were waiting," said Ottavia.

"Which he was being very coy about, Our Man. Then he starts this lousy war, England and France turn up their noses at the smell, and so do we, and only Hitler smiles. And it is a lousy war. Whatever he says."

"He," the Duce, was right there with them. Simon had chanced to come on the elementary school half day, the boy soldier's day. The loudspeaker was haranguing them, louder than usual because the recording was the Man Himself. The occasion was a victory in Ethiopia and the impotent jealousy of France, England, and

America. One wondered where the defeat had been and how bad. From powerful loud speakers, a bit distant, the voice seemed to have no actual source but to rise like gas from a swamp. With the windows shut, one did not have to raise one's voice very much.

"I cannot think as I wish about this war," said Ottavia. "My brother is an officer in it. A major. Being my brother, he is in the front line. I must think of it as my brother's war. Only as that."

Simon nodded and shrugged, together. He turned to Alistair. "A treaty of friendship now exists between Italy and Germany. Not an 'understanding.' A treaty. Not yet 'pact.' Neither country, of course, is an enemy of your country. Nor of the army in which you served."

"Does it mean anything?" said Ottavia. "Really? They're both liars."

"It is a little vague. The timing of it means Mussolini will not resist Hitler in Austria. That's new. Nor elsewhere in the East, I would say. It means Mussolini's chosen sides. I should have said, Alistair, the army in which you do serve. As reserve officer. You may have forgotten that."

Nanny came in for Giovanni, rustling. She seemed to receive applause, but it was probably for the Duce, also on loud speakers. There was peace for a bit.

"Paris will be getting cold and dark now, if I recollect," said Alistair, into it.

Giovanni seemed pleased enough. Supper, and Simon's spectacles, and now bed. The nanny seemed a good nanny. They could not trust her as they trusted Girolamo and Concetta and the girls, and by now they took account of that.

"Rain mainly," said Simon. Nanny left. Ottavia cocked an ear for continued footsteps beyond the door. Alistair saw, was unsurprised, was appalled. The night wood in the snow that circled around his head these days darted back in. Ottavia, satisfied, looked down.

"What exactly are you here for?" said Alistair.

"Pretend I'm a horse, Alistair. Should be easy for you. Something's changed in my view, and I have to look at it. Or pretend I'm a bishop. Easy too. I'm on an Episcopal Visitation. It's still easy. The Huns are not at the gate. I'm sure I'm noted, but I'm not followed. I'm looking at my friends in Italy. You're not the only ones. But you, my dears, are so . . . you. I'm American. I'm thinking about Germany and Italy. I look at you, and what do I see? America, Germany, and Italy. Very expensive figurines. Officer, nobility, scholars, important friends. Good God, you fill the room. Have you a publisher for your Goethe?"

"It's not finished yet," said Ottavia. "I've been busy. But yes."

"You will please, please finish it. It will be noted in Germany. Discreetly and scholarly. Germany and Italy. Can't have enough of it."

"I turned you down once," said Alistair. "Explicitly. At a very important time for me."

There was a crash of musketry here, startling Simon, which pleased Alistair. Target practice had started. Simon recovered.

"I remember. So important you wanted to send in the marines. I'm not worried. You seriously don't like these people. If you began to, your bride likes them even less."

"We have something else to occupy us now," said Ottavia.

"Of course. And you should. Alistair, back to literature. I admire your essays. Who wouldn't? Sometimes I think you're being too careful about your own country. It is not in me to believe that you do not view Roosevelt, the boys around him, threats to the Supreme Court, the Constitution trodden over, federal government as nanny with a club, as a sort of cancer. As grave as anything in Europe."

"You are right. Very nearly right," said Alistair.

"I think you should write it. Say so. The harder you are on your own country, the more trenchant you sound."

Alistair looked at him, saw the Palazzo Colonna, swords in racks on the wall, the face masks they wore, the chalk on the floor. It had always been quiet there, only the thump of feet and terse, low words. He said nothing.

Simon looked mildly about the room, where the fire of bright olive wood was laid but not yet lit, and the gramophone sat hushed. He said to Ottavia, "You aren't really worried that your nanny is listening outside the door? I mean, your child's nanny?"

"I prefer to think not," said Ottavia.

"I'm so glad," said Simon. "That would be a terrible way to live."

When he left, Alistair gave him a bottle of olive oil and felt a fool. Somehow, at Lucca, just after the pressing, everybody who came got a bottle of oil. Besides, he had had the label redesigned and was proud of it. They would meet again, it was agreed, but never again at Pace ed Abbondanza. With the front door open, there were feral, treble cheers. They were beyond the wood, they were not amplified, and they were much more frightening than the Duce.

The day after Simon left was for the manor court. Alistair and Ottavia sat close side by side, the long table between them and everybody else. Ottavia was composed in flowing grey, sobriety that did not quite keep from him the slight milky sweetness of her breast. This was intermittent. The man they were hearing had pigs. When he spoke, his nose lifted and flared. They did not much like him, but it was hard to say why. His smell was hardly culpable. He had hit a man with a flail once, but mainly he used fists and not extravagantly often. He was said to knock his wife about. It was a long while since they had imagined peasant life as idyllic. His work was neither good nor bad. He did a fence, or pruned, or fixed a harness decently, except when he botched it so pointlessly that it seemed a jeer. That might have been the clue. His face was crossed by ripples of a knowing nastiness, which, on the other hand, constantly bumped up against slowness of wit and ignorance. He was illiterate, obviously.

He had let a cow get loose. Anyone could see the fence was slovenly. The cow had caused damage at a neighbor's. The neighbor had impounded the cow, quite rightly. The lout had gone over, not to set things right but to grab the cow, and had done a lot more damage, most notably to the neighbor's son's head. The wife had screamed at him. The lout had replied with words described as "cutting," though Alistair seriously doubted they were much like Noel Coward's. Alistair and Ottavia inhabited this level of judicial subtlety, the present case a trifle nastier than usual. They both guessed that the wife had forced the case. The plaintiff seemed miserable. Also frightened. He had a face a little like a vole's and wore a church suit of decent black.

Only there were no witnesses. There were unhappy faces, mildly. The man was a bit dangerous. The cow was an accident. Damage was not much. Only fists had been used. The boy had bruises and cuts, no worse.

Alistair whispered to Ottavia, "He'll fix everything he and his bloody cow broke and give the boy a jar of oil for his face or pay for it all in oil, and we'll set the price. OK?"

"He might just run off to the police. I think he may have friends there."

"No. Loss of face," said Alistair.

Ottavia nodded. She spoke the judgment. A small puppy of indecision dogged her voice.

The man's arm jumped. His chest jumped. His nose jumped. Injustice it was. Favoritism it was. Witnesses there weren't.

Alistair caught his eye and held it for a time. There was a red cast in the corner of the right one. He said quietly, "We rule as we rule." Which sometimes is what a chieftain must say.

Alistair's and Ottavia's translation of Goethe's *Italian Journey* has long ceased to be the most prized in English. W. H. Auden, slightly and much later a friend of Alistair, did one which became far more read. Theirs, flinty, is greatly Goethe's journey into Goethe, though Italy is there in the end. Auden's, intended to bring Goethe to the English, which it does very well indeed, is more amenable. Alistair and Ottavia's Italian translation, which followed immediately, had much more impact, even on their own lives. It was mainly Ottavia's, from the English. The tension in its pores between German and Italian, greater than that between German and English, is probably Alistair's.

Anyway, Goethe kept them usefully busy and in a difficult time. They took their duties seriously, as he had done in Weimar, and brought rough harmony out of what was usually just rough.

It also gave them an excuse to travel, to see what Goethe had seen. They found that Goethe's sense of the cut and grain and color of stone was precise and impassioned, and his sense of plants as exquisite as Sir John Hill's. The depth of Goethe's view lay in precisely such connections, almost invisible unless you traveled behind him. They went to Lake Garda, always a pleasure, where Goethe had been taken for a spy. They went to Padova and Verona. This was not simple. Ottavia insisted on nursing Giovanni. She and Alistair drove in the new dark red Alfa-Romeo, impossibly long of bonnet and sleek as drop of oil, that had replaced the old Bugatti. They had a chauffeur now for errands. He and Nanny and Giovanni followed in a boxy FIAT, at ever-stretching distance. They needed three rooms: a suite, a room for Nanny and the cot on the same floor, and one in the attic for the chauffeur. In the mornings, rustling Nanny would knock at the door. Ottavia would put on something that rustled herself, collect Giovanni, drop the rustle, and come back to bed. Alistair hoped that his son had the sense to appreciate such a convenient breakfast out of such cute containers, which dimmed the thought that his son should not be here at all. (In fact, he got little bits of pasta, as well now, and spinach, and even tender veal cut up small.) Hotels were an exciting luxury for them. When they went to Florence, they had the two floors the family had kept in the palazzo on Via Tornabuoni. For bumpkins like them, it was a thrill to have a menu, and choice, and lifts, and waiters.

THE PEASANT WHO HAD been the cow's unwilling host did not keep large animals. He kept a hutch full of prosperous rabbits.

Every rabbit was killed. Their skulls were smashed against, if one took account, most of the walls, the chimney, the cooking kettle, the family's dowry chest, grandfather's photograph, and each of the six steps up to the sleeping loft. Which must have announced the guests. The dog had been kept for the bed head and made the bloodiest mess. There had been an attempt at fire. It had not been done well. A pail of water had put it out, but the slaughterhouse burned eyes and lungs with smoke. It was done in the middle of the night. It had been done quickly. It had not been stealthy. There had been shouted orders, and at least once, a whistle. There had been more than one motorcar with lights. Not a single peasant owned such a thing.

The peasant's house was not very near the villa, but Alistair and Ottavia had heard enough to be alarmed and up, for angry sounds do not come in the Tuscan night, and had seen the lights. When Ambrogio came running to the house and was joined by Girolamo up the stairs, they had already thrown on enough to go out.

No human being had been killed. The family had all been in the loft. When Alistair got there, two braver peasants had been up and were down again wiping their eyes and coughing. Angry, baffled gestures showed how bad it was. Alistair followed, and so did Ottavia, though told to stay down. The steps were slimy with blood, and steep, and all their clothes were smeared. They coughed with wet eyes while Alistair swung around an electric torch. The father had been beaten on the floor. He lay with his back and his hips out of plane. One's first thought was how to get a broken back down those stairs from a place where no one could breathe. Alistair told Ambrogio to run to the house and telephone.

"We'll all be dead before anyone gets here," said Ottavia. "Can't you get them to break the walls open?" There were no windows, of course. Everyone wanted to do that. They clambered up the steps, and the room was full of crashing and good will.

The son had had his nose and ears cut off, or pulled off the last part of the way.

He was lying in a ball on the floor and moaning. Alistair guessed that other parts would be missing and had him straightened a bit, but it seemed that the nose and ears were all. The smoke was clearing. When the gags were cut off the women, the wife and a slow-witted girl, there were bits of rabbit or dog behind the gags. They had quite certainly both been raped, but it was hard to get much out of them. By the time the daylight came, it came through clear air onto people who looked like butchers and wished they were any single place but where they were. The smoke had cleared, but its bitter smell remained. They heard the motor ambulance then. It bounced a little as it arrived over the tire treads of the earlier cars. The doctor, whom they did not know, and his orderlies did their proper work but kept themselves apart. They looked no one in the eye. Ottavia told some women to wash the place.

Nobody knew who it was. Everybody knew who it was. The peasant whose cow had started it all was presumably mixed up in it. It hardly mattered. He could not possibly have organized it.

"We did this," said Ottavia and said it with narrowed eyes as though Alistair were to blame. Then hung on to his hand and said, "How could we? How could we not have seen?"

16

He stood on the ridge in the dawn. He did not think they had artillery, and he was beyond likely range of their rifles. He waited for the sun on the horns. When the sun traveled down the ridge and lit the water threads between the thorn bushes, it touched first the horns, and at its touch, the antelope lifted their heads. He saw the great bows of the kudu, the spiral edges of the oryx horns, the curl of the sable, the spikes of little gerenuks all lifted a moment toward heaven, and he had stood in this spot for three mornings and waited for it. It did not matter, it was better, that the wonderful names of these creatures existed independent and in themselves. He did not know the names of these creatures at all, but he had spoken to British officers who had done Africa properly, and he knew that all these names owned bodies, somewhere. His horse snoofed behind him. Maggiore Donato Ugolino-Ferrara half turned and ran his hand down its shoulder tenderly and slowly, for they had been through tsetse country, where the horses should never have been at all, and they were sickening. A voice, also from behind but not his horse's, said, "Maggiore?"

Donato nodded.

"Do you know when they are coming?" said the voice, which was of Ipolito Benicati, the senior of his two captains.

He shook his head. The question was purely rhetorical. No one ever knew, nor could know, when the air force would come.

"The wind is ideal now," said Benicati and pointed to the wind sock on a kopje of the ridge. They were indeed upwind of the enemy.

He said, "They will not come for an hour at least. In an hour, I want the men breakfasted and in rank. We move at the first sight of the airplanes. If the wind changes by more than thirty degrees, we stand down." He pointed at the wind sock and knew that his voice acquired an edge. "And if it does change, make sure those bloody idiots notice. Signal to them. Wave it around. We don't want a disaster."

"No, Maggiore."

He was alone again. He had never moved. He stroked his horse but did not turn to him, for it hurt him to see the withering of a friend. From behind came the sounds that had made his life, the click of canteens, slide of rifle bolts, mules and the thump of pack saddles, NCOs' orders, all borne on the morning smell of smoke. Below him, the antelope took their honey colors in the sun, and the colors unmixed themselves and separated into herds each of a kind. He could feel the warmth on their backs and taste cool water in their throats. The Africa smell of dust and thorn and animal climbed from the plain up the ridge. The black islands of thorn took on weight and split the grey earth into straits between them, tempting his binoculars to no reward, he knew. The Abyssinians were there, well hid. Away, a little higher than the thorn islands, stood the rough geometry of the thorn village fortress he was tasked to take. He was not a reader, but it struck him that his enemies in this war fought as the ancient Greeks had fought. For this, he could be proud to have encountered them. Alone before his battalion, standing straight and still, he could be for yet a little while a knight himself.

OUT OF THE ENORMOUS sky, crawling like ants across a swelling cumulus, came, just at noon, six little airplanes. They hesitated and circled far away—being lost was very common for them—while the battalion held its breath and let it out when a pilot saw the flag, or the mules, or a glint of steel, straightened his wings, and flew straight toward them. Six little airplanes line abreast! Bredas, not even biplanes! Major Donato was in the van when the airplanes soared overhead. He had left his horse behind, but he carried his sword.

He marked the smoke puffs from enemy rifles and nailed them to his memory, for they would have to be dealt with at the end. They were halfway down the hill.

He saw a man drop to his right, and a mule, well to his left, but they were still at long range for the enemy. The airplanes tilted down, their shadows rushed over them, leveled over the plain, and flew low. He saw the first bombs drop, done very well, almost on the nearest puffs of smoke. They flew on and dropped others, silent as the first, and in the distance, where he could not clearly see, dropped their last load before the thorn fortress. They soared up again and made a graceful salute. He erased it from his mind. From the first canisters, he could see them on the ground, came not a blast, not smoke, but a momentary darkening of the light. And borne on the pleasant wind before them went chlorine gas to turn the bare skins of the Abyssinians into burning shirts, and enter their eyes to scald and blind them, and enter their lungs to melt them into froth, and seep between the thorns of the fortress village and lay all within it choking and strangling on the earth. The band played "Giovinezza."

The airplanes had been very late, difficulties having affected their takeoff yet again. The sun, which had softly blessed the antelopes' horns, now beat upon the plain and blasted the granite uplands. The cumulus cloud, which had already given the airplanes a tossing about as they flew past, now took wing on the heated air and soared in its embrace, swelling like a water lily, purple at the top. It drew wind behind it. In the camp on the ridge, the Arab mule handlers and camp cooks, and those wounded strong enough to sit outside their tents to listen to the band move on, saw the wind sock droop, hang down, twitch its nostrils, try the other way, undulate as it explored, then strike out behind.

Enemy fire was no surprise at all. He knew the histories of the last war. Gas is not a lawn mower. It eddies, skips pockets, and he didn't really know what the thorns would do. They were taking fire. They were taking casualties. The band stood down. They were also winning the day. Machine gun fire and grenades poured into points of resistance stamped out steadily what the gas had left. Much of the enemy fire had the sound of the heavy-caliber, low-velocity soft lead round of old British colonial armament. He winced at that thought, for the human damage it did was terrible and was cheered because it was useless beyond short range. He believed that the first victory of his sober, dutiful career was at hand.

When tears and pain dropped over his eyes and his lungs refused his breath, he did not understand what had happened. When he did understand, he found that he was on the ground. He retained some vision. His troops around him were in like state, though a few still stood, facing here and there. The gas was by now much diluted. Some would be forever disabled, the very unlucky blinded. Few would have died.

The Ethiopians came out of the thorns, to what extent survivors, reinforcements, or marauders cannot be known. Dirty white tunics and looks of loathing united them as noonday ghosts. Many Italians were able to pick up their weapons, but very few to use them well. The Ethiopians with rifles shot them methodically, those with spears exercised them afterward. The major had use of his service revolver, shot a spearman and wounded a rifleman. He was therefore shot twice. The ammunition was indeed the antique British soft lead Dum-Dum, illegal even longer than the Italian gas. The first shot tore off his shoulder. The second threw his guts out behind him into the dust.

Major Donato Ugolino-Ferrara died a couple of hours later just as the relief effort from the ridge—invalids, Arabs, artisans—began their work. A radio had worked for once, and Italian aircraft were on patrol. He was lucky. The number of the dying exceeded the number of hyenas within reach, and he was left alone.

xxx

Alistair said, "Donato has brought us to a far place."

Ottavia said, "No," and slowly and slightly shook her head. "Donato and Goethe. We were still translating Goethe then. That made it worse. All of it. And it is I who have brought us to a far place, Alistair. Through my brother and Goethe."

Alistair saw that the corner of her beach towel had fallen from the deckchair into the sand. He picked it up, brushed it with fingers, and put it in her lap, where her hand found his.

"Goethe?" he said.

"When he's in Rome and Naples. With his kind, intelligent friends. His hospitable princesses. There's the light of intellect everywhere, Alistair, never mind the bugs and fleas. Everything's getting better known. Everything's just getting . . . better. And kinder. And it always will. And everything we touched or were near got darker and more hellish. I said my own brother was tortured to death and I couldn't even mourn him because he was doing something despicable. Gas. I don't feel that anymore. I think he showed us. I think he led our way. Pray God there's going to be a war."

"It is a prayer that God shows every sign of answering."

"Alistair!" said Ottavia.

She had been watching Giovanni build a sandcastle, very seriously, with a little shovel. He was stark naked, like most of the smallest children, except for sand. Now he was making for the waves.

"Concetta's watching him," he said. Indeed, she was, sitting on a bench that looked as though it missed the schoolroom, and very fully dressed. They had gotten rid of the nanny. Ottavia claimed to think that she was steaming open letters. He thought this utter nonsense, but they were happier without her. A village girl helped Concetta in the kitchen all day long, and Concetta had become half a nanny.

"All right," said Ottavia. "So there's going to be a war. It's certain now. And that changes everything. All the stuff I said about we can't touch things now. If you can't touch things, you might as well be dead. Of course I mourned Donato. Soldiers are always doing things you don't really want to know about. All women know that."

"Donato was trying to take a troublesome fortress with the lowest losses to his men. That was his job. The gas that degraded him and killed him came from the powers we know about. It should not have been there. It would have been difficult for Donato to refuse his mission on that account. Difficult, not quite impossible. You are right about the rest."

He touched her neck, and she rubbed his hand with her chin.

"We are saying the same thing," she said.

"You feel salty," he said. There were palms and oleanders behind them and snowy mountains above. But they were not at the Lake of Geneva. The mountains were white because they were marble and Carrara was up there. They were on the coast of Tuscany. It was only the very end of May. They had swum a little, but it was really too cold, even in what would be the nice summer of 1939. The beach was busy nonetheless. Whether for a weekend celebration of the German-Italian Pact of Steel—*Patto di Accaio, Stahlpakt*—which had been all the news all week, or because of unease about it, was hard to say.

"So do you," she said. "And there's a shower in the cabana, so we can be nice and cozy. Where's Luigi? Shouldn't they be getting lunch together? Won't Simon be here soon?"

"Luigi's shy around girls in bathing suits," said Alistair. They were attended also by an odd young man, rather a fright, whose nose and ears had been sewn back on, as best as could be. They had noticed that Girolamo was getting old, so they would have an old butler, and young Luigi had been hired to polish and carry for him. He had become also Alistair's valet, more or less. They had paid for the operation and he was fiercely grateful to them, also for the job. His father was paid to sit in a chair at night in the long brick vault with the oil jars. A watchman's job is not contemptible, not for a man whose back has been destroyed by thugs.

When the gentlemen regathered, they were much more elegant. Alistair wore cricket whites and Giovanni a sailor suit. The cabana had no hot water, spider webs instead, but Ottavia had had the surprising heat of a body just out of the sun.

She said, "Is it dangerous for us to see Simon? Here and now?"

"He will have been careful. He is careful. I imagine he will have gotten a boat from Menton to Alassio or some such place then driven down the coast. He spoke of that once, for a time of need. And there is nothing illegal about his being here. Nothing out of the way at all. Nothing out of the way in an American diplomat visiting an American in time of peace. And Italians see families on the beach as the picture of innocence."

She nodded and watched Concetta's and Luigi's preparations.

"Maybe here and now are not what I meant. Are we not being perhaps a little ostentatious at least?" she said.

"Ostentatious would be a sandwich," he said. Indeed, around many families on this beach were growing umbrellas, and tables, and platters and coolers, and servants or waiters. This was Forte dei Marmi, quite ritzy. Fifty yards down, there was even a diva they had seen at La Scala, and her friends.

"There are times when one would prefer to hide," said Ottavia.

Simon said to Giovanni, who liked him, "Do you know what those things on your collar are?"

"Non. Non lo so," said Giovanni.

"Mr. Cartwright was speaking English," said Ottavia.

"No," said Giovanni. "I don't."

"Nelson's Three Victories," said Simon. "You may not know about them yet."

Which seemed reasonable. He spoke more generally. "Do you know all the continental navies put three stripes for Nelson's victories on their sailor suits. Even the French? Of course, they're French."

Giovanni had lost interest. He said to his father. "*Babbo, possiamo prendere the ball am Strand to play?*"

"Before the day is over, yes," said Alistair. "Not just now."

"I know you've been good children," said Simon.

Yes, they had been. In that dawn of blood and smoke and tire tracks, Alistair had realized they must go to the local *questura* and complain about the attack on their tenants. "It would be strange not to," he had told Ottavia. No, she had said, don't pretend we think they're a government. We should act as though we know they're gansters.

Alistair disagreed: "It will be a long, long time before they hurt us. They will hurt other people. Maybe less than last night. But they will. Maybe worse."

She thought about that. "Then you'll go."

Rodolfo, before he left, had given him a letter of introduction to the new chief of police at Lucca's small *questura* and so he had entered, distinguished foreigner, Roman suit, citizen of a great power, London shoes with chestnut glow, smoky smell and blood washed off. He stated the case. They knew something of it. Oh, but they were shocked! The chief had a face along the general lines of bull that had stopped just short of dog and retreated into frog. On his right cheek was a genial glow, the reflection of his beautiful badge of office: the coronet, laurel, acanthus, white and crimson of Lucca, all correct, and, right in the middle, a bright gold fasces, ax and rods.

Anarchists, it would have been. From Florence.

The assistant had long skinny limbs and a small head. So, in uniform, a black stick insect of sorts, and not at ease, perhaps not around bullfrogs. Nonetheless, he dared rebut.

Or socialists. From Prato. The mills there.

Alistair had not known his peasant so politically active. More rabbits, he gave as his thought.

The aura of the fasces grew a little as the cheek smiled.

No, no. Not the peasant. The peasant was a cipher. The target was yourself. And your good lady.

Well, now we all agree.

By the anarchists. Or, with a nod, kind master, to the mantis, very possibly the socialists. Of Prato.

Alistair sat enlightened. Thoughtful lips reflected the angle of his tie's knot. He tried, poor foreigner in Italy, to work it out.

But why? What would they want?

The mantis head turned ceilingward. *A distinguished family! Such envy! A foreign guest. An American. To embarrass the state even! Pray God it does not happen again!*

Or much worse. Thus the frog.

They cogitated this.

They made it so difficult. It is as though you consider your great estate a separate country. Nothing to do with the rest of us. So it is hard to protect.

And you have this court you play with. The mantis scissored it with his forelegs. *Of course, we know it is only theater. No real harm at all.*

But a very old thing. One of the traditions of Italian nobility. Responsibility. So ventured the foreign scholar.

Certainly! The jowls were as one on this. *In the days of weak, fractured, prostrate, corrupted, ignorant, unlettered Italy! But now consider! A glorious government! A leader of leaders! Unto Caesar what is Caesar's!*

In the sense of more appropriate to our ancestors' time than ours?

The nail on the head! They did hope so. And much more contact. We should all embrace each other. Right there on the wall, the Duce showed the way, crushed a Hitler to his breast.

YES, THEY HAD BEEN good children. Also there was the reception at the Goethe Institute of Rome for their *Italian Journey* and dinner at the German embassy after. Also Ottavia's nice letter to Count Ciano, their old wedding guest, for attending. Some discreet hunting parties. Ottavia's chatty letters to old German army friends, or to their wives, now getting much more senior. One could go on. With Alistair's essays, for example.

"The thing is," said Simon now, "they don't know what to make of you. It's your best defense. Your greatest value. Use that. Push forward a little."

Ottavia said, "He cannot come to harm." She pointed at Giovanni, who had his eye sadly on his castle and his shovel, for it seemed they did not consort with sailor suits. She sat up quite straight and said, "Simon will say that I am sentimental or even weak, but nothing we are to do can bring him to harm. I have thought about this. Some things are blasphemous." She was wearing a long linen summer dress, nearly white, showing some shoulder but no breast, and with "blasphemous," she looked suddenly like a young nun.

"Oh, Ottavia. Far wide. Far wide," said Simon. "Stop."

He looked down to think. He looked up. "Back to first principles." He could have been teleported from Hyannis, round glasses, button collar, rumpled seersucker. This hardly mattered. Forte dei Marmi draws from Florence and Sienna. There were several foreigners there too assured to go native. Even the diva was Swedish.

"Most of what people like me do is hypothetical. Like your grandfather."

"My grandfather?" said Alistair.

"My father had a high regard for him. Though he was well before my father's time."

"Your father?" said Alistair. "My grandfather?"

"Not quite the plain diplomat you think. Not the point. And you sound just like *The Marriage of Figaro*, Alistair. We make great preparations for what may never happen. We talk as though we know there will be war. We don't know that at all. Let alone when, who's in it, what side."

He had his back to the sea. He suddenly stuck his finger at the mountain. "Up there. Carrara. Michelangelo's quarry. Michelangelo said that the piece of marble told him what it could become. Your grandfather knew that perfectly, one of the things I've studied in him. Never force against the grain. Never force at all. Ottavia, you silly girl, do you think I'd let you run around embassies at night with a skeleton key? Hide in sewers? Keep a garrote in your bodice? You'll do this . . ." His form changed. His glasses acquired innocent merriment. He ceased to eat and prettily nibbled at the excellent lobster salad they had just begun. His head turned back and forth, and his lips moved each time it turned. "You'll give lunch parties. Just like now. It's who you are we want, and who you know. Not knuckledusters. We're here to set up ways of contact. Limits. Areas of responsibility. I usually have to say, 'terms of payment.' For when I can't be here. If that ever happens."

"Oh," said Ottavia, and got down from her pedestal, and looked a little disappointed.

"For example, what are you hearing now?"

"The army is appalled," said Alistair. "The navy is beyond appalled."

"That's from my brother," said Ottavia. "And his contacts are good."

"The country is now committed to join Germany in any military adventure Hitler starts. Without consultation. Also without steel, coal, or oil. All of which Italy imports. All of which will now have to come from Germany. Over one mountain railroad track. The Brenner."

Simon nodded quickly to acknowledge this was ground well known. "There is another line,' he said. "Villach to Tarvisio."

Alistair nodded quickly.

"There's something much bigger, Simon," said Ottavia. "Italians don't like the Germans. They're the enemy not the ally. From the Hohenstaufens through the Hapsburgs. Back way before Dante. Back to Tacitus, I suppose. Mussolini's message has been the greatness of Italy. Now he's got us playing lackey to our enemy. People won't like that."

"Too true. Too true," said Simon.

"And Germans look at Italians as court painters. Or valets."

"Oh dear," said Simon. "Of course your Goethe looked on them as teachers. Goethe and his friends."

"Are we boring you?" said Ottavia.

"Not as conversation. Never," said Simon.

It was the time of day on the beach when the shade has a different quality of being from the sun. The sea shimmered with wavelets and the sand with heat. Both were largely deserted for the time, and the main movement was the small surf. It was all close but could have been elsewhere, through a telescope. A change in the wind had brought a faint smell of lemon flower, but when the hamper opened and creaked, this was replaced by a brown and friendly smell, which would be Concetta's stuffed chicken in pastry crust. Giovanni looked at it, even turning from his shovel. Luigi removed the lobster plates. A bottle of red wine raised its neck from a napkin. Something similar must have been going on at the diva's table, for a striking crescendo passage of clinks opened up into a soft chorus of oohs and aahs.

"Two things are possible," said Simon. "We are having a lovely luncheon at the beach, and I have had a charmingly complicated trip with a boat ride thrown in. This is very possible. Or it's possible we are in a completely different world. When we first spoke of these things, that kindergarten SS day, it was quite remote. It may or may not be real now, but it's not remote. Do you know how different, Ottavia?"

"I have a suspicion you don't have conversations there," said Ottavia. "Or Hohenstaufens."

"You're saying you don't look at the stag. You look at the shoulder to see if the muscle is tensed to move," said Alistair. Or you look at a deserted Philippine village to see if the side of a face moves in a window, he didn't say. "Things look different through sights."

"You listen to what people say, and you listen to the holes in conversations. You listen to what they don't say, and you remember," said Simon. "You don't have real conversations. What you say is a nail to unpick a sleeve."

"Yes," said Ottavia.

"Yes. But we've never been there. We don't know that world."

With the chicken, a knife joined the fork. Ottavia used hers to cut some up for Giovanni.

Simon said, "In his own mind, I believe Alistair visited that world with the Russian poet. Far away in the snow. But it turned out his poet didn't want to survive. If you want to be a martyr, someone will usually help you. It doesn't count. I told him that then."

Alistair's knife stopped over his plate, but Simon softly raised his hand. "Alistair loves changing things, so you do not know where God stops and Alistair begins. He loves it that you don't know." The fingertips now rose above the hand. "It's a very dangerous form of pride. But I think it may be useful in this new world, and a pleasure of sorts. However, I don't think that goes for you, Ottavia."

To whom he turned entirely. "I was on Manfredi's boat at Capri. I've known you since the same instant Alistair did. My girl on that boat, the English one, nursed Alistair when he nearly died. It's because of me Alistair fences. We talked about boats. And I've known him about since you have too." Giovanni returned his look and joined his parents in saying nothing. "I owe you one question. Do you want to go there? You've only put your toe in. You can take it out."

She looked at the sand under their cool awning and at the tracings of the rake with which Luigi had smoothed it. Then looked suddenly up. Alistair could see from the sun on her forehead that she was looking straight at the glaring surf.

"Everything that we have done because of you has made me sick. Or not done. Will actual danger make it better? At least cleaner? I'm not stupid, Simon. You shouldn't think I am. There will be danger. I just don't see where it is yet. Yes, it will probably make it better, except for Giovanni, and there is Giovanni. So it won't. I don't want to go there at all. When I saw it in Germany, and I did, I ran. This is where people say, 'We can't keep running.' But *we* can. We could run to America now. We're among the few who can."

"You could be a citizen in five minutes," said Simon and put chicken on his fork and conveyed it to his mouth as though that were a choice of importance.

"My two families are in the blood and bone of my two countries. We gave them grace and honor such as we had, and they have turned it into gangrene. When they beat our peasant, they stole him first. They stole my brother's honor. If I run now, they steal me. I should not say, 'I will not accept it,' for I am not God. But accept it I will not. And if they steal me, they will steal my son." She picked up her glass of wine and gripped it as though it were common sense. "I know they did that to Russia years ago. But Russia's not mine. I can just be sorry. I think to Alistair, it's all equal. And who is this 'they' who does this? Where are they from? Where did they live? I don't think you can understand this, Simon. Alistair does. This is me." She put down the wine glass with care to do so gently, turned to her side, and took Alistair's hand, which she held to her knee. "I don't know why you put up with me," she said.

"I have spent much of my life thinking about this They," he said. "Back to the time Manfredi and I were boys with swords. It has not brought me understanding. Except theological, which you know too. And that coat may be too big for them. But they infect my sun, and they cannot have it. If I have to meet them finally, I'd rather have you."

Simon said, "I owed you the question." He put his plate, knife, fork, glass into good geometry, then broke it and took the last piece of chicken. "We have a great many practical things to talk about. Method is the matter, though the shape we have to learn. And now you should listen, for in these things I am well taught. Settle down, children. This is going to be a long lunch."

"I think there's pudding," Ottavia said vaguely. She picked up a pretty soft leather book. "Shall I take notes?"

"Christ, no," said Simon.

PART IV

17

He loved his wife's hair. Since he usually opened his eyes before Ottavia, it was the friend of his dawns. Her hair was the dark auburn of pretty women of northern Italy, but the fire under this auburn had a life of its own and when it drank the growing sun, it glowed like sunken gold. So it became what he loved most, a thing of contrary natures, feinting between them. Where her hair curled around her ear, itself a decoration made for a kiss, he noticed a change deep into their Roman summer of 1939: the soft Italian curl, Botticelli to be a little obvious but why not, was lifted into something sleeker and more streamlined, crisp. He was sure it was an unconscious motion of her comb. She would hardly have said to her *frisseur*, "Make me German."

Which many of their evenings, those that originated with Ottavia, were. They were also, when not actually at embassies, at villas, palazzi, foundations, concerts that rotated around the embassies, British, French, American, Spanish. And German most of all. The German embassy quite bubbled. German officers, diplomats, Germans one didn't quite ask what they were, arrived with their families every week. Some knew Italy already. Some had friends. For some it was a delicious new jaunt. They were welcome guests. Many were well-connected people—Italy was a plum—and if the little man with his moustache in Berlin was, however good for Germany, just a trifle embarrassing, well, here he was also a long way away. One did need advice here—shoes, a butler, even a lady's doctor—and from one's own kind, not a little embassy clerk. Thank God, here was Ottavia—'Stears,' was it now?—niece of a *markgraf* and sister of a marchese, knew Italy and Germany both perfectly, and with her distinguished husband had brought off the German-Italian publishing coup of the decade. And the distinguished husband, the *dichter,* was American, a country one treated with some care now, and an officer, and—though honorably taciturn about it—a known enemy of his country's socialist, crippled, Jewish president. Such a godsend Ottavia was in Rome this summer! They even had olives, it was said. *Kennst du das Land wo die Zitronen bluhn?*

Alistair walked again his boyhood Roman streets in the limitless conjecture of *avant-guerre.* What he loved in them was safe in the galleries of his mind. What was new stole their soul. All art of unveiling and surprise, which was Rome's heart, was being torn away to make avenues of bogus triumph. He walked scratching the ear of the stirring dragon whose breath would turn all to ashes. Ottavia saw the coming fire as a surgeon's, cleansing. He saw apocalypse. Hearing the approach of God's flail, he rejoiced in the nearness of his Roman tailor, and ordered a last case of shoes from St. James's. He refound Castiglione. He studied manners.

They were living with every appearance of dishonor yet without any danger to steady their nerves. Fear of the night knock at the door would have been a tonic to them. They would have known who they were. He would have been with his wonderful Ottavia with her clear brave eyes. They did know. They had to keep telling themselves. There was always one nerve that didn't hear and would keep repeating in a nasty voice that he really was going home with the little suck-up to the Germans, he the verminous old hack. "Don't push. Don't chase. Don't steer," Simon had said. "That's for later."

"You mean," said Alistair, *"if at all?"*

"Of course. Listen. Remember. Be exact. And stay busy. *What are these people doing in Rome?* is not good."

In this life, it was easy for Alistair to catch up with Curzio Malaparte, the fictional name of the fantastical journalist Erik Suckert he had first met at that long ago luncheon with Nancy at the Excelsior. He could hardly not like a man who had already been a distinguished journalist of the left, a fascist journalist, a prisoner of the fascists, a fascist journalistic superstar, who would (this was in the future but perfectly comprehensible) betray them and turn out to have been an Allied officer all along. Alistair had been some help in getting Suckert/Malaparte out of prison (a concentration camp made up of luxurious villas, for it occupied a tiny island where everybody had once gone). Suckert remembered. Malaparte was grateful. The two enjoyed the consolation of an old friendship, though it had never actually existed. Malaparte, scattering ideas all over the place now, had ideas for a magazine that would remind thinking Anglo-Saxons of their love of and debt to Italy. How Mussolini loved Hawthorne, Shelley, Browning, Henry James, Edith Wharton, Joyce, Mann (sorry!), Byron, Ruskin, Keats, tons of painters! And how they all loved him! Could Alistair find a few hours a week to be its editor? Yes, he could. Thus he was able to employ a grateful stable of literati whose art he had thought the week before curable mainly by firing squad. Its purpose was to show the busy helpfulness of the emerging traitor Alistair Stears toward the Axis.

And so walked his dear wife nearly nightly into the lion cage of the German embassy. And he did not fear for her. He supposed.

"You are," he said, "really, really sure there's nothing remembered about you, nothing seen, nothing . . . *Well, what do you know—it's her again* . . . left over? From your newspaper in Wurzburg?"

They were in their first Roman residence, an apartment they barely remembered later. Dinner alone for once, side by side, a nice wine from Manfredi still in the glasses.

She thought before she answered. She did that now. "I know now that you never know. You never know what someone noticed, someone thought. I never hung around that paper. I told you that. They didn't know who I was there. I told you that. If they did, they wouldn't have said. I don't think they would. Anyway, Alistair, it's different people here. Not the little rat-eyed Brownshirts. They were shot, anyway. There's bastards here, but they're different bastards. And it was all so very, very small. There's nothing here, Alistair. Anyway."

And at the 'anyway', he saw the face she would present to real danger. "Anyway," he said.

He still had Ottavia's hair. Which changed less than Giovanni's little hand in his when they walked very carefully by the Tiber to see the rowing clubs dashing by in their skulls. Alistair thought they looked like big, dangerous insects. Giovanni thought about ice cream. Alistair agreed, that in the stall they would visit next, it was scrumptious.

They were determined to keep that other stuff out of their real lives, lying in bed on Sunday morning, eating dinner alone, or playing with Giovanni, which they most certainly did. (A stuffed boar had impressed him, so Alistair invented The Big Black Bristly Pig, a picaresque personage who had new adventures every bedtime, in verse. Ottavia's entertainment was Grimmer.) They succeeded a bit. Their first Roman dwelling was the big apartment in brand-new Parioli. This discomfited them badly. They had thought that elevators were for hotels. Alistair tried for his mother's immense old palazzo; it was apartments now, and none were to be had. They quite soon found a small seventeenth-century palazzo in old Rome on the Via Giulia. Here life seemed more normal—though, as well as the Tiber, oarsmen in their season, and ice cream nearby, the palazzo had itinerant smells of mysterious origin, and mice. But they were home-loving people and liked to be where they first had gone to bed. It helped that their Duce had so famously made the trains run on time and that the Luccan villa was kept open. They came to know the railway line well. Concetta and Girolamo, rather old, stayed to preside over the villa. Luigi was brought to be their butler in Rome. His stitched-together face made the Lady Ottavia Stears's salon strangely suggestive of Mary Shelley's.

Ottavia would have no stranger as servant. So Luigi was not the only oddity. The village girl whom Concetta had trained now cooked for them, happily with increasing confidence. Giovanni pined for Concetta, as they sadly knew, and hurled himself at her when they visited home. He had no real nanny in Rome, but he had the close attention of every female in the house. Lucia, Ottavia's little lady's maid, much in demand here, made him laugh by speaking to him through mouthfuls of pins. Luigi, whose mouth at least had needed no stitches, sat him on his knee and turned out to have a lovely smile. The Alfa was sent home and replaced by a plain brown FIAT, their chauffeur having learned his skills on the tractor.

No danger and almost no results. They were "burrowing in," in the terms of their wretched new profession. They were not insects. One night Ottavia glowed and skipped with having heard that there were German engineers improving the signaling and points of the Italian rail lines over the Brenner and the Tarvisio. Nothing grandiose, but the lines would be able to handle a good deal more than they had.

"Aren't I your clever girl!" said Ottavia, and said it again when they went to bed, and they still felt triumphant the next morning.

There were other morsels. In August of 1939, Mussolini spread joy and light by revealing that implacable laws of physics made the presence of even one enemy bomber over Italy forever inconceivable. A week later, Alistair was able to report that the air defenses of the naval ports of La Spezia and Naples, at least, were ridiculous, useless, "like a Swiss bloody cheese." How? Through a German officer's outburst to Ottavia on the general topic of "these Italians." And by Alistair's casual meeting, which became lunch, with the naval officer who had commanded his friend the Venetian painter Pietro Vendramin in the last war. Topic: the matchless organization achieved under fascism and Mussolini's care for his military, no? He presented this to their contact.

This did not involve leaving a bottle in a tree. His contact was a sandy-haired young man whose tie advertised the brand Lux et Veritas behind a desk at the US embassy with his name for all to see, Gregory Owen. They did shut the door when Stears was there. Sometimes they met for a coffee out instead. Once for lunch. At the end of the bottle of wine, Greg, such he was, confessed his love of e. e. cummings, shyly. Alistair changed the guilty subject. That little lapse made him see that Greg's eyes never displayed by a flicker whether what Stears brought was red hot, or bromide, or wrong. He kept a list of whom they knew and what these people did.

Two evenings later, there was a little evening at the US residence. A Yale professor Alistair didn't know paid for his supper with a talk on Longfellow. They attended, of course. Over ice cream, a young man he had seen near Greg Owen's office buttonholed him with a Robert Frost doubt. How would he actually speak, enunciate, the last lines, *And miles to go before I sleep, / And miles to go before I sleep*?

Brusquely, said Alistair. And then did it.

"You mishandled that naval officer," said the young man. "Don't steer conversations. Don't catch people's sleeves. That's for later."

Alistair forbore to say, "If at all." It was nice they were listening.

xxx

German armies tore at Poland. France and England presented ultimata. Clocks ticked. France and England declared war. Their armies, five hundred miles from Poland, watched.

At the very back of the piano nobile, there was a small sitting room where the palazzo overlooked the Tiber. They used it, sitting together and even dining there alone, much like the room with the gramophone in Lucca. This it also had, and it was a radio as well. They sat side by side on the afternoon that war came. Alistair found the BBC. They listened, and as the light turned from gold to blue, they looked into the radio's purple dial.

Movement of the air caught their eyes. Above the Tiber, suddenly, starlings poured to flock for their flight south. They poured in clouds, grey smoke spinning into whorls, plunging, rising up again in strings like music on a sheet, drawn together in a dense black ball, spraying out of it again like trumpet, rearing like waves dashing upon each other, spiraling, darkening with the light. It is one of the sights of Rome's year.

But nothing happened. Nothing happened anywhere except far, far away in Poland. The Carabinieri crossed the street and stood a little closer to the doors of the British and French embassies. Their own staff mentioned the new war perfunctorily, though with respect, as the kind of thing that might interest their masters somehow. England, France, and Germany were at war, more or less. Mussolini was not.

Ottavia grew agitated. She grew furious. She slapped the lunch table and made the glasses ring. "He's going to funk it, the little beast! He's too much of a coward to go to war! Damn the little man! He can still embarrass me."

Alistair went to Zurich in December. It occurred to him suddenly that if the United States and Italy found themselves at war, bank transfers from Boston to Florence would cease. This state of affairs was so obviously improbable that he was driven to small, jerky motions that imitated what he'd do if it were true. He asked Ottavia to go with him. On the way back, they'd turn it into a Christmas in Zermatt. She wanted only Christmas at home. Not even at her brother's.

"I'll meet you there from Zurich," he said.

"No, Alistair. Come back. We shall all go together."

The servants, Lucca being their home, too, made a jolly party in a second class carriage of the same train.

That morning, Ottavia had held him longer in bed than usual. Finally, "There will be no war, Alistair. No real war. We both know it now. We will simply rot with history. That is what there is. But now we are going to be a family at Christmas."

No, he did not know. The dragon had its thoughts. She might well be right. Germany had no great weight over England and France, who besides had now had time to summon their great empires. The British, inventors of the tank, were presumably masters of its use. He doubted that Hitler could afford defeats. And Britain and France could not drive Hitler from Poland. He wondered if they would even go back to Rome.

So if the war came, he foreknew it: stoic infantry battles in northern France, the Italians scrabbling like puppies on mountain faces again, this time French, once in a while someone's mighty stroke scattering populations down the roads like ghosts at dawn. He had confidence in his judgment; his training as officer had been vastly more lavish than as poet.

War had been horror and holy to him once. Not a second time. Looking at Eastern Europe, that grubby corner of the stage reserved for beastliness, one apprehended that new torments might be in store, bombers grown huge and horrible. A hillside rocked by, and Ottavia showed Giovanni some Umbrian sheep. With them would be shepherds in the field, did he remember from last year? Maybe they'd be in the house this year again. They'd find out Christmas Eve.

GIOVANNI HURLED HIMSELF AT Concetta.

As a house that had served one family for many centuries, Pace ed Abbondanza had startling resources of stuff. There was an oven for baking a whole pig, for example, made of dark iron that had to be cleaned and warmed up for days. Nothing for Christmas trees—German blood had come into the family only with Ottavia's mother—but anything you could wish in the way of figures and camels and kings. It turned out that there was a beautiful hanging, a tapestry of the wise men by a manger in a little cave in a hill with the shepherds and angels, and a stag hunt going on outside. Concetta brought them to where it lived, in a chest upstairs with an iron lock that shrieked.

"Oh, we must have that up!" said Ottavia. "I'd forgotten it. But not till Christmas Eve."

Thus the house became full of secrets. Giovanni, whom the secrets were for, was in the way and was banished for hours to his father's study, which his father did not mind. The books Ottavia read to him were put where he could reach them. They had pictures of tailors fighting giants with cheeses and the castle West of the Sun and East of the Moon, which are particularly good when you know that everything in them is real.

His father wrote. His father watched his son's mouth and forehead move as Giovanni's eyes took in the pictures or let them go, and recognized what he could not place until he knew it as photographs of himself when very young. He wrote little poetry now. He ran Malaparte's magazine with the back of his hand. He read Edmund Burke, who preached, though in an aside, the imperative prepotency of manners over law. For manners are more subtle than the law, take their form from the intermingled breath of the best and thence spread, govern the pace of the tongue, the disposition of a hand, the word that hand chooses with a pen, give order to kindness, justice, judgment up even to the point of the rapier, fill a room with merriment and light. Law may surround a gentleman but should very rarely touch him; manners guide his eyelid in exchanges of kind harmony, and the being surrounded by law is based on flesh, to be sure, but to be comprehended in manners.

"What's questo here, Babbo?" said Giovanni. "I don't understand."

It was a plate in a book of hunting tapestries he could not possibly have carried over, so Alistair joined him and they looked at it together. It turned out to be natives hunting ducks by wading in a lake up to their necks, which ended in high straw hats with eyeholes. This took some time to work out. He could think of better methods. He turned the page to where some jolly Indians were murdering crocodiles with spikes.

"That's much nicer," he said. Giovanni agreed.

Castiglione, at the court of Urbino, had laid manners into form as reasoned and gracious as the *Principia Mathematica*. From Urbino's windy hill, one looks down at the forests of the Marche and literally at the sagging altars and miserable huts of the first destitute Franciscans, though they were gone by Castiglione's time. St. Francis in his filthy shift whose ice draggles cut his shins, and Castiglione in the joy of Renaissance geometry, much like Alistair's own house. And here the comment: both loved kindness, and slowness of anger, ripened judgment, shunned flattery and lies, love modesty and courage at its need. St. Francis, at forty-two damaged by austerities not to be imagined, hobbled by the iron nails of the stigmata (yes, they were that real), set himself to die stark naked on the bare earth. Alistair rejected that for human beings and looked up to Urbino. A discussion he was fully prepared to have with God.

He had it with Father Kirchner over dinner. The pasta was pappardelle with hare. Ottavia was smug about it, for she had shot a hare when Alistair had yet to take a boar.

"No thanks to Concetta this time," said Ottavia. "All to me."

Father Kirchner said, "St. Francis said that if temptation came upon him at the end, he would wrestle with it naked. He was also singing. Singing with joy. Is that not a little like your Russian poet, Alistair?"

"Man was born to celebrate. Suffering is at need."

"I cannot radically argue that," said Father Kirchner. "We do celebrate your hare, Ottavia. Thank you."

"It's good, isn't it?" said Ottavia. "I rather like to think that the hare celebrated something. The rising sun. Whatever hares celebrate."

"That is a thought for a painting. Each animal celebrating its particular joy."

Alistair, looking up for a moment, saw the painting there. It was like Galisteo's Irish missal.

"I'd like to paint a horse like that," he said. "If only I could."

He had not taken his horses to Rome and fell back in love with them at each return.

"You are a little hard to follow tonight, Alistair. And you are distracting Father Kirchner from my hare."

"Not so hard to follow," said Father Kirchner. "The subject is original sin. A good one for right now. We do not normally propose manners as its cure. Can they not mask evil? The goose step is also of order. Be careful, Alistair. I am your confessor."

"I understand now," said Ottavia. And to Alistair, "I should have said it at the beach."

"Ah, the beach," said Father Kirchner.

"Does he know?" said Ottavia, in a moment, sharply, to Alistair.

"Oh yes. Everything."

Ottavia tightened her mouth, then relaxed it, then stretched her bare arm a little to Father Kirchner, then smiled, then said, "I'm glad."

Alistair said, "The goose step is not order, for the goose step disrupts, while order graces. There. There is my text. There must be celebration, and only in courtesy is celebration, not the goose step. At the beach, we took service with Castiglione's Urbino. Urbino is our flag."

Father Kirchner looked down. Ottavia's eyes followed him while Alistair's, the planets. It was evident to Ottavia that Kirchner struggled with tone and that his mouth settled for the grimmer.

"I do not like countries, Alistair," he said. "Their nature is jealousy. I have been tossed between them. I was Austrian, and I honored my emperor. If you make your Urbino a country, it will be jealous. Your real country will be jealous. All of Ottavia's are jealous. I think of you as my children, and I am worried enough about you already. I am easier with St. Francis's bare earth, though I understand your objection. It is true that all we fear may not happen. It has not yet. This war may still die unborn. That is our prayer."

"That is not my prayer. It is my fear," said Ottavia. But then clapped her hands in authority then spread them wide in peace. "It is much too near Christmas for this," she said. "I have a son upstairs dreaming of sugar plums, I hope, though they are actually Karlsbad plums, sent by my uncle from Wurzburg, bless him. And for putting up with my pasta, you have a lovely pudding. And then we can go next door and see the nativity hanging. It will be so nice for Giovanni. I have had the servants light the room with candles, for it is Christmas Eve tomorrow."

"Karlsbad plums. Oh dear, how I remember them," said Father Kirchner.

18

Germany moved. France groaned. France whimpered. England swam home. That was that.

Except not. Mussolini surprised defeated France, suffered sharp defeats from France's defeated army, but prevailed in the end.

"Christ, is there no limit?" said Ottavia. "Are we jackals now?"

"There is no limit," said Alistair.

The RAF bombed Milan. The Royal Navy savaged the Italian fleet.

German invasion barges clustered like mussels in the Breton bays.

So in from a mild sky blew myth again, and not an Italian hell of starlings, even driven by hell's gale, but out of the north, Odin's bane, the night wolves who would eat the sun. They had England by the throat. He had thought that countries faded into mist. Now he saw that their bowels could be torn out on the grass. The wolves had gorged on his Paris. Of Sylvia Beach, God knew Traitors and their molls in the Closerie des Lilas. James Joyce was in Zurich, thank God, but near death, they said. He did not like to think of Nancy. And he, American, though a willing knight, rode against the wolves on a dead horse.

The French and British embassies were no longer there.

His own was there and open for business. The German embassy was very open indeed.

The atmospheres there had changed. At his own, there was a retreat into what he himself called "Protestantism": shorter sentences, more closed doors, papers gripped, not allowed to flap their wings. He still had a role here but felt not entirely welcome. This went well beyond Greg Owen's merely tactical, "We'll have to make different arrangements for you. You'll know in a few days. We don't want you around here, Alistair."

At her embassy, which is what he called the German embassy, though he knew it wasn't (whatever her mother, Ottavia was of Italian father, born in Italy), there were balloons of mirth, and belches of boasting, and a swing to the booted step. The war was going well for Germany. There were certainly no problems here. This was a little noisy. It was entirely superficial. For the real German diplomats and real German officers, who were not at all lacking and whom Ottavia knew much better than the *landsknechts* beneath them, this was serious. War was serious. Wars went both ways. War with England was serious. War with England with America looking on, however far behind the Atlantic's rain curtains, was very serious indeed. On the upper floors, there was a retreat into order and into craft. And one sought out even more one's own kind, such as Ottavia, daughter of officers.

The first question is the beginning of the end, Simon had said on the beach. Never let it be asked. Know exactly where the unraveling can begin. Never step out of character. And don't be too much in it. People change a bit in war. Normal people.

So who were they? And where were the loose threads?

Alistair was American, not so very bad yet. He was still, technically, an American officer, though that defect was indefinite for now.

Ottavia was much rougher stuff. Associate of state enemies. Propagandist against the state. Was this true? Ottavia thought, Alistair thought, Simon had said that even Hitler's weasels might stifle a yawn at an upper class young girl's very short flirtation with a minor publication in the tamer circles of dissent. If that same girl turned up at the social heart of a German embassy in wartime, married to a foreign officer, and made a profession of knowing everybody, that yawn would show teeth. Though it still seemed possible that that was all unknown.

And then Alistair was an eminent poet. He was of distinguished family at home. His father was a senior judge. He had private means and was said to be deeply conservative politically and an enemy of the Roosevelt regime. This last was a little hard to pin down, but it seemed to be in accord with his literary persona, presumably hard to fake. He had grown up mostly in Italy. His mother was something of a heroine of the last war. He had married an Italian noblewoman, sister of a childhood friend. Her brother had done respectable and useful things for the party though could not be called an enthusiast. Her second brother had been decorated in the Abyssinian war, posthumously. The wife was, of course, half German. That half was Catholic higher nobility, important people in the old Catholic archduchy, politely pushed to the side during fifty years of Hohenzollern Protestant ascendency. There were cousins scattered through the officer corps, none especially remarkable. The couple had an agricultural estate, which they were accustomed to supervise themselves. The subject was a colleague of the prominent fascist journalist Suckert/Malaparte, who vouched for him. Much better, he was the present and childhood friend of Rodolfo Pallandra, just back from extremely successful service with Generalissimo Franco's circle, and now eminent in the major fascist stronghold of Florence. Rodolfo Pallandra had a high opinion of him and expected to see him more.

Not too bad, they thought. Not too bad, Simon had said. They did not know where Simon was. Maybe still in Paris, no real reason why not. But they did not know and were not told.

They reassured themselves of these things in bed, safe right in the middle of the Duchy of Urbino. Discussing them there, they could still sleep afterwards. Things could not be really, really bad with Ottavia's breast in your hand and her thigh against yours. It was always late.

"But I only work at night," said Ottavia.

Daringly, for Urbino, Alistair said, "So do a lot of other ladies," got a kick and a promise it would be aimed higher next time.

"Because it's not all a joke. I am a kind of whore, Alistair. I spy on my friends. And some of them must be fighting and dying somewhere now. It's not funny." But snuggled up again, thank God. They lay together. The night wolves circled Urbino's walls, close enough to smell but not yet to feel the chill in their veins.

THE YOUNG MAN PUNCTILIOUS about Robert Frost was finishing his coffee outside on the Piazza Navona as Alistair walked by. This was a Friday evening. The bombings of Milan and Genoa had made an impression, but the pope had forbidden Churchill ever to hurt Rome, as was known, so the generous space, always so handsome, was convivial, relaxed, and crowded too. The Roman summer had not noticed that August was over. Outdoor shade was happiness. The young man caught up with him in the little Piazza Pasquino.

He asked, "Were you followed?"

"I don't think so," said Alistair.

"I'd be amazed if you were. If you had been, he'd have to come through that narrow funnel we just walked through, and he'd have to have been close to you in the crowd."

"Or to you," said Alistair.

"Yes. But I'm trained."

"Ah," said Alistair.

"You should start to think about it. Did they teach you in the army?"

"Not exactly," said Alistair.

"No. It's pretty much common sense. Unless you're dealing with experts. The Italians don't have experts. Watch who's behind you. Shop windows are a godsend, but choose them sensibly. Lady's underwear. Books. Hunting things. Motorcycles if you're lucky."

"One is so various," said Alistair.

"You must buy Ottavia things sometimes. Is she the only one?"

"The only what?" said Alistair.

"The only female. You would buy panties for?"

"For Christ's sake," said Alistair.

"Oh damn. We didn't think you did. Think there was. Don't bridle. We have to know, and we don't have all the resources we should have. Would it be in character for you to go to the country now?"

"Do you mean Lucca?" said Alistair.

The young man glanced at his notes, which were invisible. "Yes. Lucca. That's it."

"In late summer? Looking to the harvests? Yes. Of course."

"Is there a place you could go by bicycle? Private and not on your land?"

"I don't have a bicycle," said Alistair.

"Oh." And the young man's notes were of no avail.

"I have a horse. And from the road to Mutigliano, which goes past my gate, there is a little road that goes sharply uphill. A gravel road. It would be hard to mistake. There is a wood at the top. And a house, but it is abandoned, falling down. It is a pleasant view. I often ride there. By a way quite different from the road. And very secluded. If this is supposed to be a meeting, I imagine it would serve."

"Can you be there Thursday next week? Midmorning? At eleven? If you are followed, skip it."

"I shall be alert for banners behind me. Or hussars. But understand there are no shop windows."

"Aha," said the young man. "That's funny."

"Do you seriously think that I would have told you?" said Alistair.

"Hussars? Oh, I see. About the ladies? Not really. But I've asked, you see. Now I've asked."

Alone again, Alistair observed that the *pasquino,* the blurred little statue for which the square is named, had heard all this without any suffering any diminution of reality at all.

IT WAS A PLEASURE TO be on land not his own, for he could behold it without thought. The track was narrow through the unkept high meadow. Boromeo's hooves brushed aside poppies that crowded down from the wood, favoring a fold in the hillside friendly to water. There were cornflowers mixed with the poppies. The path was steeply up. His saddle creaked. Boromeo sighed to show that it was hard work but that he was a horse who did not complain. He looked down more than up. In the light that enveloped the flowers, the wings of wandering insects winked. He did not need to look aside or behind him, for the first of the climb had given him a good view of his own estate, and he was warmed as much by that as by the sun. He heard a motor climbing the road on the far side of the hill. His contact, then, would be there in the warm blue haze of Roman pine a very little before him. He did not push Boromeo on.

In the wood, at the end of the road, was a car, and a man inside it, face unseen.

Simon said, "This is a hell of a lot of trouble. Sorry."

Alistair said, "More for you than for me, I think. I had a pleasant ride."

Simon got out of the car.

Alistair dismounted. "Where are you now?" he said.

"Lausanne. That will change. Because you think. That answers your next question, which is, 'Why are you here?' Because you think, Alistair. Very dangerous habit. Could we sit on this rock, do you suppose?"

Alistair tied Boromeo's bridle to a shrub but only lightly, for he was a well-mannered horse. The rock was warm in the sun, but the air, which smelled of pine and thyme, was not overheated. The view was the spires of Lucca, quite far beneath, and strung to them by rows of olive and vine. "I do think," he said. "I think we are standing on the hinge of the world, and my country does nothing."

"There are Rolls-Royce engines for the RAF made in Ohio and not much talked about. That is why they have doubled their aircraft production and are winning that war. Hitler has three weeks of summer left to invade England, and he won't because he can't. His first defeat. The US Coast Guard and the US Navy shadow convoys until the Royal Navy meets them beyond Nova Scotia. Our airplanes go a little further. We sold them fifty destroyers on very easy terms. That is a lot of ship, Alistair. None of that goes to the other side. They're on their own. My service passes everything it can to the British."

This for attention, which Alistair gave, and now remembered Simon in fencing whites at the Palazzo Colonna putting on his mask and with that movement changing from puppy to cat.

Simon leaned forward, spoke of Congress, foreign entanglements, the Irish vote. Out of the shrubs beneath the pines, a veil of gnats was conjured by the sun. It had shape. It was here, not there, and though it rippled, it did not much move. It had no color but changed the colors behind it: moss turned black, but some little trumpet mushrooms presaging fall in the loam, more gold. He had made a demon out of Roosevelt, he was told; the man was much more complex.

"So when do we fight them, Alistair? We'll have to. Germany does not have an off button. Do we start when we have no allies left and no base over here, or much sooner? But there needs the moment. The moment when all that is plain. We cannot see that moment."

"The point of next intensity in a poem," said Alistair. "When you do not see it, you still know that it is there. You have to act upon it, step up on it. There is courage also in art. We know there are poems of wars. I think war is a poem. It has form, it seems." He had decided that it was time to look at Simon.

Who said, "If we and Italy came to war, would they arrest you the next day?"

"The next day, I doubt. Things are personal in Italy. The policeman. The barber. Probably the hangman. Rudeness would reflect badly on them. I doubt the next day."

"Not the right answer, Alistair. It can't happen at all. We'll get back to that. There are things I have for you right now. Spain was the nursery of this war. Our friend Rodolfo did very well there. Which is nice. And he stands well with two of Italy's point field officers there. I don't give a damn about the generals. These were colonels. One's a general now. One will be. They are cutting-edge Italian army. We'd like to know more. And one made a point of being independent of the Germans there. So it showed. Rebuff. I can't tell you how interesting that is. Develop this contact, Alistair. Cultivate it."

Alistair nodded. "I will do that."

"And travel," said Simon.

"Travel?"

"Just that. Move around. Find any excuse. Military installations are difficult to hide if you know what they are. You're a trained officer. You will make connections others wouldn't. Defensive points. New factories without much access. Military units. Added rail lines. Connect the dots. Move around."

"As I can," said Alistair.

"Of course."

"It seems little."

"Your point of next intensity. Which you must mount up. And I thank you for those words," said Simon. "You have positioned yourself wonderfully, Alistair, as I never doubted. Olympian. Opaque. They wonder, are you with them or not? And still a very captivating fellow to have lunch with. You're all I hoped. You're such a question mark that people can't resist trying out their thoughts on you. Do you see where I'm going?"

"We try to please, Simon. But no, I don't."

"You're a question mark. That is your value now. We are not at war. We will be at war. There is no room for question marks in war."

The stance to meet threat is stillness. He had learned that on Vipero long ago. He watched a beetle, gold and green, walk on Boromeo's bridle, and wondered if he would persevere to Boromeo or fly off first.

"You are right," he said.

"And so are you, Alistair. They will not arrest you the first day. You're quite an old friend. I am not sure they will arrest you at all. House arrest. House internment. The Hermit of Lucca. Very likely. But that's the Italians. We had not expected the degree of German influence in Italy. We expected it at the top, but it's seeping everywhere. The Germans will want to arrest you. Just to make sure. They do that."

Boromeo took control of things. He snoofed. The beetle flew. Alistair saw only to nod his head. Which disturbed no stillness.

"And how does the belle of the German embassy in wartime look with a husband arrested as an enemy alien? We lose you both. You're gone, poof! Just when we need you most. I need you to go beyond the question mark, Alistair. I need you to see the light."

"Meaning?"

"And having seen it to start talking about it. Your magazine, Alistair, your and Malaparte's, it's pabulum. Mussolini's debt to Robert Browning! Querulous remarks about the British Empire, poor downtrodden Hindoos! Snipes at America for mistreating its negroes! How Romans civilized Britain, for Christ's sake! Chalk dust stuff. Yale stuff. Half the British Socialist Party would sign on for that. Ninety percent of the French Assembly. It's all right. Keep on doing it. It helps. But we need the Thunderer, Jove, You. Alistair Stears has wavered. He has nobly thought. And Alistair Stears has discovered the heart of fascism. And He Loves It. Vergil dumps Aeneas, roots for the Greeks. They'll never arrest you then. You can do anything."

"I'm to be a traitor."

Simon said, "No. You are an American patriot. This will be a ruse of war. Think Odysseus."

"America is not the point. You are asking me to be a traitor to myself."

"Alistair Stears cannot be a traitor. You will be a traitor to treachery. How Alistair is that?"

Ottavia's voice drifted through the pines, *I am a sort of whore, Alistair.*

"No question mark. Exclamation point. Fascism's English trumpet. You'll probably save your wife's life."

So the whore and the strumpet, he thought, and therefore smiled when he said, "A traitor to all my work then?"

Simon said, "A traitor to yourself because you did this yourself. You imagined yourself into the heights. Really imagined, because you really became it. Dante, Virgil, almost. But you never noticed that other people were imagining themselves too. There was a little man who saw his moustache sticking out of a knight's helmet. And there was the schoolteacher's son with the chin we all love who knew he was a Roman emperor and adored salutes. They found friends and they worked very hard and now they are bigger than you. Much bigger, and quite unlike you, and very nasty. And they want people to be like them. They want people to like them, Alistair, to believe that having them on top of the world is normal. If you shake their hands, they'll believe you mean it. And then you have a position here that is unmatchable. 'The hinge of history,' Alistair. I'm not going to insult you by asking if you mean what you say. This is the shape of reality. It's not any cleverness of mine."

"What would you have me do, Simon, just what?"

Sounds returned, above Simon's prescription, mallet on vineyard stake, wheel on rock on road, sudden and big and close, Boromeo's hoof punishing root for his patience was wearing out, a high hawk. He heard all. He said, "I am leaving now. I must think of my horse as well as the world, and he needs water. I need time. I suppose we can communicate?"

"Use the embassy. You know how. They will cooperate."

"The man I last saw from there is a fool."

"We are a small service, Alistair, not like the British. We don't have an empire to play with. That will change. We need you, Alistair. You should know I am not an amateur. You have a right to know that. You will use the embassy. But it will be for nothing important. One day, they will kick you out. It will be obvious and rather crude. I think you won't be told when. Then you're to be a traitor."

He said, "Then there will have to be another method. Will I not be told that either?"

"I do not know what face your contact will have. Or faces, maybe. I do know who will choose him, ultimately. He will be put in place by Cardinal Guzman. Whose predecessor you knew so very well."

Because he felt fear, he said, "The cardinal certainly does not obey you."

"No, indeed," said Simon. "He was asked. For his cooperation. Not by me.

Very high up. You were part of the answer. He would do it but only with you. Not otherwise."

"You should have said this first."

"We have our little pride. I hoped to call you to your loyalty to your country. It looked pretty close. Because now there's no question, is there?"

Alistair shook his head at the obvious.

Simon said, "All the other things are still valid. You'll take up Rodolfo?"

"Yes. First. I should anyway." He said, "My horse still needs water," but smiled. "And I still need to think how. Very much. Though not if."

Simon opened his hands. "We're finished," he said. "No loitering in this game. The embassy will serve while it serves."

HE STAYED BOROMEO ON the far side of the hill. Simon was his guest. He waited for his departure. Engine, brakes, tires on stone, back, clutch, and turn. His guest left his care. He turned Boromeo down to water, and watering his horse restored sweet nature, which reminded him that his responsibilities were small and real. He had a good ride home and then a late lunch for both of them, and for him, there was his Ottavia. They might be in hell's own situation, but he was husband and father still, and of Urbino. A saddle is a good place to think. He began to figure their chances.

There is a thing about mazes: to get out, you leave something behind. He could run and leave the war behind, but he doubted that Ottavia could or would do that. More: Ottavia had not truly met her love, who was himself. She had conjured him together bone by bone through the thoughts of a lonely childhood. She had ended up with a fairly decent likeness of him. By now, she was the companion of two thousand nights, the womb of his son, his delight, his best friend. But right at the center of all that was her imagining of him, which was his second self. Which was what would be left behind in the maze if he pulled her from it by force. So the decision was already made, was made the moment Simon spoke: he would give treachery everything it wanted.

19

Extra pounds became Rodolfo, thought Alistair. Was it four years now? Rodolfo's self-importance no longer jumped and barked; it moved smoothly on the broad plains of his shooting suit of loden. They were indeed shooting. This was Alistair's land, his birds, his dogs. Two setters crept forward on a scent toward the left, Rodolfo's side, so it would be his guest's shot, almost for sure. Rodolfo's eye followed, his feet obeyed, his shoulders moved. The grouse, Hungarian and big as a small pheasant, clattered, cockbird rocketing. The gun rose without haste. The grouse fell straight, out of the puff cloud of its feathers. One setter accepted it. He did some shooting over in Spain, thought Alistair, who had seen already that Rodolfo's gun was Spanish and very nice. His guest looked to him and smiled. He saw gratitude and pleasure, no conceit. He smiled approval back.

He was not pleased. He needed the Rodolfo he had known, for whom he had always had a side-glance of scorn, whom he had fitted into his plan for this day as a rabbit to be baited. He clutched at scorn. The loden coat, cut so, was wrong for Tuscany, and the feather in the hat was absurd. There was a sheen of sweat on the prospering cheeks. But the lard in the cheeks would not chuckle if poked. Its weight was power. It could stifle. He was ill at ease and had not expected to be.

Shooting, not "a shoot." Walked-up birds, no beaters, no other guests. Alistair and Ottavia had bundled Ottavia off for a day with her brother, in truth a little overdue. "Truth" had slouched into their conversation; after the session with Simon, it had sat down with them. Truthful people, they had never seen the point before in declaring truth. Rodolfo's invitation had been a tangle for them. Decision: the squire, confident, four-square, invites his old friend, been too long. And serious things on his mind in this serious new state of affairs. No harm in that. The calculations made their poor heads ache.

The motorcycle outrider was in the kitchen with the chauffeur of the big black car. The secretary, clerk's business suit cut thin and plain, was in the morning room. There was a telephone there if needed, no? The bodyguard stayed fifty yards back, part of the trees, really, not bothering the gentlemen at all. Rodolfo had blossomed.

They walked the fields line abreast, Alistair right, the gamekeeper with the setters, Rodolfo left. Too far apart for talk, and too many ears. They walked mostly through plow, maize and millet harvested, food for oxen, but the stalks not yet sere. The ground was crumbly. One thought of vipers. One wore boots. The birds flew and fell, here and there, but in sufficient rhythm. A mule pulled the lunch wagon and the afternoon. Both would catch up. They'd talk at lunch.

It was easy to begin. Their lunch was a tray of prosciutto and pâtés, good bread, and the year's last perfect tomatoes, a wine chosen to be light. The attendant from the wagon brought it and retired with the bodyguard and gamekeeper. No fuss. They ate with bread and napkins on their knees. Rodolfo beamed at the tray. No doubt where the pounds came from. That Franco was Good King Wenceslas compared to a Stalin satrap did not have to be argued, so nor did the virtue of those who had helped him to Spain. Alistair said so.

Rodolfo said, "Thank you. I did not like the communists. The men from Russia. Italy did well by that."

So Alistair moved. "Stalin is to the east," he said. "We can almost see him. And to our west, Roosevelt is a socialist now, if he ever wasn't. The people around him now are even worse than they used to be. Churchill has turned to the socialists, offered them power. You could never trust the French. Spain was important, Rodolfo. We should all thank you. What is there? Spain now, Italy, Hungary and Romania. Germany, of course." For he was convinced that as bait for a rabbit, mostly true had the sweeter scent.

His rabbit sniffed but did not quite take it. Rodolfo said, "It was valuable for me. The men from Moscow were about power. Italians always have some excuses, some exceptions, even your enemy should think you're pretty decent. Not there. It's like arguing with a slicing machine. You learn from that. But we beat them, Alistair. We beat them." His hand settled on Alistair's shoulder, became comradeship, and squeezed hard.

Alistair jerked, then smiled.

"And there's something else," said Rodolfo. "The Spanish like to kill. I'm glad I saw that. Made me realize I don't think I do. Now I have to think if that's a weakness. A fascist shouldn't flinch. But they're a lower race, of course. The Spanish are."

Alistair said, "Italians don't like to kill, on the whole, I think. Not many of them. Not much of the time."

"Italiano sono," Rodolfo said—I am Italian. Said it like the the old Rodolfo, loud and spiky. And then he veered so wildly, Alistair couldn't see the turn. "I'm sorry about your man here. The peasant they beat and nearly killed. That wasn't right. Of course I know about it."

Judicious Alistair said, "No one was killed. Got out of hand, I imagine. Someone excited in the night. You're right, of course. It wasn't very good. Ottavia took it quite badly." Implying, *But we are men.*

"Fascism is grace through order, justice through strength. Not crawling around in the night beating people. What good is that? It's weakness. It's disorder. If a Spaniard kills because he wants to, does that make him a better fascist? In the early days, of course, we had to make our point. You could be killed for being a fascist once. Not now. We're the guardians."

Given that chance, Alistair jumped again. "You suggested once that I should have a role in the party. We had that lunch in the Via del Corno." In the amazing time when days stretched between sweet dawns and guiltless sunsets and war did not sit across the room.

Rodolfo seemed not to have heard. He turned on his haunches so his face looked straight into Alistair's. He said, "I'm very successful, Alistair." He said it quietly. "I'm honored, even." He looked at that in silence as though he had found a pearl in his napkin, then at Alistair. They were very close. He could see the spittle on Rodolfo's teeth and a scrap of ham caught fast there. "I didn't think I would be. I never thought

I'd be as good as my father, who was just a good captain who died too early. I'm much more than that. Spain topped it off. I thought you'd be something, and Manfredi, though he doesn't have to do much. Simon was always smart and funny. Now that I'm successful, I'd like to be sure what I'm successful at. So I think." He raised his eye. "It's funny how I can talk to you, but I can. I always could, Alistair."

He leaned forward. Musk on his body, as though the bottle had just now been cracked.

Alistair longed to rise and walk. He found this intimacy shocking, sexual, dangerous. He thought suddenly, this is how a woman must feel under a man she doesn't want. He nodded seriously into what he supposed were soft brown eyes. Out of the soft brown eyes burst an air-raid siren.

Rodolfo said, "What does Simon do now, Alistair?"

Do not, do not, do not deny you've seen him. He probably knows. But he didn't ask that. "He's American government. Like his father. Foreign service." And now what? Your rabbit's a weasel and here are the teeth.

But maybe it was not. It only nodded and ran off down the strangest burrow of all. "Franco took away the laws against the Jews. Laws since 1492. Am I supposed to think Franco's not a fascist?" Now he looked at Alistair as if Alistair were being slow. "The party used to be full of Jews. I never minded them much. I don't think the old man minded them." And since Alistair was apparently being not only obtuse but argumentative, he went on, "It's not Italian. If I was Romanian, I'd be happy to hate Jews. It's what they do. I don't think less of them for it. I don't look down on people. But I'm Italian. So I don't. Not much. Not enough to go to all the trouble of running around being beastly to them. If it made Italy stronger, I'd be for it. A fascist doesn't flinch. But I don't think it does. And if it doesn't and it isn't Italian, it's stupid. And if it isn't Italian, it's from someone else. The Germans aren't bosses here; they're guests."

He looked down. Into the silence, Alistair scribbled reports. Rodolfo looked up. So did the two setters, encouraged by the thought that lunch seemed to be ending with spare food, pâté at that.

Rodolfo said, "They are guests. And we are little Italian innkeepers. And they tip us in steel and coal."

How Simon would love this. How interesting his report would be.

"Italy's the thing. Italy and fascism. Fascism and Italy. They're the same now. We've won our battles. That's what I've been thinking, Alistair."

Alistair said mildly and quietly, for things do change and what we thought once we may no longer think, and they were men who talked of serious things, "You suggested once that there could be a role for me in the party, Rodolfo. I have thought a great deal about it. I did not have an Italian wife then, nor an Italian child. Italy is my country now. I have no other. My wife is Italian first, like you. She has her German loyalties and connections, as she should, and our son will know his German heritage. I am not without standing. I feel the world is confused about my views. I like, 'Fascism is grace through order, justice through strength,' Rodolfo. I would like it to be easier for it to be known that I think that. And I feel a little the guest at the Italian dinner who never pays the bill. If I could contribute something to the party's thought, it would salve my conscience. These are difficult times."

He ran his fingers over the grain of his gunstock, a gesture of simplicity. He said, "To be thought about, only. Perhaps you would consider. Nothing to rush." And opened his hands and said, "And we have fields left to shoot." Stretched his hand toward his preferred of the setters, half to point and half to cajole, "And these gentlemen should earn their keep."

The shade left them as they rose. The dogs forgot about lunch and peed instead. The gamekeeper hoisted up the ammunition bag, shook the dog whistle out of his shirt. Alistair picked up his gun and in its balance found elation. He had Rodolfo. Had him by luck. It was clear that Rodolfo intended to mark his new estate by becoming a voice; and in that case, he could not fail to see the advantage in having a private laureate. At this thought, scorn lifted its sharp nose and banished unease. Banished fear. He could handle Rodolfo.

They walked on. His gun was smooth to his hand, pleasure to his eye. His dogs were handsome. Birds would rise out of the cover, each one a moment of sheer joy. Beyond the plow, the olives of Pace ed Abbondanza spread over the hills like mist. All were his delight, if they would ever forgive the insult of today.

Writing lies, he needed the truth. Poets do need truth. And the truth he kept before him was that in this war, he was a traitor to both sides. Or he was not. There is treachery only where there has been allegiance. And he knew that his allegiance to the US Army was to itself and the craft of war, no more. But what about his true allegiance—to the world of fairness over form, kindness over truth, adequate means over joy, the decent democratic Allies? No. His masters were Burke and Castiglione. He was very nearly sure that he and Ottavia were risking themselves to pass to their son a world in which his soul would starve in drizzle.

He wrote in the room where the BBC and starlings had brought them the war. The view was the Tiber, and he liked moving water. Shift the eyes to the right, and there was Castel Sant'Angelo, the pope's castle.

So Castel Sant'Angelo became his compass. It was harmonious, asked no understanding, and guarded what truth was left. He looked to it as he put the period on each sentence. *All right?*

Alistair and Ottavia joined the reception line at the Villa Wolkonsky, the German ambassador's residence, out of a Roman night of the newborn 1941. Epiphany had yet to come. A Christmas star still hung in heaven. One seemed to lose it on the way. It was not a great way from their Via Gulia, but it seemed a weary one. One left Castel Sant'Angelo's Rome behind, Mussolini's lit up the Piazza Venezia, gladiatorial ghosts grunted and bled in the Colosseum. You ended deep in the Rome of the caesars. Where Ottavia had conversations over her bare, jeweled neck. They shuffled past footmen and SS guards all polished up toward the ballroom door. Reminded Alistair of an abattoir.

But Ottavia greeted host and hostess in the manner of *jeune fille de la maison*. It was true that the ambassador, though Protestant and Prussian, was a close army friend of her uncle's, and his Wini a chum of her aunt's. Ottavia took Alistair's hand a moment then let it go. "Fish to fry," she murmured and went off into the crowd. He looked after her dismally and smiling. His own world was still almost entirely Italian. He handled it with only occasional dread. He thought her German one vastly more dangerous. He hated to see her sink into it, undefended, and with so much bare skin.

He did not speak German. What he knew he hid. Language surrounded him like glass and let him look. He truly did not understand most of what passed in his earshot, so he heard beneath words, which is a basement poets know.

The spores carried to Rodolfo on his breath were ripening underground, he was sure. He felt, as he made politenesses around the room, that he carried a new scent, meatier and less abstract. His two "new" monographs—he called them "the Devil's Verses"—would have had some effect, but hard to judge how much. They were in English. Simon had placed them in American publications whose expenses he assumed were carried either by Berlin, or, depending on the steepness of your view of the world, by his own secret service. They were not "Nazi," they were not rants—they would never be. They were the views that a man of honor might possibly hold, but they had crossed a line.

Still, when the acknowledgement, for that was what it was, came, it surprised him by its economy and even elegance. A young officer, well read he had learned, SS he knew from Ottavia, a gentlemen he believed—they did exist—caught his eye, detached himself from a group where he was the junior and feigned humorous relief. Putzi Hasseldorf. They talked for a while of horses, for the young man had several here, and wanted advice on winter management in Italy, so different from Silesia.

"And just because you're south, don't skimp on the blankets," said Alistair. "Italian cold is damp."

"Do you read P. G. Wodehouse?" Putzi said. "I've never dared ask you, Alistair. I thought you might think me just silly."

"As much as I can get and with huge pleasure," said Alistair, entirely truthfully.

"So do we. He is something that we and the English can share, it seems."

P. G. Wodehouse, swept up unwittingly in the occupation of France, was doing radio talks and writing squibs from his nice house, and they did not reflect at all badly on Germany.

"There is a great deal we can all share. Most of it's the best," said Alistair, who would even have agreed.

"And it must be brought forward, not hidden. Look at you and Ottavia. An Anglo-Saxon American in marriage with a German, as I prefer to call her, giving Goethe to the Italians. The apex of civilization."

"Thank you," said Alistair.

"Though giving him to the Italians might have been a miscarriage of effort. What was it about pearls?" But with this, a pleasant laugh.

For that was the strong wind in this room, much more than anything to do with him. This Christmas had begun Italy's agony. In November, Royal Naval aircraft destroyed its fleet. The Italian army attacked Greece, was magnificently repulsed, and now was fighting for its life on the Albanian coast. Just after Christmas had come the day of shame: Mussolini begged Hitler to save Italy from Greece. The British took Italian Libya, Somalia, Eritrea, and Abyssinia within two months, annihilated four Italian divisions, and took two hundred thousand prisoners. Catastrophes on the scale of Caporetto, though much further away.

So he listened, beneath the words. The Italians were in pain. The old general over there, moustaches like wings, was twitching his nose so that they all but flapped in defiance. Some had put on the Italian worldly look: we all have runs of luck.

Very interesting. Simon certainly would think so, building on his quotations from Rodolfo. He himself was much more interested in his Ottavia, whose neck just then sparkled as it tuned, revealed for a second within a forest of uniforms.

He was not deeply concerned for her this evening. Just listening is what a bright young woman did. Dropping grains of bait to keep the conversation where she wanted it needed no great magic. She really was who she was. He was starting to understand the mathematics of their position. Listening was safe. Writing lies was safe. Returning to a topic, sniffing at it, chivying it, chasing it was where traps stood open. The first question is the beginning of the end. She had done this on the matter of synthetic gasoline in Luftwaffe engines ("How clever of them! Is it just as good? Oh, how awful! And how many of them have there been that crashed? Do I know any of them, the poor boys?") and over the mole in Livorno harbor. And would again, for she entirely lacked his respect for odds, though he thought she weighed them just as consciously. Then his ignorance of German turned its brighter vowels into snapping teeth, and its gutturals into the breath of wolves, and the dark uniforms around his lamb into shaggy pelts.

In fact, in the car home, some noise and traffic around them, the glass partition up, and their chauffeur only young Basilio from Lucca, she said, "Something's going on." Then pulled her coat tighter around her throat and took his arm. "A lot of people are expecting people they know to start turning up here, by and by. So it becomes a buzz, and then everybody's coming." She shrugged, and her shoulder rubbed his arm. "It doesn't matter who's right and who's wrong, precisely. People are coming. The embassy's getting bigger."

"It is hardly a desert as it stands," said Alistair.

"It's going to be the biggest God ever saw when all this happens," she said. "Big enough to run the country."

"You don't think," said Alistair, "that they are losing confidence in their Italians?"

Her chin agreed vigorously. Then she looked up at him. "Oh God, how I love it when bad dogs fight!" And laughed when he smiled.

A report of consequence. Highly conjectural, to be phrased with great care. To be considered by minds he would never know, weighed with a balance he would never see. But important, yes. At this date, his reports still went through his embassy, though at such remoteness that fingers barely touched.

HE WAS EXTREMELY SURPRISED. He was to meet Greg Owen of the embassy, unmet for months. He was to meet publicly, luxuriously, at the Hassler, for lunch. Literature was promised. "A friend from Paris." *Hardly Nancy*—if only, poor girl.

Very little had changed at the Hassler since Manfredi, Helene, truffles, and Champagne, though a different headwaiter bowed to him. He saw Greg with another seated across the room. He signed to the headwaiter that he saw his way and saw in turn the man's surprise, unease. The walls were still carmine and white. A trolley made way for him, bearing its scent of duck. He had a memory of his mama in her Easter dress, their *canard presse*. This was one of his good places. Many more uniforms than he had known at the Hassler. Outnumbered, ladies now looked as tender and delicious as the lilies. He understood the headwaiter's dismay; Greg's table was as yet set for only two. Soon he would see a waiter running. He nodded to Claus von Stierberg, counselor at the German embassy, friend of Ottavia's, and two unknowns. He did know Greg's company though not well. He had been a *habitue* at Sylvia Beach's, pretty decent poet of somewhat populist bent. They had spent pleasant moments together, and he was suddenly, surprisingly warmed to see him, for nearly all the American birds had flown home and there were times, as he would never have said, that he felt alone here. The waiter arrived at the table and seemed to cause some fuss, even be chided. Anyway, took their attention. They had not seemed to see him. He could surely ask about Sylvia, did anybody know? Even about Nancy?

He said, "Greg, how pleasant. Not late, I hope." Though he wasn't.

Greg looked at him. Steven Belkin, that was the name now, last seen at Fouquet's, looked at him. He made for the third chair, still unfurnished. The waiter seemed to despair.

"Is this who I think it is?" said Belkin.

"We are busy, Alistair, I'm sorry to say," said Greg.

"Then it is who I think it is," said Belkin. "The former Alistair Stears. The American Nazi in Rome."

Greg Owen appeared to deprecate such bile. But said, "We were having a private lunch, Alistair. Talking about rather American things. Not much to your taste, I imagine."

20

1943

The fist of German ascendancy dawdled inside its sleeve. Alistair and Ottavia often wondered about that. Now he confessed it, on his knees, before the confessional, in his boyhood's Santi Apostoli, where his mother had talked to Mary after she rose from Maggiore's bed.

"I have committed sins of impurity, Father."

"With yourself or with others?"

"With others, Father."

"With how many, my son?"

"With three, Father." Which was the code number of the week, assuring both priest and penitent that they were impostors.

"Proceed, my son."

"I have been to Naples and Capri. An exchange with Curzio Malaparte was the stated reason. He has a villa there, as I have said. I see no significant movement of German armor or ordnance south, nothing on the scale to repel an invasion. I find no major works in progress in Naples that I would regard as defensive. The Italian officers I talk to seem on edge. All the African coast is Allied now, all Patton. Rommel's a memory. I'd be on edge, especially if the Germans were not moving in behind me. They go together. Ottavia says the same. No major German movement. She does report more Gestapo, civil SS—SiPo types—moving in. You can take that as a fact, though she doesn't know why. You can—

"That's a long enough sin."

"Yes, Father." (A little bit louder.)

"You were not used to weekly confession, were you?"

"Not weekly."

"They're worried about that. You're still watched?"

"No more and no less that I can tell."

"We can do this once more at least. Maybe you've had a crisis of faith. And they weren't always watching you. They wouldn't know when you confessed."

"No, Father."

"I must ask. Do you wish to confess, truly? I may not deny that to you."

"My confessor is Father Kirchner at home."

"Of course. I forgot. Better to keep it apart. Pray for me, my son."

"Pray for me, Father."

His name was a stained card on the confessional, Father Signoli. He had never seen his eyes. Alistair rose. He dusted his pants legs but still looked down humbly, then up at Our Lady behind her beautiful hanging lamps. Outside, the Piazza Santi Apostoli was full of March sun. He let it bless his shoulders. The man who had prayed across the aisle from the confessional came out behind him. Shocking bad manners it would be to acknowledge him. So long as he stayed in character, they barely seemed to care. Italian, of course. Would Germans be invisible? Read minds? Read Ottavia's? Read a woman's mind? Now really! He needed to go to Sicily and could think of no excuse.

His boyhood home, Palazzo Odescalci, still ruled the square. It was still there. It was all still there. The RAF bombed Italy with increasing venom but not yet Rome. The huge hard fist of America stayed still. It would not stay still for long. How heavy it was, he knew. Rome of two thousand years was a stage set now, could be gone tomorrow. He had truly scratched the dragon's ear.

xxx

BACK IN NINETEEN FORTY-ONE, now two years gone, they had heard nothing about it the evening before it happened. Busy hobgoblins had hammered though the night. He had sensed nothing from the Via Gulia, shutting out the mild December air as they arose, but the Via Gulia can be unclear about the century. The newspapers knew better. The hobgoblins showed off their work at the breakfast table, littered with broken battleships and reeking smoke under a sky of thunderous headlines: *PEARL HARBOR Giappone Distrugga la Flotta Americana. Arrendersi Roosevelt?*

"Oh, Alistair!" called Ottavia, who was first down, back up the stairs.

He had sat and read the front pages as though sucking at them.

He looked up at Ottavia, she still standing. "The Lord hath delivered mine enemy into mine hand. Cromwell."

"But you've nothing to fight with. It's all destroyed."

"We have my country," he said.

She smiled. He frowned.

"Only to think of Simon hearing you say that."

"But where is Simon?"

"Yes," she said.

He put his finger over "*Arrendersi Roosevelt*?" Will Roosevelt Surrender?

"Merde. Cambronne. Anyway, it's only one fleet."

It was also, they quickly realized, only Japan.

"It's a matter of hours, isn't it, Alistair? He must declare war on us and Germany, no? Should we send Giovanni away?"

Not hours. That breakfast was December 8. The next day, nothing, and nothing the tenth. They lived inside a cold, wet cloud: What happens if Roosevelt closes his eyes to Europe? What happens to us if he doesn't? If he does? They were not ready.

On the eleventh, dear fatherly Hitler did the decent thing. He declared war on the United States. Mussolini trotted along behind.

He lived with a space in the air behind his shoulder, for the hand to grip it suddenly.

The stairs were hushed at night, waiting for the front door to give in and the many feet to rush up. Neither happened. On the tenth day, Ottavia said, "We must take action, Alistair. We cannot sit and shiver. I have a thought."

She did. They invited their embassy friend Standartenführer Putzi Hasseldorf of the SS and his pleasant wife, Renate, to dinner. Also Ottavia's distant cousin Manfredi de Ricasoli, who worked closely with Galeazzo Ciano, foreign secretary and their old wedding guest, and Manfredi's wife, Poppea. And others, for the evening was purely social.

"I am sure you have some English editions of Wodehouse," said Putzi. "We cannot get them here anymore."

It was a pleasant dinner. They had grouse sent down from Lucca, on purpose.

Over brandy, after the ladies had withdrawn, Putzi said quietly, "I know you are doing valuable things with Curzio Malaparte. And you are an old friend of Ezra Pound's. I would like to have a lunch party for you both at the embassy. Some of our more literate people. Of course, it is difficult to get Ezra away from his castle."

"Let him be," said Alistair. "Mr. Pound and I never got on very well."

NOW, EIGHTEEN MONTHS AFTER America entered the war, they thanked God they could still go to Lucca. Had to go to Lucca. It was their normality. It was also a labor now. Trains ran when they could. Once they even had to stand, even in first class, with flies under the window and cigarettes under the seats, all dead. Another time, the train came to terrible stop and people fell around. The track had been bombed. This time, there was fuel for the little FIAT that came to meet them but not promised again. The Alfa, his crimson teardrop, lay empty in a barn.

Giovanni, now of seven dignified years in tweed jacket and grey shorts and polished leather shoes, did not run to Concetta and bury his head in her lap. He shook her hand firmly then buried his head in her lap. Later he said, so quietly that his father barely heard, "Daddy, I don't like it a Roma."

"Why, old son? Rome's beautiful."

"I can't talk to Solferino and Boromeo and Paolo there." They were in the stable together, sitting on a bale of hay. Paolo the groom had become as much of a friend as Luigi of the stitched face. Giovanni sat very close to Alistair and gave wistful look at the lap he had forsaken. He said in an even smaller voice, "You promised me a pony, Daddy."

Since he in fact said, *"Du hast mir einen pony promesso, Daddy,"* translation gave his father a moment to think.

He said, "You'll have one, old son," though in Italian. They had given up on his English, just for now. "They're harder to find these days. I'm sorry." For why feed what you can eat?

"All right. And I like what Concetta cooks better. It's nicer here."

"There's more here," said his father. "Most people in Rome have nothing now. Not enough to eat. They're hungry. We're very, very lucky. All of us." He meant their people.

"And you and Mama aren't the same in Rome. Especially Mama."

Oh Christ, he thought, tell her! Who else sees that? The canary in the coal mine!

"We're just the same both places. We love you here and we love you there. Mama and I. They're just different places, old son."

He didn't tell her, for he loved and honored the change. Here, Ottavia entirely cast away the brightness and the antic sexiness she wore like a rubber skin in Rome. She became the Italian chatelaine in time of woe, holding up a tottering world. She climbed down into storerooms and made lists, then hid them: how much oil, grain, hay, potatoes, ham remained, how much stolen by soldiers, how much by police, how much deeply hidden, what could be given to the most in need. She sought out the cottages through mud on foot, who was truly suffering, who might be shirking, what children really had to see the doctor, which young mothers were simply overwhelmed. This was not remarkable: her ancestresses, who had done all this since the wars of the Guelphs and the Ghibellines, would have been shocked had she not, but Ottavia did it well. In the evening, he dined with his exhausted waif in her dressing gown after her bath, straw, cobwebs, mud, and even coal washed off. He told her she overdid it.

She held his eye. "I have so much to get clean from, Alistair. So much." Then, thinking that too dramatic, looked back at her soup.

It ended, even when they were too tired to do anything but hold hands, in their nightly wonderland of bed.

The third evening, she said, "Some of the people have had contact with . . . they're not brigands, exactly. I heard them called 'partisans.' Men in the hills. Like the old Carbonari, really. They're boys avoiding conscription. Deserters. Two men back from Russia where they say it's horrible for our people, Alistair, horrible. Even some communists, I'm afraid. I think you ought to find out about it."

The days when they had no secrets from each other were over. Wiser so, now. She told him what was ready to be passed on. He told her what she needed to know. But he smiled to himself at this. It was why he was here.

HE HAD TOLD PAOLO, Paolo on a hunch, where he would be that afternoon, up on a hillock, never honored as such for it rose within the woods, cleft by what long ago had been a quarry. He thought as he rode. Time was moving backward. They had worked seven years on Pace ed Abbondanza, and it was going back to what Manfredi had given them. Their tractors made nests for swallows in empty sheds. Trellises sagged; olives were crudely pruned. Half his young contadini, if half of what one heard were true, were corpses on the Russian steppe. It seemed an eddy within a broader backward stream. He had a cardinal again. His current go-between, his human drop box to that cardinal, was a priest of the Santi Apostoli. His horses were ill fed, though their coats were not as poor as Vipero's had been at the end. His car, like the old Hispano-Suiza, was forgotten in a shed. He was seeing in Ottavia the fine etching of strength used up he had seen in his mother among the chickens at Buttrio by Udine. They were just the same age. He saw in himself tics he had seen in Maggiore. Fondness fell on him as a bolt, and he hoped that they had found such solace in the night as he and his Ottavia yet did.

He checked Boromeo at the hillock, told him he was still on duty, not to ask questions, this might take a while. He dismounted.

This was a far province of his land. Years before, he had tracked a wounded stag here and today had had to puzzle out the way. A flat stone from the ancient quarry lay beneath a beech. He sat. He listened. In due time, Boromeo gave the expected sign, a low whinny. He believed it impossible that he had been followed from the house. On what horse? What horse here? No hoof fall, no answering whinny. The wood was mostly of ash trees. The breeze sounded among them, rising and falling like very distant surf and fanning the young leaves to a green smoke. Of the copse above him on the slope, the smoke seemed denser, but only at a second call from Boromeo, and following his eye, did he form within it the shape of horse and rider, still. He waited for the trick of eye to fade, but it did not. And then he stood.

And by his standing made the shadow stretch tall, then break in two. The face and body of a young man appeared on the surface of the leaves and then approached, carefully, downhill, on the spongy, stony ground.

The first words were, "Three men here: *nobiluomo*, poet, and they say American officer too. Is that all true?"

"There is only one of me," said Alistair and slightly smiled.

"That may almost literally be true. But I wonder if there is a fourth of you that brought you here. Which side that might be on, I could not start to guess."

"My horse brought me here."

He did not know him, to his surprise, really did not know him, knew him from no fair, no hunt, no harvest. His Italian was a gentleman's, of Tuscany. His carriage agreed. His clothes had come to know the woods. He was a younger man, no boy. He would have guessed midtwenties.

"And told your groom where you were riding to. Always a wise precaution. You are right. He is one of us, a little."

"And who is us?"

"A very, very good question. But one that will not be answered now."

"Let us not begin with errors," said Alistair. "You may be too young to understand time. When I was an American officer, you may have been born but not much more. I am an Italian landowner. Italian husband. Italian father. That is why I am here. Mainly the first. As to American officer, things change. Countries change. Ideas."

"And German officers have been guests in this house. Not to mention leading fascists. Being here is not the least brave thing I have ever done. I would like it more if you were here as a poet. Two unknowns meeting in a deep wood. Two horses. We should ask each other riddles. Very Ovid. Or discuss the nature of these stones. Very Goethe. I have read you only in Italian, of course." He was, Alistair saw, one of those who can smile with only his voice. "But your wife's is the feudal family here, I know. That does give you some right to ask for me."

"As it were." And then Alistair said, though mildly, "But then why have you come? I could be a trap."

"I thought about it and did not believe it. So I am here and you are here. What you want, I do not know. What you think I am, I do not know."

"You are one of armed strangers moving around the land. A risk to my people. That is my business." And, making mildness yet more mild, "I suspect that you are poaching my game."

"Pig and deer are nice once in a while," said the other. "That really is a remark petty enough for a landowner. Do you know how impenetrable it is back there?" He pointed north, toward Alistair's Monte Prano.

He did know. For his house, however urbane it might seem and mildly ecclesiastical as Lucca's spires might be, backed onto a wilderness of tens of thousands of square kilometers where mountains rose to six thousand feet, rivers scampered like mice through twisting chasms, the roots of firs split marble, and winter snows drifted shoulder-deep. There were hill towns, but they were spaced wide, and the roads were threads. In truth, Alistair did not know where his own land ended that way, though there were cairns here and there.

"There could be men in their hundreds back there," the other said. "A less petty man would know that. They could have trucks, though surely not enough. They could have machine guns, for certain far too few. The Americans have a great many. And airplanes to carry them."

"You don't seem to do much with your trucks and guns. That I have heard. Are you their lord?" And chose the word for its flick of dismissal.

He was not to be dismissed. "Even if they had all those weapons, they could not fight the armies of Italy and Germany. Perhaps they would just be hiding. A wood is better than a prison. And they might know that Africa groans under the weight of Allied armies. Armies can cross water, they might reflect. Then they might both hide and wait. I would not have to be their lord. I could be their messenger. Who scents an American officer who has been asked to find him. And that is much more tempting than pig. And that I can believe, when police spy I cannot."

"There are things I must require of you," said Alistair. "You must not steal from the contadini. Especially food. They are hungry already. You must not force them to go with you. You must not shelter with them, for you will draw the police or the Germans there in the end. If you do these things, I will have to side with the authorities. I would have no choice."

"Very honorable of you. As a landowner, of course. But consider. Men in their position," he gestured behind him, "would want to make friends, not enemies. Any commander they could have would see that. I was an officer. I think we left the service at about the same age. Do we get anything in return for behaving?"

"That is a very, very good question. Which will not be answered now. I am here alone. I am no police spy. You are right, and you get that. And Paolo, my groom, seems to know where we both are. Do you have a name?"

"After you talk to your people, you mean? I have no name yet. I am sure a poet can make one up. Better than 'Nemo,' I would hope."

"Good day," said Alistair. And turned.

HE WAS SATISFIED. No, he was pleased. No, he felt something tantalizing, dangerous, and alive within him. For three years, there had been only apprehension and care.

He knew the country there behind him. Manfredi had told him right at the beginning. He had been there as hunter. He had sought it as explorer of an Italy very old and very harsh. He had been ready to hear the footstep of Ovid's satyrs and spiteful nymphs. Back to Roman time, at least, cutthroats and the pursued, running slaves and serfs, Carbonari (Ottavia was quite right) had crept there, and with them, bands who hated Genoa, hated Parma, hated Florence, hated emperor or pope. The people there, priest, peasant, even shopkeeper, sided by reflex with anyone who fought authority outside. He lived at the edge of the Wild West. The Abruzzi were as harsh. But the Abruzzi were not by the big cities, and this country touched the spine of Italy, the roads and railways from south to north.

His report would carry a good gloss with good faith.

All true things, even the abstract, have a gesture, a voice, a face. That is where one looks for trust or turns away. He trusted his Nemo (the name would do for now), and that fact would go in his report. There was something else, and he had to look for it. And then whistled and made Boromeo raise his ears. Far beneath what had passed between them, he had heard an echo of himself.

He waited for the slightest sound of bridle, for a host should not leave first. He made, and hid, a gesture of farewell. He turned to Boromeo and checked his girth.

21

This confession was short: the partisans exist, are perhaps capably led, are advantageously situated, desire contact.

He could have added a night's weeping from Ottavia. A girlfriend of her schooldays, now one knew part of the insanely brave White Rose Party, an anti-Nazi group deep within Germany, had been uncovered, caught, killed—tortured, one did not bother to add. This she learned in a late night call from an embassy wife, to all appearances entirely loyal yet a friend of those same days, who had wept as well, drawing Ottavia all that night into a dark German landscape, far from him. He himself had passed a hollow night, for the body beside him seemed barely his Ottavia. In the first light, she opened her eyes and said in a voice of cold ashes, "I must find out how to use that woman," got up, and left the room.

This was too inconsequential to confess. More consequential was the design of future contact. He envisaged reports of greater length: troop strengths, munitions, more names, landmarks and coordinates. Did one take the terrible step to paper and now in a time of tightening peril? Well, he would be told. One ray of clarity. Ottavia learned, and this he could report, that the object of the Allied legions in Africa was not believed to be Sicily and mainland Italy, too hard a target, but Greece and Jugoslavia. So that was where the reinforcements were going. Which made sense.

And explained, as April warmed into May and then June and even July, why his masters' interest in his Nemo seemed polite but hardly passionate. So their future had been changed again. It was hardly theirs.

THEY HAD AGREED VERY early that if there were anything sympathetic in the actual enemy you were talking to, some friendship should be felt as well as feigned. This, Simon had said, is the principle of all great con men, a term Alistair had not known. He hated the German embassy, hated its boastful flags, its varnished guards, the portraits of the Führer within. Its evil was palpable and grew monthly as creatures from the most diseased parts of the German body were drafted in, for it seemed that as Germany slowly weakened, it also rotted. Near it, he fingered every image he could form of German cities turned to pits, ants, and ashes. He so hated to see Ottavia enter it alone that he usually made excuse and joined her. And then quite often enjoyed his evening.

As this one. He spent most of it with three men in the armchairs of a small drawing room. There had been thunder. Now it was cool for early July. The windows were open, and birds had come out after the storm, though they might have been only starlings. There was Standartenführer Putzi Hasseldorf, whom he thought was all right, more or less, a young diplomat he knew less well, and General Frido von Senger und Etterlin, older, regular army, a Catholic nobleman from Ottavia's uncle's province whom Alistair liked with warmth and respected without doubt.

The discussion was again of Italy and Germany. "So what of us?" von Senger und Etterlin had ventured. "What are we doing here? And should Italy bless us or curse? They don't seem to like us."

"We are here because we have to be," Putzi said mildly, to the obvious. "And are lucky to be, of course, for ourselves. And I agree they do not like us much. I myself like them, as Goethe did, and I cannot despise a people Goethe admired. If Alistair and his wife are right. If Italy would only fight, we'd leave her alone."

"But fight whom, precisely, and precisely why? Many, many Italians have gone to America and have done very well there. Many, many Italians fight in the American army. I am told they fight rather well. Why should the Italians want to fight America? England I find a little more understandable. Yes, Lord Nelson was a bully to them." So von Senger und Etterlin, who looked at Alistair then but would not meet his, nor any other traitor's eye. Then smiled to the room and said he was a simple soldier who fought whomever he was told to.

"And remarkably well," said the diplomat.

Still a pleasant evening. Nothing deep, no real scholarship, but voices agreeably tuned, and very good German, as he could now know. He had been apart from Ottavia too long. He made his apologies, rose, and took his leave.

He did not find her quickly then remembered she liked a smaller room off the main salon. There was a picture of the Führer over the fireplace, but it was charcoal, and positively calm, and made him look almost like somebody you could have lunch with. He quickened his pace as soon as he saw her, for her face was oddly focused and her neck seemed stiff. She was talking to two other women but made excuse as he entered, and turned toward him as though movement were uncommon for her.

"We should leave," she said, "but properly, of course." Which they did, and it took time, for she was more vivacious and chattery than usual. It ended with the ambassador inviting Alistair to shoot boar, which happened every single time, and never in reality, and the ambassador never looked at him as he said it.

Outside, she said, "Thank God!"

"What?" he said.

"Later. In the car."

Later in the car, she said in what might have been one breath, "There's a new man there, a policeman, who knew me in Wurtzburg when I lived with my uncle when I was a girl. He knows nothing about me, so don't worry. He was a young Nazi thug and then he was police, Gestapo. He was the one in charge when they burned down the newspaper and beat the people. He came to my uncle's house to ask for money. For the party. They still had to then. I've never forgotten him. When I told you about my little dog full of maggots, it was him that I was talking about. Really. His eyes. I know he recognized me. He knows absolutely nothing. So don't worry."

Back at Via Gulia, he got her a glass of milk. She said, "He knows absolutely nothing," and drank it down. They went to the back sitting room where the starlings had brought them the war and had become their friend in time of disaster. She sat on a sofa, and he held her hand.

"I do know this," said Ottavia. "I am not someone who can be picked up and made to vanish at an underling's thought. The ambassador served under my grandfather, and they do treat me a bit like a niece, even if he is a bastard."

"You refer to his suggestion to The Chin that he shoot several hundred prominent Italians at random to get the attention of the rest?"

"It did stick in my memory," she said. "And Kesselring being a friend of my uncle's and then introducing him to Manfredi. Which was your idea, I know, but he is my brother. Military hero and all. And quite a lot of them, even some of the SS, really are friends. Putzi really likes us, I think."

"This is a time for clarity," he said. "You're in danger."

Her hand in his agreed too quickly for her to tell it to behave.

The defenses she believed in were not entirely nothing, he could agree. The upper class can close ranks. They were far from Berlin here. She was in the last resort Italian, not German. Which might help. A very little bit, all of it. A very little bit.

"Am I?" she said. "A lot of me says I'm not. He knows nothing about me except who my uncle is. I'm not just saying that."

"Think very carefully," said Alistair. *And it won't be enough.*

But she did lower her head to look at memory, while he remembered that her neck, which bore with it her warmth and scent, was most often what he saw first on waking and never without joy.

"When my uncle turned him down," she said, "he did not bite the carpet or anything like that, of course. He stayed polite. The temperature in the room fell a few degrees. But he did look at me, which he had not, except to photograph me with his eyes. He said, 'I expect your friends would applaud that, young lady.'"

"Oh Christ!"

"But it doesn't mean anything, Alistair. My friends were my friends. Our lot was not pro-Nazi in those days, very few of them, and everybody knew it. My real friends were the ones who even opened a book every now and then. The Nazis were so vulgar, we made fun of them. A few officers joined the SS, but that was for promotion, nearly always. And anyway, that came later. It doesn't mean the newspaper. I was very careful. Even then."

Yes, he knew about the dumpy clothes, and never any makeup, and the bag she had, like a sack, she said, for books, if any. *And I hardly ever went there, only twice I think. Very wise. In one so young.* He was terrified.

"And I make far too much of him. He's just a common little man. 'The temperature in the room fell a few degrees!' Really! 'Photographed me with his eyes!'" She looked at him carefully, more carefully than at memory, and all at once she turned, her arms were around him, and they were touching all up and down.

She said, "Alistair, I'm frightened. It's nothing new. I've been frightened every day since Simon on the beach. We live in fear. You and I. I and you. Do you think I can't see the mirror? Do you think I can't see you? It's changed us. We're in winter, and we're too young, my dear. Every time you're inside me and it's over, I think, 'Was that the last time? The last time ever?' That frightened, darling. And every time I see my child, but I can't talk of that. So what's a little more? But one thing's better now. It won't be forever any more. The Americans and the English will come, and they will trample all before them. It won't be straight to us, they say now, but they will come. Maybe even soon enough for us. We can't know that. But we will help them. Can we agree on that? We wait, and we are clever?"

"Yes," he said. And then, "It's better that you're frightened. I'd be even more frightened if you weren't."

"No," she said. "It's better because being frightened makes me less ashamed."

SINCE OTTAVIA HAD SPOKEN on the fifth of July, she had to wait six days. She would have waited only five had the Italian press found the invasion of Sicily as dear to its heart as Pearl Harbor. Given that the mighty bombardment by air and sea could be heard through much of Calabria, comment seemed nonetheless required. It was an Allied fiasco, of course.

She was down first, as was her habit. Alistair came down the stairs and saw his wife's back leaning over the breakfast newspapers supported by straight arms. She turned, and he found himself faced by a dangerous smile.

"Vengono," she said, They're coming, but they rarely spoke English now. The smile turned more wolfish.

"Sie kommen." But she put her hand on his when he reached the table. She pointed at the lines describing the Allies' quick defeat, the mopping up.

"I have my doubts," he said.

"The BBC." She looked at her watch. "Ten o'clock, the next. We'll dare it, no?"

He nodded.

It was not a fiasco. Syracuse was in British hands already.

IN THE GREY DAWN after the embassy evening, Ottavia had wanted to send Giovanni away, to Manfredi and Claudia.

"You can't say that on the telephone. You can't make that call. And sending him away would be an announcement. We need a reason. An air raid would do."

"He's our child."

"Any move against this house will come from the Italians. This is still Italy. Manfredi would be told immediately, and he will certainly act, and the Marchese Ugolino-Ferrara will not be stopped from taking his nephew. And if we did not come back from the embassy, Luigi would call him."

"All right," she said. But it hung between them, a half-made reproach.

Now, in the back sitting room again, as the big radio's dial changed from the dangerous BBC but still glowing purple, he said, "Rome will be bombed now. The gloves are off. I will surely be ordered to Lucca. The partisans are in the game. I hope the bombing comes first, and I hope it's awful. Everybody with money will run out of Rome then, like the other cities. Above all, the children. We take Giovanni to Lucca, of course, and somehow to Manfredi. Yes, he's safer there. Claudia will be dear to him."

She looked over the Tiber and Castel Sant'Angelo and thus toward the sea. "Let the bombers come," she said. "With flaming wings."

And so, very nearly, they came. There had been a small raid on Rome a month before. They had been in Lucca. They had seen RAF light bombers in twos and threes, angry hornets to trucks and tanks on the Tuscan roads. They had no inkling. They awoke to madness. The sirens' screaming had not died when a huge sound rolled inland from the sea, two thousand engines of five hundred heavy bombers. It came upon them, and the jeering of hell swallowed the night. Dark shapes swam fast above while the very few searchlights raised weak vague fingers, and all over the city white light flashed and grew into blooms of flame. He held Ottavia, who held Giovanni whose face was in her nightgown. Even with mouth to ear one could not talk. He was finally seeing, it passed though his mind, the blind ogres he had written in "Tagliamento." A bomb hit the Tiber embankment, and their house shook. He turned Ottavia's face silently from the window glass.

In the morning, most of the city was still somehow there. Coffee existed. For two hours, their fear had been the same as every single Roman's. Knowing that, they sat in sweet lassitude.

At noon the bombers came back for the San Lorenzo freight yards. They bombed the ghosts of Vipero and Pompey who had just been loaded into their sweet-smelling car by their young master and Manfredi for the long trip to Venice. Their young master carried Manfredi's bright, sharp sword.

WHATEVER THE CIRCUMSTANCES, BECAUSE of the circumstances, he had to go to his mailbox. The stately succession of penances at SS Apostoli worked well enough for communication in normal times. For dire or tremendous things, a second course existed, never used until now. He set off for the Campo dei Fiori.

He was not greatly reluctant to leave his family for half an hour. He was clear more than ever that any move against their house would come from the Italians. He knew firsthand about German worries, increasing every month, of the skittishness of their one European ally that could, with some wit, be called a first class power. Germans had been beaten up in Rome, and Germany could not retaliate here according to her taste. That German police, on this day of days, would drag a highly connected Italian lady from her palazzo in the middle of Rome was simply not credible. The Italians had other things to think about.

He reached the Campo. Giordano Bruno waited, as every day, for his pyre to be lit. Alistair was glad that Giordano was not alone and that the horrors of the night had not emptied the square. This part of Rome did not, in fact, seem badly hurt. His mailbox was well placed. There were bakers and butchers here, selling anything they might still have to sell. The trickle of vegetables that still reached Rome was sold in the stalls at awful prices. The space, therefore, was cluttered, and nobody could watch it all. He walked this way and that and tried to look hungrily at dandelions and chicory whose journey had been hard.

The drop was exactly as the photograph had showed it, in the cavity made by a small group of figures on a wall on the side of the Piazza della Cancelleria. His wise masters had even told him what to do: barely break stride, and stick your hand in while your back screened your hand. He did just this, took it out empty, walked on, and silently swore. His wise masters became instantly part of the roiling clouds above an agent's head: they had abandoned him, the method had been changed and he not told, the drop had been discovered, he had it wrong. Most implacably, he would have to come back later to exactly the same place, which might now be watched. Everybody he loved needed desperately for him to be dismissed from Rome and sent to Lucca.

When he got back to the house, he shook his head. Ottavia pursed her lips and said, "I can't just not go back to the embassy."

"You bloody well cannot go back to the embassy. It's the one place you're in immediate danger. Except you're not going out on the street alone, either."

She said. "What does it say my not going? I see him, he sees me, and I vanish. It's almost a confession. Anything he has on me, if he has anything at all, is old and hazy, Alistair. He can't act quickly. Maybe against a little clerk. Not against me."

"He won't know you're not there. He won't be there. Gestapo gumshoes are not invited to the ambassadress's soirees. He was there because it was his first night in Rome. They do that. It's called, 'not snubbing the lower classes,' their leader being one of them."

"You see?" she said. "The little man passes on some old, stale gossip, if any, and I act as though nothing could possibly be wrong. Nobody pays him any attention then. And there's no danger. And think what I could hear. Are they moving in or pulling out? That would be worth anything."

He looked at his Ottavia and felt himself engulfed in half-logic like freezing fog. He said, "We are going to Tuscany very, very soon, and for a very good reason. Sicily's over. It will be over. It's ours. It will be ours." He found that he was making points on his fingers, and folded them. "Everything now depends on routes north-south. Brenner to Naples. Our people are not stupid enough to make the next landing Naples. They will land at Ostia and Pescara or even Livorno and Ancona and cut the country in half. Anything that impedes the Germans moving north-south becomes vital. That's where I can help. Rome's over for us. We're Tuscans. Don't go back there. It's stupid."

"All right, Alistair," she said. "But I think you're wrong."

He went back as the walls began to be pale gold, and swallows sailed over the Tiber, and window boxes grew shadows. He took a different way and entered the Campo from the Piazza della Cancelleria. The vegetable stalls, threadbare as they might have been, were gone. There were a few stalls selling well-worn boots, dresses, trousers, and shirts nearly ragged, and no lack of customers, and no lack of haggling.

He returned home with a lighter step. And a paper in his pocket. He would have to decode it, but that was laborious, not difficult.

She had used her best paper, from Pineider, with the arms of Ugolino-Ferrara. She had written:

I have gone there. For all the reasons I told you, and one that I did not. I will not stay very long. Do not come after me. I know that I am right, but, if I am wrong, take our child at once, and go. We will meet again somewhere.

He looked into darkness. He had never seen her nemesis but distilled him as firm as flesh out the corruption of years: a fat, black fly sitting on their souls, rubbing its busy little feet. He looked into darkness and drifted into clichés out of a different tale, how he loved her, how could she have done it. He looked into darkness and realized he must find a plan there. Go back twenty-five years and take Giovanni to the Grand Hotel des Isles Borromées, get a boat and row to Switzerland, like the young man there and his girl. The idea was asinine, and always had been, and those two had probably drowned. Good shoes. Something with pockets. Some food. Gold coins from the safe. Their almost-sane plan had once been Forte dei Marmi and a motorboat. That was from Lucca, close, not Rome, and he would never get there. If he did, where was the gasoline? Take Giovanni to . . . He realized the problem was himself. Don't take Giovanni. Give Giovanni and plenty of money to Luigi, a sensible man who loved them, and tell him to go to Umbria, to Manfredi. Nobody would look for a servant and a boy. A servant and his son, for if a little boy happily holds the hand of a man who looks like Frankenstein's monster, it has to be his daddy. With Manfredi and Claudia, he would have a perfectly happy life, and then nothing mattered. He and Ottavia had happened once, and now they were gone. He dreaded to imagine what was in store for her. He supposed there was a remote chance, alone and with gold coins, he could wander into the countryside and find some sort of guerillas and stay with them until the Americans. He supposed there was a remote chance that Ottavia would come back. She had been sure she would, and she was not a stupid woman. Here, they had until morning. The Germans would still need the

Italians, and Italy was very, very busy. And what would they do to her meanwhile? What were they doing to her now? It would take twenty minutes to wake Giovanni, make up some kind of adventure, and send Luigi on his way. Possibly, better than darkness, on a busy morning street.

He had learned, in the first darkness of his boyhood, that if you have only dry stones to look at, you must start to sift them and make patterns or go mad. He had a message to decode, and knew how to do it, though he never had. He was almost sure the message belonged to a different story, but it could be done. If he had respect for hope, it should be done. Hope made him ache for his Ottavia. It was a key code, dependent on the coder and the reader having the same edition of the same book. Harrison's eighteenth-century English translation of Castiglione. He went to the next room and brought it back. 143. the page. 8. the line. *in public spectacles with or without arms there is no fitter way than that.* 8. the word, its first letter. The message began with "T." Maybe it worked.

He heard the door. It was certainly not a storm trooper. He did not dare go to look.

She sat down softly beside him and said quietly, "I was right to go. Nothing happened. Nothing happened at all." She put his arm on his. He could drink her scent but he could hardly look at her, for he was too close to tears. She said, "Poor Alistair! Poor Alistair! But you have to listen now, because I did hear things. There are no Germans in Palermo. Patton is aimed at it, and they do not think it can hold."

He made himself nod sagely. He imagined that Patton knew that quite well. He had no interest in Patton now that Ottavia was back and could not imagine why Patton existed.

"They're not reinforcing, Alistair."

He supposed that the Allied aircraft that now ranged Italy at will had observed much the same. He nodded sagely.

"They'll hold Messina long enough to evacuate." That, he thought, would be sensible of them.

"Alistair, there's much more. They are saying that if Sicily falls, Italy may leave the war."

Now he did look at her, for he had heard the same straws pattering in the wind himself. "What do the Germans do then?" he asked.

"I was talking to women, not prying from the men. I do have some sense. So a lot of it was, what's going to happen, where are we going next. Last night shook them. There was damage around the embassy, and a lot of them live nearby. The windows were open, of course, July, and I could see people listening to the night then looking sheepish about it. They've heard about it from home, and now its coming for them. The Luftwaffe can't protect them, and they know it now. So suddenly it's not 'What shall we do?' but 'What's going to happen?'. I don't suppose anybody really knows what happens if Italy turns. But there is one plan that is being talked about. Move everything back to the Alpine wall and seal it. Take the units that aren't needed there and send them east to Russia and west to the Atlantic wall. Lose Italy but turn the tide in the east and seal France."

"That would be very, very intelligent of them," he said. More intelligent than he could imagine in a nation at war. Even if Hitler let them.

"So it may be almost over for us, darling. Very nearly over. We'll have to build Pace ed Abbondanza back up. Do you think our tractors will work again?"

It was a lovely story she told, and it made him happy to give it thought. "It depends," he said. "It depends on rust. In the engines. Nobody's looked at them for years."

"Poor little tractors! I'm not too old to have another baby. Would you like another son? Would that be fun?"

He could not touch such a lovely thought except with a smile, and touched her hair as well. "I think I'd rather have a girl. A boy should have a sister."

"Then I'll try for that."

"Ottavia," he said. "What was the other reason?"

She did not misunderstand him. She said, "We let them become masters of the world because they frightened us. That's the only reason. They had nothing else. Too frightened even to fight back. If the people at the newspaper had smashed typewriters over their heads, broken their teeth with rulers, if thousands of people had done that, they'd still be in the gutter, my horrid little man, and all his friends, and Hitler. Hitler most of all. But they didn't. I didn't either. I ran. That's what Sophie, the girl with the White Rose Party, must have seen, though by then it was too late, and she must have known it. I knew her very well. She wasn't amazingly brave. I don't imagine anybody wrote 'Heroine' on her cradle. But she was a heroine. I had to salute her.

I didn't go back to prove I was innocent. Or to prove I wasn't afraid, because I was afraid. I went back to prove I could. So Sophie wouldn't be alone."

He put his hands on her shoulders, looked at her a long time, and kissed her gently on the mouth.

"I have my orders," he said. "We're going to Lucca."

"I somehow knew that."

"Tomorrow night. In somebody's car. No one we know. As far as Pistoia. Why Pistoia, I don't know, but after that, we shift for ourselves. We can't take a servant. Good shoes. Clothes with pockets. Some food that keeps. Money. It won't be cold."

"It shall be done," she said. "I'm very tired." He took her arm. "I really will try to do a girl, Alistair. After it's all over. She really will be a baby sister. It's a huge big gap. Like I was."

22

Amelie said to her friend Ottavia, "Do you remember how it was the last time, when we were little girls? The kaiser was winning, and suddenly he surrendered?"

"Wasn't in Germany," said Ottavia. "But yes, a bit."

"It won't be like that this time. It will be slow and awful. Of course we won't surrender. That never. But I don't think we can win."

Ottavia, who did not want this conversation, not even with Amelie who had wept with her over their White Rose friend, not even looking at Amelie's baby's crib, not even with Amelie's husband far away in Sicily with his SS, decided on nostalgia. She said, "My uncle told me our men threw away the kaiser's flag. They marched all the way back to Wurzburg for their own archduchess to dismiss them. She dismissed them, and she got on her train and went away. They say she was crying. She was a nice lady. She gave me a chocolate once."

"Oh," said Amelie, "Do you think my servants will come back?"

The apartment, though desirable, was not well ordered, and the baby's blankets were crawling out of the crib.

"What's wrong with them?" said Ottavia.

"They haven't been here since the bombing. Maybe they're dead. A lot of people are."

Amelie gestured to the apartment building across the street, like hers in the general area of the German embassy. One entire wall had been ripped away, leaving the apartments intact and furnished, though smoky, like a tableau in a museum, *Scenes de la vie Bourgeoise.*

"They sent a woman over from the embassy to help. She was horrid. I got rid of her. Probably works for my husband. I don't mean Heinrich's horrid."

When they were both in pinafores, Ottavia and Amelie had thrown bread into lakes for ducks. This did not stop the SS from drifting in this apartment like a gas. *He wouldn't have a microphone in his own flat, would he?* thought Ottavia. *Maybe he would. Protestant and Prussian, and why the hell did she marry him?* For lack of anything more encouraging, she looked at the piano, an old friend. Amelie's family was musical. Its curves gently flirted and its grain ignored the frowsy room. The old silver frame on top it now held Heinrich. He strode forward in SS black as though his boot were to kick the music stand. His jowls were leftovers of the successful businessman; the rest of him, the aspiring thug. She looked at the other Heinrich, the baby.

"Are you still breastfeeding him?" she said. *Get to it, you goose!* she told herself. *You know what you're here for.* And then, what was now her mantra, *We don't expect to survive.*

"Yes, but it's not time. He's fine. I may have to get that woman back though. I can't clean. And the Italians all hate us, anyway."

"Oh, I'm sure they don't," said Ottavia. "I'm Italian."

"You're different," said Amelie. "And you're going to be American, anyway."

"American?" said Ottavia, so startled she sounded wonderfully shocked.

"Your husband is."

"Amelie, they hate us. We're traitors. We're not socialists. Roosevelt hates us." *And please, please let there be a microphone.* "If the Americans get Italy, I don't know what's going to happen to us. They won't, will they?" For Amelie, she knew, loved secrets, so she could tell them.

"Mussolini's coming back this evening. He's been with the Führer. I'm sure they've worked something out. Heinrich's coming back too. He's too important for Sicily. It was worse than you know, Ottavia. When the Allies came, at dawn, they say the whole horizon was battleships and the whole sky was airplanes. And the Italians aren't helping us at all. They're betraying us, like last time. That's why Rommel says they're not worth defending. It's only Kesselring who likes them. I'm sorry, Ottavia, I don't mean to hurt your feelings. You know Kesselring, don't you?"

"A bit," said Ottavia. "Don't know Rommel."

"So I suppose it depends on which one the Führer chooses. Do you think he's told Mussolini already?"

"I don't expect they talked about the weather," said Ottavia.

"So if Rommel comes, I suppose we'll pull back, and if Kesselring stays, I suppose we won't. I don't know where that leaves you, Ottavia. I'm very sorry."

So Kesslering, who likes us, will destroy us, and Rommel, who thinks we're dirty servants, will save us, thought Ottavia. *Oh well.*

But it was a pretty good haul she had, and Amelie, she had to say, had never been very notable even at throwing bread. With that thought, taking her leave, she hugged her fiercely, for she loved and feared for everything that was still kind and weak.

"I'll try and find out something about your servants," she said, at parting.

She herself was hard and venomous and counted her friends like change and hated it and hated Heinrich seeping through Amelie's life and the black smoke still leaking from the sores of Rome and the barbed wire that stood between them all and summer and lakes and pinafores.

If they kill me, just let me be myself for a moment first.

xxx

THEY HAD GONE NOWHERE. Their good day for travel, the day after the bombing of Rome, had been preempted. Mussolini had gone somewhere. Hitler had gone somewhere. One now knew that both somewheres were Feltre, in the Italian Alps.

Morale. Reaction of Italians to the bombing of the one sanctuary, the Holy City. Reaction of Italians, once promised all the Mediterranean and its fabled lands, to the fall of Sicily, now certain. Reactions of the German official class, off the record best of all. Everything they could, please. And positions, strengths, and preparedness of German and of those Italian units considered strongly fascist close to Rome. One last Roman push. Then they'd be able to go to Lucca. Promise.

Alistair was appalled. In Rome, he felt eyes in every wall, heard rats stir under every floor. That they sniffed most greedily for Ottavia brought him shame, though that his downfall would follow hers by an eyeblink lessened that. He longed for Lucca. On Pace ed Abbondanza's hill above the spires, they could be taken as wolves, no doubt, but not caught as rabbits. He missed the valleys and the woods. He found that he missed his Nemo. He knew that their duties in Rome mattered. Their judgment was asked for now, as well as eyes and ears. If he and Ottavia could bring it off, they'd be given the key to Urbino, even dead.

The day following the fall of Palermo (not complete until the evening of that day), he walked the city. The news came to the Campo dei Fiori with the lettuces. The vegetable woman said to the bric-a-brac man as they pulled the ropes outside their stalls to steady the shelves for their poor stock: *They say they shook hands with them, even the officers, even the Carabinieri.* And he and Ottavia had hurried before dawn barefoot in pajamas to the dangerous radio above the Tiber. Palermo, it seemed, had less fallen than been inhaled. Patton was beyond it already, storming toward Messina. The herb man, hands yellow with melissa: *They have so much chocolate, they throw it like confetti. Even chocolate!* sighed his customer. *It's over for them, down there*, said Herbs, and, better yet, looked nearly straight at a Blackshirt as he spoke.

Mussolini came back to Rome. Mussolini called a meeting of the General Council of Fascism. The council had not met since 1939. Alistair knew this. Alistair roamed the streets. He should be talking to people, if only a sentence at a bar. He knew men on the council. He knew Dino Grandi. He knew Federzoni. He could find nobody. Malaparte had left for the south the week before. He could of all things not leave Rome. Cabinet posts seemed to have changed overnight. He went to the Circolo della Caccia, the august Roman club in the Palazzo Borghese of which, thanks to Manfredi, he believed himself the only foreign member. He found silence under those grand ceilings, but a most odd one, as though behind every lip there were a flood of words, but no lip quite dared open. He sensed that the floor of the world was slippery as grease, and one wrong step could end anywhere. And so could bring Ottavia down.

He left his club, and power, behind and walked the streets again, Castiglione's high councilor as hobo. Bombs had fallen lightly by the Corso. The tramlines were broken, a window at his shirtmaker was broken, his mother's old palazzo seemed unhurt. In sight of Mussolini's place, the Palazzo Venezia, and in sight of its guards, he slowed his pace as much as he dared. He could pay a call on Prince Colonna and watch the Palazzo Venezia from the Palazzo Colonna, but he was not on close terms with him, and the action would seem odd. He noted more of the fascist honor guard than usual around the palazzo. From the movement of cars and transport, he divined more within. He went to a cafe in a corkscrew side street off the Corso and pretended to loiter over a pretense of coffee. He loitered in a bookstore. Books, at least, were still real, and he bought an early work by Ugo Foscolo. He doubted he would ever open it. He crossed the Corso again, went around his mother's house. He was shocked to find a crater in the middle of the Piazza Santi Apostoli, which he still felt he owned. He had loitered enough to fill the time. He went into the church. He prayed in hurry but not pretense.

This time at confession, his priest said, "You can't have gotten virtuous this fast. Now you're too quick. Say more."

THE GRAND COUNCIL OF Fascism met at night in the bowels of fascism, the Palazzo Venezia. As late as he dared, Alistair walked the Corso and had the impression that the council still sat, now very late. The walk was dangerous enough. He dared not linger.

Very early in the morning, while Alistair and Ottavia still kept the day at bay in each other's scent, a car made the short drive from the Palazzo Venezia up the hill to the king's Quirinale. It carried the order of Mussolini's firmest friends, his Grand Council, the Men of Steel.

The next day, the leader was not to be seen. The Palazzo Venezia closed upon itself.

In the afternoon, three powerful cars climbed the same hill. The late sun was strong enough upon them to turn the pennants of the fasces pallid. The windows were closed. By the time they arrived, the faces within began to shine with August sweat.

Late that night, a Red Cross ambulance skipped down the hill. It contained Benito Mussolini, stripped of his power by the king, by the king arrested, and bound for an undisclosed prison.

The next morning, Marshal Badoglio was the king's prime minister. Alistair and Ottavia knew this at exactly the same time as the king of England, President Roosevelt, Generals Patton, Eisenhower, and Montgomery, and very possibly the pope.

La comedia e' finita.

"So let's go home," said Ottavia.

22

They arrived, exhausted, after a drive of thirty-six hours full of frights, and bombed roads, and frantic hunts for petrol. They were not expected. There was no coffee. They could not face bread or sleep. Home at last, they touched Pace ed Abbondanza at first as though it had been the last watercolor from their childhoods and on paper cracked and dry. Then saw each other thus and smiled. It had not been very long. In due time, they drifted into the dining room. Giovanni had pled to stay in the kitchen. Concetta brought pappardelle glistening with the fat of the last boar ham and afterwards a shot rabbit with a salad of arugula from the fields. Girolamo, all a to-do and smelling of silver polish, served them. The Galilean planets held their appointed courses over them. Some accident yet untold had made the sideboard split. The sun made the carpet warm. He kicked off his shoes and found Ottavia's toes.

"Did Luigi go to bed?" For they had brought him after all.

"Yes, Signora Ottavia. I fed him first."

"Thank God. Can you keep Giovanni?"

In their room, sleep wrapped them like the blanket the summer kept aside.

"Petrol out of paint buckets!" murmured Ottavia. "My God, where are we now?"

"It got us here," said Alistair and almost slept. Then, "Worth any Titian," he said and did.

When he awoke, late afternoon but still high sun, he woke to duty. He let Ottavia's hair on the pillow, an autumn wood in sunset, fill his eye for a moment but quickly let it go. They were still under orders, never any doubt of that. He got up gently, not to wake her. Their trip had not been nothing. And when they had been waved to the side of the road by a German force—not large, a company—moving by truck and motorcycle, what had that cost her? He pulled on trousers and a loose shirt. Kept bedroom slippers for a reason.

The placing of the transmitting radio had been the last thing that he and the real, identifiable Simon had discussed. It had been provisional then, for their field was Rome, and Lucca, little more than an excuse to travel.

"In the house itself? Really, the house itself?"

"Can't be the stable, Alistair, too much going on there. You can't control it."

"Yes, but . . ."

"A shed, Alistair? A hogpen? A pump house? Why do you keep going there? On an odd schedule? Sure to be noticed. Easy to watch. And somebody could get in and you wouldn't even know. The house, Alistair. The house. Be clever."

In fact, there was an attic, locked for years. Old trunks, old uniforms, old swords, old pistols. Some family papers. No one's business. They called it "Bluebeard's attic" and laughed. So there it was, and not much at all. A black box, some wires, an earset, a Morse key he'd better get better at.

Morse was in the world of meter, and easy for his brain. He smiled at that. Castiglione would love that the courtier's mastery of verse, a mastery commanded, would give the courtier a tool for espionage five centuries later.

He stopped on the third floor, only for a moment, to begin a new habit of listening for a footstep that did not belong. Still the real house, here, lower ceilinged, little visited but there for guests. Frescoes only around the windows here to greet the sun with grace. So up to the wildernesses above. The key shrieked.

He felt no present anxiety. The radio had barely been used, and that months ago, and then on a transmission schedule long changed. He had to send only the merest chirp: where they were—which would have been guessed—and await instructions. His greater fear was that a mouse had taken some part of the apparatus for nest or lunch.

But the dial lit up. He connected to the time signal and reset his watch, spies being the very best people to ask the time of day. He had seven minutes to wait.

They would be listening. His masters would guess that they would come here, even if they had not yet been missed in Rome. It would occur to Simon immediately.

It would occur even to the ghost of Simon. It was a ghost he dealt with now and could be nothing else. The time when Simon could appear, take East Hampton shape down to circular glasses and buttoned collar beside him on a warm rock beneath a pine, or by a hamper on a beach, was long gone. Even individual voice was too broad to push through the bars they lived behind. Block letters to be deciphered through the pages of a random book, apparent nonsense to be memorized at blasphemous confessions, were the phantoms that kept him company now. Even so, the Simon he knew had long been present, often in turns of thought and sometimes even phrase. For long he had assured himself that the attenuation of Simon was due simply to time. Now in this attic that ticked to the summer heat, among leavings of old wars where a spider's web made the face beneath a hussar's helmet, he knew suddenly and surely that Simon was gone. Had been gone for months.

He looked at his watch. He set the frequency on the apparatus. He set his finger over the key, made his ear take heed, and tapped the simple message needed. He tapped too slowly, but would improve.

Ottavia was up, and Giovanni, returned to them. Her son perched beside her on the chaise longue with a jigsaw puzzle. Both looked up at him, and his heart devoured it. Here with his family, in the old house just shaken back awake, with its battle standard just hoisted, as it were, in the attic, he felt suddenly that in this new void he could bring his family, his contadini, his valleys into the order that his life, his art, had set forth.

Ottavia looked up from the jigsaw puzzle on the table among picture frames. She looked toward the grove of chestnuts that had shaded their wedding, now a bit taller. She said quietly, "And to think that we are still at war!"

He shook his head, for they had had this conversation. She had been livid that Badoglio, the new prime minister, had vowed to continue the war beside their German ally.

"Poltroon!" from Ottavia.

"Meaningless!" from Alistair.

With two hundred thousand German troops in Italy, the Italian army disorganized, and Patton no closer than Messina, what was Badoglio supposed to do? The last fight had gone out of Italy with Palermo. The Campo dei Fiori had told him that, and to doubt it would be to doubt his own eye, his own muse. Patton's preparations should be swift. They would still give the Germans time to withdraw to the Alpine line, if that were their wish, which he himself doubted. If not, Patton would strike, not to play, God forbid, with Naples—his masters simply could not be that dull—but to use the might of sea and air to come ashore at Rome and Pescara, split the country, or even La Spezia and Ravenna. The Italian army would drift to the Allied standard. And the partisans, much fiercer dogs, would maul the German thigh as it tried to move north or south. And the poet courtier Castliglione said it, must first of all be warrior.

THE NEXT DAY THEY celebrated. They had a pony cart cleared of birds' nests, scrubbed and aired, and greased about the axles. The pony it belonged to, a Presbyterian sort of animal imaginatively named "Grigio," was told he was back in service and put into the shafts. Their goal was Lucca and lunch. They hoped they could find Father Kirchner to join them. The telephones didn't work. They could not spare their quarter tank of gasoline. But they had woken up with a feeling of peacetime and did not want to let it go. They agreed that, coming home, they would walk the steeper parts to spare the pony.

The road smelled of dust and August. Ottavia drove, far the more skilled. She left the brake to Alistair, who sat beside her and contemplated the warm flesh in the modest cleavage of her day dress. They could not help being landlords. The vines and olives prospered. July had fattened them, but they prospered like street boys—too few hands to train and trellis. A ditch had fallen in.

But they trotted into Lucca smartly. Their hoofbeats rang off the walls. The pony trap had cleaned up nicely. The arms of Ugolino-Ferrara, though discreet, were not too badly scratched on the door. When they dropped the reins at the restaurant on the square, the owner and his wife and all the waiters came out to make a fuss of them. They walked back to the chapter house to look and found Father Kirchner, who had leisure for them. Just as lucky, the restaurant had a fish, a big orata. In its honor, pasta and vegetables being what you got those days if you were fortunate, they had a white wine from Elba before a Sangiovese from Siena.

"Thank you," said Father Kirchner. The fish spine on his plate was white as milk, clean as fossil.

"Not long before the boar," said Alistair. "October. I'll send you the first one."

"You may not find so many," said Kirchner. "The men in the hills." He looked at Alistair more straightly. "They might serve you some."

Alistair nodded distantly. Ottavia did not look up. What Kirchner guessed right about them had lost the power to surprise.

Instead, Ottavia said, "Those poor men!" and looked away from Kirchner at the plane trees on the side of the square where Ezra Pound had found his trouble. A number of beggars sheltered there. Most seemed to lack a limb.

Father Kirchner said, "One hopes the men in the hills do not just become robbers. If they do not have to fight. That has happened in Italy before."

Born up by the wine and the fish and their holiday, Ottavia smiled and touched his hand and said, "Surely you will instruct them on that point, Father?" But then looked back at the plane trees with clouded brow and said, "I thought I knew the beggars in Lucca. I don't know them."

"Oh, but you do," said Kirchner. "Just not quite like that. One was the young butcher's boy. One brought you telegrams sometimes on a bicycle. The one leaning on his crutch is the son of the man who kept beehives, remember? The rest were contadini, not yours, I think. They came back from places. Libya. Greece. Even Russia."

"Oh God!" said Ottavia, grabbed her handbag and nearly rose, but Father Kirchner gently eased her back.

"They're not going anywhere," he said. "You can give them what you want later."

"Oh God!" said Ottavia.

Pasta with mushrooms came. For mushrooms had become a meat these days.

"And there is quite a good chance they will not have to fight," said Kirchner. "Hitler's mind is not a place I would wish to be, but the roof is falling on him in the east. The Afrika Corps is gone. Italy has left him, whatever Badoglio says. I do not see what he wants with our poor hills. Maybe north of the Po, Milan. Patton has shown what he can do. Better to look after his own garden, surely."

"It feels like peace," said Ottavia. "It felt like peace in our room this morning."

"Everybody agrees," said Alistair.

"And those poor people. Can the Church do something? A hospice? Even if it's over, they will still be there," said Ottavia.

"It is being talked about. We have our hands full with the orphans just now."

Garibaldi across the square observed them, recognized them, and wished them well. They became aware of motors, heavy and authoritative, not a common sound those days. Around the corner, from the back of the square, entered a German unit. Ottavia stiffened, but it could hardly have come for them. An infantry transport, with cab for driver and officer, maybe forty motorcycles, two antitank guns behind light tractors, another transport. A force like the one that had pushed them to the side the day before. Moving southwest, which made general sense, at least to a pessimist. It stopped in the middle of the square but left motors running. The square trembled to their noise. The officer and his sergeant got down from their vehicles and consulted with pages—maps, he guessed. Both were young men, the officer the slighter. They were close to the contingent of cripples. Consultation over, the officer looked at them, quickly looked away, and walked back to his truck, keeping time with his map against his thigh.

The sergeant paid them much greater heed. He walked a little up and down the line of trees as though making an inspection. He put his hands on his waist and arched his back so that one saw well-muscled shoulders and arms in short sleeves tanned by the sun. He fished in his pocket and tossed a coin, so it did not land close to any of the cripples but more or less in the middle. He turned and walked back to his truck. His face, which seemed open to sullenness, was blessed by pleasure, granted freely by the day. There was a movement of crutches toward the coin. The sergeant stopped a moment and quickly, gratefully laughed. Then picked up his pace and swung up into his truck. The choir of engines rose in pitch, and smoke shimmered above it. The convoy moved and passed out of Lucca.

"One could have wished them going the other way," said Kirchner.

Ottavia's gaze hung on the empty spot where a sergeant had been. She spoke to the air beneath her chin.

"They will not stop," she said.

Her husband looked a question.

"The maggots," she said. "I'm sorry. I'm sorry. I meant my little dog full of maggots all that time ago. They will not stop. The people who made this war. In

Germany mainly. They love cripples. They love ruins. They love corpses. We're their food. They will keep on until every one is dead. They do not really care if the corpses and the ruins and the cripples are Germans or something else. It is all to eat, and even their own death is to eat. We will have to fight for our lives, Alistair. It is not over. Not even a little bit. We have barely even seen it."

He knew that The Men In The Hills, for he liked that name over "partisans" or *partigiani*, knew he was there. Therefore he waited. When there is force, not law, manners matter most. He, and his Nemo, knew that he would return not as cautious pilgrim but as quartermaster: that is, inquisitor, bit, and goad. The radio in the cobwebs had woken to his touch. First, a new schedule, then a crisp reprimand for changing his base, then business: strength of the free forces' matériel and personnel, whether augmented by deserters or POWs (this latter surprised him), possible drop zones in that tangled country, apparent threat by government forces. He waited upon Nemo and let his masters wait.

He was called to the pantry one day to an impossible scene. Ottavia must have been rehearsing a pantomime, happy children to arrive later. Two bearded Hindus sat side by side like birds on a perch, still in bits of uniform, struggling to reconstitute their turbans while wolfing pancakes.

He got there as Ottavia said, "English would surely be easier for you, as I suppose?"

"Oh yes, ma'am, thank you very much. Patveer Singh and Tagh Singh at your service, sir and madam," said possibly Patveer Singh.

"King's Peshawar rifles," said Tagh Singh, perhaps, who had anchored his turban and seemed much relieved.

"POWs?" said Alistair.

"Yes, sir. A regrettable moment in Somalia, sir. But we were undoubtedly the victors, sir."

"You escaped?" said Alistair.

"It was not difficult. I do not think they really cared. A camp near Altopaschio." Which he pronounced not so very badly. "Others, too, of course. Quite a lot remained. They do feed us, they are not bad fellows, and Italy is strange."

"You are very brave men," said Ottavia. "Were you all Hindus there?"

"We are being Sikhs, excuse me, ma'am. But Hindus coexisted. Also Tommies. Mainly Tommies."

"Americans?" said Alistair.

"None present."

"German guards? German officers? German vehicles? Anything like that?"

"The Hun was not in evidence, sir."

He looked at them. The last pancake went, cut neatly in half by Patveer. Ottavia had found tea, it seemed. Birds or not, and travel-torn, they seemed taut and capable. They had good, neatly moving hands.

He said, "How did you get here?"

"The common people were beneficent, sir," said Tagh, was it. "They sent us here."

Oh, Christ, he thought. *Hang out a shingle, "Allied Business Conducted Within."*

"I cannot keep you," he said. A shadow fell. There was uneasy shifting on the perch. A cat. "But there are men in the hills." He motioned. "They are the enemies of your enemies. They are warriors."

"We are good men," said one. And the other took it up, "Give us a Lee-Enfield .303 and we will show anybody what is what."

"I think so too," said Alistair. "I think that they will receive you. You have some Italian. Go to the stables," he motioned again. "Someone will tell you where to go."

They stood in unison, and spoke in counterpoint. "Thank you, sir, madam, for the excellent pancakes."

"And for the unusually delicious tea."

Ottavia pressed upon them a big loaf of bread.

"Fare forward," said Alistair. "We may meet again."

So the pantomime closed, leaving after it a scent of lemon, and of Darjeeling, and of the scent of their bodies, which Alistair thought like the smoke of beechwood.

Messina fell. Scylla and Charybdis, snaky monsters of its strait, intimidated the Royal Navy with their tides. They liked Hitler. The narrow passage to the mainland was stitched tight with antiaircraft guns and field artillery. USAF and RAF were warned off. The German evacuation barges sailed smoothly. Lacking such accommodation, the Italian army fell prisoner.

August established itself. Alistair began checking grapes for sugar, walking through the heat in boots for vipers and hat for sun. He carried a notebook and a little tube. It was what one did in August. Patton stood on Messina's cape. He wished that he could see his eyes.

Quite appositely, Nemo said of this season, "This is the difficult time. When nothing happens."

"Every officer knows that," said Alistair.

They were not then looking at grapes. They were in the tangled valleys and the mousehole roads. They had exchanged horses for a car about twenty minutes beyond their first meeting place. A line of trucks stood within the forest. Onto the track near the road, boughs had fallen, and stones had rolled down from the mountain.

"How do you get them out?" said Alistair.

"Takes twenty minutes to clear. Enough men," said Nemo.

In the back of each truck was mounted an Italian army machine gun, fifty-caliber. Metal plates had been pasted on the sides as armor.

"These we really do have to hide," said Nemo. "But we don't have enough of them. And a snack for a tank anyway. No antitank weapons. We need them. We need your bazookas."

The curator of the trucks just now was a young man with eyeglasses and a hunting jacket. Alistair saw the book in his pocket: Ugo Foscolo, itinerant revolutionary, but no bandit's book. And there were women—but not what he'd thought. Of women in the hills, he would have expected camp followers with loud laughs washing britches with their sleeves rolled up. He would have expected officers' doxies. He did not expect a crisp young lady with excellent English who had learned to set up a detonator.

"Where do you get these people?' asked Alistair.

"You want a robber's cave full of bravoes in sheepskin? We've got some of those. We've got deserters on the run who can't write. Mostly we have modern Italy. Mainly socialist. Students. Mechanics. You don't understand. Elena, whom you liked, thinks you're a marvelous poet and completely out of date. Sorry."

No, he did not understand. "Do you have many of her?" he said.

"Not enough. Let it go. You don't have to understand. You're an infantry officer who understands that part. You have contact with the Americans. You'll never be a traitor. I can't tell you how wonderful that is. Maybe you're the parting gift of the old order. You might even like that. Get back in the car. We have other places to go."

They had come out of the barn of a farmhouse above a small town, though it would have been a village elsewhere. The barn held rifles. They were mostly of 1914–18 model but neatly stacked and with bolts sweetly oiled. His guide claimed two hundred. Alistair thought somewhat fewer. There were cases of ammunition, and all that he looked at were full. He had noted all these points. Outside, he looked down at the town and saw an Italian flag, the royal flag again and without fasces, flying on a house, a cheery peasant apron in the stony streets.

"That's Carabinieri," he said. "What are they doing here?"

"We don't bother them, and they don't bother us. It's good they're here. The government's officially in control, and we go about our business. I was saying, this is when everything should happen. We should be moving pieces on the board. That camp where your Indians came from. Several hundred trained soldiers lacking only rifles. Mouthwatering. A quick nighttime raid. We can't. We don't have enough rifles for them, and if we got into that flat valley, we might not get out. So that plum will shrivel. For your Indians would not make it now, Alistair, even so soon. The Germans are thicker on the roads every day, and the Italians are getting scared of them again. So the Germans get stronger, and we don't. And you are in danger, my friend. You should pray that none of those nice Italians who sent Allied soldiers to you talks to a German."

"Drop zones. Parachute drops. We haven't talked about that," said Alistair.

"We will," said Nemo.

So, that evening, 20:06 being his call time, Alistair faced the enormity, the monstrousness of having the radio in his house, over his family's head, sucking demons out of the ether. The danger of the radio lay in transmission and increased with length. So he faced a matador's version of art's great question: scale. He could put into three lines the partisans' needs (rifles, machine weapons, antitank, radios, waste of time to talk about trucks—they wouldn't get them), resources, personnel quality and morale, coordinates of possible drops. Thirty seconds of coded transmission for his too slowly loosening finger. But everything that mattered—the untried enthusiasm of the bright young students, the bone-weariness of the deserters—what of that? The dispersal of the weaponry, the loose communications? The narrow drop zones, inviting heavenly, lethal manna to roll off precipices, hang from trees. For in battle, theory is a pit to fall into; everything is the least you need. Does your boot slip or hold? Is the man to your right twenty feet too far behind? Are the woods thin, with flickers within, or a green cloak?

He cut out, put back, sought to imply, cut again but less. At 20:06, he sent. A three-minute transmission. His family could die by his slow hand.

He listened to the August cicadas in the still night as Italy lay in its spell. In the night woods, he imagined the brambles grow, their stems thicken, their thorns crawl out, and the homeward fox jump higher every dawn. Woken by dry thunder, one had dreamed of guns.

The news, because from privileged sources, always required attention. A country neighbor, a colonel of the old war, came over expressly to tell them—this straight from Rome they understood, finger on lip, wink of eye, glance around for listening servant—that the king had reached London. There he and the English king were arming the vast force of Italian POWs and would lead them back to Italy in English battleships from Malta.

And the English landed in Reggio di Calabria with no resistance from the Italians.

August ended.

The airdrop to his partisans, remote as the Second Coming, happened. His radio told him this in the language of insects: Morse. The transmissions were quite long, but reception was safe. His replies were terse. Terse were his words to Nemo. They met horse to horse and had no need to dismount. Sites, time, quantities. He was to be at his own house, near the radio, for the drop.

He had imagined the drop as a vast event, the fist of the sky, like the bombing of Rome. It was nothing of the sort. From the attic, he counted two Dakotas. They came at an angle past Lucca toward the hills, made no fuss, and were quickly gone.

It turned out that the English really were in Reggio di Calabria. And in Tarranto too. The Americans were in Salerno. No shots were fired. Eisenhower announced that Italy was now an ally. The Germans occupied Rome. Evading chains, the king ran away. The prime minister ran after him.

The German army disarmed the Italian army. One Sardinian regiment in Rome died to the last man resisting. Most of the rest, without orders, without a government, with a coward for a king, surrendered. The army that Alistair had seen claw its courage back inch by inch after Caporetto, that had been promised the fabulous Orient, the Balkan valleys, and all the empires of the wine-dark sea, was packed into freight cars for Germany. Enough slipped away to flow like a torrent into the partisans.

The ear in the attic was all business, therefore stingy. They knew what the BBC told them. The BBC even added, just once, a short coda in Italian, "The old friendship now restored." So said many, many leaflets dropped by the RAF, along with bombs for the old friends. None of either, as it happened, fell on them.

In the afternoon, in the cool and loamy flower room, Ottavia arranged wiry little cornflowers with great care because they were blue and hopeful.

Alistair, whose soul thirsted as much, looked at a wall in his office in the hope of seeing a new poem's face. He found none. A car arrived. Since both were preoccupied, neither heard.

Girolamo answered the door. He ran to two doors successively and said, "Two officers, sir. Two officers, my lady."

"Invite them in, of course," said Ottavia.

Alistair caught up with her as they entered the salone whence you could see the front door and the entering silhouettes, sharp and black, of two SS caps. Ottavia caught his hand.

"Alistair, they're German," she said.

He had caught a glimpse from his window. "No men with them," he said, "and not armed."

Putzi Hasseldorf said loudly and cheerily, "Alistair! Ottavia!"

The caps lost their iconic shapes carried against britches, and immediately regained them, right side up on a side table.

Ottavia, very straight, said, "Such a surprise, Putzi."

Putzi said, "My friend and colleague, Obersturmbannführer Haffner. Rudi. Whom I have told about you already."

All inclined.

"There is no coffee, regrettably," said Ottavia as they sat. "Champagne will have to do."

"We can't stay long," said Putzi. "We are on our way to La Spezia. The Italian navy sailed away to Malta, most unfortunately. But there are some of their officers there, under arrest. We knew you were holed up somewhere around here." He turned up his palms, innocently pleased. "So we winkled you out."

Haffner smiled too. The caps looked on like Siamese cats.

Putzi went to the window. Alistair joined him and found himself with Putzi's arm around his shoulder as they looked down upon the spires of Lucca.

"I can see why you like it here," said Putzi. "In Rome, one forgets how much Italy has. But are you safe here, you and Ottavia? One hears there are very bad elements very close to here. Very bad indeed. You should come back to Rome. It is quite safe there with us now. There has not been another terror bombing. Roosevelt is afraid of the pope, they say."

"We are safe enough," said Alistair. "Living cheek by jowl with bandits is rather an Italian tradition. There is a kind of etiquette. Ottavia's family is respected. I do not expect trouble."

"I hope there is none. I hope they never ask anything of you. You would refuse, of course, and report the contact to us. And then they might turn nasty. Maybe even against Ottavia most of all, do you think? We are masters of Italy now. I did not expect that. I was romantic, no doubt. I thought Italy was our friend. A false friend is a traitor, Alistair. The worst thing there is."

"Indeed," said Alistair. "The worst."

"And we are the masters here. As those Italian naval officers in La Spezia will find out. That we are masters, and that they have become traitors. That is really Rudi's affair. I am just the translator, the cicerone for things Italian. Rudi has by far the heavier hand. His Italian is terrible, so it is nice for him to meet Ottavia. Come to think of it, now there is really no Italy, Ottavia is finally German. And to know where you are is pleasant, of course. You have a beautiful city. I can see that. They say the duomo is quite lovely."

"A very fine St. Martin," said Alistair. "And a maze, on the facade."

Putzi raised his eyes and laughed light surprise. "A maze?" he said. "That is almost too appropriate, for now." Then looked back to what the caps were watching, which was Rudi and Ottavia.

"He had the power to frighten," said Ottavia. "Not by anything he said. He was quite polite." She took her fingers off his wrist. "Just like the man in Wurzburg."

They were sitting very close, knees touching, the shadow of his chin upon her cheek. He saw them for a moment, the two mice trying to plan after their fright. That eye would be German.

He edged a little further from the window. To cover it, he said, "What did he talk about?"

"Friends at home." She spoke pedantically. "The pleasant experience of receiving news. Was it the more difficult here in the country?" This time her fingers met around his wrist. "Oh, Alistair, do they know about my friend, the one they tortured? That she was my friend?"

His shoulder said they couldn't know. "It was Putzi who led, then," he said. "Putzi almost said things."

"Putzi thinks he owns us. He always did."

And there she had it, he thought. They were Putzi's asset. And if that had come about by chance, it no longer mattered.

"They may know just enough to take us in," he said.

"Then they will. It's as simple as that." She put both her hands around his now. "We always knew it would end like this, Alistair. And now it has. Now I know why they were here. It was to see us like this, as we are now, so they can think of the difference when they see us, later. It's a game, Alistair."

He looked into her eyes and nodded, for the truth she had just faced was terrible, even if it were not true.

"It could be something else though," he said.

He put it to her that they were now Putzi's, very well might be, and that Putzi was very much not all-powerful. If something were known—take your choice from the list—that would drag them into the slaughterhouse, Putzi would lose them there.

She stopped him. "Then it's about me," she said.

He considered that and thought again that she was right. If his transmissions had been captured, if he had been seen with the partisans, if his confessors in Rome had been turned, then the pack of hounds that would have descended on them would have no ear for Putzis. A finding of youthful indiscretion, Putzi could probably control. And there by his own window, he had just linked Ottavia's name with danger, three times.

"If he thinks that I'm a contact, he'll want to turn me. Better that it comes from me, that I turn myself and come to him. That's always better. It would be a very big thing for Putzi. So it gives us a little time."

"Time for what?" she said.

"Time for Patton."

"Alistair," she said and now tapped his wrist, the schoolteacher, "Putzi's not the only German."

THEY LEARNED NOW THAT fear has a rich landscape, like storm clouds, not just darker and lighter, but with pustules of sickly light, ragged arms that stretch out, and whirlpools to suck you in. Ottavia had given it very nearly a face: every action he took (the radio, for listeners would be silent, was worst) came with a photograph of Ottavia battered and stick-limbed in the corner of a cell. They could not talk about this and so talked less and less. He had known fear as moments on a horse, watching for watchers in the streets of Rome, a snake, as fire and freezing both, fusing into their own cure, judgment and skill. The fear that seeped through the windows now had joined with doom and was chilly as lead. The airdrop to the partisans had been largely a success. This he knew. This, with fingers that would not go fast enough, he had reported.

They had taken a small and obscure railroad bridge in the Apennines, but not too small and obscure to carry trains with some twenty thousand pounds of shells and companies of infantry. All, and the very roots of bridge, had gone in one stupendous annihilation. For a month, trains would have to take a main line much more exposed to the RAF. This was considerably his doing, and he could not look at it without seeing versions of their own fate. He did not know how far Putzi's patience stretched. He did not know who else was looking. He could only guess Ottavia's thoughts.

They sat longer every evening into the night. They sat at first in silence, for putting on the gramophone seemed to risk jogging fate's arm. This was the bottom of cowardice. He could endure it no longer, and one evening they sat born up by the majestic inquiry of J. S. Bach in his cello suite No. 4. That night they went to bed arm in arm. He began to name evenings by their music and so remember them.

The Neapolitans looted armories and rose against the Germans. Southern bloodlust turned into a blowtorch by desperation yielded three days of glorious courage and ungodly horror. The Germans left. Patton arrived. Neapolitans threw flowers. Patton moved north, with Montgomery to his east. Whatever his subtlety, Putzi had very soon to call in any cards he held. His partisan band held a fine position. He was told to organize the details of another airdrop, had meetings with Nemo, and greatly increased radio traffic. So he was busy as he waited for the sword to drop.

They came during a Dvorak cello concerto, late. They must have come fast, for the noise of engines flowered suddenly, and then there were voices, not hidden. He found that Ottavia had risen and was standing very straight, as for an expected guest. He joined her and took her hand.

She said, "Remember that we did everything we could, and it was a great deal. We must remember that through all that comes."

He nodded. He found that they were standing together in the back of the room. She said, "As for you and me, Alistair, it was wonderful. Thank you."

He looked at his Ottavia and had suddenly to restrain tears, which had nothing to do with fear but only with sorrow.

"Yes," he said. "It was."

From the door behind them, Girolamo, collar loose and really half asleep, flustered in and made for the front door. Ottavia motioned him to her. She gripped his wrists until his eyes were wide.

"Take Giovanni. Hide him. Take him to my brother's. Take Concetta. Let Luigi lead. Do not fail me." She released his wrists and spread her hands. "Thank you for your long service," she said. "Thank also Concetta. Thank Luigi. You have all a home at my brother's. Now leave us."

The front door bucked, and half opened. Alistair remarked, as to a botany class, "They're Italian." It opened all the way. Two officers of Carabinieri stood in it. They were young. They looked awkward. One nodded at them, for lack of a better gesture. The other looked behind him, toward a confusion of uniforms outside. A fat colonel came in behind them quickly. They stared at him. All of his old succulence of manner had dropped away. He seemed both peremptory and uneasy. He stared at them, erect and hand in hand, immersed in a cello playing in a different universe as at an inappropriate charade. His shoulders relaxed a little. He turned to the two officers, spoke to them, motioned them back, and waited long enough to close the door that it was not quite in their faces. He turned back, and in doing so he seemed to have taken back his old magnificence like a cloak. He took a step toward them.

Rodolfo said, "We all need a drink. Before you take me to the Americans." He sat down on a sofa. Domesticity joined all the other props. He sat up properly. "You are under arrest, of course. That's necessary."

PART V

23

They started down the hill road in the dark, in Italy now very dark. The car was a black Alfa-Romeo with pennants. They could have been a party of admirals taking the air. Alistair and Ottavia, however, were handcuffed and fell over each other on the first tight bend. The seat smelled of gasoline and leather.

Rodolfo passed back a little silver key. "Works for both," he said. "Sorry about that. You never know who's on what side these days."

So that was better.

"I didn't know you were Carabiniere, Rodolfo," said Ottavia.

"I haven't been very long."

They were in the back. Rodolfo was in front, with a captain of Carabinieri, who drove. The road twisted tight again. A shrine jumped to life in the headlights, white and small, blessed them with its halo, and was extinguished. He must know it by day, thought Alistair, but could not place it. They could not be going down much longer.

"You should have questions," said Rodolfo.

"Who was going to arrest us?" said Alistair.

"You mean SS or Gestapo? That is a bit more than I know. Gestapo, I believe. It seems that it was connected with Ottavia, mainly. That's all I know."

Supposing he was right, Putzi had been trumped. If Putzi had been trumped, it was by Ottavia's ferret. If so, his transmissions were undiscovered. If his transmissions had been discovered, he would be now as fox under a pack of hounds. If it were Ottavia's ferret, the matter was still a young girl's indiscretions, disturbing given her marriage to an American and her connections. Disturbing, and very unsure, and very, very embarrassing to well-placed Germans who had found the pleasure of a nice cigar in the knowledge that you could be Hitler's minion and the friend of civilized foreigners, and that German girls of family bred loyal and true. And the Germans right now were busy. No matter. No matter what came, Putzi or weasel, and they had fled, and their flight was discovered, as it certainly would be, connected with a raid of Carabinieri of which the Germans' loyal Italians had no knowledge at all, then their status would very quickly change. Then grim men would come, and the radio would be found. And then he and Ottavia would change from Putzi's possible tea-party spies to the high nobility of treachery.

"More important just now," said Ottavia, "where are we going?"

"To the Americans."

"Geographically."

"Do you know Graziani?"

"Is he a place?" said Ottavia.

"He is a general, the last I heard," said Alistair.

"He is an Italian general who is loyal to Mussolini. He is a true fascist. Therefore, he continues the war. I am a true fascist."

Alistair said, "The Carabinieri are the king's. As is the army. Therefore the Germans are your enemy."

"Graziani is more loyal to the king than the king."

"But we are going to the Americans," observed Ottavia.

"Because I am more loyal to Italy than to Graziani."

"We are getting off the subject," said Ottavia. "Where are we going?"

"Graziani's division is supporting the German east flank somewhat east of Avellino. That is where we are going."

"He has a division?" said Alistair.

"He has men. Their numbers are growing."

"That is quite a lot of sides for you to be on, Rodolfo," said Ottavia to him, who did not answer. He sat in silence. His grandness leaked from his shoulders, and his head lowered. He said something to the officer driving that they did not catch.

Alistair said, "Rodolfo, when we get to this place, whatever it is, how do we make the crossing? I am not familiar with that theater."

But when he spoke, Rodolfo said, "These things happen to Italy because she is weak. I became a fascist so that she would never be weak again. And now our ally has occupied us, and we beg an enemy to save us. And as the lady says, I am on at least three sides. And my father was a gallant officer and of noble blood."

The driver, who was in front of Alistair, put back his head and said quietly, "You are an American officer?"

"I was a long time ago."

The officer nodded. This was good news, it seemed. Alistair considered that, looked at the dark beyond the window, and was appalled. The officer, he was perfectly certain, was a good, plain soldier. An honest soldier should have nothing to do with this except drive. He had thought that they had slipped off the cross of their doom at the house into a warm, stale intrigue. He trusted Rodolfo's intrigues. If this officer could be reassured by another soldier's presence, then there was no intrigue. Or there were the materials for intrigue, but they had not settled into place, or had settled into place once and now had unmade themselves, and their rush down the night road and the milestones lighting up like sparks were just what it looked like, flight.

He said, "The plan, Rodolfo?"

Rodolfo spoke looking levelly to the windshield, with the very smallest turning of his head. "You of all people should know, Alistair, that one keeps a certain flexibility. The rigid plan breaks on a pebble. I am well connected in Graziani's circle. Much of my work is special. I have complete ability to move around. The names would mean nothing to you, and as you just said yourself, you do not know that theatre. The point now is to get there. When we do, it will be up to you to follow my lead. Which I am sure you can do." He turned his head a little more, as grace note. "And I will follow yours with the Americans."

This was all right so far as it went, though it dragged behind it Rodolfo's tone to him: indignant schoolboy to rigorous master. Alistair said only, and mainly to himself, "This is no time for wishful thinking."

Which it seemed was too much. Rodolfo now spoke to the roof. "When I came to your house, you two were not looking very happy. I was not what you expected. So we agree that I have saved you. Do you have any idea how long I have saved you? I've always known what you were. You pulled the wool over the Germans' eyes, Alistair, never over mine. Years ago, before Hitler, before Jews, before any thought of war, I asked you to stand—not with us, goodness!—but by our side. You were intrigued. You were nearly with us. But you wouldn't do it. So why would you snuggle up to the Germans? Beautifully done, Alistair. Our old friend Simon. That church you used to go to in Rome, just because it had once been your mother's, of course. I am sure there was some skullduggery there. We nearly pulled you in. I nearly pulled you in. Not with pleasure. I like you, Alistair. And then, I always thought you might be useful. And, Alistair, we're being very honest now, from the first day America joined the war, I didn't see how the Germans could possibly win. Last time, Italy was on the winning side. Even that almost killed her.

"You have to know what drives a man. The big thing. I'm a patriot. Italy's all I've got. My only home. Italian's the only language I speak. Nowhere to run to. You're not. You're for the *bella figura*. Yours, of course. We weren't quite good enough for you. Not the right tailor, not quite the right cologne. Your Ovid, your Urbino, your Castiglione. God, the Germans lapped it up! And then your Goethe. Good God, you two, your Goethe! And horses, of course. You could have run against Hitler, I shouldn't doubt. You would stand near us, because really you agreed with us. But not so our shoulders touched. Your own country's nothing like good enough for you. And the Germans? The Germans aren't even good enough for me. The truth is, Alistair, nobody's good enough for you, except yourself. Yourself and," courtly, he bowed to the window, "the Lady Ottavia, no doubt."

"Oh, pish, Rodolfo," said the Lady Ottavia. "What balls!"

"You don't know him like I do. When we rode together as boys. That damn stupid jump he made thirty years ago. I've seen through him since that moment. He wants to cover himself with clouds of glory and then gaze at them. D'Annunzio and Roland at Roncesvalles!"

"Courtesy toward your guests, Rodolfo. I do not accept D'Annunzio," said Alistair, who found the rest reasonable as far as it went. "I am far the better poet."

But now suddenly there were lights ahead of them, and not just down the road but spread out, lights much too white for an Italian village. A crossroads, then, and traffic assembled. Then they were in it, and it was German. It was transports, the inevitable motorcycles, even a force of tanks on carriers. Dozing engines shook the air. High vehicles loomed darker than the dark. Legs, cut off at the knees, busied themselves, for though the lights were white, they pointed only at the ground. The RAF was never far. He thought, *Wehrmacht,* and thanked God. An MP halted them.

An officer came out of the dark, a young major. Alistair said to himself, *Soldier,* and thanked God again. The major looked at the car. He looked at the pennants as at an unexpected carnival. He looked at the papers the driver held out. He looked at portly Colonel Rodolfo. He went around to that side of the car. Rodolfo spoke. Whether it were German was quite unclear, but the self-assurance was satisfactory, and "Graziani" came twice. Ottavia had already opened her window. She spoke to the major as though they were rather good friends. "Something you never thought to see," she said. "A decent Italian." Her neck and her chin and her smile rose up into the cool empyrean of her German. Her index finger hovered at Rodolfo. The major snorted amiably. His eye fell again on the papers but glanced them.

"You'll have to take the Avezzano-Benevento road," he said. "Capua's too dicey." He saluted, mainly Ottavia.

The MP stood down. They drove. Alistair took Ottavia's hand, which shook. Shook rightly, for the matter could have turned like paper in a breeze. They passed the last vehicles, guns behind tractors pointed fingers at them.

In a little while, Rodolfo turned his head as best he could. "Thank you, Ottavia," he said.

Though her hand still shook, her voice was as a girl's who's won a dare. "You weren't so bad yourself, Rodolfo."

In this also, he thought, she was right.

"We can't do many more of those," she said.

So, Avezzano and Benevento now, east, the mountain roads. Alistair had the impression that they might be driving through a hole in the war. The German forces, confronting Patton, would surely favor the coast, from which the mountains they were about to enter would effectively isolate them. He doubted they cared whether Graziani lived or died, but he presumably gave some slight assurance to their eastern flank. And Montgomery, as he understood, was far east, the other coast, in fact. He dared hope there might be no one around the way they were going, except Italians, and that Ottavia might get her wish. Daylight might be different. It was two o'clock in the morning. Ottavia's cheek began to press his shoulder.

He said to the driver, "Spell you?" who shook his head.

OTTAVIA OPENED HER EYES before the sun, in the luminous dawn of Mezzogiorno fall. Small roads had taken them around Avezzano, and small roads through the mountains here, picked by the driver without a word. This was not the wilds of the Abruzzi; there were villages, and far off the campanile of what should have been a town. There were also acres and acres of stony slopes, and spiky bushes, and scruffy sheep. No war. Nothing here to bomb. No troops. Partisans, maybe, he imagined, who would not much like Rodolfo's flags.

Ottavia moved her shoulders and said quietly, "Alistair, can we stop? I need to pee."

There was nothing near but the thorn bushes, at that fleeting hour touched with rose light and delicate as thistledown.

He said to the driver, "We need to stop." And was met by manners good enough not to ask why.

They stopped. Ottavia touched the door handle.

"Be careful," said Alistair. "Vipers."

"Oh, for God's sake, Alistair," said Ottavia. And then, huffily, "I'll watch out."

Ottavia's need not being unique, they gathered shortly around the car.

"No vipers," said Ottavia. "Just sheep shit," but took his arm.

"We should keep on," said Rodolfo.

"Maybe," said the captain.

"There is no obstacle. There are no troops." On the dawn hillside, in his *diviso di colonello,* he appeared to be in fancy dress.

"Troops, no," said the captain. "The Germans would not move troops across the mountain ridges, and they will not move troops from the east when they are facing the British Eighth Army there. The Americans are certainly busy on the coast. They will want to get past Monte Cassino before the Germans fortify it. And I do not think the RAF will bother us just here. Though they would like this car."

Well done! thought Alistair.

"So?" said Rodolfo but not peremptorily.

Alistair looked at the long lines of the hills, and stones of walls and distant churches now sharp in the risen sun, and threads of smoke from unseen chimneys, for the night had been cold.

"There are eyes," he said. "We have certainly been seen. If there are partisans, I would rather they have to come to us than that we run into an ambush. I would prefer a halt, with some concealment if we can find that. It will be a long and hungry halt."

"Not that," said Rodolfo. "Trust me. Then they ambush us at night."

"If they do not come today, then they are not interested or there are none. They would not fear one car. Would the Germans be hunting us?"

"Not yet, I think, and why here?"

THEY FOUND A BARN, far from a farm. An old track led to it from the road. The roof had fallen in. They had to clear some tiles for the car. They were well hidden. The watching eyes, of course, would mark their earth. There was a well too.

Out of the car came ham, a roast of pork with herbs inside, cheese, bread, and wine, all from a hamper with willow hoops for handles. Rodolfo looked pleased. Ottavia said, *"O, dio!"* profoundly. He looked more pleased. Alistair wondered if this were a regular accommodation when one was fleeing the Gestapo with Rodolfo.

So they ate.

ALISTAIR AND THE CAPTAIN alternated as sentries. The barn was on a prairie of grass colored between olive and smoke, with not many bushes. It went up unchanged to a rounded ridge, so that one felt slightly dizzy, as though standing on a ball. Though night belonged to the fall now in the Mezzogiorno hills, summer came by ten o'clock and took back the key. This turned on the cicadas. One did not see villages from the barn, but there was an excellent line of sight from the campanile of the town in the distance. They thought it might be Faicchio.

When Alistair had been there an hour, Ottavia came out and sat beside him. In a crack in the stone they sat on, there were crowds of pinhead flowers, blue and yellow, on stems like paper. She looked at them, and he watched her.

"Sempervivums," she said. "Or something very like. Didn't know they got this far south." Then, "Do you think we'll get out of this?"

"We have shed our chains," he said. "Meaning our duty, of course."

"Through Rodolfo? I expect he's rather good at ditching duty."

"We are in motion. We were tied to Lucca. Arrest cancels that. Your German major gave us the right road. Since he didn't know who we are, we got it by chance. Chance and motion double each other. I think our chance is good. The war we volunteered for is won."

"In case it isn't, we don't have a gun, do we? I really don't want to do the gestapo thing."

"No," he said. "The captain must. Rodolfo probably."

"Might be hard to get," she said. Then said, but only quietly and to the flowers, "If Giovanni's safe, we've lived. If he isn't, there's not a lot of point in it. Can I stay here, Alistair?"

"Of course. Of course. Of course," he said. And put his arm on her shoulder and down her flank. "But you do have to help me watch."

"If we do die, have we bought him a decent life?"

He looked toward the sempervivums, but when he spoke, spoke to Apollo, whom he had known since dawn to rule this country naked to the sky.

"The lute will not be strung again, and the music is scattered. It was broken before it was passed to me. But the echo has lasted me so far. I think it will last me for my life if I live. I think that it will last Giovanni, just. He will live among enemies—but we will have taught him to know his friends. Castiglione will fail him, as he has failed me. Manfredi will teach him more, if it comes to that. Claudia will give him modesty and kindness."

"A peasant concubine? Yes, I suppose she would," said Ottavia.

"He will live on mean streets," said Alistair, "for that is what there will be. But there will gardens still to find. And he will have been taught to find them."

THEY WOULD HAVE SEEN military traffic a long way away. Time enough to hide. Or a truck bouncing down the road full of patriotic brigands. Nothing like that came. A mule cart came, hooves clip-clopping like a lazy clock. Two hours later, another came, the other way, for proper structure. Church bells came on the unchanging wind, unexpected every time. From very far, and very faint, came sounds of heavy battle, concussion of ordnance or bombardment touching the ear. It was from the west, and the wind was not helping. He suspected they were east of the American front even now and would soon pass behind it, but this hope seemed too flimsy to feed to Ottavia now. The sun smelled of dust in the grass, and the air was sent by the sun. If the cicadas had suddenly stopped, it would have been terrifying. He became aware of a poem and sat forward, pricking at the scent. It walked arm in arm with *Here at the quiet limit of the world, a white-haired shadow roaming like a dream* . . . but it had its own distinct face, and he knew that he could distinguish it in time. He stretched his back against the sun that fed it. He suspected he was seeing his last poem.

At the change of watch, the captain and Rodolfo both joined them. It was late afternoon. Birds were beginning to fly again. The captain said, "I think we can say the partisans have no interest in us. If there are any."

"But I would still prefer not to enter a new country until dark," said Alistair.

The captain nodded, though he said, "You are a little more impressed by them than I."

"Because he knows them better. That's what he was doing up in Lucca, I am absolutely sure," said Rodolfo.

The captain nodded again, more thoughtfully.

They took the road again when the western mountains were darkening toward sunset and those in the east were sharp. They finished Rodolfo's nice picnic, though Ottavia said, "You can't serve pork that's been sitting here all day, Rodolfo. You'll kill us all." It sounded as though she had been pulled out of a hole, and gladdened Alistair.

"We do not really have so very far now," said Rodolfo. "We should begin to find Graziani's units in three hours or less. No reason for Germans here."

In dusk that was almost dark, they took small roads, though for all he knew, they could have been main roads here. There was no incident and no threat. They began to pass shreds of a military force.

They passed a checkpoint under a flag Alistair had not seen before, the royal flag hiding behind the skirts of a strapping fasces.

"I think you must be home, Rodolfo," said Ottavia.

But Rodolfo, now fully inflated again, said nothing.

They left the main road and drove uphill. Rodolfo motioned their driver to stop. He turned around and crossed his thighs to do it better. He said, "I must set things in order tonight. I must find things out. Where we are going, you belong to me. You will never be far from me. You do not answer questions. You refer to me. Do you understand? You are at ease. And serious. And silent."

"Just where are we going, Rodolfo?" said Ottavia.

"Headquarters. A headquarters. I do not think General Graziani is here."

Alistair drew in breath, but Ottavia spoke first. "We are not two little contadini you picked up on the road, Rodolfo. If this is a headquarters, there are people in it who know us, I should think."

"Yes," said Rodolfo. "So they will know your views. If they don't know you, they will still know your views a little. I have done some work on that. People do not want to be alone. Alistair's views, Mr. Pound's views, M. Celine's in France, even some of Mr. Eliot's are well known in our circle, perhaps a little clumsily. There are many who feel warmed to see Mme. Chanel by German shoulders at the Ritz. You give comfort. That's the psychology—you mustn't forget psychology. And people do not question me. Alistair just has to be enigmatic. Second nature. He is a sympathizer observing the meticulous organization of free Italy's reborn army. Easy. Though he won't say it. I will. And Ottavia's her haughty grande dame. Haughty but pleasant, I mean."

"Thanks for that," said Ottavia.

"We're both actors, Alistair, confess it," said Rodolfo.

They drove up steeply. There was a castle, castellations all medieval under a waning half moon. There was a barrier and a brightly painted box for a sentry to pop out of. What Alistair chiefly saw was Rodolfo's body's ability to change its substance, portliness to vague menace. Even the uniform, sent in by a backstreets theatrical outfitter on the sheep hill in the dawn, drank in salutes and clicks of heels and rose around the neck like a bull's throat. There was grand door with steps. The captain opened Rodolfo's door, not theirs. Rodolfo ascended. They were drawn in his wake.

There were men in uniform. Rodolfo was greeted. Rodolfo greeted. But at the top, he paused and spoke to Alistair. "I am looking for a place to cross. Notice what you're allowed to notice. Don't look interested."

"He really is at home here, thank god," said Ottavia. But that was sotto voce.

There were rooms of officers. There were telephones. There were maps squeezed uncomfortably among the castle tapestries. It was hard to keep track of the uniforms. There were the old Italian army ones he knew. There were the flashier ones of the fascist guard he knew less well. Those officers whose military tailors had the fastest fingers had brand new ones on which a swastika and a fasces held hands across the breast. There was a good deal to eat and drink. He was passed a cup of wine, respectfully. He picked up a ham sandwich as he sidled behind Rodolfo. He could not imagine what was going on. He had expected the drowsy nervousness of a night headquarters, subalterns at lonely desks, a telegraph breaking into chatter and quickly quiet. He reflected that this was the first time in his life he had been in a headquarters in time of full war. He reflected that it was not at all late for an Italian party. There were some quite pretty girls, presumably who worked the telephones, which lay unattended.

Everybody was alight with medals. In a kinder time, one could have settled back and enjoyed oneself, he supposed, almost. In fact, he found it less a night in a castle than on a Naples street where the eye of the jackal showed through the fun. He thought the smiles reached for a sneer that had lately been scrubbed off. It was a nasty place, and dangerous.

He looked for Ottavia. An officer had found a glass of fizzy wine for her and was looking unutterable things from his soft, possessing eyes. He remembered the Italian army he once had known. He remembered his stepfather, Maggiore, and his colonel's cloak smelling of the dust of the trenches, and his boots cut by sharp stones, and his tired, kind eyes.

He supposed Rodolfo was studying the maps. He wished forlornly that their captain of Carabinieri were there with them but supposed he must be sleeping.

Rodolfo was suddenly with him and whispered, "They are under great strain, these officers. You must understand that. They are waiting for their moment to attack Patton's flank." He was entirely serious.

Rodolfo's movements became more random and more urgent, both. *So he's looking for someone he can't ask for,* Alistair thought. He kept silent until a major buttonholed by Rodolfo stepped forward and said to him straight, "So you will tell the world that Patton was not crushed by Germany but by Italian valor rekindled in the ruins of Naples?" His eyes were clear, his gesture was gracious, in this castle of conceit he spoke with the crystal exaltation of pure insanity.

Alistair liked him at once. "Indeed," he said, "for I know. I stood with Italy also after Caporetto."

"I had not even thought of that," said the major, as though a meteor had landed at his feet. Then he saw Ottavia and said, "Your lady. A warrior's lady," and swept her a lovely bow. But the major, though delectable, was not Rodolfo's man.

Then Rodolfo was reading papers between a piano and a bookshelf in the dimmer half of a room and handled the whole matter with expedition, for Alistair did not realize it was taking place at all. A piece of paper was shown but not given. Rodolfo peered. An index finger tapped. The paper was withdrawn. Rodolfo nodded. The other man did not.

"I have what I need," said Rodolfo. "Tomorrow night. We do not stay here."

24

The castle kept guard over them until a swoop of the road erased it. They all felt better; Alistair's hand, at least, loosened on the car door. In the westering sun, the turret was a head, the arrow slits, angry eyes. They were glad only at the passing of a bogey, and they knew it. Casual observation was not their great peril. But now they could seek cover to wait for full night, when leaving the barracks would have been too clumsy a sign.

Cover they found, a stream margin with gravel dry enough for the tires, screened by stiff rushes of late summer in which nymphs snickered to Alistair in the puffs of breeze. Not much was left of what had started at Pace ed Abbondanza. Rodolfo had put on officer's khaki. Their captain wore fatigues. Their car had changed into an open box, khaki with liver spots, big tires, severe headlights, and a muscular toolbox growing from the running board. His Ottavia, still a belle of the castle the night before, was a military waif now, in a boy recruit's uniform shirt and pants ending in cheap new boots. Only Alistair remained in his character: litterateur, sympathetic observer, traitor. This, Rodolfo said, and Alistair supposed he believed, would satisfy casual observation. Their plan, trump card of duplicity clutched in sweaty hand, was simple: continue along a minor road through the generous no-man's-land, past a forward observation post which would not be manned tonight, and so to the American lines. Their real protection, Alistair was sure, was that this front was a fraud, that no real army was as lax as Graziani's, whose defense was not in vigilance but in being too unimportant to annihilate. Their real protection, Rodolfo was sure, was that, should the forward post, through whatever mistake, be manned after all, Alistair's sympathetic curiosity would be invoked: he could not bear to miss seeing the absolute front incisors of Graziani's new jaws.

THE LIGHT VOICE OF flowing water came from the middle of the drawer. Veils of insects rose and sought the skirts of night. It was probably water rats in the rushes.

"I was given twenty-three hundred hours," said Rodolfo.

"The moon will be up by then," said Alistair.

"It is much less than full, and I will not need lights," said their captain.

"But why would an officer like Rodolfo drive without lights?" said Ottavia.

"I think I would though," said Alistair. "And, anyway, he mightn't want the Americans to see."

There was a thermos jug.

"It's coffee," said Ottavia. "It really is."

No one commented. What one could have said was that tonight would bring them to safety or to wreck, and no magic would make it otherwise. That, one could not say.

Something splashed heavily in the running stream. They were all proud not to have jumped.

Alistair looked at Rodolfo and knew himself humbled to find it odd that a plump man whom he had often mocked stood in exactly the same peril as themselves, and had so far carried them from doom to hope. A nymph who listened inside skulls thought that was funny. There had been a puff of air.

Their captain looked at Alistair and Ottavia. "I would like you to know my name," he said. "It is Lorenzo Mutti." And thus said exactly what they all meant.

GRAVEL RATTLED UNDER THE tires. Rushes crashed against the doors. They rose out of the creek bed, out of the vegetable dark and little wings against the cheek and noises that might be anything onto a tabletop. One mountain to the east glowed in the climbing moon's cold fire.

Captain Mutti handed Alistair the map. "The topography is accurate. The positions are approximate," he said.

"Where is the post?" said Alistair.

Mutti's right thumb quickly stamped the map. Alistair held it up to his eyes in the still too dim light and was for a moment seventeen again, in the lead car of a medical convoy, with Udine burning to the north. It seemed to him that the contour lines crowded up where Mutti's thumb had been.

"Steeper there?" he said.

"Yes. You do not see it from here."

The road was very nearly straight. It seemed to have joined in the game of driving-with-no-lights and glowed in front of them as though taking its cue from the book covers of fairy tales, where the road goes on forever. It was not paved but recently made and, in the rainless weather, smooth enough that one felt stones one by one under the tires. It crossed a wide, moderate valley. Far behind, they could see again the castle turret, Childe Roland's, fire now in its eyes. Even further, on the opposite side there were vague structures, presumably in American hands. On their side, they had passed through hamlets, deserted but otherwise unharmed. In the moonlight, beginning now to be diffused by high cloud, the grass looked like the sea, and the clumps of thorny bushes, clouds upon it. At the bottom of the valley, there would surely be a river and a bridge. If the bridge were down, at this season the river could surely be forded.

He tapped that line and said to Mutti, "Mines?"

"If there are, they are recent. I do not think so."

The absurdity of this front stood revealed now, not by argument but by the hand of God. In all the valley, there was cover for no more than a platoon at a time. To force a crossing, the Italians would need air cover to drive the Allies from the sky, tanks to force back Allied armor, guns to overwhelm ours, all a fantasy even for the Germans by now, and for Graziani's forces, beyond imagination. Graziani could not even pretend a threat, could not harass, and could not concern a flea. This quieted one of Alistair's many fears: of jumpy American sentries, a danger he had thought of no way to deal with. Thinking about all this, the space of that simple, particular fear was taken at once by a cold and hollow one he had not had time to explore.

Rodolfo, not talkative of late, looked at his watch and spoke. "We should stop. We will be there before twenty-three hundred. We should wait."

Alistair heard himself say, "No!" And surprised by the force of it, said again, "No! No!"

Even Ottavia looked surprised. Captain Mutti looked at him and said, "The colonel's is the better order, as you know. More military. The colonel is right."

Alistair said, separating words like milestones, "There is not one thing sure here. I would not be the only known quantity. No."

Mutti looked at him directly and without haste, and very slightly narrowed his eyes. "Very well," he said.

It was in Mutti's eyes that Alistair realized the conviction of the whispers he had not quite known himself to hear in the dark streambed: that everything they thought was otherwise.

It was not easy to determine position or distance. Alistair took Mutti's compass and made an effort to triangulate from the castle and a summit shown on the map but found that he had long forgotten the trick of it. The slope increased somewhat.

"Does this go on?" he said. "This gradient?"

"Yes," said Mutti. "And picks up a little."

Alistair gestured toward the ignition key and flicked his wrist.

"Very well," said Mutti. "Even that," and put the car out of gear and switched off the engine. They went more slowly, but they went and would not stop.

Ottavia took Alistair's arm.

"Will you recognize the post?" said Alistair. "In the dark?"

"I have certainly been there," said Mutti. "Not in the dark."

They watched. Soon, a line grew up in front of them separating two shades of dark, as two depths of sea.

"There is your change of contour," said Mutti. "The post is not far, but you must be closer to see it. Even when it's manned, there's not much. It is hardly a fairground. But you would see some light, and the shapes of vehicles. The Americans have never bothered to shell it, so they allow themselves that much. The western side is better protected."

"Of course," said Alistair.

And then, "I have it," said Mutti. "There is a kind of dome, a mushroom. It is actually the entrance to a bunker. It is not a natural shape. Do you see it?"

Alistair saw it.

"There are some sheds, but they are much harder to see. There is no light. I see no vehicles. It is as it should be. Nobody."

"Nobody," said Alistair.

It was not necessary to invoke demiurges. Demiurges he had certainly heard, but they spoke as echoes. The castle was enough, whose degradation the spirits of the mud rapturously applauded. He knew, of course, all the sufferings, all the stumblings of the Italian army. It might have fled from the Greeks, been netted like quail by the British, deplored by his brother-in-law, thrown like chaff from its own Sicily, disarmed and put into cattle cars by its ally, but to Alistair, it was still at its heart Maggiore's army, brave in misfortune, bright in honor. An Italian, in this year of 1943, would have seen the castle as another manifestation of his state, farcical and criminal, shrug your shoulders. To Alistair, it was the opening of a lazar house, and from the breath within, nothing but treachery could form. It had attached itself to the poem growing in his mind, giving it a violent charge of dark and light. The poem cast forward its own lines of telling. He was in a state of exalted prescience. He knew also that perfidy, betraying all, must betray itself.

The sheds now existed as panels borrowed from a darker night. In the opaque moonlight, the roofs were brighter, like paint with a little milk in it. And then, at the center of a shed, a blade of light opened, turned, and sheathed itself again.

Mutti, good man, moved quickly to the brake.

Quicker, Alistair said, "No! Off the road!" which with a thump and a buck they did, undamaged.

Alistair said, "Can you get to those thorns?" indicating bushes that were not far and were downhill. Mutti's arm stretched for the ignition, and Alistair snatched it back. "Think, man!" he said.

They reached almost to the perimeter of the thorns. There was an unseen hollow, and they stopped. Mutti lifted his hands, helpless.

Alistair said, "But good enough. It's between us and them." They sat. Alistair murmured to the night, "You have faithless friends, Rodolfo. But who would eat you whole?"

Replying from the night, Ottavia said, "Rodolfo? Not us?"

"Hardly needed for us. Much too elaborate. But a high officer of the fascist army escaping into the American night with two agents. And caught in a trap. Now that's a downfall. That's a chance. Who would it be, Rodolfo? Do you know or care?"

"They've seen us," said Rodolfo.

"The door that opened had light inside it. They have no night eyes. Maybe he was going out to adapt. And we, no lights, no motor. And twenty minutes before our time. I think it very likely not."

"You knew about this," said Rodolfo.

Alistair said quietly to the night, "I was told. In the streambed. You had to listen."

"This car can handle this terrain," said Muttti and patted the steering wheel. "I can do it without lights if the cloud doesn't thicken. At least as far as the river. I think the bridge is down. But then we are nearly safe. It will not take long."

"Only with the engine, though. Which you would have to start." And now, the light crunch of the tires silent, it was extremely quiet. The wind, almost constant in that country, barely stroked the grass. There was no noise of water here. Insects barely spoke. Far to the north and west, heavy guns, perhaps bombs, touched the ear. Later, they knew they were the opening salvos of the battle for Monte Cassino, but they were inconstant and would not cover present noise.

"They may be night-blind, but they're not deaf," said Alistair.

"You were a good officer once," said Rodolfo.

"I was well taught," said Alistair.

Hunched as though in pain, Rodolfo raised his face like a sorrowful plate to Alistair. "Alistair," he said. "What game are you playing? You knew. You knew. And you were the one man I could dare to treat with honor. And I did. I did."

"Thank God I've got boots," said Ottavia.

"I only knew your friends, Rodolfo. I have no game. We'll get out of this with good sense. You've brought us a long way already. We know that, Rodolfo."

They moved to get out of the car, and, having once moved, scrambled.

Mutti said, "If they had seen us, I think we would know already. If they did not see us, and this is a trap, they will be careful not to show their hand. The time for our arrival is approaching. At some point, when we are quite late, they will want to take a look. They will drive up the road. Then they will see the car."

"Can you get us to the river by then?" said Alistair.

"Maybe. Or nearly. It is not very difficult walking. There is no path, so they cannot know exactly which way we go. And the moon is dimming. When they go to look, we may see their headlights."

"Speed above all," said Alistair. There were many uncertainties, for he knew by now that intelligence in wartime has wandering paths and that ears can be deaf as well as pealed. Nonetheless, so comprehensive a betrayal of Rodolfo as this must very likely have gotten to German ears. It was true, thank God, the Germans here did not seem close.

The grass sprang underfoot. Neither roots nor rocks impeded them. The temperature, a little chilly in the car, was pleasant now. They kept by Mutti, walking together. Still, nobody spoke; a flock of sheep, some distance ahead, drifted gently in front of them and were a kind of company.

One would remember such a walk in the dark, all down a life from childhood, the night the car broke down. They could make out the line of the river now, straggling trees, white stone, sometimes a glint of water. Above it were the happy lands which no fear haunted, where no love died in dungeons. Behind and around them, demons roamed and sniffed for prey. It barely moved. There was the element of nightmare. They seemed to walk fast, and it barely moved. Khaki was almost the color of the grass. Alistair could suppose that they were very hard to see. One was allowed to look back.

So Mutti did and said, "There they go." All turned. Where the road was, a scintilla moved, wavered, went out, was brighter, stopped. They had not heard the engine. They heard car doors. Did not hear voices. They had come, one saw, thank God, quite a long way.

"They're patient," said Mutti. He looked at his watch. "Twenty-three twenty-six."

"Italy," said Ottavia.

"How many would there have been? Do you think?" said Alistair.

"We are wasting time," said Mutti. They walked on.

Alistair answered himself. "This was organized on the sly, I think. Not many. Not a truckload, surely. Enough to arrest four. One civilian. One woman. Maybe someone armed. A sudden roadblock. Rifles around the car. Six would do it."

"Maybe," said Mutti.

"Do they go for help?"

"If you are right, they have a problem," said Mutti. "They do not know where we are. This army does not seem to have flares. If they split up, one of them meets us all. In the dark. If you are right. If they send for help, it will take time to come. Even if their radio works. Even if their radio works and somebody is listening."

"They do have a car, and we do not," said Ottavia.

"No, marchesa, we do not," said Mutti.

"I'm not a . . ." said Ottavia, but Mutti went on, using rank for the first time.

"Captain Stears, I think you are right that this force is very small. I doubt it has valid orders. All right, maybe six. There is certainly a second car, maybe truck. They would not all have gone to look for ours. They probably do not have a portable radio, but it will not take them long to get back. The second car is at the post, with men to drive it. That is not very far away."

"Where is the American post? How far up the hill?" said Alistair. And added, "Captain."

"Captain Stears, the American force here screens the ports, Salerno and Naples. Your main units are miles away. They are not interested in this country. Graziani is a nuisance, and they have to watch him. They have a sub-command in a castle, and the watchtower is permanently manned, we think. But it is quite far. You have patrols, of course, but no fixed point. So far, they have not crossed the river. That is the only thing that makes it a frontier. Our men could cross it, too, but they do fear the patrols."

"I thought we had the Americans at our fingers," said Ottavia.

"No, marchesa. We have their influence. I had thought the captain would have known."

"I'm not a marchesa," muttered Ottavia, but they were moving again. Downhill, as fast as they could go, on ground less even now, misstepping; under a fading moon, this had every feeling of flight. Was flight, was all they had, but Alistair tried to hold it from his brain.

"Can they get the cars across the river?"

"I doubt it."

"Then we are equal there."

"And I doubt they would want to drive with lights there. We have two pistols. The one I gave you, can you use it?"

"Oh yes," said Alistair.

"I'm armed," said Rodolfo. Alistair turned. Rodolfo was behind, doing better than one might have thought but stout and not fit. He himself nearly fell, foot on a queer stone, put out his left hand and tore it on a low thorn. Ottavia pulled his other arm, and he was righted.

"And the colonel is armed," said Mutti.

But Alistair had seen the scintilla that had gone up the road turned around now and bright, coming back. This he said.

"Damn!" said Ottavia.

"They will take a few minutes to get organized," said Mutti. "When we see the lights start moving, we have to use the bushes. They will slow us down a little. They will hide us rather well."

They were acacia, maybe. They were damnable. They were not dense. Sheep easily traversed them and left tufts of fleece on thorns. They had hard, knotted roots. If you threw up your arm for balance, a branch would bite it. There were sprays of thorn one did not see, though at face level. There were brawny louts that tried for your thigh. God knew what they all looked like. It was pretty good cover.

They could see stones in the river now, grey melons. They could see the riffle in midstream around the stones and that the stream was nowhere deep. They already knew that artillery had eaten most of the bridge. The thorns shrank, thinned, and ended before the bank. Stands of rushes reached out to them, but there was still more than fifty yards of open ground.

"I don't think I like that gap," said Ottavia. She was bleeding from her forehead, and her boots seemed not to fit.

"If we were facing good soldiers, marchesa, it would be our doom. I would put one car exactly there. Even now, he can get there before us. The other would zigzag down the valley. If one sees us, he signals, and the other takes us from the rear."

In fact, the lights behind them seemed to enjoy each other's company and to progress in fits and starts, as though peering as far as the headlights went.

"And many of the officers you met last night know less about warfare than a Boy Scout, and plenty of the men are jailbirds. We go for the rushes. Look for anything moving on the American side."

The thorns gave out. The grass thickened toward the river. One did not see stones. Ottavia bled and sucked in breath at each footfall. Rodolfo struggled but was there, and, head down and snorting, even bull-like. This, Alistair saw as he looked back before the dash to the rushes. The two sets of headlights were closer, but not close, and proceeded still like careful children.

And behind them, six more sets, widely spaced and moving fast.

"Run!" said Alistair. "Run!" Ottavia stumbled. He grabbed her arm. "Run!"

But she had looked. "Oh Christ," she said. And ran.

So they blundered into the dark. They could hear engines now, not automobiles but loud and military. Where they put their feet was inky, between the lighter river and the pale thorns. They stumbled but did not fall. A cold white light overpowered the tired moon. It was far behind them, but its light touched the rushes. The next flare showed them. The third gave them shadows. The rushes were there, and they threw themselves into them. A machine gun began behind.

"Down!" shouted Mutti.

"Move!" said Alistair. "Cross! They will not kill us. They want us to stop." And indeed, the bullets seemed to strike not even the rushes.

They slid the few feet into the streambed, which sloped down. Round stones were murderous to haste.

"We don't even have flares," said Mutti.

"They're not Italian," said Alistair.

In the water, the stones were slimy and unseen and reached with soft, retarding hands. Climbing out, they slipped back. There had been a respite, no flares, no firing. The Germans, he had no doubt, at that point could not see them. Slime or not, they came out of the river, Alistair and Mutti with Rodolfo by the arms. There were rushes on this side too.

It could have been choreographed. Just at this, the vehicles reached the far bank. It could have been admired. No hesitation, no confusion at all. Men jumped out, four or five to each. Something bulky came out. In a moment, a searing light swept the stream bank, and stopped at their rushes. A good dozen men slid into the streambed. Again, the machine gun.

"Get going!" said Alistair. "Ignore that thing!"

They climbed. This side was steeper—one used hands. They climbed, grasping at vegetation, sobbing for breath, Ottavia moaning, he supposed at her feet. They climbed though sweat filled their eyes.

They climbed for good manners. Alistair certainly knew this and supposed they all did. It was pointless. What were they? A poet, a lady in bad boots, a stout desk colonel, his desk captain. Behind was some of the best of the SS, clean of limb, bright of courage, black of heart. They had crossed the stream in half their time. The distance closed without let. He had a minute's hope, which a gesture from Mutti confirmed: the contour above them, and there would be there some kind of hollow, cover, a place from which to fight, a place to hide, at least for minutes. It was no good. Such was their pursuers' luxury of speed and soldiery that they were already beginning to form a bull's horn, already grown from black shapes to arms and faces, to rise up and encircle them.

Ottavia saw it. She stopped him by his arm. For a moment she was only breathless prey, hanging to him, but regained herself.

"Alistair, they are not going to kill us. You know that too. So make them kill you by shooting at them. Kill some, maybe they will. But kill me first." She stood in front of him quite straight now. "Now, Alistair. I'm your wife, damn it. Don't let them have me. One shot. Now."

And now, at their last extremity, they were assailed closely by a terrible roar and then by a clanking of chains and then a shrieking as of a titan's ghost. And that was the final seal upon them, for he knew, though did not know how, one could not think, that they had gotten some devilry around and in front of them. Their remaining moment had been snatched away, and they would be taken right then from all sides. He did in the tempest of that din draw the pistol and pulled back the bolt, the longest motion his hand had ever made.

Ottavia's lips said, "I love you." She shut her eyes.

And Alistair looked through tears or sweat at his wife's breast and the Germans' backs.

For the Germans were running away. A dagger of flame stabbed his eyes, and a concussion tore at their skulls. Ottavia stared wide. The searchlight and its vehicle on the far bank exploded. They were under machine gun fire again that shook the night and made the German one a toy, but it passed above them. German bodies flew here and there. A beam like the searchlight came on above them, and behind it a vast, roaring shape slid down. He threw himself from its path, but it was not aimed at them. He shielded his eyes to look up at it and very nearly sobbed.

For even if you had spent the whole war in Italy, it was not very difficult to recognize a Sherman tank.

The main gun fired again, not quite as bad, for they were behind it now. Another field vehicle blew up. That seemed to satisfy the monster, for the hatch opened and it grew a head with binoculars.

A voice said, "A nice quiet night, and then all that goddamned ruckus. We saw them Krauts chasing you so we figured you were OK." And then, "Who the hell are you, anyway?"

Alistair stood up. He shouted into the din, "Captain Alistair Stears, United States Sixteenth Cavalry, retired. I am under special orders, OSS. Colonel Rodolfo Pallandra, His Italian Majesty's Carabiniere. Captain Lorenzo Mutti, the same. The Lady Ottavia Stears, my wife. I report to Intelligence Officer Simon Cartwright, OSS."

25

Fear had seeped into them for years like cold dew. Lack of fear came like a summer evening.

They were left alone at last. They were in a cell but a monastic one, and not too terribly small, and overlooking a battered garden, and with a little faded fresco of St. Francis and the leper. There was a guard at the cloister gate, but he neither stamped nor threatened. A polite young soldier brought them a dinner to remember: a clear, bilious broth in which floated letters of the alphabet (construed by Alistair as a personal salute from a literary chef), of which the color set off nicely a pink, chilly, sweating slice of what was possibly meat kept company by a salad of fruit covered with jelly and mayonnaise, they thought. Coffee came with dinner in determined mugs. The young soldier affected to take Alistair's pointed question as to wine as good-humored badinage and smiled as he left.

"Is this how you used to eat?" said Ottavia.

"I don't think so," said Alistair.

"You'd hardly forget. One could try taking off the jelly. Perhaps."

Left to themselves on the summer evening of lack of fear, they, who for a month of evenings had scarcely risked speech, fell into a bed, and, since it was made for one, became one. He found places of her he more remembered than still knew, the underside of her breasts where he could scent and see nothing in the world but

Ottavia, the buttons of her spine that made her arch into him and moan, the first thread of damp to his fingertip between her thighs. His heart soared when he felt her convulse before his own time came and heard her sob and then mew almost inside his ear, then draw him deeper in until his flooding into her was magnificent, and long, and much too short. They were completely surprised. They were amazed. They were terrifically impressed.

They lay in the dark a long time with their faces touching.

Ottavia said, but so quietly that he could barely hear her though his ear was at her lips, so it was like hearing thought unspoken, "It wouldn't have been quite dying. You see that, don't you? I'd have been dead, of course, but it wouldn't quite have been dying. I felt very close to you when I was standing in front of you and you were about to kill me, and that's not quite dying. Maybe it's a little how the saints feel. A little. It's love maybe. You were saving me. And I knew you would be all right. Somehow you'd have made them kill you, or you'd have killed yourself. You'd have leapt into death. I can't do that."

He said nothing but held her closer.

She said, "That was only yesterday. And now today."

She put her chin on his shoulder blade and nudged in a new topic. "Alistair," she said. "Do you know we may just have given Giovanni a new brother? I know we don't think about this anymore, but I'm supposed to be terrifically fertile just now. How about that? Conceived in liberty."

He kissed her eyes in turn and said, "A hell of a lot better than just before."

"Oh God," she said. "Yes. Think of that. I'd have given birth to a griffin, I expect." And then, "But it's probably nothing. I was never very good at conceiving, was I?"

"You were amazing. It's meant to take a lot of practice. And it did."

She squeezed, in fact, his member, then nudged another topic with her chin. "Giovanni's all right, incidentally. I know it. I'd know if he wasn't. I'm starting to know things." And then one last, "That's all. I'm sleepy after all that. You're a lovely pillow, Alistair. I'd forgotten."

He saw her shut her eyes, and felt her body change, and tried to think about their state. But the dark folded him into her soft and odorous body, and he fell into both and slept. Her warmth kept nightmare away, for now.

She was taken away in the morning. And he, a few minutes later.

He had given the army in its time all his loyalty. It had given him its heart, like a tart apple. They had parted friends. On the night when all light died, his army had stepped out of the dark, taken him in its arms, and said, "I never forgot you." So, hanging to a tank's bitter hide and breathing the engine smoke, he had imagined, and by it was moved close to tears. He held to this like a blanket on waking, in his debriefing.

For he was debriefed by two strangers when he had imagined Simon, spectacles round and collar buttoned down. They sat at either end of a table, determinedly at ease, and lepidopterally labeled West Point and Yale. West Point was softly brown in well-cut uniform. Yale wore a shirt he could have borrowed from Simon and a blazer and held his fountain pen straight up and down, like a dagger. They had come from North Africa, whence the broken half-province of Italy was ruled.

"This is old material," said Yale. "Your last word-of-mouth reports from the Santi Apostoli before you . . . relocated yourself. The day you said you went to your club in Rome and did not see Count Ciano, were there present any unusual number of members with known pro-German loyalties?"

He thought. He thought with care, for this was not quite unlike beginning a poem, when the young poem, like an adenoidal child, asks you answers to questions you didn't know existed.

"No," he said. "I don't think so. I have no memory of that." Then, still thinking, caught at a word. "There would not be many such members. The Roman aristocracy does not give its loyalties freely. It is not an easy club to get into."

"But open to you, of course?" said West Point.

He accepted it. He assented with no expression. So he, for four years and more every year, had looked stonily upon brave men making the first offer of their conscience. Even his Nemo, whom his understanding had reached to at the first moment, he had probed for collusion, self-aggrandizement, simple plunder, an elaborate trap.

He said very mildly, "I would like to know whether Father Signoli, if that was ever really his name, has survived. At the SS Apostoli. He was a brave man."

Which brought a cool stare from Yale and from West Point. "General Fridolin von Senger und Etterlin was also a member. You mentioned him. Twice."

"There were a very few Germans. He was . . . appropriate."

They were in a room embellished with an archbishop's crest, not abbot, not cardinal, and he had no idea why. Part of a suite for visitors? The monastery was large and Franciscan, as he knew from certain paintings and bits of della Robbia over doors and doubted his handlers knew at all. It had been eviscerated by the American army; not violated, not damaged in any major way, but simply stunned out of its substance by a power so vast. Jeeps flew around like swallows, staff cars prowled in and out, one saw bits of herb garden under the axles of huge trucks, rumbles of feet were heard as unseen detachments flowed down corridors. An airport had grown up next door full of roars and speeding shadows. Beyond the coastal hills, the sea was barely seen between towered warships. The power he had rejoined was oceanic. He was glad for it. He could be proud of it, proud for it. Yet the lingering tang he had loved of horse and leather on the air was gone forever, and he sensed chill where comradeship had been. Every question about Simon had been ignored, like an embarrassing superstition. Their war, it seemed, had been fought by chess pieces on a glass board.

West Point, "We have an impression that you and von Etterlin were friends."

There had been a time, before the cornered fear at Pace ed Abbondanza, of the shameful fear of a sleek rat at the German embassy. He had forgotten it. He remembered it now and spoke through it.

"I was a traitor. General von Senger und Etterlin does not like traitors. I was no friend of his. I was in his company more than once at the embassy, among others. Those names were in my reports, I think."

"If there were a putsch favored by the Germans against possible waverers such as Ciano, it would be logical that von Etterlin would be present. He would be an asset for them. You suggest they did not have many. At that level. You agree?"

Alistair put his hands on the table. He would have preferred to put his forehead there. He said at length, "Count Ciano was a serious man. Too fond of parties. A snob. On the wrong side. But a serious man. An Italian patriot. A real diplomat. He saw everything his master did not. Von Etterlin would have respected him. So should you, since he was shot for you. If you are able to see von Etterlin skulking in club corridors to undermine Count Ciano, then I cannot imagine what else you see. All men are not devices."

He foresaw the flat stares this would bring and raised his eyes to meet them. He saw Yale, who had sat forward, convert his fountain dagger into a baton and count the points with it.

Yale said, "They are not. Most are. You have to know which are which. Someone has to tell you. You have. That is what you're for."

Alistair said, "Why Etterlin? Why Etterlin, Etterlin?" and told his hands to acquire humility.

West Point said, "General von Senger und Etterlin has been appointed commander at Monte Cassino. Monte Cassino holds the Mountain Line, alias the Winter Line. The Winter Line holds Italy. We do not know much about him."

"Then you are fighting Parsifal," said Alistair.

Their circumstances improved. They were moved to an apartment in a villa shared with other distinguished oddities, such as an art professor given colonel's rank and tasked with unstealing art. Ottavia found an Italian girl, apparently living in the garden, who could get into the kitchen and cook for them. Given the season and their own shorn state, they found her a coat closet to call a room of her own. Ottavia was told about the PX, a kind of military store stocked mostly and uselessly for Americans but where one could also find things like chickens. They found where to buy wine. Their rooms had billowy, dusty drapes. Their bedroom had a ceiling of smirking swains and worse sheep. But it was in their language, however debased the vocabulary. From one window, one could watch warships in the bay creep in and out and bombers leave and come home. Over all of it, for Alistair, stood distant Apollo, silent. His poem claimed but did not answer.

After two days, Alistair did accomplish one real thing. Captain Mutti was back in the Italian army, under General Mark Clark (alas no longer Patton), but serving nonetheless his king, and with a company, which a captain should have, of surrendered Italian volunteers. They were to begin retraining the next day and then join the assault on the Winter Line, which loomed before them in the mountains. The captain was allowed to come to their rooms that evening. They shook hands, drank wine, kissed cheeks. He saluted Ottavia. They never saw him again.

So much for that simple, honorable, and effective man. Alistair was examined on what he knew of Rodolfo, and on the much more that he surmised, while Rodolfo's fate hung like a smoky question mark. It was clear that his questioners here (not Yale and West Point, and they had probably never seen either place) found Rodolfo much more interesting than himself. Whatever, Rodolfo sank like oil into the secret machinery around them. They did not quickly see him again either.

To his surprise, Alistair recognized his old friend and sometime colleague in fascist journalism, Curzio Malaparte, walking down a corridor looking more domestic in an American uniform than in the SS one he had affected the year before. He came for dinner, a chicken and extra wine, and told jaw-dropping stories of evenings in Warsaw with Arthur Greiser, the Gauleiter, the "King of Poland." One never quite knew, with Curzio. He was on Eisenhower's staff now, having left the Gauleiter's. The dachshund under his arm, who asked politely for a chicken wing, was a different one but with a similar mien. They were humans again, with a dinner guest. Back in his company, charmed by his storytelling, Alistair was shocked by a memory. Writing fascist journalism with Curzio, a part of his mind had been sufficiently taken by its claims that he could write with eloquence, even while the rest of his mind looked aside in scorn. He was falling into the same state here now.

In his debriefings, he was now where he had yearned to be for years, able to communicate the hide and the scent of what he had witnessed as well as the skimped shape. His handlers were often patient. He was ashamed to have thought them obvious. They had names by now, real or not, but he preferred the ones he had started them with. They attended gravely to some elaborations and asked odd questions. They stared down others. He gave up seeking their logic. They chose, and they prevailed. He knew that he was being given his proper degree, far above most agents. He felt more and more like a schoolboy.

The power around him, awesome, grew. He knew that it grew also in England, looming above the grey channel, grew in China, grew in the remote Marianas, grew in air fleets, grew in ships, grew in endless files of healthy, muscular, cow-eyed young men. It would change the world. By merely existing, it would change the world. He knew from Curzio that half the females in southern Italy now whored for the Americans in Naples, which would have surprised not even Nestor, but that they spent their earnings on Coca-Cola, which would. No more emaciated Picasso whores over absinthe. A Coke!

So it was benign, was benign in every fiber, and did not even need the advantage of enemies like rats in tombs to look benign.

He turned back to Castiglione, of course. Even in debriefings, even bringing to memory the play of expression between Putzi Hasseldorf and his Gestapo second at their own villa during what he now called their pre-arrest. To wit: Putzi was disturbed by his second, was disturbed not just socially but at his center, not just by his intentions but by his nature; and this made no difference because Putzi would go on doing exactly what the other called for, and that Putzi could be multiplied a hundred thousand times, and therefore there would be no general movement against Hitler except just possibly by conclaves very brave, very small, and perfectly placed. Not Stalin either. And this West Point and Yale did gravely listen to, and the fountain pen made neat stabs.

He had nearly parted from Castiglione. When he had said on the sheep hill, pausing in their flight, that Castiglione would fail his son as he had failed himself, it was because Castiglione rejected the existence of evil. Castiglione insisted that what we call evil was ignorance, or hastiness, too much animal spirits, bad tutoring. For most of a fairly blessed life, he had been able to pass over that, only mildly censuring his humanist for his humanism. No more. There were all the things he had seen, all the tales he had heard of real demons under the midday sun. No need for recount, because there was much closer. There was as close as bedsheets. He and Ottavia had been happy people and still saw patches of happiness in the sky. The nights were not their friends. Both had become prey to nightmares, risen in thin wisps during the Roman years, in ranker coils in the house that became a trap at Lucca, and turned lurid since their near capture or death. Any night, either one might wake to a troubled bed and need to drag the other drenched and thrashing from the jaws of sleep and hold the other until it calmed. So it was as though a foot beneath one's dear bed evil had left a compost of misery waiting for one to sink.

But what remained in Castiglione, and paid for all, was the knowledge that only spirit, the afflatus, had right to rule: warrior, artist, and saint. Warrior, artist, and saint do not fit together, the three daemons, but the small space between them is a circle, through which shines the light through which Leonidas, St. Francis, Monteverdi, Homer see the world in a dance of thought and vision, which in certain lucky times and places it does, though very badly. For only a daemon sees through the world's fog to see an ideal's heart, and if you can aim at an ideal's heart, you may possibly catch its feet. It had been settled in him since early youth that only the wasteful virtues earn the sun. But the wasteful virtues—courtesy, merriment in peril, love for love's own beauty, language for its spell, a happy, handsome list—by no means had to caper in motley. Baldassare Castiglione, analytical chemist of the wasteful virtues, loved the absolute grandeur of the Spanish style, white on black carried to grace by the spine of the sword. The new Europe, raised from the plague pits, held back from the sugar of entitlement, should be ordered by keepers as sensitive as girls and as grave as hidalgos.

Yale was to return to North Africa. West Point would remain, though handling other game as well as Alistair, most of it fresher. For his last two days, Yale took over the sessions. It was clear—Yale alone in a bulked-up sweater (the Mezzogiorno's winter had finally come) in as close as a monastery comes to an easy chair, with a copy of Alistair's Ovid that might not have been a prop—that different rules were in place.

With his own book, Yale waved him to another friendly chair. He said, "The elephant in the living room. It's time. You are completely exceptional. Let me count the ways. And we have been treating you more or less as an ordinary agent. Which we should have, by and large. But it is unprofessional to ignore what must be there. I want you to talk. I'll prompt you if you want. Whatever. What passes, Alistair? What passes? It's also called 'evaluating the agent,' so we don't have to be embarrassed."

"We'll talk about Simon. We will talk about him first. He is the one of you I know. The one I trust. And he is my friend."

"He's dead. We very, very much hope he is dead. By now. Sicily, at the very end, near Messina. He was trying to make contact with a local asset. He should not really have been there. He should not have been alone. Some peasants captured him. Pure opportunism. They sold him to the Germans. The peasants did not know what they had, of course. The Germans eventually did. Anyway, the Gestapo did."

"When?" said Alistair.

"Now about three months ago. Did he give you to them? The dates could work. Only if it took them a long, long time to get you out of him. He gave away some minor networks first, which we do have reason to know, but even that took about a month. Which is a long, long time. You were important, and you were close. He might have held on to you until the very end. Which, as said, we sincerely hope has come."

"Dear God," said Alistair.

"If you think you owe his memory, I will not stop you. Now let's move on." He tapped the Ovid. "You believe in putting things together in odd ways."

In shock and grief, Alistair believed in putting things together in anger. He said, "How are you enjoying fighting Parsifal? You are not getting very far, I think." For indeed, General von Senger und Etterlin, with his much smaller force, had turned the Allies' vast array into something like beagles snapping at a boar in the mountains. Snapping at his feet, every Yank and Hindu, Englishman and French Moor, Pole and Jamaican, Aussie and all.

"It's 'We' not 'You.' Are you pleased?"

"No," said Alistair. For the news from Italy, the Allies halted, the Germans secure above a people to them traitors, the Italian fascists revived and filled with venom, was horrible, worse than anything he could have conceived at Lucca. Von Etterlin was killing the American army, which Alistair still loved. And Alistair had come to love von Etterlin.

"Good," said Yale. "Is that what you call 'moving on'?"

"But I will move on," said Alistair.

THE NEXT DAY, ALISTAIR SAID, "Hitler turned the world into a black and white photograph. It got sharper and sharper. There was brown in it once, but it went. It got so sharp and cruel that it got brittle. You are bringing back color, the color of candy and of soap. You smooth with fat and sugar. Hitler turned us into skeletons. You'll smother us. I'm sorry. 'We' will smother 'them.'"

"I wonder about that," said Yale.

"About what?"

"This 'we,' this 'them.'"

Alistair said, "You should not have said that."

"If you only knew the things you shouldn't have said," said Yale. It hung there but not terribly.

"Ottavia wants you for dinner," said Alistair. "Tomorrow evening, if you can."

In fact, Ottavia, hearing of his yesterday, had said, "You cannot turn your colleague and superior into an enemy out of pique. It is unnecessary and it is stupid. He must come for dinner, like a gentleman. I believe he is one."

"It will be a little scratch." He smiled. "We do not quite have our staff from Lucca."

"You bet," said Yale. Then reordered himself and made a flourish. "An honor, signore. I am your lady's slave."

He smiled at his own wit. Alistair smiled. He would have liked to have liked Yale. It came to him that in some American scheme, he was supposed to like him. If they had fenced at the Palazzo Colonna, walked in the Boboli Gardens, talked on the beach with Ottavia, if some distillation of Yale had lingered in coded riddles from a priest in Rome, it was very possible that he could have liked him. Simon was gone, and gone horribly. He was alone in his own country. He clung to Ottavia. Apollo smiled and did not speak. He had begun to fear his country.

He was a poet. He was quite sure this was what had given him the prescience that had saved them all. Apollo, also of the lyre, gives measure and meter. Therefore, it was precious and therefore dangerous. He had divined thus far: the poem was neither in Apollo nor the traveler but in the space between, the silence between the notes, the second before the lightning. Lines came but did not fit together. He remembered, told Ottavia, and laughed in telling her, that his state in this was as bad as on the day he first saw her in the woods in Lucca.

She always gave attention. "But that didn't work out so badly, Alistair. And you'll make it work. You always do. You're the best. It's quite simple. Not like my problems."

Which he would like to know, please. They were sitting at the window end of the salon watching starlings and sometimes bombers while Annunziata, the little girl from the coat closet, set the table at the other end.

"What to feed your American. It'll be another damn chicken. There's nothing else. I look for veal. Annunziata looks for veal. There's none."

"They don't eat it," he said. "I don't think they know what it is."

"Annunziata knows some farmers. But they have no animals. The Germans killed them all just as they left. All. All our meat's American." She repeated this, in Italian and a louder voice, and ended, "*Non e' vero?*"

Annunziata straightened herself, curtsied, and said, "Sì, signora," then mumbled something to her feet that Alistair strangely caught.

"There you have it," he said. "There's rabbits again. Give him rabbit."

"Do they eat them? Maybe I should do what they gave us the first night. They eat that. In our room with St. Francis, you know."

He looked out of the window a long time. He heard perfectly well, far to the side, Ottavia and Annunziata lay plans for the obtaining, skinning, and cooking of rabbits. The farmer would want payment half in dollar bills and half in American cigarettes.

But he murmured to Ottavia, "You have cured my deafness."

In the little fresco, St. Francis and the leper were painted before the embrace. The eye was drawn, now he remembered, to the space between. Was drawn because the space is not empty. The space is where all is that can be, for out of the space, as once the universe itself, arises grace, or courage (prismed forms of one light), or subsides instead back into nothingness. The kiss arises in that space. St. Francis does not conceive but receive. The kiss therefore is not an 'answer to leprosy', but complete in itself, requires no repetition and no result and is *sub specie aeternitatis*.

It does not matter to Apollo what the traveler does. By consenting to exist, Apollo has opened a space from which the traveler may receive prophecy and measure, or the prophecy of measure, and the acquiescence of the physical world to his need. To the result, Apollo is indifferent. The space will close and will never have existed.

He said to Yale, "My work here is over. I came as a messenger from myself. Not with much choice, of course. The message is read."

"I'm thinking you could analyze the reports of other agents in the field. You know the field. You know Italians. You know the curves. You could be valuable."

"I want to go back to Lucca."

Silence from Yale, then amusement to cover annoyance. "You can hardly walk in the front door."

"The partisan army," said Alistair.

Silence again, then soberly, "You really don't like us, do you?"

"Your front is stalled. You should be in Florence, and you're barely off the beach. You are nowhere near done with von Etterlin. Do you know how many more mountain ridges run west to east in Italy? Have you counted? You should have used air and naval power and attacked far up the coast, pincers east and west."

"We did. It was a catastrophe."

"Anzio was a catastrophe in execution. Meanwhile Italy is dying. You're bombing it. The Germans are shipping it off in railroad cars. The fascists are eating its guts. The hope is the partisans. They can counter the fascists. They can hurt the Germans.

It was the partisans who drove the Germans out of Naples, not you. Don't forget it. I know that group outside Lucca. They have proved themselves. They can expand. I need to talk face to face with the officers here who deal with supply. If they're in North Africa, I need to go there. The Lucca group can expand based on supply. I can give you Tuscany, with a little luck."

"With you as *principe,* Count D'Annuncio?"

"I loathe D'Annuncio. But well done." He scored a fencing point with his finger. *But if I could, I would. Because that's the point. Different principalities, republics obeying different versions of the proper code. Not the blob these people will make.*

"You really don't like us very much."

Alistair said, "Europe has to be remade. There is no choice in that. Europe has been defiled. You will do it wrong. Not just the wrong shape, the wrong substance. You will not know what you are destroying. I do not want to be a part of that. Let me be on my own."

"Expatriates," said Yale. "I knew some in Paris. I left."

"So did I," said Alistair. "It's why I'm here. I am here. I do not hate America. I have shown that twice. What you are grew up with you, probably, I think. There is a lot to admire, but you're not for us. You will protect us. So our swords will rust, and we will learn the patience to swallow insult. You will teach us kindness, so we will let every lout think his opinions matter. You will teach us the wrong ambitions, so every shepherd will prostitute himself for a motorcar. You will teach us sincerity, so you will destroy manners. You will probably even send us that damn mouse you love to laugh at. You will bring out our most common, our most crass, our most cowardly." He said formally, "I will not be a part of the Americanization of Europe."

"You are under orders," said Yale. "I thought that might mean something to you. You will do as you're told. And we have a fine and victorious army, I might add. I do not know what is cowardly about 'Americanization.' Maybe 'Frenchification.'"

"My stepfather said that a conscript army was a brothel. It does not make warriors."

Yale put his hands flat on the table and looked at him. "That's so nice of him," he said. "God, he must have been brilliant. I'll pass it on. To the girls up at Monte Cassino. They do obey orders once in a while. You might try it yourself."

"But why not give me something I do gladly? It's not a soft option. And your position in Italy is terrible. You'll win, but it will be terrible. And, just think, I can be your Lord Byron. You need one."

"Ha!" said Yale.

"And I'm a much better poet."

"At least you'll be dead," said Yale. He looked down to his desk, and to his hands on his desk, and picked up his fountain pen and threatened the desk absently with it. "Alistair," he said. "I haven't heard much you said this morning, so it doesn't matter. What you're asking for is not deranged, whether you are or not. We do need help. There's even been talk of a landing at La Spezia, good port facilities if they don't blow them up. I don't think it will happen, but then you'd really be useful. And we'll know how to keep you on a leash—don't worry. I'll put this into channels, with recommendation. The army will remember you're West Point. West Point takes care of its own. Thank you for not bringing that up. And you're Alistair Stears, for God's sake. You'll probably get it."

"Thank you," said Alistair. "You'll have to take care of Ottavia."

"I don't see why. She refuses to become American. God knows why. It's all anybody in Europe wants."

"Her family were Dukes of Ferrara once. I understand perfectly. But you do have to. Take care of her."

"She can stay where she is. We will."

The room grew quiet and then did nothing to help.

Alistair said, "Aren't you supposed to have one last line?" He changed his voice. "One more thing, old chap. Don't come back."

"That's the Brits, you idiot. You can't even keep us straight."

26

The sea was not far, but the road was twisting, dense, and steep—to aircraft, nothing. The supply flight from Sardinia would be overland three minutes at most, time for two sharp zigzags. Dawn would put sun in the eyes of an observer from the west. The mountain wall would screen from the beach.

Fear, two days of hiding, forty-three-year-old legs exhausted in night woods, quarrels with his compass, Ottavia's tears, Ottavia's anger were set aside in Alistair by beauty. The drop zone was on the heights of Cinque Terre, still wholly wild and awaiting spring. Lucca was under snow. They looked down on oranges and flowers, and dawn's first rays scattered the lemon leaves into diamonds. The sea was pink and crawled. Far below, birds greeted the dawn with flight.

"There," said Nemo. Under shading hand were two silver dots, out to sea, aloft, approaching. Nemo threw out his arms. Three boys ran out of the woods to the center of the mountain meadow, gripped edges of folded canvas, and drew out straight and wide the guiding white cross. Nemo quickly waved them back.

The aircraft were among them absurdly soon. They passed to the right, circled, climbing, screaming like motorcycles, and lined up on the canvas. The light flicked as they passed overhead. Already canisters thumped. This was no high drop. Though on parachutes, the canisters fell hard, and bounced, but were made for that. Nemo jumped up and waved. The aircraft sank again, and swept out over the sea, became fiery points in the dawn. Very professional. They likely did this somewhere every day by now. There was not much risk in it for them. The coastal batteries were around La Spezia and Genoa. The Luftwaffe no longer dared the sea.

The meadow was full of brigands. Nemo shouted, "If it won't open, cut!"

Muddy, bearded, quilted partisans attacked the canisters like hungry rats, thought Alistair, and approved the image, dime store though it was. He himself ran out a little stiffly and began to pry open a hatch. Three vans emerged from the woods: a baker's, a cattle dealer's, and one from the Sodality of the Cult of Saint Anthony of Padua, the better to assist the aged infirm to Mass. It was dangerous but not extremely so. The odds of the Germans having a large force near at hand were minuscule, since they had none within fifty miles. An opportunistic patrol, even by Italian fascists, was possible though very rare. They had enough sentries, machine guns, and hard hearts to deal with that. The point was to gather and quickly disperse. This was done in all ways and by every path at hand, definitely including boots, big knapsacks, and strong legs. The canisters remained, like the debris of Christmas morning.

In the truck, Nemo, who drove, seized Alistair's arm and shook it, actually tousled his hair, and slapped such shoulder as he could find. The van flirted with the precipice.

"You got them! You got them!" said Nemo. "I saw them. Bazookas! How many?"

"Twelve, I think," said Alistair. "Should be."

"You got them! Now we do not run from tanks. We kill them."

"Careful, Nemo," said Alistair. "Not Tigers."

"No Tigers in Italy. They need them too badly in Russia."

A little later, Nemo said, "This Nemo name has to stop. It's stupid now. You're one of us."

"I was never sure if it was the submarine on your mind or Odysseus."

"The submarine. I like that book. I thought it would intrigue you, as a poet. My name is Captain Alfredo, as I am called by the others. Of course it isn't," said Captain Alfredo.

"Of course," said Alistair.

"I am not trying to mystify. Our place, my mother, is not a hundred kilometers from here. We have a little title, which means nothing, but it makes the name recognizable. When I was a plain deserter, I did not want the army visiting my mother. I certainly do not want the Gestapo or the fascists visiting her."

"You certainly do not," said Alistair.

The road had relaxed a little and so had Captain Alfredo. "I never knew my father," said Captain Alfredo. "He was killed well before I was born. He was a major of Bersaglieri, my old brigade. I have his guns and his land and a saddle I don't use and a smoking jacket and his books. And a signed score by Puccini. That western girl. And his title, which is worth less than any of them. When the Savoias came, they needed a friend or two around here. So they made my grandfather a baron. It means nothing. I have told you much too much. More than I tell. Somehow I tell you things."

"They will remain here," said Alistair and touched his forehead.

THE GROUP OF WHICH Alistair was now a part had three separate though linked tasks. The first was to oppose, confuse, mock, and kill unrepentant Italian fascists. This was no slight task. Mussolini, after the king's magnificent arrest, and after being bundled out of the palace strapped into a small FIAT ambulance, was incarcerated in a mountain fortress. This happy fairy tale ended when a superbly able Luftwaffe pilot got him out. Hitler set him up as dictator of the Republic of Salò. He was the most straw of puppets. Salò, a pretty little place on the banks of Lake Garda, could not have held off one Allied regiment for five minutes. But the gallant rescue, coupled with His Italian Majesty's remarkably not gallant cut and run for Bari had the effect of drawing the fascists from the holes where they had licked their wounds since the Italian surrender out and into and under German skirts.

It turned them into werewolves too. On the whole, for twenty years, they had been small-time bullies, loudmouths, and profiteers. A very few had been honorable and serious men. A sufficient number had been hooligans. Now, all who retained the allegiance dived for the bottom. Their beatings and insults and rapes, often committed against gentlemen and ladies, disgusted and dismayed even the German commanders who sheltered them. They roved in squads and commandos. They burned farmhouses at night and brutalized the families. They filled union supporters, as of old, to the gills with castor oil. They beat priests senseless.

Against this, the partisans responded with venom and glee. Assassination suited best. For practical reasons, it had most often to be by gun, from a car into a cafe, from the back of a rally, once from the confession box in church. All this was second best, however. The purpose was not just to show that no fascist was safe but also that no fascist had dignity, or worth, or could live for a day without a German nanny. Picturesque was best: disemboweled to linger in a ditch, for example, outside a burned farmhouse. Or hanged. A plain hemp rope, from a bough over a country road, to kick and dangle, best if the victim were stout, even better if well-dressed, superb if you could get one wearing spats. This last trifecta was achieved only once. All this made Italy lively.

Beastly, barbaric, and necessary if fascism were not to be an available choice in the new Italy. This bloody work was carried out by partisan groups all over Italy, many of which could do nothing else and, being socialist, were little better than the fascists, or communists, or no better at all. For the Lucca group, which could do much more, this was a minor function.

The government of the group behind Lucca was made up of Captain Alfredo, former Captain of Bersagliere and son of a major of the same until his death in battle. There was Elena, the explosives girl, face like Athene, fingers like a violinist, first class degree in chemistry from Bologna, and a father who owned a company that dug Alpine tunnels. There was Henrico, who had a magisterial sense of road and railroad movement, the effect of one bridge or switching station's failure on an overused and faltering transport system. They had an excellent movement and supply man, also regular army. Now there was Alistair Stears, who possessed, for the moment, the confidence of the United States Fifth Army. There had recently walked in a young, decorated British tank officer who at first seemed to claim descent from Eton by P. G. Wodehouse. His mild eye contradicted this, and Alistair already suspected there was a great deal more there. By comparison with most even of the braver and more decent groups, this was government at the level of the Imperial General Staff.

At all events, they were doing better than General Mark Clark and the Fifth Army, still stuck in front of Monte Cassino. By explosion and ambush, they had made the roads and rails in the mountains and foothills unusable. This was a secondary network, obviously, to the trunk routes running down the valley, but it was almost impossible to attack, and very difficult to survey, from the air. Everything now had to go through open country, to be picked at by Spitfires and Hurricanes and Typhoons, and through city marshaling yards, to be hammered by heavy bombers at night. Germany had no capacity to supply by air or sea.

Elena's packages became smaller and smaller and just as deadly. Two young men, two young workers on the hunt of a job, could carry material to destroy what mattered of a switching point or bridge. You did not need to blow up all Tuscany. They had watchers posted to time traffic and observe schedules. The magician Henrico wove this into his web. A line from Bologna to Florence and the south passes through Pistoia on the edge of their mountain duchy. Three teams of two were sent out. Traffic stopped at Pistoia for three days. Enough. Trains stopped, stood still to be attacked, struggled in reverse, were rerouted clumsily by routes to the east. Far to the south, the fighting front was starved. One team, and one boy alone, got back.

Elena and Captain Alfredo were the *principessa* and principe of their world, thought Alistair, and could be, as they should be, though were not, mated. Virginity surrounded Elena as though through concentration of the mind on other things she drew it from the ground. It was the virginity of a goddess, Diana, and it rejected utterly boorishness or mannishness, or a collar that did not properly show off her throat, or a voice that did not hold merriment. She sat at her hellish workbench looking like his old love Nancy painting a babe in watercolor. You saw her, loved, and despaired until you saw a gold light like a lily's stamen far inside her crystal eyes and knew that virginity had an end. She would do very well for Captain Alfredo. Captain Alfredo's gaze upon the world, if badly drawn, would have been purely arrogant, but the humor in the mouth and thought in the eyes made something quite different, still impressive. He found that he usually foreknew Captain Alfredo's reactions and expressions before they happened. This puzzled him, but he supposed it came from similar officer's training.

Himself Alistair put in the role of elder statesman of Castiglione. His knowledge of the new weapons was not good enough to trust. His contributions to council came from the classical curriculum of West Point, lessons from Hannibal, Scipio, Wellington, Lee, and not necessarily worse for that.

They did not live in caves or sleep on skins or cook on bonfires, though some of the outlying sentries might have. The officers lived in farmhouses outside very small towns. Mornings brought smells of manure and cattle. When game was shot, it was hung on a barn beam to cure, and someone had to push through sheep to cut it down. At least one still ate well for those days—cheese at breakfast. They changed the houses fairly frequently, usually putting a ridge between the old and the new. Alistair, Captain Alfredo, Elena, and Henrico were normally billeted together but were very rarely all in the same place: Captain Alfredo circulating among his men, Elena distributing infernal devices (she was never allowed to keep her kitchen in the dwelling) and instructing in their use, Henrico looking at railways. A series of sentries and watchers, beginning at the edge of the highlands then on heights and crossroads in very roughly concentric circles, guarded them. That, and being able to travel light and move fast. That, and few and narrow roads each giving a hundred chances for ambush. That, and history. From runaway slave to recalcitrant Gaul, this region had defined itself by enmity to every lordship that looked at it. Fascism had been loathed from the first, especially as it seemed to emanate from the detested city of the Medici. Communism was checked by a rough respect for the Church, as long as cardinals stayed away. The Germans, of course, were simply hounds from hell. Treachery was unlikely, and any neighbor who discovered it would cure it with death.

The men were first and foremost deserters, including some officers, and escaped POWs, likewise. These had military discipline and training. Plenty had escaped the German labor dragnet, mostly young workmen and peasants. There were old socialists and unionists, university students, the disappointed in love, the disappointed in art. There were about six hundred in all, who never, ever assembled in a body. Sympathizers were much more numerous. There were arms for all.

The third task of the whole force would come at the moment of an American or British arrival. It would take the form of savage attacks on the German rear. Casualties would be high. Among the leadership, none really expected to survive the war. They expected to be extremely difficult to kill.

Behind the farmhouse of the moment was a torrent in a valley steep enough to have ideas of a ravine but south facing and quite sheltered. Now in March, it was still cold in the hills, but very early spring was on the march in Italy and the air from the valley had changed. Alistair sat in a protection of rock in the sun on a blanket and was warm. He had dealt with the code transcripts from the Fifth Army's last transmission. He had brought his notebook in which Apollo's poem, line by crossed-out, moved, overwritten, changed, asterisked line painfully arose. A west wind he could not feel overbore the sky with huge clouds, dark at the edges. The tops of the forest were very high above the ravine, overtopped it, and tossed in the same wind. A little fancy could turn the farmhouse into a shepherd's bower, which, as a matter of fact, it was. It had been a long time since he had set eyes on a painting by his joy of joys, Fragonard. Knowing this, the master from time to time sent him paintings created out of nature to enjoy while they lasted. *Just thinking of you,* he now heard Fragonard say. He saw Captain Alfredo come out into the farmhouse yard, which was convenient since he needed to communicate the transmission to him. Then he saw Captain Alfredo look toward him, seem to make a decision, and walk toward him. He sat down on a bit of Alistair's blanket and glanced at the notebook.

"It must be a great thing to write a poem," said Captain Alfredo.

"It can be. Mine tend to take a while. More like building a house. No sonnets on napkins. Not since I wrote for girls." He smiled, of course.

Captain Alfredo did not. Did rarely. "I love the great paintings, too, but for me that's a conjuring trick. I cannot imagine the act of painting. Or music really. There's a piano at my mother's house. I even had lessons. But my playing never sounded real. Even to me. I read quite a lot of poetry, though, for a soldier."

He never referred to himself as anything else. The officer's training had gone deep. Alistair thought that he found little difference between his bearded ragamuffins and his old regiment. He thought that he himself and the new Englishman had been all that was needed to reconstitute an officers' mess. And the ragamuffins might be better soldiers than the regiment.

"Who gives you most pleasure?" he said.

"What everybody likes. I'm not original. Leopardi. He seems to be my age most of the time. And a young squire, like me, though a lot grander. At least he knows what shepherds and peasant girls are really like. And Orlando Furioso. It's old, but it's terrific. You can sit by a fire and see all those wizards and knights."

"You certainly can," said Alistair.

"And I read French. My French is not bad. I like Valerie. Baudelaire's too nasty. I can't read English. When I was in the real army, I tried to read your Captain Liddell Hart. I couldn't."

"He's English, actually," said Alistair. "Not ours."

"Same thing," said Captain Alfredo.

Alistair laughed.

"I've got some English poetry though. Had it for years. I don't even know what it's about. Maybe you'd read it to me one day."

"Be glad to," said Alistair.

"I read Tagliamento. In Italian, of course. I told you that. I had to know who you were."

"I have very little idea now of what that man was like or what it was like for him to write it."

"You seemed all right to me. It is why we are here now." And then, "The transmission?" said Captain Alfredo.

"It is quite unusually general," said Alistair. "It says that they soberly expect to dislodge von Etterlin within a month. A month. I think it cost them some pride to say that, so I believe it. They say that we should expect 'considerable resupply'—their words—about that time. That's all."

Captain Alfredo looked up at the moving trees a long time.

"Then they are thinking as I do," he said.

"And I."

"What do you think?"

"That when the Winter Line falls is when we should expect real trouble. And a real job. When the Winter Line falls, they can't hold Rome. After that is the Arno. After that, it comes here. There will be a moment when they are not holding a major line and may have more resources than now. They might like to get rid of us then."

"Yes," said Captain Alfredo.

THIS HAPPENED EARLIER THAN either imagined, earlier and possibly less. Their efficient watchers gave reports of an assembling incursion, certainly involving vehicles and light guns, possibly armor. It was clear, hardly a surprise, that it would begin up the valley of the Seronio from Lucca to Borgo a Mozzano where the Seronio is joined by the Torrente Lima. These streams, and the roads that ran beside them, form a pincer at the southern end. The country inside the pincer is a very hard nut indeed, impassable for armor or guns. Captain Alfredo, however, with the concurrence of the whole directorate, had ordered that villages as low as possible on the massif should be protected, protection being the mother of loyalty. Captain Alfredo took command of the western flank, between and above the very small towns of Barga and Coreglia. This was the first time the group had been put into true military order. There were about two hundred men concealed in difficult ground, most with light machine guns but also mortars, two heavy machine guns in armored vans, and three bazookas to be used in absolute necessity. Beside Captain Alfredo was a medium machine gun on a tripod, an English Bren, and its gunner.

The difficult ground occupied by Alistair and Captain Alfredo was a v-shaped cut in a very small ridge, well concealed by second growth. It was a forward position. A force of about twenty trusted men with similar vantage points was ranged within fifty meters of them. If this group, on Captain Alfredo's order, opened fire, it would be the signal for engagement.

Captain Alfredo said, and sounded hesitant, "Alistair, I have those English poems here."

It is common, when action is probable and the stakes rear much higher, for men to want to close one thing they think unfinished. Alistair knew this very well and knew that his friend's focus was not proved the less by it but the more. He did not move the binoculars from his eyes but stretched out his hand for the book and said, "Give." Then discovered it was not a book but a sheaf of papers, not at all thick.

"The other problem is," said Captain Alfredo, "it's in that damn handwriting you all use."

He skimmed the first line:

In dark eyes are intimations of immortality,

Thought left him. He knew he put his hand over his mouth. He took it away with great gentleness, as though it stuck. He knew the next line but had to be sure. His fingers had remembered the paper instantly, Pineider's finest, cool, heavy, and smooth. He used to filch second sheets of it from his mother's escritoire at the old palazzo.

Warmth in dark hair steals life from death

What he had in his hand was unmistakable, like a stone tablet fallen from the sky. He had no thought of how it had gotten here or why. Those two lines were charged; he remembered he had been proud of them once. He skimmed the page. Poems to a girl, to Her, to Serafina, from that time.

He said, and forced his voice to be merely extremely curious, "Where did you get this?"

Captain Alfredo said, "My mother gave them to me."

She was a pretty, middle-aged country gentlewoman whose photograph he had seen and several of whose sayings he had heard.

He said, much more mildly, "She bought them for you? How did she get them? This has never been published."

"No. She got them from my mother. My mother gave them to my mother to give to me. I'm sorry. I'm confusing you. I'm confusing myself. My mother, whom I call my mother because she is my mother, did not give birth to me. That was another woman, younger. She died. That was when she gave my mother these. I never really knew her."

Now he noticed marks at the bottom of the page he had not first registered as writing. Two letters caught his eye. He puzzled at it and felt his heart and his chest turn cold.

He said, "What's this? Your name's not 'Alisto.' Alisto's not even a name."

"I know. I think she used to call me that. I have a vague memory of it."

The writing was as of a person drunk or very weak. What it actually said was, "Alisto, addio, addio." The "o" of the second addio went flat.

Now he shut his eyes. *All right. It's you. It really is.* He looked completely away from Captain Alfredo. He remembered the binoculars and put them over his eyes. They might as well have been a pair of shoes. A voice said, *Whatever you do now is going to be wrong.* In the dark by himself, he thought. He found a sentence and rehearsed it several times. *Addio to which?* he asked himself. *Both of us?*

He spoke the sentence, "That is more interesting than these poems. Tell me. Tell me."

Captain Alfredo said, "I can only tell you what my mother told me." The subject had been changed. He sounded a trifle annoyed.

"Well, then," said Alistair.

"So," still stiffly, "my mother told me all this when I was sixteen. By the fireplace. Made a point of it. My parents, my mother and father, that is to say my not-father and not-mother, were married in 1916. He went off to the war very quickly. He was a pre-war officer anyway. I suppose their marriage was consummated, I hope so, but there was no thought of a child. He was killed. My mother was alone. It was very difficult for those women, I think—this is me now. They had to show untold reverence for their dead hero, whom no doubt they had loved, and all the other men were going or gone."

Stop chattering! thought Alistair. But the stiffness was gone from Captain Alfredo's attitude. He was telling a story and telling it, in truth, as fast as Alistair could hear it. His first love was still a powerful magnet in his mind, but the face had been worn very flat. Serafina seemed most to have disappeared from him, as though that were the substance of their love. Very slowly, color returned.

"She wanted a lady's maid. Myself, this is me again, I suspect she was already starting to hope for a friend. She interviewed the local idiots, half of whom smelled. Then this other girl turned up. She was nicely dressed. She was intelligent. She carried herself well. Nobody knew her. I gather her references were a little vague, but I don't know much about that stuff. My mother took her on. Worked like a dream.

"Soon the age of miracles began. It turned out—I really do not know how, Alistair, I was not there—that this little peasant knew all the major Italian sculptors and painters, then the poets too. I think that is when things began to change a little. When your lady's maid is the most cultured woman in twenty kilometers, she isn't quite a maid anymore. They began to talk and so forth. Because my mother loves all that. And we live in a backwater. Maybe even started to have tea together, or that came later."

Oh, Serafina, you trained on Anna Stears in Rome. You trained on me. This was a piece of cake. Pity there was no son in the house. Irony brought back actual affection, very different from mythic love. He added to himself, *my dear*. Suddenly he saw Captain Alfredo's hand move on the rock, tendons precise under the fluid skin, the forefinger catch at a nub of lichen, and thought, *This is my son. My son's hand moves.* He could not face that thought whole and added, *And I bet you were running the house by then.*

"So it was wonderful for my mother. She had a friend of sorts by now, and the girl was even running the house, and very well, too, I'm told.

"But, then, Alistair, this little miracle showed she could do one other thing, and this thing is one that lots of girls can do. She could be pregnant. My mother told me about this part. She's not really a prude, and she does have a sense of humor. It started puzzling. Then it became embarrassing. Then it became obvious, and she had to speak. Tears, of course. Her husband was missing in action. She was sure he was dead. She had needed a job so terribly, terribly badly. And for the baby. She was sorry, sorry, sorry. And so happy here.

"Now, Alistair, it seems there were pregnant girls running around all over Italy then. You were here. You know better than I do. Some really were war widows. For some, the husband was missing—the record keeping was terrible. Some were war girlfriends, man dead or missing just like the other ones. Some were probably a bad lot. But nobody, except very nasty people, was nasty to these girls. The war widows of course you honored. And if a girl gives herself to her boy before he goes off to war, does she need to be spat at? Or given a medal? I think my mother would have gone for the medal, though she wouldn't have pinned it on. So there was never any thought of throwing the girl into the street. If she wanted a dead husband, she could have a dead husband. There were millions available. Maybe she really had one.

"So I was born. With the doctor and all. And then my mother was my mother's lady's maid, and housekeeper, and friend. And then my mothers really did have tea together, every day, there are even photographs, and played with me, I suppose. And I suppose they talked about Dante and Michelangelo and all of that. And my mother learned to drive the car, and took it into town every day, and did the shopping. And I suppose my other mother babysat.

"Of course it gets bad, Alistair. You know that. Ninteen eighteen. She caught the flu. I was a year old. She did. Maybe she caught it in town. It was very quick, I'm told, and very horrible. I suppose she knew she was dying. She became hysterical, maybe. My mother finds this part very sad, I know. She started raving that there was a powerful American woman in Rome who knew who her baby was, and find her, find her. But nobody could understand her; there was no sense to any of it. And I have been told that not everything she said, my mother, was always absolutely true. So she died. But she gave my mother these first and said I must have them. So I've had them since I was sixteen, that talk by the fireplace. I cried a lot, I'm told. But then I forgot."

He looked at Alistair, with a smile, or maybe was just surprised. "Something I never thought of. She couldn't have read them either. They've been dumb for years and years. So what are they?"

Oh yes, she could, thought Alistair.

"They're not important," he said. "I think they were by someone quite young. It's not all bad. Some's good. But some of it's awkward. I doubt they would ever have been published, like this. They are in the form of love poems. To a girl, of course. Maybe he got better later."

You did what you did best, my dear, and it worked until the very end. I don't think you were unhappy. I'm glad. And here is the eldest son I promised you I would give precedence to. Isn't he? And was he a trick, those last nights together? Was I meant to be told later? At my wedding? I don't care. We made a beautiful son, my dear, but he will not be mine. Eighteen years a girl. Less than a year my love. A year a mother. And twenty-three years a corpse. I will pray for you. You made people happy. Usually.

Captain Alfredo said, as though his thoughts walked on stones, "Alistair, if these are love poems, were they to her? To my mother?"

"She kept them." He saw the delicacy of the cheek, in what was, after, a sunburned officer's face, the lift of a corner of the mouth in shy question, the clarity and depth of the eye. *You knew who he was, the first day. No. No, you did not, but you knew something. There were too many horns in that wood.*

"Was the man who wrote them my father?"

"Poets have girlfriends. Girlfriends have babies. That is all you know."

"And desert their girlfriends when they've got them pregnant?"

"That you even more don't know."

"I can make a very good guess, Alistair. It's not a nice story now. My father's a bastard."

"Why make your mother a liar? The English and Americans had armies too. There were poets in the armies. The poets got killed. If a poet was your father and your mother was his mistress, you don't know what happened between them. They're gone. You're here. He seems to have loved her. So you were conceived by love."

But Captain Alfredo's head had turned. He said in a very different voice, "Alistair. Your binoculars! Something's moved."

27

With the binoculars, Alistair saw at once. At the lip of the slope below them, down a somewhat open couloir, the top of something small and brown and box-shaped with antennae and a gun was surmounting the lip. It looked like a cockroach climbing onto a tray. Whole, it was revealed as a small armored car.

Captain Alfredo said under his breath, "Italian. These aren't Germans. Fascists." Then summoned the boy who served as runner and ordered, "Tell the bazookas to stand down. Don't touch the bloody things. Tell the fifty-caliber to keep the car in its sights. Hold all fire until the order."

Slightly behind the car came a line of infantry strung across the couloir, with a half rank behind.

"Bloody idiots," said Captain Alfredo.

And now with a sound more of fireworks than fury, small eruptions occurred around, alongside, and a few times within the patches of cover that dotted the couloir. The car and the infantry advanced, about at a fast walk. There were probably two hundred men involved. To Captain Alfredo, they were a light force, lightly equipped, neither well trained nor well led. To Alistair, yearning now for reflection and quiet, they were the vanguard of the hosts of hell, pushed in venomous defeat north through Italy, into Tuscany, into Umbria with his young and defenseless child, and now guided by scent of malice to where the new son he had found stood paladin.

Captain Alfredo said, "Seventy-five yards." He called the runner, "When the Bren gun fires, fire at will. The fifty-caliber fires only at the car until the car is dead. Everybody else takes the infantry. They're below us. No high aiming. About one minute. Hurry."

Now the fireworks, in fact a light mortar, had begun to fall very generally on their line, though often deeper into the wood. They were too thinly spaced to do damage except by bad luck. One landed close enough to dust Alistair's sleeve with pine needles. He was appalled to have slightly flinched.

"He did at least two weeks of officers' school, their commander," said Captain Alfredo.

One could see the features of the infantry now and see the moon of a face within the visor of the armored car. Its gun pointed here and there like an old man's stick. The infantry had now reached a point where some small rocky and brushy places were littered in the couloir, and the line was slightly confused. Captain Alfredo lowered his hand to the Bren gun.

At seventy-five yards, one could see faces, not expressions, certainly no wisp of the soul. What Alistair saw seemed deeply ordinary, humanity reduced to cotton wadding pushed up the valley. This intensified his loathing. To be overcome by what approached would be like being eaten by a slug. He disliked machine guns; he carried a hunting rifle, hunting sights, sweet to the shoulder, flat of trajectory, lethal. As the Bren shook, as the fifty-caliber woke like an iron foundry and the sound of its bullets hammering the car echoed back, he let his sight find targets. A man is easier than a boar; what he shot at fell. The bolt ran smoothly. He became aware of men leaping from the car and saw a glow of orange under it. Three of the men went down in the hornet swarm of machine guns, but one, still on the roof, was thrown from it by his shot, for one photographic moment horizontal in the air. A second armored car stuck its beetle legs over the lip of the slope, seemed to take a look, and scuttled back. He stopped shooting.

The half turn of the head to sight the car had shown him his son's face beside him. Away from the cool optics of the sight, the scene was vile, a shambles. The remaining enemy now ran. Bundles of clothing slick with blood lay on the ground or crawled on it. His son's face had no trace of bloodlust, could have been a concertmaster's alert to the whole. His mouth retained the considered judgment that had accepted Valerie, rejected Baudelaire. His skin, very close to his own, reflected no heat but intense engagement. Alistair heard his heart say, *I made this? I and a girl long dead?* Seeing the retreat of the second car, Captain Alfredo made a motion to cease fire that could have been a priestly benediction, and his eye showed relief. He turned to Alistair. "Good shooting," he said. He rose to go among his men and seemed to praise.

There was a whoosh and a dull thud in the air. The car became invisible in flames, and light ammunition began to rattle its hull from inside. Alistair looked into his own hands to seek grace until all this, he imagined months or years of this, was over. He thought he heard a single high screaming from inside the car.

When Captain Alfredo came back, he said, "The wounded?"

"The boys will shoot them. We'll collect the weapons. Boots as needed. The farmers can have the rest."

Alistair nodded. He said, "There was a German observer with them. I am almost sure. In the scope. He stayed back. I could not get a shot at him."

"Thank God you couldn't. He will tell his friends we are limited to light arms and one heavy machine gun. And they will believe him because that is what most of us have."

THE GENESIS OF THE attack was now easy to unravel. Mussolini and his general, Marshal Graziani, chafed in the Republic of Salò under their slavish estate beside the Germans. Relief from it required some sign of military prowess. Graziani's southern army, whose heroes Alistair and Ottavia had encountered in the dark castle, had by now entirely gone home, gone over to the Allies, been arrested by the Allies, or had signed on as German snitches. Far from the Allies, the north was different. To join the arms of the New Rome, the Army of the Socialist Republic of Italy (to give Salò its party name), was for many young Italians the only alternative to joining the men in the hills or cattle car service to German work camps. Some were the old army, who brought with them an enthusiasm verging on the postmortem, an absolute expectation of yet more cruel defeats, and what remained of their training. There was the muscular wing of the old fascist party: dues collectors, boys handy with a rubber truncheon or castor oil can, jailers, and breakers-up of printing presses, with their specialized skills and a positive attitude that set the tone of the enterprise. And there were thousands upon thousands of bewildered young road-menders and goatherds, penniless and famished, with no training whatsoever. The vacuum of officers was filled by old civil servants resolutely loyal to the party. The brains of the attack that day, though the partisans could not know this, had become rich as a customs collector in Domodossola. It was quite a big army.

The Germans would have had no objection to letting this new ally stretch its wings, nor in finding out, at no German cost, what the partisans could do. Captain Alfredo, therefore, could tell Alistair that his success lay not in shooting fish in a barrel on the slope but in having shown almost nothing of his hand: not the new mortars, not the new bazookas, not their antitank gun. Captain Alfredo was pleased with the day.

The partisans knew by the smoke and firing, and were told in detail later that evening, that the retreating fascist rear guard had chosen to believe, though it was quite untrue, that the very small town of Barga, through which they retreated, had furnished the men who had mauled their friends. They therefore shot thirty-eight men, mostly at random but more specifically the doctor, the priest, the mayor, and the schoolteacher, though the last was in fact a lady. Most women not too old and unattractive were raped through the afternoon. They set numerous houses and businesses on fire, including a lumberyard, which in turn burned up a neighborhood. They took, the least they could do, all the money and food they could find.

Over the next four days, about twenty young men from Barga came to join the partisans. They had now no food and no livelihood. A hot meal and revenge appealed. They were given the dead fascists' weapons, their boots as needed, and sometimes a warm blanket.

THE MEN WALKED BACK from the victory though cold woods that nevertheless showed, in rocky places or where a hillock protected, the brand new white and cerulean fragility of iris and violet. Talking was in intense short remarks but quiet. For many, though neither the POWs nor the deserters, it was the first actual battle they had known. Most of them were a little shaken by their victory. Belief in Allied victory was general among these men, was probably utterly necessary for them, though a few might have qualms. Alistair's belief was of a different order.

At the head of this, here and now, prince and paladin, was his son. He knew resolutely that Captain Alfredo son of his loins would never be the son of his house, nor of his fireside, nor of his deathbed. He yearned for his Giovanni, solemn to horses, bright-eyed over a book, who smiled goodnight. It was Giovanni who fueled the fury in battle he knew would stay with him in this dark wood. But Giovanni had arrived in the proper train, cherished pregnant wife. The doctor, a good quail shot, so known by his first name. The heraldic cradle. First step, first words, first book, first pony. Even poor dead Simon holding him awkward on his knee. To this, this new son had something of the miraculous, the heaven born, Sarpedon or Achilles on the plains of Troy.

Sarpedon, or Achilles, said to him, "The fascists will not try us again, I think. The Germans will. Not tomorrow. They have their hands full getting trains to Monte Cassino. I intend to make their hands even fuller. Your job's the Fifth Army. I'm all right for small arms. Elena needs detonators, the new ones with the radio signal. She can make them, but it takes too long. Antiseptic powder, sterile gauze, and morphine would be very good. Then, grenade launchers, more fifty-calibers. Three or four more mortars. More rockets for the bazookas; they're tricky to learn. Anti-tank guns are worth their weight in gold, and I've got trucks to pull them. Even one more. Will you do that?"

"Of course," said Alistair.

He wrote the transmission. Sometime in a different cycle of history, an Alistair Stears had transmitted by sliding creamy papers into an envelope of shiny brown to decorate with a French stamp for his publisher. His pen had loved to trace the smiling and buxom shape of 5, for Fifth Avenue, and the twin skyscrapers N and Y. Now the codes were torturous. Since Salerno, the code depended on encoder and decoder having the Oxford Dickens volume of *Our Mutual Friend*. It began with counting letters. Since Alistair liked to use a pin, whole chapters looked like victims of some bibliophobe sadist. Proper names, the impossible Veneerings, the awful Lord Snigsworth, switched on different fountains of arithmetic. Numbers, as of times and coordinates, had their own codes, separate from letters. Common phrases, weapons types and calibers, type of terrain, had their own two-character codes, hugely compressed. The system he had started with at Lucca now looked like a schoolboy's dodge around a Latin master. It was hard work. He had to check three times. Homer's man with a chisel on marble for taking shorthand had had a cushy job, he thought.

He went out to the FIAT van. The radio, another huge improvement, was mobile, and instead of broadcasting always from fifteen feet above Ottavia's sleeping head was driven on twisting tracks to a different site each time.

So in a glade but screened by trees quite high on the mountain, he stopped. There was a faint, never constant, sound of wind in pines. A small hawk piped overhead. A light sound of water came from where a seep traced by irises ran over a little rock. He listened a few minutes for alien sound. He restarted the engine, which wiped away all of this, turned the switch, and waited for the radio to warm.

He waited to call a country no longer his, though it had kept its present bargain very well. He did not even have for it the warmth of dislike. He called from a country that was not his, was the more not his because thirty years of fantasy had told him that he was Italy's and Italy his. Three weeks of cheek by jowl with Italians had shown him that he barely understood them, did not intensely like them, and barely cared. He risked his life, and would probably lose it, between two ciphers. His adored wife, whom he had clung to in Salerno as America drifted away, was beyond his reach, maybe forever, and had shouted her anger at him as he left. His real son, just as beyond reach, was in danger he could not effect or even gauge.

He lived now wholly in poetry. So he lived in poetry's time, which is not earth's. Dead women brought full-grown sons. Figures from Tagliamento, the officer kneeling in the mud, the Umbrian girl, rose out of the mist. Serafina stirred in her grave and looked over her lover and her son. Unfulfilled promises invite the dead. He talked to Nancy in Paris and moved her back from wherever she was safely into her nice little flat over the grocer's on the Rue du Seine. He wrote various ends for them here, fine and awful, filled them with incident, and lived them all.

The radio warm, the time exact, he transmitted. The nice thing now was that he tapped his transmission into a recorder that then played it into the transmitter at ten times the speed, and it was caught and calmed down again at the other end. He tapped the one character "Ready?" and received it back. The transmission, which once would have been long, lasted six seconds. He waited for the one character "Received in order." He turned off the radio. He got into the FIAT and drove down the hills.

THE RAILWAYS WERE NOW a battlefront of their own. Bridges, tunnels, and major switches were impenetrably guarded, tying down a large part of the German strength available for northern Italy. The military trains now ran down the valley lines at night. The main line from Bologna to Florence was out of reach for Captain Alfredo's band and anyway ran mainly in tunnels. There was a secondary line, but larger than the one that ran though Pistoia, that reached Florence through Prato. This, with great care and risk and by virtue of the extent of the mountains, they could reach. Henrico's intelligence revealed that at least one heavy German train could be expected down it each night. Unfortunately, small, meaningless traffic also traveled it. They believed that this traffic was a bait, so that a mine carefully, dangerously laid for a German war train would harmlessly annihilate an Italian switching engine and its crew instead.

Elena, therefore, burrowed into calculations of fuses and annunciators she had never visited. A bomb was made that would fit over and resemble six consecutive railroad ties, quite obvious to close inspection but not otherwise. Twenty men were needed. The best were chosen. They would travel in much smaller groups, almost entirely in mountain country, and assemble at an unremarkable stretch of track between Vernio and Vaiano in the Bisenzio Valley. Shortly before they set off, Elena, distracted in the morning, silent through the afternoon, attended a last rehearsal with the men, came to Captain Alfredo, and said, "These boys can't do it. They don't understand the fuses and the timing. I can see it in their eyes. They'll do everything but bring it off. I have to go too." There was discussion. There was even argument, but a slim waist in a silk scarf and legs in long boots left with the laden men.

A certain train was made up, long, heavy, and black near Essen in the Ruhr Valley and its flatcars loaded with forty new panzers, themselves under black shrouds. It went east and near Munich received thirty 78mm guns and eight boxcars of ammunition for tanks and guns. Double locomotives took it over the Brenner. It reached Verona by day, still out of range of likely attack. But, now a hunted species, it received searchlights on the locomotive and the middle cars, six machine gun posts on top of the cars, an antiaircraft gun at the back, a car for eighty Wehrmacht to alternate and man all this, and an officer to join the crew on the footplate. It left Verona well before dark, for there was little danger yet, but it passed Mantua in full night. It got green lights in the Bologna yards and barely slowed as it was routed around bomb damage. Then it was free to thunder though the dark heart of Italy, through the Apennine galleries and into the valleys of Tuscany, where a half moon floated. It was easily seen by Elena and her men. Who easily saw that it was the real thing and not a switching engine puttering down the track.

They were quite a long way, three hundred yards, from the track, where they had laid the bomb and three small radios and switches well after dusk. They were in a coppice of olive trees, not much but enough to make them hard to see even with the searchlights. They had, the part that mattered, three radios and two stopwatches.

The officer on the footplate, a good man but quite young, was rapt in the many impressive noises of a heavy steam locomotive at speed. One got a much more vivid impression of speed in a valley than in the dead open. He played with the thought of this mighty German beast plunging south. He played with it as the leading wheel squeezed a steel ribbon feeding one of the transmitters and cut the current until the weight was gone. The radio to Elena's right flicked off. Two stopwatches were started. The captain was leaning out around a slight bend for a fine view when the second radio flicked. The second stopwatch kept on. Elena made a lightning computation of time, distance, speed, distance, and time. Twenty-one seconds later, she detonated the bomb.

The locomotive reared like breaching whale, pouring its burning bowels out across the footplate and crashed onto its side, still at nearly sixty miles an hour. Boilers burst, cars of well over one hundred tons tore into each other, capsized or bounded left or right for half a mile up the track. The gun crews were hurled onto the rails where cars crashed over them. Tanks were ripped off the flatcars, skittering away and landing often on their backs like beetles. A few tanks survived the flailing cars; the guns and their barrels did not. It was a wholesale, a glorious destruction. Word had been passed to the USAF, whose Typhoons came in early morning to devil the wreckage with rockets and strafe the repair crews.

The proud and happy partisans, now unburdened, split up to get home more safely. Within an hour, every German with two feet would be hunting them. A surprising number came back.

Elena did not. All loved her. All prayed that she was dead.

LIVING IN POETRY'S WORLD, Alistair began to feel poetry's secret winds. What is interesting is the places the unfelt winds have the power to move us to. He had first met Serafina above Lucca, that is, he had met her naked body in the nymph's figure by what became his own canal, and her naked body was absolutely the strongest force between them. It was well within the wind's strength to carry her in turn to Lucca, a thirty-minute train ride from her own Florence, a town of good reputation, a place for a new life. She had had some small money then. She could have waited for word of a decent job. Easy for the wind, too, to use Manfredi to carry him here from Paris, to carry Nancy back, and put a dryad in the wood to become Ottavia. And for poetry to use poetry to spring the trap with his son was simply poetry with her most Apollonian smile.

28

Only after the irises faded and the poppies came did General von Senger und Etterlin abandon the ruin that the USAF had made of Monte Cassino. It had been founded the year that the Platonic Academy of Athens closed. It died in a pandemonium of bombs, screams, and tumbling stone as loud as the monstrous blasphemy behind the act. General von Etterlin had never been so impious as to make any military use of the monastery at all. The mountains of rubble the wanton destruction made provided cover for regiments of Germans for weeks to come. General von Etterlin began an orderly displacement north. There were minor holding actions on possible ground, but it was clear that Rome could not be held. A German departure from Rome began, without outward panic. They were even able to take the Jews of the Roman ghetto with them, though they traveled more economically.

A THREADBARE COAT OF late snow cast a light on gun barrels that made them colder than the air to the touch. The airdrop ordered by Alistair alone among the pines came to pass, successfully. Its fruit was transferred from canisters to vans as breathlessly as the last time but much more slowly, for a fifty-caliber machine gun takes two men to move it, and a mortar, three, and even a light antitank gun must be surrounded as though by ants. Feet made greasy smears in the wet snow.

"You did well," said Captain Alfredo to Alistair. "The Fifth Army must like you."

"Or they think the more they send, the less likely I am to come back."

Captain Alfredo smiled perfunctorily. He said, "So this is what we have to fight the German army with. I do not think there will be more."

"Not soon," said Alistair.

"Not ever," said Captain Alfredo. "The next help the Allies will give us is themselves. Our duty is to fight and survive until they come. Until they roll over us like thunder, spreading the New Jerusalem behind."

Captain Alfredo's face, like the gun barrels, reflected the weariness of the snow. So did his phrasing and his voice. Alistair had no doubt why. His son had been in love with Elena, a bride whom Alistair would have escorted with tender ceremony into the household that would never exist outside his mind. His son, commander, could never deny to himself that the gold light far inside Elena's eyes was worth less than a train and tanks and guns. He could, after all, have stopped her.

In a better voice, Captain Alfredo said, "It's not all bad. They don't know we've got this stuff. And we have our real friends, the woods."

An Indian in a turban detached himself from the men, came up to them, saluted Kensington Barracks style, and reported that the matériel was trans-loaded.

"You can move off then," said Captain Alfredo. The Indian saluted again, impeccably, though contriving to convey to Alistair a memory of Ottavia's tea and cake in the kitchen.

"Thank you for those two," said Captain Alfredo. "Nice to see real soldiers."

Now that the hubbub had ceased, they heard the voice, fluting among these mountain boys, of Captain Alfredo's new field adjutant, the British officer, ex-POW. The Italian was not bad, though it ended curiously in an authoritative *"Dicedemus!"* Let's go, in Latin.

He motioned Alistair toward the car. The vans breathed exhaust into the snow and crushed it to mud as they moved. The antitank gun left its separate tracks behind its van. They got in the car. Captain Alfredo shut the door, turned the ignition, and began to speak, and his actions in sequence did not interrupt.

"I was not West Point, but they taught us theory too. And I read more for myself. Guerrilla war we learned from the other side, necessarily, how to deal with Arabs and suchlike, but it's all the same. The romantic idea is the corsair, running, and dodging, and stinging until the big force bleeds white. Might work against stupid troops. Your Captain Mahon explained all that. The corsair cannot meet the battleship, so the battleship takes what it wants. In the end, the corsair is still running and dodging, but all the good places are gone. Then the mop-up begins. So forget the corsair. We have to stand and fight. It's not hopeless. The Germans will not have unlimited force to send against us, and less and less as the Allies approach. We have to fight using surprise and terrain as quantities of one equation. But we cannot keep fighting, for they will always be superior. So we fight and vanish. Reappear and fight. Fight units, not six German boys lost in the wood. And always time it so that when the Allies engage, we have the force to fall upon the German rear. I just have to be better than their commander. It's a dance, Alistair. A dance to death."

A bet of which outcome he had for the moment, his love dead or dead and tortured, little care for himself. Alistair reminded himself that this was the remedy for the soul he had chosen over American balm, and would again, and wondered what his own payment would be required to be.

He said, "Such real soldiering as I did was against guerillas. In the Philippines, we were nursemaids to the fleet. No war to fight. There was an insurrection of a tribe. We overcame it, of course. I was never very proud of it. But such warfare as I know personally is a little like this."

"Well, good," said Captain Alfredo. "I thank that tribe."

VIGILANCE, THE PERIPHERY, BEING more important now than ever, Captain Alfredo decided on an inspection in detail. He took Alistair and two boys from above Pistoia. They would spend the night in a barn in the valley of the Lima. Overall command at home was given to Henrico. Henrico was a civilian, so tactical command devolved upon the new adjutant, who was Lieutenant Catsmeat Pastmaster, MC, (high decoration for his subaltern rank) of the Royal Scots Greys, so keen at declaring everything a "wizard ops" that he put it into Italian for them, *manovra di mago.* Amateur theatrics, that. As well as a Military Cross, he had a soft, inquiring eye and lips that moved to silent thoughts. One day he handed Alistair a verse translation of Horace's "Ode to Mt. Soracte," not bad at all, and encouraging, considering where they found themselves. The two Sikh NCOs revolved around him like adoring moons. Captain Alfredo complained once and peevishly about the Latin lapses.

"But it lends tone. Surely," said Alistair.

Captain Alfredo snorted but nodded. And added, "You sound just like him."

It was too far for horses. They drove where there were roads and then walked paths as needed to remoter stations. The snow, never invited, had had the grace to leave only damp around rocks, balm to crocuses in deep shade. It was May. When the lowlands came into view through woods and valleys, one saw fields bright green before the summer sun, lambs, new wheat, all among the grey smoke of olives.

A bitter spring, 1944. In the lower hills, villages were burned or broken, church towers above empty lanes, farmhouse cellars like the sockets of pulled teeth. The partisans could not dare protect this country. They ventured out of the woods like snowflakes into sunshine.

To the captain, Alistair said, "We should have kept General Patton. Italy dies while Mark Clark thinks."

"General Patton went north, to higher things. Italy has to wait her turn as usual," the captain said. And then, "But you are wrong, Alistair. This will not kill Italy. This has been going on since Hannibal. It is what war is here. Montefeltro. Belisarius. All the Sforzas. Charles V. Julius II. It is all the same. Italy never dies. She is just always sick."

"I don't even like to use the binoculars," said Alistair.

Which one did not need to glimpse stone-built mountain farms, still whole, or hills so graced that an abbey crowned their heads, or streams starting small and bright toward the Arno. There were no vines or olives up here, but quince trees flowered around the farms. They were on foot now, and quite high, toward an observation post directed at Lucca, whose spires they began to see well below. It had a heliograph, and Captain Alfredo wanted to be sure it was hidden and still worked.

It was clear to Alistair that on this mountain path, he was holding the party back, not much but perceptibly. The Pistoia boys could have pranced off like goats. He saw this with dismay, as an infantry officer must. He saw Captain Alfredo looking at him and nearly flinched before rebuke or—much worse—sympathy. The look, however, was just that, no more, then moved beyond him, and his own moved with it. And then his step faltered. Then stopped.

"Yes, it is," said the captain. "I wondered when you'd notice."

They had turned a mountain flank, and well below, thus as visible as from an airplane, was a canal with one small white object visible beside it, a nymph, then graveled drives, the roses and the rosemary, and then his house. His hand moved toward his binoculars then refused them.

Captain Alfredo said, "The devil is not behind us, Alistair. You can look." And then, "I think you should." So, though the binoculars had been the eyes of hell this morning, and he feared them here, Alistair looked.

The house was deserted. There is no disguise for that. One attic window was broken, as he moved the glasses down, and broken glass crows like a raven at ruin.

And then fair walls, and the windows neatly shuttered, and the outer front door held firm in place by the cast iron bolt. He looked at it with astonished gratitude, as though it had fallen brand new into his hand. It was not, for Tuscany, a house of great grandeur, but it was in every gesture a house of grace, and the grace saw him now and smiled.

"Do you see the way you rode when we first met?" said Captain Alfredo. "It's rather clear from here till it gets lost in the woods."

He did not answer, for a single broken rail on the veranda above the gravel showed the rest whole, and now his glasses picked up like a spring breeze and flew here and there among the gardens and the fields. The paddock fence stood. He could people it with two horses but did not dare. Some olive trees had been pruned for the spring. Not very well but done. Done. Done!

Gone, fled, they had been nurtured. If they walked in the front door, Giovanni, Ottavia, himself, there would be chaos—the search would never have ended at the radio—but the front door was there. The Galilean planets kept their paths. He put the glasses down. He found himself overcome with humility and could look only at the ground. He had driven the house from his mind, less afraid of destruction by an avowed enemy than by a winter of small greed and spite, railings taken for burning, doors forced, silver pilfered. Not one hand had touched it unworthily.

"One could think something was deficient in your map reading, Captain," said the captain. "Did you really not know where you were?"

"It is because I never learned to read," said Alistair. "It is why I am still a captain at forty-four. It is hard."

The observation post was in good order. The heliograph was an Austrian assembly of lenses and mirrors and smooth-running screws, hidden and ready. It would signal a buildup of forces in the flat country and roads and railways around Lucca. There was nothing now.

IN A BARN HIGH and drafty enough to allow a fire with no chimney, Alistair sat on old sacks. His thighs ached from the day. A farmer had supplied an only moderately senior goat, faro for polenta, thin wine, and fiery grappa. There had been a moment of excitement when the unfolding fire caused a big snake to fall off a rafter, but it was only a grass snake and ran away. Alistair sat alone in half shadow.

The gift he recognized made the preservation of his property a bagatelle. The gift was to and of the soul, to and of the republic for which he was now at forty-four crawling around in the woods like a red Indian. His people, unurged, had given to him and Ottavia and Giovanni their loyalty and valor and showed that the world he prized was not laughable but stood, existed, and was firm. Not urged and not driven, law had not protected them but grace. All over Europe, he knew, must be men and women like himself; when the smoke rolled away, they would find each other and join hands, for law is imposed, but grace is touched by hand.

Thus the house required from him everything that he was spending here and now, for a house so given must be lived in with courtesy and lightness, not assumption and superfluity. He was right to be here. And on that, he slept.

He woke even more lightly and went out of the barn and away from the soured woodsmoke and stood in the cold and slanting light within the trees. He had still tatters of a dream of Solferino, one of the horses not in the paddock yesterday, with Giovanni in the saddle (not a complete fantasy by now), Ottavia, all against the Roman Campagna where he had ridden Vipero so very long ago. The Germans were not going to hold Rome. Umbria, immediately to its northeast, had no good holding line for them, and they would not waste time on it. The British Eighth Army was moving in force behind them.

So (even in two weeks?) it would be easy for Heaven to engage a British officer much like Catsmeat Pastmaster to salute his way into the villa of the Marchese Ugolino-Ferrara and his lady (you could hardly tell the difference by now between Claudia and a pretty, middle-aged marchesa loyal to her lame marchese), and two little boys, one called Giovanni, and give official notice that Hell had been shown off the map. All the country between Umbria and Salerno would be Allied then. Then they would go, Manfredi, Claudia, and Giovanni (In a car, even? Would they have gasoline? Would they take Girolamo and Concetta too?) safely to Ottavia and walk in from the sunshine, and at that his heart paused at the apex of its arc like a rocket, and like all the very best fireworks threw out garlands of blue, gold, and emerald shimmering joy.

Alistair was even more encouraged that morning than Captain Alfredo, who had found his whole southern periphery sound, and, having gotten rid of one fellow with two empty jars of grappa on the floor, well-manned.

He would be sniper. Not an officer's role, but, telescopic sights and no bad shot, he would be sniper. He needed to zero in the rifle before battle, not his rifle, but Captain Alfredo's father's. Lieutenant Pastmaster attached himself, and Sergeant Petveer Singh attached himself to Pastmaster. They chose a place somewhat off in the woods so sound would mislead, not lead.

Catsmeat Pastmaster said, "Beretta, is it? Don't know them, but the Eyties seem to like them. Did you get it in Italy?"

"Not mine," said Alistair. "Captain Alfredo's father's. Mine's London. It's handsomer than this, but this is a very fine weapon."

"Useful caliber."

"The best for boar," said Alistair. "A man and a boar are about the same size. A boar has a tougher hide."

"Exactly. Was my Soracte ode all right at all?"

"I liked it," said Alistair. They were stepping over a brooklet now, Alistair a little carefully with the rifle, when a bramble curled around his leg. Pastmaster steadied his shoulder while he unhooked it. "You got *Dissolve frigus* right. 'Beat back the cold.' Horace's rhythm, and there's a reason for it. In the last quatrain, we were looking at a frozen mountain. Now we're suddenly in a mountain hut or something, we don't know, and our host has fire and wine. We need a drumbeat. *Dissolve frigus!* Beat back the cold! Very good, Lieutenant. Written by a man called 'Catsmeat'? Truly?"

"I'm stuck with it," said Pastmaster. "Real name's Clarence. I loathe it. But that's what I was trying for. Thank you very much, sir. What range do you want?"

"Not 'sir.' We're not at Eton. Two hundred yards, then three. And I liked 'full hearted wine,' for *merum*. That's the important thing in that couplet, that the wine's uncut. Good again."

"Thank you . . ." *Sir* was wrestled into Stears in the back of Catsmeat's mouth. He added, "I can't help 'sir.' Eton and army. I've been saying 'sir' all my life. To my grandfather, actually. Of course, the other half has been calling me 'sir' all my life. Since I was five, anyway. Is that a German sight?"

"Austrian. Don't know a bit about it. We shall find out, Lieutenant. We shall find out. Why do you do this stuff? Translate Romans?"

Catsmeat Pastmaster seemed in pain but then brightened. "Look, if I have Singh put the target in that tree, the beech, you'd get an avenue there, three hundred yards easy. Would that do? Shall I tell him? Shall I pace it off? I'm quite good at that. Singh can stay here and call the shots."

All this took some time. Then they were downrange from the beech, and Singh was still up it, hammering the target. New leaves, the color of smoked salmon, grew from his turban.

"Not unbecoming men who fought with gods," muttered Catsmeat to the leaves on the forest floor.

"Umhh," said Alistair.

"Because it's difficult as hell. Because you aim to perfection. Horace is perfect. It's made of perfection. Perfect out of nothing, it's light enough to float. Perfection's the thing, isn't it? If you can touch it, even once. I've known fellows who could do it with a cricket bat, but I'm not that good at that. And I thought maybe as a soldier, Roland, Achilles. My father was with the Khyber Rifles, when he was ensign. He has stories not so unlike Arthur and all that. Which is right, because truth doesn't change, does it? I mean, Achilles is still true. But, still, it's messier than that. So it's Horace. And it's partly the messiness, soldiering. If I go in some stupid way, and I probably will, I'd like to have done something really well. At least tried. And I mean to go on. So if you liked it, it really matters. And you did all of Ovid, sir. Sorry. Look, Singh's ready, Stears."

He would lie as a sniper. So he lay there, shoulders on a swelling of the forest floor. He breathed twice and then forgot his lungs. The stock came to its home in his shoulder. The bull's-eye floated over the crosshairs then sank into them. A tendon in his finger knew it was right. He heard no shot, felt no recoil. Singh's right arm pointed up. His left counted five. Singh's right hand pointed left. His left counted four.

"Five inches high, four left," said Pastmaster, all business.

"Help me with these damn screws," said Alistair, of the sight.

"I READ YOUR OVID all a summer term. I was sixteen. I never dreamed I'd be walking in an Italian wood with Alistair Stears. Good lord, never! But it's right that it's in a wood. Because a wood's not quite real, is it, the greenwood? Even if we're all here. And I never dreamed you'd be a Yank. Oh, sorry, sir. I mean sorry."

"Is the dark wood real?" said Alistair. "Which do you think Achilles went to, to be taught by a half-beast? The dark wood or the greenwood?"

Lieutenant Pastmaster looked at the sight, which they had finished with and closed up.

"I don't know that, sir," he said.

"Nor I," said Alistair. He took lightly the rifle by the stock. "I think we can go again."

This time it was one inch high, no windage.

"Good enough," said Lieutenant Pastmaster. "Heart lung shot at two hundred, smack on. Anyway, it's not Kenya here. Wounding's fine. Wounding's good, actually. Not a lion, after all. Disable a man completely and leave him on their hands. Pain in the neck for them. Do you want to try three hundred? Good sights those. I like the Austrians. Good ski guides. Not like Huns a bit."

"Sixteen's good," said Alistair. "You need balls for Ovid. Lots of girls there. You have to love them. Horace, too, as you've noticed. Are there many like you? In your army? I'm curious."

"I don't know," said Pastmaster. "I'm only an ensign. General Wavell's a poet. Have you read his 'Madonna of the Cherries?' Maybe not. It's very new. I'm sure there are more. There were some at Eton, I think. I say 'I think' because very few could bring themselves to go over the top with it. Because they didn't know what there was without it. Because there's nothing. Is there?"

"Where in the world did you read that?" said Alistair.

"I didn't. You're not going to re-zero for three hundred, are you? Not much point in these woods."

"Just want to see what happens."

At three hundred yards, if he dropped the sight three inches, he would be all right. Lieutenant Pastmaster was correct, of course; it would not be a common shot in this terrain.

"There's something I don't like," said Lieutenant Pastmaster. "You're setting up to be a sniper, sir . . . Stears. That's obvious. It's the only place inches count. The other side doesn't like snipers. Really cheeses them off. They seriously try to kill them. I wouldn't like that. You can do another Ovid. You can do anything. You could do the *Amores*, speaking of girls. I think I'll put Singh with you. He doesn't belong to me, but he thinks he does."

"You carry the MC, Lieutenant," said Alistair. "How? Where?"

Lieutenant Pastmaster studied the leaves again. "Operation Compass. Beda Fomm. Against the Eyties. That was General Wavell too. I'm a tanker, of course, worst luck, all the horses gone. We had the Italians, but they were trying to break loose. We were outnumbered, actually. They say I held a corner of a battlefield. Tank was on fire, or bits of it were, a bit, but we could still shoot. Lucky that. Just a corner. I can barely remember it. It can't have mattered much. But General Wavell spoke to me. That was before 'Madonna of the Cherries' though."

"Battlefields are made of corners. And you do remember it. And you should. It mattered very much. And the battle be damned. A battle can be a poem. Homer showed me that. A long time ago. And that is why Achilles is still true." He looked at Pastmaster's face again and though it was still studying the leaves, said, "In fact, you remember it very well, Lieutenant." And without quite meaning to, smiled.

Catsmeat Pastmaster saw the smile, and surmised his own face, and now looked as miserable as though caught with the colonel's wife.

"I think I'll take that shot again," said Alistair, to spare him. "That distance might have been a fluke." He picked up the rifle again.

AND SAW THE HAND steal out of the pit, through old leaves, sleeve stripped bare from flesh, corpse hand reclaiming life, and then, alongside it, the rifle pushing, cold snake. The shoulder rose suddenly. No head, the rim of helmet only, too skinny an arc in his sights to dare a shot. He was sure the Germans had not counted on another ragtag band of bandits to need so much of their care and skill. The 50mm roared to his left, and Germans dropped as they came over the ridge, but only one hit, he thought. The 50mm was concealed, but something of a man must show, for that was the angle the enemy sniper was moving to. And now the head, jowly for a warrior. And now the rifle was held and raised, a sniper's slow hand, he knew his own, and yes, toward the 50mm. He was sure he himself had not been seen. He had the advantage of time. While the sniper found his aim, he sharpened his own on the face. He shot. The head flew back, broken. The hand followed it, back into the grave. At seventy-five yards, it was not a shot to boast of. But it was not bad.

Withdrawn from the sight's cool cell, he could admit to himself that he was shaken by the ferocity of fire. The attack, its high probability, had been signaled by the very heliograph he had met. Company strength, or two companies under strength, Pastmaster and Captain Alfredo agreed, and he concurred. So we could just fade away, said Pastmaster, surprising at least Alistair by his caution. We could and possibly should, said Captain Alfredo, but they would take positions and hold them. We could give them hell when they try to resupply, but the loss would be permanent. We fight. So they fought.

Sergeant Singh, by his side, touched his arm and pointed twice. A light truck appeared at the right of the German line, carrying a heavy machine gun. It was no better than their own, but their own, thought Alistair, was terrifying. One of the bazooka gunners moved forward to counter it. The bazooka had a deadly failing. It left a trail of smoke behind it that pointed straight at the weapon. Until the gunner could move away in the undergrowth, it was the sniper's task, if the sniper could, to preempt focused interest in the bazooka. His own present position had apparently not been marked. This was his third in two hours. This one would be. Such trust as he could have, he put in Sergeant Singh's quick dark eyes.

The bazooka fired, more fizz than bang. The missile was all but visible as it flew. An orange star broke on the truck's side and was erased by a rich bloom from within. The truck must have been lightly armored, at least. The machine gun toppled. The truck burned. Sergeant Singh seized his arm, pointed hard. A light machine gun on bracket pointed its muzzle at the smoke trail. The gunner was visible but thin in side view. Alistair fired much, much too fast. The gunner jumped, the bullet had surely struck iron an inch from him, but stayed upright, and, good German, bent to his weapon again. Alistair damned himself, worked the bolt, and this time let his eye flow into the sight. The gunner slumped. Not dead, he guessed, but done for now. The bazooka gunner had scrambled away. He hoped.

This was their third position. There would not be a fourth. The steeper slopes were behind them now. The Germans, who could read a contour map in any terrain, knew this too. They would crush them here. The third withdrawal would be a monkey-rush, pell-mell up the hills. As with all the other bandit groups.

He had seen the strewn entrails of the fascists with little but contempt for their stupidity, unpleasant as it certainly had been. For this enemy, he had nothing but respect. No juggernaut, but care. No dragon's fire, but fencing. Loss, but not waste. He could see Senger und Etterlin's eyes, intent, patient, slightly amused at mankind's place, and the exact placing of his fingers behind it, though he could certainly not be there, or even know about them. Now that these partisans, rather troublesome ones, had been ushered into position, the blast would come.

And so would their own, back. They had been modest as spinsters so far in showing what they had. In a moment or two, they would show it all. Captain Alfredo's gamble: if they could fight a German unit to a standstill and then be absorbed again by the wood, if (and Catsmeat Pastmaster's and his Sikhs' lapidary drilling would have a lot to do with that) the Germans might conclude that destroying these people would cost more than their limited forces could afford. Elena's bombs had done their work. The rail lines were still in chaos. Two battered alpine passes had to supply three German armies. A mighty host approached from the south. Poland and the Ukraine were old, old history now. There was little left to gamble with. There was nothing to waste.

But there was a tank. No monster Tiger, but certainly a tank. There was a drum-roll, a murderous passage of fire on the late position of the bazooka (surely their only one). Then the German groupings drew a little apart (Act Four: Conclusion), and there it was, machine gun port open, the dragon's snout, the main gun, looking them in the eye. The machine gun went to work. The main gun toyed a little moment, looked here and there for the most delicious morsel. Stopped.

And the tank, not the gun, exploded. Metal shards flew up like the spent casings of the machine gun. Fire poured from torn steel. And a little way under the cover of the wood, Lieutenant Pastmaster, who had command of the Fifth Army's antitank guns (for what a desert tanker does not know about antitank guns is not written), gave his assessment to his Sikh corporal. "Nice, that," he said.

So, no more fencing.

You can't hide the flash of an antitank gun. A mortar got the range, too close. Again, Patveer Singh, the eye, pointed. The mortar was those three men, huddled around their cauldron. Just the job for a sniper, and a compass swung joyfully in Alistair's head to point to the friend he was protecting, Pastmaster, not just comrade. One down. He was too deep into the second shot, target around the fallen man, his back to him, to know his luck had run out, that the skittering of the earth was bullets. The tripod gun, remanned, had found him. Singh emptied a magazine of submachine gun at it and rolled left. "Sir, follow!" Saplings and brambles to cut the light. Lead hornets followed them. Blood on his cheek his tongue could taste. A fallen bough. A stray bullet ruled a crease in it as he mounted it. A spur of wood hurt his haunch as he rolled over it. Behind it. Sergeant Singh unhurt too.

He breathed deep, discovering his body, and crawled toward the end of the bough. Pastmaster's lightning had dealt with the mortar, though a foe beneath it. Certain parts of the enemy force were accessible to him also from here. The tripod gun still probed for them but did not know a foot of beech was in the way. Their own fifty-calibers fired, an endless uproar, into the far woods, the right of the line. He did not understand, then did. A German flanking movement must be moving through the woods, precisely toward the guns. He heard the bazooka's voice, no, voices, one, two, three. Must be something important, but he could not see what. The Germans had gotten their heavy machine gun off the burned truck and set it up. Apparently it still worked. Evidently it was firing bursts at the men resisting the flank attack. That, he had a shot at. He prayed that all the rolling around had not disturbed the Beretta's sight. It had not. The gunner fell. He uttered another prayer, mentioning Swarovsky by name and all his sons. And now he knew a sniper's worst nightmare: he was heavily under fire and did not know from where.

So, the other end of the bough. Singh rolled left and vanished. Singh had found a pit. He thanked God and followed him. Wait a minute or two then look around again.

He could not have said when it began to wane. There must have been a structure here, long, long ago. There were scraps of wall, of skinny Roman brick among the tree roots. He could raise himself on them and peer over the bough, but, as though a mist had formed, there was less and less to see. Clearly, the flank attack had been driven back.

By the German front, stretcher-bearers began to creep about. Their own killed or hurt, no few, would be largely in the wood, invisible, and would have to be gotten back to the country doctor who served them, just adequately, or buried against wolves and foxes. He was bottomlessly tired. He stood stupidly on his crumbling wall. Singh, now nanny, pressed a handkerchief against his face and took it away crimson. "Not bullet, sir. Only thorn. But not good. You need iodine." He winced in foretaste. The grey German tide receded now, leaving behind it black hulks of scorched metal. On their side, there was a movement back. Sergeant Singh motioned for him to join it. It occurred to him, but as simple fact without any gilded frame, that by being here, and still largely alive, they had won.

The wood received its creatures back. So rash of them to venture out! Blood turned to copper beech, and gouged earth to oak branch. He found Captain Alfredo, who looked at him without expression as he approached. For the moment, the captain was alone.

"I hope they do not know how little we have left. I suppose not, or they would have kept on." And in the same tone, "You did good work. I thought you had been killed near the end. I'm glad Singh took care of you. I have lost my adjutant, you know."

Alistair did not register the words. Thus, wandering a little east into what must have been a pocket of heavy fighting, he saw, and did not believe he saw, then saw, the body of Lieutenant Clarence Pastmaster, MC. His death wound was clearly to his chest, for a blanket lay over it, stained and beginning to seep at the center. His face was unblemished. Over it, Corporal Tagh Singh wept openly.

Captain Alfredo came up behind him.

"Do we try and get him back to his people? I do not quite know how."

"Better here," said Alistair. "With the men he fought with."

He would make a memorial one day, he promised, right here, where no one would ever see it.

29

Florence fell. The bridges staggered. People clambered across the Arno. There was no drinking water. It was August.

Long and heavy, an extraordinary hoard of ants for such a hole, German columns poured out. They went straight north toward Bologna and northeast to Forli and the Adriatic. From their easternmost hills, Captain Alfredo's band could watch the westernmost fringe of it pass Pistoia. This was a small overflow for clogged mountain roads and rails. It passed for a day. They watched as ragged shepherds, the imperial banners. Even if their Elena had lived, she could have done nothing against rail lines guarded shoulder to shoulder.

BEHIND THEM, IN THE northern Apennini, ants were busy too, soldier ants and slaves. Along the Gothic Line, Kesselring's last defense of Italy from coast to coast, fifteen thousand slaves had dug and mixed and blasted and poured and shaped some two thousand pillboxes, machine gun nests, and gun positions. The discovery of this had actually been theirs, when a Calabrian deserter of no prowess whatsoever had been looking for a rabbit he would not have to share. He found instead, in a place where nothing had happened in the history of the world, two hundred human scarecrows digging trenches in limestone under German rifles. He got back with his life, though still hungry. Captain Alfredo had put his whole remaining force into a delicate and dangerous discovery of the woods. These works were far from the Fifth Army and largely invisible to aircraft. The Fifth Army had been very nearly grateful. Partisan groups to the east had been given the message. The shape, extent, and depth of the Gothic Line was now known.

Alistair's weapons now were a sighting compass and binoculars. His companions were Monte Cimone, 2,165 meters, and Monte Cusna, 2,120 meters. At the easternmost extreme of the country, he changed Monte Cusna to Monte Giovo, 1,912 meters. It was rarely difficult to find a place whence these summits were visible.

His vision of himself as sniper had opened a trap door into loneliness into which he slipped without effort or bruise.

He crawled up a short slope, insinuating himself through brush. At the top, he heard easily sounds of pick and shovel, a rumble he guessed as a cement mixer, occasionally, the exclamation point, a drill. He was in no danger of losing such sounds and dismissed them. He tuned his ears like a hare's for small sounds behind or beside him, for the danger here was capture. He felt very much at home. Alone, the slow penetration of meaningless shapes of brush, attention at a hair trigger, then sound, which was the intimation of meaning, and now, his chin on the roots of pines, the meaning itself, the thing, was solid ground for a poet. He had seen it before but only as a hole. They had quickly built.

It was a gun emplacement, of course, the road that it overlooked being too distant for anything else. It was nothing much, a small defense for an exiguous line of attack. Two guns at most, and maybe only one would be supplied. It faced east to the small road probing north toward Bologna. It would make life miserable for a column of armored cars. With care, he took bearings on Monte Cimone and Monte Cusna and then on the lower but closer Monte Cantiere. He noted them and would draw them later on the ordnance map. He had a pleasant sureness that they would lie exactly over the lines already there. He triangulated his present distance from the target as 190 meters, bearing 033. This would be precise enough for American or British guns. The last line was written, the work complete. He would not come here again. He heard a closer sound.

It was not very close, and quite indistinct, but it could have been a voice, and then the clink of canteen on rock. In these woods, he guessed he could escape a patrol. He was a poet, not a rabbit. He gently withdrew.

But he had marked the beast for death, and he took a last look. He foreknew his distaste. It was grey and grainy. Slovenly building had smeared cement dust into the torn earth around. The corners were jagged. The grey slaves moved viscously, like snails on rock. The soldiers had the look and clubs of kennel hands. Death should come only from beauty, a Mycenaean bronze deadly leaf, his own rifle, a Spitfire. He knew this already. He left with quiet steps.

In three days of patrol alone, drinking from streams and eating dried venison, now scarce, and hard cheese, he had examined three such works. All were at the extreme eastern edge of their kingdom, impeding the secondary roads from Pistoia over the mountains. Behind the mighty mountain woods that had begun as their salvation and became their universe and souls, there was nothing. He could report that what he had seen was within days of readiness. It was now early September of 1944. Captain Alfredo expected the Fifth Army and the British Eighth at the mountains in early October and to overwhelm them by November. By December at best, mid-November very likely, all movement would be impossible. Some German units might be left over winter but only in the far north where the Alps were consanguineous with their race. The work of harassment that would be asked when the hard fighting began would kill most of Captain Alfredo's band still left. This was discussed between Alistair and his commander and son. He hoped no one else talked about it.

For now he was at ease. Smell of hot pine in the woods. Beside him, he had his friend's (he could not call him "Catsmeat") Horace and Martial. They were the first books he had had since Salerno, and he could not bear to open them. In camp, the smell of unwashed bodies. The streams were low, but he had contrived to bathe. He sat under a tree, the camp just visible through the woods. He usually slept out there, alone. His son and commander came sometimes to speak to him. They were most of what was left of the old command.

From the moment he had known his son, Serafina's ghost had stirred. Now, as he was so solitary, she was all but palpable. She wanted her son back, and, if her son, why not his father. She troubled him at night. He would have bid her go. She did not seem a wicked spirit. She never spoke. Her shadow nearly melted into a tree; in the dark she was the bare profile of her face and breast. If she were more real to him now even than Ottavia and Giovanni, and he acknowledged that she was, it was only that she was dead, and the wind was taking him there, and was probably taking her son as well, and Ottavia and Giovanni were living and would live. He had discovered the idea that he had killed Victoria by holding her in his thoughts when near death, and he would not kill them. Anyway, the woods, their gracious mother, rustled with the dead.

Cold came before the Allies. They heard (a friendly postman from Castelnuovo) that Rimini had fallen after a great battle. Nothing much seemed to come of it. Rimini was far away. A Fifth Army transmission told them that their coastal plain, from the cliffs of which they had watched the silver angels from Sardinia bring their first amazing supplies, was firmly in German hands. They knew this. They had begged Fifth Army for supplies, not for what they knew, and these were not mentioned.

Their own accomplishments were real though not big. A Luftwaffe general was known to travel by resplendent car to inspections along a certain supply road. A tree felled at the right moment stopped the car, and one round from a bazooka killed it. They destroyed a bridge vital to that same road. Best of all, they found an exposed new gun emplacement too lightly guarded and destroyed it and its people and its gun a week after it was finished. Captain Alfredo's triumph in all this was that not one of his men died.

There was no more game. A stag stepped out of a thicket one day in front of Alistair and raised its noble head. Astounded as Count Hubert, he shot badly and had to shoot twice more to kill. Rabbits were prized. A badger was not refused. Marmots were choice. There were acorns.

On the day that ice first breathed on the shoulder of a creek, he finished the Apollo poem. That is, he wrote it down. He wrapped it with his maps in a canvass case.

Since it was a poem of empty space surrounded by the invisible, or, if visible, the protean, it was *sub specie aeternitatis,* and all movement in it was imputed, not physical. He was writing of a connection, never more than possible and evanescent, between this world and another to be permitted only by stillness: no cards, no chant, no spinster holding hands, no medium, no shaman, no hoax. That is, he was writing of the change in the world that such a connection implied. His point of concentration was still Apollo, unreachable on the bare hills, and as instantly present and gone as a spark. Technically he was aiming for Dante's feat in the Paradiso, though at much shorter length. Hell is a prison hulk, curses, farts, and blows. Busy Purgatory buzzes with self-improvement. Heaven is eternal. Eternity does not move.

The poem was an accident, of course: a moment of intuition in their escape across the lines (he had no doubt whatever that this instinct, or whatever it was, had saved all their lives), a faded fresco in a monastic cell. The immediacy of Apollo was the sun over those dry and empty hills.

All his great poems were accidents. He easily admitted this. Tagliamento was a girl seen from a train and a murdered officer seen from a truck. His great Ovid was a naked mistress entranced in the moonlight and a stag hunt gone half wrong. His woodcuts of Italian history—apparently a remarkable number of people liked them—were findings on the floor of a bookworm's mind. Poems were millraces he slipped into; he had to contrive each rapid, weir, and whirlpool (he had never quite failed to do so) until the current very suddenly softened and let him go. This poem was brittle. He could easily say that too. That it was surely his last did not give it a heavenly light. Writing it, his back against a tree, feeling the bumps of a log, rifle beside him on the ground, he had been close to his old Paris streets, his walk down the Rue des Saints-Pères with freezing fog's magic on wrought iron balconies in the time when his poems had become bleached seashells. This was not them. The energy behind it was not formal; it was furious.

In midwinter, the trees of grace, oak, elm, ash not only lost their leaves but shrank. Their boughs were like turkey bones, their trunks starved. There was space for fields of metal sky. The pines sharpened into pencils. Their mother had turned aged and poor. Snow, very heavy this year, was common. Cold was always. They had firewood without limit. They could not show smoke. They lived in a cave and kept the smoke with them. Alistair went there only when chilled through, then only to its mouth, then sat with back turned.

But one day he sensed Sergeant Patveer Singh beside him and very slightly turned his head. Both kept silence. Since the roof was entirely black by now, the fire had abandoned even its one poor parlor trick with reflected flames.

Singh said at length, "Permission to speak, sir." And then, "It is a strange thought, sir, that my own men are less than a day's march away. Even in these strikingly inclement conditions, sir." This indeed was true. There were six Allied divisions within ten or fifteen miles of them. "I believe that it is even the case that my own Peshawar Rifles are present."

Alistair said slowly, for so one thought now, and quietly, for he might be teaching treason, "I do not see that you could be blamed if you went there. You are in the service of your king, who is not His Italian Majesty."

"Emperor, sir, of India."

"Emperor. There would be risks. There are still Germans. You would be shot if captured. But you are a skillful soldier. I believe you could do it. Will you?"

"It is difficult. Captain Pastmaster was my officer, my leader, my chief."

"And he is long dead."

"And therefore you yourself are, sir. For Captain Pastmaster held you as his teacher. I cannot desert my chief."

"I absolve you," said Alistair. "My church can do that. It's useful."

"My own faith includes also Krishna, sir. I am a warrior. A warrior does not leave a battle. He told Arjuna that. Emperor or here? I tell you one thing, sir. It would give me great joy to leave with you after a just victory and be your companion to your house, sir, and take a cup of tea from the hand of your gracious lady, sir, one more time before we part."

Alistair turned on the ground and inclined his head. "It will be my great joy, too, my excellent warrior, should that day come. I had thought that we would all die here. Now, if our gods are very good, I believe that such a day may come for some."

For the Gothic Line in fact was broken. In early November, the Fifth Army and Indian brigades of the British Eighth had, by the hardest fighting, overwhelmed the Apennino passes even to the plains of Emilia-Romagna. The destruction by artillery, bombers, and sabotage of nearly all of Kesselring's hidden forts, their positions exactly surveyed by ragged partisans, had soberly and actually turned the balance, and the armies knew it. At the plain, they stopped. The rains came. Rivers swelled beyond their bridges. The rain came more. Mud washed from mountains and buried trucks. Jeeps sank to their waists in fields. Supply lines now stretched all the way back to Florence, challenging in sun, dismal in swamp. The Po, their next real obstacle, was a mile wide and no bridge attainable without a boat. The armies lay sodden and exhausted.

The Allied air forces, however, could now bomb the Brenner and Tarvisio passes.

Singh said, "You should look to your lady, sir, and to your house. The latter entity, to see it at least, is not so very far. You should do that, sir. A house is part of a man, as is his lady. The gods are tired of this war. They need to know that you have heard them. I will go with you. We can break the snow by turn."

"That will come later," said Stears. "And it will be as it will be."

xxx

IN THE MIDST OF Captain Alfredo's band, on a stump facing Alistair and the captain, sat an exceedingly dirty Franciscan who wanted protection. On his shoes and stockings, he had mud, successor to snow, on his habit, thorns, on his shoulders, the sticky ochre pads that would be beech leaves one day, and on his hood, some dead leaves and a caterpillar. Theologically more interesting was that just behind the friar's head hung down a spray of wisteria none of them had ever imagined to exist until it had suddenly bloomed.

Captain Alfredo said, "I cannot fight troops. Not even Italian ones. Once. Not anymore."

Inside the hood, the monk's face resembled a rabbit's painted in timorous smoke but a rabbit's desperate and driven to bay.

"No troops, I am sure. Jackals. Lickspittles. Probably cowards. But women, children, old men, sick men cannot fight them. Nor can we, a bunch of monks, of course."

It was true that German and fascist forces in Liguria had counterattacked, threatened even Lucca, recaptured Barga. They were being beaten decisively back, but it had been real. One had heard that the werewolf packs that ran with them had taken heart.

"If I do anything, I would have to reconnoiter first," said Captain Alfredo.

"There is no time. It took me three days to find you."

"Good. Then the Germans won't. You are sent by your abbot, I take it?"

"My abbot believes in protection by God alone. So do I. But I believe that God's protection may sometimes be found in the hearts of men like you. Or that there is the closest place to look. Is the master of Pace ed Abbondanza here? I was told he might be."

As though hearing his name from a foreign language, Alistair sat stupidly and stared. Then stood up.

"I am he," he said.

"Then I see you are alive. I have a letter for you."

From the filthy habit came an envelope white as snow, for his name in a hand he knew. Father Kirchner's. He turned his back to the men and opened it.

"My dear friend and child in Christ, greetings. With this is a letter from the office of Cardinal Boccherini, whom you well know. Regard it as an instruction to those who owe it loyalty.

Your wife, your children, are well, safe, and need you. Children, because you have a little daughter you do not know, conceived at the American base, I think. All, and I myself, pray for your life and your swift return. I pray that this reaches you."

He read the second sheet. It was in Latin, short, and to the point. The Church had no further interest in influencing the strategies of this war, the end of which seemed preordained. The Church's duty was to succor Christian souls trapped in its remaining hells and to prepare the ground for Christ's grain when it had been ploughed by the soldiers' feet.

So to this savage and hungry lair came a voice that was the successor to Cardinal Galisteo's, the first and highest of all his masters, the voice above the orange trees in Rome, and spoke his own thoughts. Into this savage and hungry lair came Father Kirchner's news, which he buried for this present time like a violin in a coal mine, for it seemed to him that this was much more than another child, that his family was now complete, and that when he could look at the violin, it would play of a daughter music that Mozart barely wrote. He thanked Ottavia, life, and God.

Captain Alfredo said to the friar, "What have you got there? Terrified peasants? A school teacher or two?"

"About thirty. It varies."

"Women too?"

The scarce face incredibly blushed.

"Our abbot said, 'How feeble are you?'"

"Of what sort are they?"

"They are Christian souls."

Captain Alfredo looked at him. Not quickly, he said, "In what do these Christian souls employ themselves while still on earth?"

The rabbit wavered then plunged forward. "If I told you, your decision to save or not would be wrong before it was made. I might even endanger your soul."

Captain Alfredo looked at him more bleakly.

"Most are simple peasants. What do you expect? Some are hunted because they helped you. Some were simply starving."

Captain Alfredo nodded at both possibilities and did not move his eyes.

"A few are from cities, I believe. Genoa or Florence. A few arrived in suits, clothes like that. There is a woman who writes in a journal with a pen. There is a doctor, I am glad to say. He is Hebrew."

"Possibly not a Christian soul," said Captain Alfredo.

The monk smiled as improbably as he had blushed. "I think God might like him though."

"Names. Can you give me names?" said Alistair, intelligence officer.

"Oh, certainly. Of course. There is Carlo. There is Bartolemeo. Anna-Lisa. Gugliemo, he is a lovely old man."

"Real names," said Alistair.

"Those are the real names. God's names. If I knew their other names, I would not tell you. God is not interested in who your friends might be."

"Or I in comedians. Even in God's comedians. Do you know what you are asking?" This from Captain Alfredo.

"No. I know only what I am offering."

Captain Alfredo said, "Tell your abbot there will be no attack. The American front is within twenty miles of your monastery. You may not know this. You or your abbot. It will be with you in five days. The stupidest fascist will not paint himself crimson when he is about to be captured. You do not need us." He turned away.

"That is not what the Italian officer said," said the friar to his back.

Captain Alfredo turned. "What officer?" he said, without tone.

"The one who came to the monastery three days ago. An Italian officer in proper uniform. He asked for four people by name. He, too, believed that what matters about a soul is its name. My abbot, in fact, had hidden these four when the officer's car was seen. He said that he had never heard of them. The officer asked again. He said that he had never burned a monastery before, and that he could be sorry for hungry peasants. My abbot repeated himself. The officer said, *'Bene. Arrivederla.'* He smiled. It was not a very nice smile."

"Or God's liars," said Captain Alfredo. "Why did you conceal this?"

The friar said, "Because it is not what . . ." *matters*, presumably. But Captain Alfredo had already motioned Alistair away.

The era had changed. With the wisteria had already come the new hatch of bright silver airplanes, Typhoons, Spitfires, Hurricanes, Mosquitoes sweeping in from the south. New in Italy this year were the huge Flying Fortresses still thundering up the hill of the sky to the Brenner, Munich, Berlin. The guns had woken up, alternating with hot quarrels between particular spots. The sounds came from the same places always. Neither army had yet moved. March is known for cold, dry winds that drink mud. None yet, but soon, and with them, tanks would labor out of fields, and the Po would be hugged again by its banks, and its bridges filled with trucks, maybe filthy as the friar but moving inexorably north.

It was clear to Alistair that whatever the band did now would be its last act. The poem was about to end; but poems do not merely end, in the mist of their dissolution, their perfect meaning glows like a sun. They close, and in their closing consume the lice, the too-near latrine, the tired quarrels, and the broken rifle sash whose webbing got stained with baked beans.

Thus he said to Captain Alfredo, "Not difficult. Not far. The very worst. Slavering wolves. No, drooling hyenas."

"Graziani's units, what's left of them. Proper weapons. Conceivably armor."

"Why, under the noses of the Americans? You said that. Anonymous jackals, maybe."

He saw his son lower tired eyes and sigh. *He is far too young to look like this.* Seeing his nostrils flair over the arch of lip, he thought, *Did I make such a perfect head? His mother, too, of course. No wonder she wants him back.*

His son spoke. "Evil does evil. Now I sound like you, Alistair. But now that monastery is still well within the territory of the Germans and the fascists. A last playing out of hatreds? Or maybe they want to murder some now who might bring them to justice after the peace? And they all hate us, Alistair. We have been the worst of the thorns in their side. And they are stronger than us. I see two possibilities. We go for nothing. Or we go to our own end." And then, "You want this."

"Logic wants it. And that is a feeble word. Shape wants it. Light must have darkness. Here is darkness." *And amid the richness of God, one cannot whine like a pauper.*

"I am a merchant with my books and my scales, Alistair. A good commander must be. You are the poet, not me. I have brought my men through nearly three years now. Can we do it? Is it worth it? The battle with the Germans was inevitable. But many of us are still here, and none of us need be ashamed. That did not happen by itself. This has no known shape. Of risk or benefit. And the monk is a liar."

"The time has changed. This is the end."

Captain Alfredo looked at him with no haste while he himself with no haste sought the thought within his son's face. The thought was not in the words he spoke.

"Maybe we can do this. There is not much left of Graziani. The Germans do not seem to be part of it, which makes sense. The German commander must be thinking of a decent surrender. Our presence itself may stop this. I must ask the men. I will order no one. I will shame no one. Maybe those days are over too."

But in fact, gauntness and raggedness, the norm for months, and beards, for razors and soap had mostly died, and an ill-spaced column down the paths, which the Sikhs tried to shore up but couldn't, turned the march into a medieval woodcut: they were merry pilgrims, merry tumblers, merry something. *Or God's comedians, in fact*? silently asked Alistair. Rabbits can frolic; the friar turned most frolicsome of all. None of this was very strange. They thought themselves the best partisan band in Italy. The greater victories had pushed them aside into a narrow, hungry hole. The path lead gently down. Their wisteria's family began to show themselves here and there, a wonder every time, and then its circle of friends, iris and crocus. They walked in a cool, pleasant, rising breeze that had already turned the crests of the paths from mud to soil and stone. They, clean-limbed hounds, were going to the aid of such as they could probably like against the worst leavings of all they had hated most. And they were going not into the German dark but into the American dawn. In this, Alistair thought they were probably, in fact, quite right. A woodcut can make a scarecrow with a submachine gun jaunty. In this time of passage, he allowed himself to look at the violin. A child conceived the night of their escape, for that was certain, conceived by salvation, a new Ottavia conceived with wings. For Ottavia herself was a gift of grace. His finger had been tightening on the trigger. If God had delayed a second longer with His eye Ottavia and her empty womb would have been killed by his hand before the saving tank. The monastery had its back to the woods but looked on a wide bay of upland pasture, to the left and right of which the woods went further down. If not as vegetal as their friar, it was certainly agricultural. There were ghosts of Italian chickens who long ago had pecked corn by empty stables strewn with straw. Incredibly, there seemed to be a pig in a sty. There would be apples in six months if no one cut down the trees for fire, for there was apple blossom now.

Alistair said to Captain Alfredo, "No cover in front. A glacis. So they can't creep up. I don't think they'll use the back."

"So they don't come at all, or they come motorized. How nice."

The friars had made a generous vegetable garden, he now saw, with evidence of potatoes and such in quantity. Perhaps they did have something to eat.

No frescoes in a place like this, no Ghirlandaio for sure, no della Robbia either, Franciscan though it was. He'd guess it was a manor given to the order, not very recently. The bare walls of the room assigned to them nonetheless had the light he associated with monasteries alone, stillness, and some order of the nacreous, distant mist, as though by great blessing you could see completely through. Bread had been brought when they arrived and just now a boiled potato for each man with some thin red wine. The daylight now was lowering.

The partisans had this room to themselves. Arriving, they had seen the refugees scattered around like a stage ensemble, peasants indeed, a few clerks or workers from a town, three more and a lady might have been "professorial." The ensemble was quickly gathered in. The abbot spoke to Captain Alfredo. The abbot was a bent scholar, courteous in voice and manner, who had once, thought Alistair, been a strong young man and would have liked to become one again for this hour but could not quite remember the trick. Alistair could not hear their words, but on the abbot's face, the reception of near two dozen fairly young armed men showed reluctance, holy dread, and, far back, a tremulous ripple of gratitude. Their commander did not object to his men's segregation. He had never encouraged mingling.

Like the abbot, Alistair now studied them. In the days of the old command, he had had friends, had loved dead Elena as a future daughter-in-law. Now he knew only the two Sikhs (both on reconnaissance duty now), an RAF flyer they liked but thought too jangled in nerve to be a useful officer, and a squat Sardinian sergeant who had clawed his way out of Russia and who fascinated him as might have an order of indestructible beetle. The rest were bodies to carry rifles. So he could see them new. He understood the abbot's holy dread. To a quiet man, they would have seemed savages. But they did not jar against the monastic light. They had an intensity and stillness most men lacked, even the friars, and a way of looking sometimes at the edge of something over the world.

Captain Alfredo said, "The abbot's not a comedian. There is a former magistrate from Genoa here and the mayor of Parma who barred the bridges from the fascists twenty-five years ago. Old men now. They matter as witnesses. The woman was a journalist who knows things too. The doctor's a scientist. He matters, though no one here knows why. The rest are just what they are. He's got those four hidden again."

The scouting party returned, reported the lay of the land. The two friars who had led it looked positively smug and borrowed a military swing. Corporal Tagh Singh, the younger Sikh, had a not bad hand for sketching and was proud of it. Captain Alfredo made a map behind a frowning brow then drew it out roughly. He made dispositions. A motorized attack was now the assumption, since its purpose would not be mayhem only but kidnap. The men formed groups and went out into the dusk, beefy and hirsute now, for two friars had brought a pile of blankets. Each group took one flare from a vanishing supply. A friar brought candles into the room.

Captain Alfredo said, "It will be a dark night. No matches. You need your eyes."

He said it as though in benediction, for he himself remained within the walls with half a dozen men.

It was a dark night. The woods that embraced the sleeve of meadow were already black. Alistair, his familiar, Patveer Singh, and four more arrived on station as the last shape of the country was being drawn into night. Now they could clearly see the road, or track of earth and pebbles, and the black mass of the hillock it wrapped around, passing out of sight a hundred yards from the monastery. Another patrol was situated around the bend, where its flare would easily rise over the hill. The monastery was almost as dark as the hill. Another group was placed in a small concavity in front of it and just to its side. Alistair and Patveer were in the central position, for command.

But night abstracted this. They were left with the road, become a sinuous undersea creature with a faint and chilly phosphorescence, and the monastery, where candles only, and deep inside, glowed like failing fireflies. Alistair had suddenly a memory of the road. It was the same flesh as the road through the valley of death they had traversed with Rodolfo, this the paler and more toxic. They waited, magazines full but still on safety, a pile of cartridges in Alistair's hand. He raised the rifle, looked into the telescopic sight, and found his eye pulled into darkness. Dim as it might be, the road's glow would surround the silhouette of truck or car.

Midnight, when the sound of motors rose through the gathering insects of spring. He chambered the first round. He thought two of his men had slept. He waited for the flare. Too long—were they all asleep there? The flare rose and brought with it a quick storm of rifles. He ordered, "Fire on sight. When they round the bend, try and kill the drivers. If they turn on lights, fire between and just above. No flare! No flare!"

But, as Patveer cursed, the flare rose straight above them, and its unnatured light bathed all, bathed a car and a truck, no lights, coming fast around the bend. All fired. He could see in the instant no clear damage. The vehicles might well be lightly armored, and they had no heavy caliber. Then the flare died. All died with it. Their adaption to the dark ripped away; they were left with the dark alone.

The road should have showed the shapes still. The road showed nothing. And out of nothing, Alistair had a vision of teeth and claws, which was intelligence in the foe and a soldier's craft, for they had driven off the road and into the pitch night, and were between them and what they guarded, and their own force was small, and its weapons light. And knew as he saw it, which was truly the teeth and claws, that if the trap they had built faced the wrong way, he was its champion. He ordered, "Back! The house! Fire at sight!" He amended, "Fire at backs, not faces!" and saw Patveer quickly nod.

A hedge of sparking muzzles from the concavity near the house. Bullets flew over them. They were taking fire from their own, good God! Nobody down.

They nearly fell over the truck. Its doors and loading ramp were open, all gone. Patveer, always the best of them all, rolled a hand grenade within. While the truck erupted, somebody shot the tires off the car. A few more bullets flew overhead, God knew whose. They ran toward the monastery, stumbling here and there. The beggarly light of candles showed the door smashed open and black figures crowding in. Patveer Singh cried, "Down! Fire from prone!" before his officer could get it out. Brighter sparks than candles now flashed inside the monastery, whose walls reverberated like a gramophone with din. Their fire told. Bodies crowding the door began to fall or ran off to the side to try windows. Alistair consulted with Singh, who called, "Forward! Keep low!" Shutters in the wall opened, and they were under fire again, while those firing at them fell here and there, but whether shot by them or from inside, they had no idea. Alistair, telescopic sight useless, was down to three rounds in the magazine and two in his hand and kept them for better times. They arrived at the door.

Churchly light glowed over carnage. There were peasants dead, peasants dying, fascists dead, a fascist with a pitchfork through his chest, a fascist with a sickle halfway through his throat, partisans dead, partisans still firing from corners, fascists turning from the window to fire back into the room. He took out two, point-blank. The floor was all over blood. He looked for his son, who was somewhere else. He did not see Patveer. He registered the astounding sight of two young friars bursting out of a trapdoor, wielding flails. One went down at once. The other split a fascist's skull.

A deficit suggested itself. There seemed no more fascists. He looked around. There were no more fascists. In a sudden silence, from well outside, a car started, drove a little way making strange sounds, then stopped. Someone from the door shouted, *"Sargento Singhi!"* Alistair went there too.

Sergeant Singh was quite dead. Though a small man who had surely kept low, he had taken a bullet in the head. He had probably not gone another step. Alistair took the small, brave body in his arms and through the door, found some floor with no blood, and propped him carefully by the wall. His commander urgently needed to know this. He set out to find him.

His son, by contrast, was not quite dead. He was in a kind of shallow alcove, good choice of position but not good enough. It, too, was plentifully supplied with blood. There was a hole just off the center of his chest not much smaller than a fist. His breathing whistled. Alistair threw himself beside him but did not dare hold him.

Captain Alfredo looked at him with eyes just alight. "I'm glad you're my father," he said.

Alistair made a noise like *"How?"* His son's hand was very near his and was laid softly and lightly upon it.

"Oh, Alistair, your son would not be stupid. Handwriting. How much does it change? And that 'Alisto' thing, that name. She named me after you. And the way you looked. And all the boys started to joke about it. Does it mean anything? Did it just happen? I'm sorry it's ending. It's all ending, isn't it? The war. Me. All this. Did you love her?" He rested. Alistair said, "Very much. I loved her very much," but he was not sure to whom.

Alfredo whispered, "My mother. The living one. She's the Baronessa Corvino-Matesto. Not 'Maltesta.' 'Matesto.' The farm's a little below Carera. Could you find her?" He smiled faintly. "My real name's Donato, Daddy."

He was silent again and seemed to be in deep sleep. Alistair felt intensely cold and knew he shivered.

His Donato said in quite a different voice, "Where's Singh? He should have reported by now."

Alistair absurdly said, "He's sitting outside." And looked for the reaction, and saw none, and then knew his son would never hear again, and lost the room within his tears.

A little later he saw that there were other people there. The remaining partisans surrounded them, a frowsy honor guard. The abbot was there, frail inside his habit. There was a lady in a stained good dress. A slender man in a neat beard and pince-nez knelt beside him on the bloody floor. The man said, "He would really have been dead the moment that happened. An operating theater, a good supply of blood, a heart surgeon—then maybe. I can't even tell. But they aren't here, are they? Nobody could have done anything." He looked at Alistair. "It is good to love a chief."

One of the men said, "His son. We know now."

"Oh," said the doctor. And took Alistair's hand.

A number of things now seemed to decide themselves. The old jurist and the old mayor belonged with the Americans, whose tribunals would write down their stories. The precise location of the nearest Americans was not known, but the direction was south and not so very far. The monastery owned an old van, empty of fuel, of course. Someone had the clever idea of siphoning gas from the fascists' car. The doctor and the lady journalist spoke good English. Alistair put them all in the van with two strong, well-armed partisans to drive and protect. It seemed unlikely that the fascists would make an attempt again. Every single one of the four left with dignity and sad modesty, but they left a chilling place. The friars, nearly all of them peasants, were realizing that several like them, and one of their own, had died for people who dressed as they never had, and the reasons for whose greater worth were barely knowable. Alistair felt their chill in himself; their vegetal friar's theology being sounder than his abbot's.

The abbot, however, knew just who Donato's mother was. He could very possibly once have known the family, thought Alistair. He undertook to convey the body, waiting perhaps two days for the last fascist or German to surrender or disappear.

Alistair would make his visit but another day. He could not bear the thought of more weight than was upon him now. He did not need to tell himself, though he knew, that they who had died had died in the name of justice against infamy and had fought as knights. He himself was spared from sacrifice. He, the unsacrificed, had killed his own son, who had become his chief in heart as well as duty. He had brought slaughter to a modest and holy place, all in the name of an epic that might very well be nothing but noise outside himself. Moreover, he knew as well, he could have done nothing else but to surrender to something formless and barely known even to him. He was commander now and felt his place like a barren hill. He would lead his remaining men back to their old camp. What possessions they had were there, maybe even small sums of money, and his own poem in its leather case, and the things of those who had died. If there was an iota left of duty for them, they would do it in Donato's name. They left, not a merry woodcut now but a silent fourteen, not defeated, not cowed, but moving toward the face of a future each only saw in his own imagining. They walked the woods through a hard, dry wind, like the wind that dries the hams above Parma.

Three days later, he gave the command to Tagh Singh. He wrote a letter for him first, to his British officers, narrating his deeds and service, and those of the dead Patveer. It was a small command now. Several of the fourteen had already slipped away. The war had slipped away. The guns were distant now. He liked to think of them cannonading the walls of Bologna and smiled at that simplicity. Since the wind came always from the east, they could hear the rumble of moving traffic from the roads below. He thought that the men left had perhaps nowhere they knew to go. He gave Tagh Singh the money, quite a lot, he had long kept about him, told him to make arrangements for them and then to rejoin his own.

On a day of strengthening spring, he took the path toward Lucca, and walked, and did not look back.

WITH THE DEATH OF her son, Serafina had flowed back into her grave. She had left no message in the air, no color of light except the indentation of a tree, somewhat suggestive of a breast. He decided that he had been entirely wrong about her. She had not haunted them with covetousness of life. There had been no claim of debt. She had come as a woman because the two men she loved were improbably together in great danger, and, if she could do nothing else, she could at least watch over them.

Very near the edge of the wood, he hesitated, and while he stood there heard a sound behind him like a clumsy step. He turned, prepared to smile if Sgt. Patveer Singh, the boundary between life and death not being very distinct here, had decided indeed to join him and take a cup of tea from Ottavia's hand. There was nothing, maybe a falling branch. He moved decisively then, and this time did not stop at the fringe of the wood, but stepped out into full sun.

The sun sparkled on the grass, and the trees singly in the meadow cast clean shadows, as never in the forest. A sparse embroidery of spring flowers began at his feet and became denser as the field descended and crocus gave way to daffodil and, far below, his canal looked like a blue seam cut through iris. His angle of view was not quite the same as from the wood. He moved his eye quickly down the canal, past peach in blossom, past the nymph, to the house.

All its chimneys were alive: into the sky rose the faint veil of ash wood and birch from the salon and bedrooms, the hearty torrent of oak from the kitchen ranges. The glorious and brave ascent drew his hands with the binoculars up to his eyes. The shutters were open and he could see sun and shadow in the rooms. He looked in hunger. A form passed quickly by a window and was gone. A dress only, he could say no more, but the dress had the scent and footfall of Ottavia.

He started down. The meadow at first was steep. His mind tossed between different continents of matter. On the highways around Lucca, as the hills let them go, he could see lines of traffic, supply and reinforcement, funneling into the mountain roads for Bologna and Milan. He did not count or even raise the glasses, for all this could be assumed. On this side of the mountain, he could hear no guns. It occurred to him that he had torn himself from a dark and savage bed, that Ottavia's dress would wilt at the woodsmoke and grease of his clothes, and that his tongue would find only barbarisms to speak to her; he thought that, and thought also exactly the opposite. For he knew also that the poem was closed, the seal locked by blood, and he longed to usher his son into a Europe of warrior kindness where he could grow as knight and poet and his daughter in laughter and truth. It was not extravagant that a world of survivors of a gallant war could buy a world clean of greed and envy, in which St. Francis could stand with knights in poetry and merriment. A groom came out of the stables with a bucket in each hand. He strained his ears for a neigh or whinny. He forgot his clothes, knew his tongue to be his own, and drank the thought of Ottavia. He did not need the glasses now to see the small, dim shape of the salone like a photograph behind its glass, and could have marked the spot where Ottavia had stood slim and straight the night Rodolfo and his men arrived. The way being easier now, he began to run.

FINIS

CPSIA information can be obtained
at www.ICGtesting.com
Printed in the USA
BVHW031646180820
586739BV00001B/33

9 783951 979601